Tanneheuk, Montana appears to be an idyllic small town. There's no crime, no poverty, and no racism. The town is overseen by a small group known as "the elders," a tribe of people who have watched over Tanneheuk for hundreds of years. The elders are shapeshifters – **werewolves** – and they protect the townspeople from the corrupting influence of outsiders. In return for their protection, they only require one thing:

Every year, on the first day of Autumn, they want to hunt a human.

Drake Burroughs is a young minister with a checkered past. Newly assigned to the Tanneheuk Church, he knows there's something dark going on beneath the surface of the seemingly perfect little town. When he discovers the truth about the elders, he convinces the townspeople that the hunt is a sin against God, and they should break their pact with the werewolves.

Roman is the Alpha Wolf, the leader of the elders, struggling to keep his pack together and his leadership unquestioned. Roman knows the annual hunt is archaic, but also understands the importance of tradition for a race of beings who live on the cusp of extinction.

Added to this volatile mix is a family of con artists hiding out in Tanneheuk;
A town deputy, torn between her unrequited love for one man and her burgeoning desire for another;
A young girl training for the annual hunt, determined to be the next chosen;
A restored 1970 Dodge Charger;
Karaoke night;
A lot of guns...

It might be Judgment Day for Tanneheuk.

"Autumn Moon is a sultry, breathless read that appeals to the beast that lurks within us all. Memorable characters with distinct voices, harrowing action, and some great plot twists compelled me to keep turning pages into the wee hours of the night." - Sean T. Smith, author of *OBJECTS OF WRATH*.

"Go ahead and pick up *Autumn Moon*, but you'd better have the next two days off because you're not putting it down. Slade Grayson's writing is sharp and visceral; he doesn't tell you a story, he engulfs you in it. A breakaway from all the tropes, *Autumn Moon* is a reinvention of the genre." – Nick DeWolf, author of *FRIGHTFULLY EVER AFTER*.

"Slade Grayson does a masterful job at setting up and defining his characters in this wolfish adventure. The plot line is steady and keeps the attention of the reader all the way to the end. I found this a great read and I'm looking forward to more from this author." - Deborah D. Moore, author of *THE JOURNAL*.

# Autumn Moon

## SLADE GRAYSON

A Razorwire Publishing book
An imprint of Vintage City Publishing
ISBN: 978-0-615-48772-4
*Autumn Moon* copyright © 2021
by Slade Grayson
All Rights Reserved.
Cover art by Dean Samed, Conzpiracy Digital Arts

# September

Slade Grayson

# Chapter One

He wanted to stop time. More than stop it, he wanted to turn it back two hours to when he still held Charlotte in his arms and she had whispered sweet endearments in his ear. Her words had been filled with love and promises... and regret. Regret for the wasted moments when perhaps she had failed to make him aware of how much she loved him. The words she whispered were the words you would say to the love of your life — if you fully expected to never see them again.

Despite the bittersweet moment, it remained precious to him. His heart had swelled at her words and at the way she had rested her head on his shoulder, the smell of her hair and the comfortably familiar way her body nestled against his. If there had been any lingering doubt about his decision, it had been instantly washed away when his arms encircled her. That was the moment he wished he could freeze and relive, over and over until the end of time.

He checked his watch. Twenty-one minutes to go.

"Sheriff, how about letting me have a head start." He phrased it as a statement rather than a question, perhaps because he already knew the answer.

"Ya know I can't do that, Randy," Sheriff Creel said. "It would break the pact."

They sat in the front seat of Creel's patrol car, parked on Lawson Road at the site where the paved part ended and the road became a dirt path that curled up into the mountains. It required a four-wheel drive vehicle to proceed further, and even then, the path was filled with downed trees and fallen branches. Although Creel owned a jeep, he chose to use his patrol car because he knew he wouldn't have to travel beyond this particular point. This was the point on Lawson Road where he was instructed every year to discharge his prisoner. It never changed and never varied. It was always this place, this time of year, and always at midnight.

Randy said, "You know, it wasn't fair. There wasn't..." He hated that his voice sounded whiny. "There wasn't but maybe twelve people there. How can it be fair if there's only twelve?"

"It's never fair," Creel answered. "Doesn't matter if it's twelve or twelve hundred. It's never fair for the one who gets picked." He refused to meet Randy's eyes.

Sheriff Creel did not fit the mold of a stereotypical small town sheriff. He was neither fat nor racist, didn't chew tobacco, and he shied away from the use of "good ole' boy" idioms when he spoke. Instead, Creel was tall and lanky, rawboned, with steel gray hair and a neatly trimmed gray beard. He wore gunmetal aviator-style wire-rimmed glasses, which he would push up at times to rub the exposed part of skin where the nosepieces set. His glasses weren't tight or uncomfortable; it was a nervous tic Creel always had, even during the years before he was appointed sheriff.

Creel's attire was usually a denim shirt, worn jeans, and a battered pair of brown leather cowboy boots. He kept his badge clipped to his belt along with a .45 in a side hip holster, but only when he performed one of his sheriff's duties. His day trade was a carpenter, which kept him busy most of the year. The stipend he received as town sheriff wasn't large, so Creel earned a living doing what his father and grandfather had done: building things.

Truth be told, his duties as sheriff were quite simple. He had to be available to investigate a crime (if one occurred), run a background check on any strangers who came to town, and arrest any lawbreakers. But there were very few lawbreakers. The town had a way of dealing with that outside of arrest and incarceration. Chiefly, Creel's primary responsibility was to ensure that a pre-chosen person, once a year, was transported to the end of Lawson Road and released at the stroke of midnight.

"You want to hear something funny?" Randy asked in a tone that suggested he didn't really find it all that humorous.

"Sure."

"It wasn't supposed to be me," he said. "I mean, I walked into the school gym and I remember thinking how it was a low turnout. Twelve people, you know?"

Creel nodded. They were covering old ground.

"I saw Charlotte and I took a seat next to her. She grabbed my hand right away. Her hand was damp and kind of cold at the same time. I remember thinking that. I told her... I told her how there should have been more people there, but you know, Pete broke his leg last week, and John and Marlene had that bad car wreck. Josh messed up his knee during football practice last summer..." He shook his head and whispered, "Fuckin' cowards."

Creel looked at him. He said quietly, "Ya can't blame them. Sometimes they're influenced by their parents. Or their loved ones."

Creel liked Randy. He thought most of the younger generation was lackadaisical and nihilistic, but Randy was different. He was hardworking, responsible, and generally acted respectful to everyone. It was those qualities that had inclined Creel to hire him as a carpenter's apprentice the previous summer.

"It used to be, they only picked from the eighteen year olds. But people stopped having kids, or the kids started having accidents, and the pool to pick from dropped. So now it's eighteen to twenty-one, and that pool has dropped. Soon they'll expand it again, maybe to twenty-five. Or thirty." He patted Randy's shoulder in a paternal way. "That don't matter. What matters is, ya did your duty. You were a man."

Randy let out an exasperated breath like Creel was missing the point.

"It wasn't my number," he said. "They called the number and it was like you could hear everybody sigh at the same time. I stared at my ticket, thinking, Thank you, God. Thank you. Around me, I heard people breaking down into tears of relief. Then I realized Charlotte hadn't made a sound." He shook his head at the memory. "I looked at her and she was chalk white. Her hand dug into mine like…like she was on the verge of a seizure or something. That's when I knew. It was her number that was called."

"So ya switched with her," Creel said.

Randy nodded. When he spoke again, his voice shook. "Funny thing is, for that split second, that one tiny instant, I was glad it was her and not me. Just as long as it was not me. You know? Then I took her ticket, gave her mine, stood up, and announced it was my number. Now I wish...now I wish..." The words caught in his throat.

"No, ya don't. You'd do the same thing if ya had to do it again. It's like I said, you're a man." Creel checked his watch. "Listen, son. We have a few minutes. I can't let ya go early, and I can't give ya a weapon. But I can give ya advice."

They sat in near total darkness. There were no streetlights this far from town, and what little illumination they had from the full moon and starlight was periodically obscured by a slow moving cloud cover. The murky gloom of the interior of the car gave it the intimacy of a confessional booth, so when Creel offered Randy advice, he paid attention as if the words were coming directly from God.

"Tuck your pants into your socks. Ya don't want getting caught up on something and taking a fall. I see you're wearing hiking boots. That's good. Ya came prepared. Most come wearing sneakers, I guess 'cause they don't expect to get picked, or maybe they figure they'll be running, so... Thing is, you're running over uneven ground, so ya need sturdy shoes."

As Randy tucked in his pant legs, Creel thought of the girl last year who had worn flip-flops. He had shaken his head at that, but the girl had been too stunned from being picked to realize what a detriment her footwear would present. Before he sent her out, Creel had retrieved a pair of hiking boots he kept in the trunk of his patrol car, along with several pairs of boot socks, and had instructed her to put them on. The boots had been too big for her, but three pairs of socks made them serviceable.

He remembered she neglected to thank him. In fact, she had remained silent the whole drive up. When it was time for her to go, she simply walked off into the woods. It was the only time Creel had not seen one of them run. He wondered if she did later, or if she kept walking like that, dreamlike, until... He shook his head at the memory.

Although Creel was careful not to break the rules of the pact as set by the town charter, he had no problem in occasionally bending them. For instance, keeping a pair of hiking boots and a pack of boot socks in his car trunk, just in case, or giving advice, as he did now.

"You're gonna head north," he told Randy. "If ya can, keep your eye on the North Star. But it's gonna be hard 'cause it's cloudy tonight and you're heading into some dense forest. The trees will block out a lot of the sky. Best thing to do is, keep track of whether you're running uphill or downhill." Randy's eyes were locked on him. Even in the dark, Creel felt the boy's intensity as he soaked up every word. "It's a steady three hours of runnin'. That's runnin', not walking. Believe me, son, ya can't afford to walk. Now, you got a light on your watch?"

"Huh?" Randy said. "Oh, yeah." He pushed the button on the side of his wristwatch to prove it. The face lit up in a blue glow.

"Good. That's how ya keep track. The first hour, you're on level ground. The next hour and a half, you're running uphill. The last half hour, you're heading downhill until ya reach the river. Once ya do that, it's over. You've won. Ya just have to get to the river. Okay?"

Randy nodded.

"Now, it's not exact, because everybody runs different, but it's how ya keep track. If more than an hour goes by and you're not heading up, or you're close to three hours and you're not heading down, then you're heading in the wrong direction. Got that?"

"Sheriff? Has anyone ever gotten to the river? Has anyone ever won this?"

Creel considered lying. Would it be wrong to give the boy hope, even if it was predicated on a falsehood? He decided it would be, just as it would be wrong for a prison warden to tell a condemned man that the governor might call with a stay of execution. It was best to let a man know what his chances were and what he was up against.

"No, son, I've never seen anyone make it. But, and this is the God's honest truth, it doesn't mean you can't. I've seen ya move on the football field. You're quick and you've got endurance. This thing can be won. Understand me? Someone can win this. No reason why it can't be you."

Randy felt his heart race. He knew it was almost time. Any second now, it was coming. His breathing picked up, faster and faster, like before the start of a game when he heard the crowd cheer and he pulled on his helmet. The blood would rush through his ears and the din around him assumed an underwater quality.

"Just get to the river," Creel said. "Okay, son? Get to the river. Three hours. That's it."

Creel wanted to tell him, *Please win this. Please make it. Because tomorrow, your parents are going to come to my office and ask me what your demeanor was and what we talked about. They're going to want to know what your last words were and whether you were scared or not. I'll tell them the same thing I tell all the parents, that you were brave to the end, cracking jokes and passing on messages of love to your friends and family.*

*Except in your case,* Creel thought, *I really won't have to lie.* Not like some of those other times when the kids spent their time whimpering or outright crying and begging for their lives. Like the Beardsley boy one year who acted brave in front of his family, then broke down into tears and refused to get out of the car. Even when Creel told him what would happen to his family if he didn't go, he still refused, and he had to pull his gun and force him out. Or Reggie and Becca Foster's daughter four years ago, who'd offered him all sorts of sexual favors if he would let her go and take someone else in her place.

*No, Randy, in your case I won't have to lie. But I will have to see your parents in town from time to time and see that look in their eye. I will have to see how they deal with their loss, whether they divorce or stay together. Whether one or both of them turns to the bottle as many of them do to ease their pain. I'll also have to watch what happens to that pretty girlfriend of yours—Charlotte— whether she goes on and meets another young man, or whether she turns into the town slut. I really want you to make it,* Creel thought. *Even if you're the only one who ever does.* His watch beeped. It was midnight.

"Time to go, son," Creel said, but Randy was already out and running for the woods, not even stopping to shut the car door behind him.

\*\*\*

He ran. He ran until his lungs burned and his legs trembled. Branches reached out and clawed at him with skeletal fingers, but still he ran. Tree roots and rocks threatened to twist his ankles, but still he ran. His shoulder smacked a tree and sent a bolt of red-hot pain through his body, but still he ran. He ran with the palms of his hands out in front of his body to deflect potential obstacles rendered invisible by the dark. Soon, the clouds dissipated and his visibility improved, so he was able to foresee the vegetation that blocked his path and the uneven terrain that threatened his mobility.

When the ground turned slightly upwards, Randy checked his watch. Fifty-one minutes had elapsed. He was on schedule and headed in the right direction. Just two more hours, he estimated. Maybe sooner. He ran on and gradually his trek became more difficult as he scrambled uphill.

Forty minutes later, a far-off sound brought him to a dead stop. It was the unmistakable howl of a wolf. Not the melancholy wail of a lost or distressed animal, rather, it was the cry of a wolf sending a message to its pack.

Randy had never been camping or gone on a hunting trip. He'd gone fishing maybe three or four times, and hiking once. His experience with nature and animals was minimal. Buried deep in his subconscious, however, was the fight or flight mechanism all humans possess — the primal part suppressed by thousands of years of evolution that was quick to analyze potential dangers and give back an assessment of a perilous situation. Randy knew, without having to think about it, that the wolf had picked up his trail and had signaled the message to its pack.

His chest burned and his head felt heavy. He realized he was holding his breath. He gulped air and ran. He ran up hills, sometimes hitting level ground for a few minutes, but ultimately, he resumed an upward path of flight. His shins sent sharp bolts of pain that overshadowed his other worn out muscles. At times, he stumbled, and used his hands to claw his way along, going on all fours like the hunted animal he was.

When he felt he had to stop for a few seconds to catch his breath and wipe the sweat from his eyes, the world spun and he sat down— hard. *Maybe I should give up*, he thought. *Just sit here and wait. I'm never going to make it. My lungs feel like they're about to burst, and I've still got, shit, an hour of running ahead of me. Just give up. Maybe...maybe it'll be quick.* He thought of his parents. And Charlotte.

Randy was up and running again when he saw it. A flash on his right, a shadowy blur that could have been a bush or a boulder. It could have been one of those things, but it wasn't. Randy knew what it was. It was a wolf. A big one.

He kept going and tried not to look anywhere but at what was in front of him. He topped a ridge and felt a moment of elation. Then he saw them.

There were ten, maybe fifteen of them, vague outlines in the moonlight that circled from both sides to cut him off. They were bigger than any wolves Randy had ever seen, but by their shape and gait, he could tell they were wolves nonetheless. The darkness concealed their individual characteristics, but he could see the wolves didn't all share the same color fur. Some were light brown, while others were gray or black. One or two might have had a reddish tint to their fur, but under the circumstances, it was difficult to tell.

He turned to run back the way he had come. Not that he wanted to backtrack, but his choice in the matter had been made for him. If they were in front, Randy had to go back. Unfortunately, as he slipped and half slid his way back down the rise, the wolves were behind him as well. At least two dozen of them picked and clambered their way up the slope towards him. Their features were hidden by the murky gloom cast by the canopy of trees, but their glistening eyes were surprisingly visible.

He spotted a tree with a low-lying branch and sprinted to it. His first leap brought him up short, but with his second leap, he was able to get his fingers around the branch. It bowed dangerously under his weight, but stopped short of breaking due to the toughness of the tree. Or maybe it was Randy's mental plea that kept the wood from snapping.

His hands clutched the branch and his nails dug into the bark with frantic desperation. Randy swung one leg up and managed to hook his right heel over. His left leg still dangled in space. Before he could swing it up, a blur shot out of the shadows and clamped down on it. The weight pulling on him mixed with the sudden burst of excruciating pain made him release his grip on the branch. Randy dropped to the ground with a bone-rattling thud.

He screamed out in pain and anguish. The wolf held his leg in its massive jaws, its teeth sunk firmly into his flesh and leg bone. Even if the wolf released him, Randy was in too much pain to stand, let alone run. It was over, and he screamed out at the night to vent the hours of fear and frustration.

The wolf stood with Randy's leg in its jaws and stared at him. Its coat was a shiny silver that gleamed in the moonlight; its eyes were glacier blue. It regarded Randy with a look of detached curiosity. It was much bigger up close, too. Its four legs were hugely muscled and its body was twice the size of a normal wolf. Randy knew, however, there were no "normal" wolves within several hundred miles.

Without a growl or a move to bite him, the other wolves encircled him like a rapt audience. Many of them had eyes the color of coal, but Randy caught flashes of other colors: green, blue, light brown... One black wolf, smaller and leaner than the others, had black eyes with an amber ring around them. It stood farther back than the others and acted hesitant, as if unsure if it wanted to commit itself to the pack.

Randy's leg throbbed. He felt the warm rush of his blood run down his leg and soak his pants. The wolf's jaws were an iron clamp. His body began to shake from the trauma of the blood loss and the fall, but the wolf simply stood and passively watched him.

A figure walked out of the darkness. It was a naked man with an easy manner about him. He moved like a man who was accustomed to being naked in the woods in the middle of the night. He stepped fearlessly between the wolves, walked to Randy's side, and crouched down beside him.

"Hello," he said.

Randy recognized him. Everyone in town knew the man, or at least knew of him. He had thick black hair, long enough to reach his shoulders, although it curled up at the base of his neck. He wore it brushed straight back and behind his ears. His eyes, like the slender black wolf, were also black with amber rings, and his clean-shaven face was sharp and angular.

"You gave us quite a run," he told Randy. "That was a good idea you had, to climb the tree. It's been tried before. Not often."

His naked body had a surreal quality. It was disproportionate,

Slade Grayson

or so it seemed to Randy. The man's torso looked elongated and his arms had a gangly, stretched appearance. The man smiled and cocked his head, as if to say, *Isn't this a fine mess?*

"It wouldn't have worked. We would have just climbed up after you."

Randy cried unashamedly. "S-so wh-what ha-happens n-now?"

He couldn't keep his voice from shaking. His teeth chattered, either from terror or from the coldness that was rapidly seeping through his body.

"Now?" The man said, "Well, now we eat you. But don't worry." He stood up and his face was lost in shadow. Only the amber rings eyes remained visible. "It'll be quick."

The man lied. It wasn't quick.

# April

Slade Grayson

# Chapter Two

From the outside, it had the appearance of a typical Azure City eatery, one of those walk-in, closet-sized places that changes its name every two years. The menu hardly varied, however. It consisted of hot and cold sandwiches, soups, and an assortment of salads, all culinary delights designed to entice the business lunch crowd.

The interior of the establishment was more spacious than the exterior would lead a passerby to believe. The floor was a dark wood that matched the chairs and round tables. A long bar took up most of the left wall. The right and back walls were dotted with booths. Hanging lamps cast the decor in spots of warm gold.

Drake was afraid he had underdressed for the place, but he spotted other diners in casual short sleeve shirts and jeans, along with patrons in business attire. Drake was dressed in a white oxford cloth button-down shirt, dark blue jeans, and white high top sneakers. He was trying for a clean-cut, yet casual look. He wanted to appear relaxed, despite the fact he was far from it.

He checked himself in a mirror inside the front foyer. His blond hair was freshly cut and he had shaved extra close that morning. With his young countenance and peaches and cream complexion, Drake thought he resembled an altar boy more than a minister.

The hostess was pixie cute. Although she acted pleased to see him, her smile failed to reach her tired eyes.

Drake said, "I'm meeting someone. Reverend Daniel Goodis?"

"This way," she said and picked up a menu. Her heels clicked loudly on the wood floor as she led him in a serpentine fashion past the other diners to a table in the back.

The place was alive with conversation, but somewhat subdued. Despite one or two boisterous voices, soft piano muzak could be clearly heard over the restaurant sound system. They reached the table where Daniel waited with a man Drake had not met before. His stomach knotted; he had thought this to be a private lunch so they could discuss his options. The addition of a third party was unsettling.

The hostess placed his menu on the table, gave him a smile, and left him to his lunch companions. Daniel and the man stood. Drake noted that the two men had stopped talking when they saw him approach. Not a good sign, he concluded.

Daniel smiled warmly and shook his hand. "Drake," he said, "this is Reverend Harker Lang. Reverend Lang, Drake Burroughs."

He shook the man's hand. Daniel had failed to introduce him as Reverend. He wondered if it was foreshadowing.

Lang smiled genially. He was a solid four inches taller than Drake, which Drake estimated put him at around 6'2". Although Daniel had gone the casual route as well, Reverend Lang wore a black suit and clerical collar. His skin tone was dark and his hair was the color of charcoal. It made Drake think the man was Hispanic, but when he said, "It's a pleasure to meet you," he detected a distinct British accent.

"Same here," Drake replied, although he had no idea who the man was or his purpose at the meeting.

Daniel was several inches shorter than Drake and was just beginning to get some of his weight back after undergoing chemo and radiation treatments for cancer the previous summer. After he lost his hair, it had grown back a coarse gray, so Daniel had taken to regularly shaving his head. Drake thought it gave him a youthful appearance despite the lingering pallor to his complexion from the cancer treatments. Still, for a man in his fifties who had skirted so close to death, Daniel had an air of exuberance around him.

Once the three men sat, a bored looking waiter appeared and took their drink order. Daniel ordered an ice tea and Lang said he was happy with his ice water. Drake wanted something stronger, but ordered an ice tea. He failed to stop an involuntary glance at the bar, and hoped Daniel missed it. Alcohol was one of the two vices that had led to his current predicament, and he had promised Daniel he would abstain.

Lang said, "How old are you, if I may ask?"

"Thirty." He wondered what that had to do with anything.

"And you've been ordained now, how long?"

Daniel answered for him. "Drake has been ordained five years. He came to the church right out of law school." He seemed to take paternal pride in the matter.

"Really?" Lang said. "That's wonderful."

Drake said, "Law school was my parents' idea. From a young age, I felt a calling to do something more fulfilling. So I naturally gravitated to the church."

Why did it suddenly feel like a job interview? This was all personal background information Daniel knew. And for some odd reason Drake attributed to intuition, he had the feeling Lang knew everything there was to know about him. Maybe it was the way the man stared at him, stared through him, as if he could read signs in the air currents throughout the room.

The waiter arrived with their drinks and asked if they were ready to order. They all agreed they needed a few more minutes.

Drake picked up his menu and went through the motions of pretending to consider the lunch selections. *Might as well get it out in the open*, he thought.

"Daniel," he said, "I know what this meeting is about."

"Maybe we should order first," Daniel replied softly.

On cue, the waiter returned. Lang handed him his menu.

"Nothing for me, thank you," he said. "I'm fine."

"Well," Drake said with a light laugh that sounded uncomfortably forced, "I'm hungry, so I'm going to order something."

If the church intended to let him go, and he certainly had that impression, he was going to make them pay for his last meal. He ordered a hot roast beef sandwich, a side of steak fries, and a bowl of vegetable soup for an appetizer. He would have ordered lobster if it had been on the menu.

Daniel ordered a salad. He had converted to vegetarianism after his cancer scare, part of his new healthy lifestyle that included regular exercise and yoga.

At least he wasn't one of those staunch vegans who would have rolled their eyes and clucked their tongues when he brazenly ordered a meat dish in their presence. Daniel was tolerant. It was one of the qualities that made him a good minister. And a good friend.

When the waiter left, Drake said, "I made some bad choices this year. I know that. I was thinking that maybe...maybe a move should be in order."

He didn't really want to move, but it would be a better option than excommunication.

"Really?" Daniel said, "Well, that's…" He smiled. "That's basically the reason why I asked you here. I'm glad you agree." He exchanged a pleased look with Lang.

Drake was relieved they were all on the same page. Sure, he knew what he had done was in some circles considered not only immoral, but also unpardonable. It was the type of act that could cause an irreparable rift in a church congregation. But did it mean a man's career, his life, should be forfeited because he gave in to temptation? What about forgiveness? It was a subject Drake had preached on many times, as had Daniel.

"I want you to know," he directed his words to Daniel, "that I haven't had any alcohol in over a month. Not even a sip of wine. Not that I was an alcoholic or anything, but I think the fact that I allowed my drinking to get out of hand was one of the things that led to what happened."

"You mean the affair with the married parishioner?"

If not for Lang's stinging comment, Drake could almost have forgotten the man was there. Now he was unsure as to what stung worse: Lang's remark, which brought back a healthy dose of unpleasant memories, or the fact that Daniel had felt it necessary to share the information with an outsider.

Daniel was apologetic. "I felt I should inform Reverend Lang about everything, considering the fact that he's offered to help us smooth the situation over."

*Smooth the situation over.* Drake liked that. As if he had accidentally insulted someone. The truth was, he had carried on an affair for four months with a married mother of two, a woman he was supposed to have been counseling for depression.

He had counseled her all right. He counseled her right into bed.

Not that it had been his objective, at least not in the beginning. She was attractive, certainly, but his intention had really been to help her overcome her periodic feelings of despondence. His counseling sessions had worked, too, although he noticed her happiness increased proportionally to the amount of time she spent with him.

She had been the aggressor. Of course, it was his responsibility to remain strong in the face of temptation. So why had he faltered? Why did he cross the line?

*It was the drinking*, he thought. His once a week libation had turned into a daily, then a twice daily, then thrice daily, and oftentimes more. The drinking contributed to his bad decisions. It had stripped him of his moral character and wiped away his inhibitions, which was why he had to stay away from alcohol in the future. He couldn't afford another fall from grace.

"I was thinking," he said, "that I could move to a church upstate. Or maybe even Pennsylvania or New York. I know of—"

Daniel cleared his throat. "Actually, Drake, there is a church in need of a minister. That's why Reverend Lang is meeting with us. He's visiting from out west and he told me of a church that will be in need of a new spiritual leader very soon."

"Oh, really?" That perked him up. He had gone from scrounging to stay in the ministry to being offered his own church. The Lord really did work in mysterious ways. "Where is it?"

"The town is called Tanneheuk," Lang answered.

"Is that in New York?"

Daniel cleared his throat again. "Actually, it's Tanneheuk, Montana."

"Montana?!" It came out as a near yelp. Drake saw several restaurant patrons look in their direction. When he opened his mouth again, he made it a point to keep his voice low.

"Why so far away? Daniel, everyone I know is on the East Coast. I grew up out here."

"This isn't a punishment," Daniel said. "It's an opportunity for you."

Ostracized was more like it. He was being banished to the far reaches of the country. Daniel must have read the stricken look on his face.

"Really, Drake, you're looking at this all wrong. There's a church that needs you. And quite frankly, you can't stay here. The scandal won't go away as long as you're out here." Daniel took a sip of his iced tea, wiped his mouth with his napkin, and said, "Her husband…" He made lines in the condensation on his glass. "…has made remarks about the possibility of a civil suit against the church."

"Civil suit? For what?"

"For abusing your authority. He alleges that you were in a position of power and you used that to take sexual advantage of his wife."

"Sexual advantage?!" Drake's voice had risen again.

Daniel nervously glanced around as people at some of the neighboring tables suddenly took an interest in their conversation. Lang appeared neither embarrassed nor uncomfortable. If anything, he appeared ambivalent.

"I didn't take advantage of her, and I didn't abuse my authority. It…it just happened. It was a mistake between two consenting parties."

Daniel waved his hand dismissively. "The husband is understandably upset. As, I might add, are many of the parishioners. We're simply saying that perhaps if we put distance between you and them, the situation might work itself out." He shrugged. "That's all."

Drake shook his head. "But Montana?"

"It's a very nice town," Lang said. "Small. Cozy, really. Just the one church. I think the town has…" He thought for a moment, "Twenty-six hundred people according to the last census."

Drake had the impression Lang knew exactly how many people lived in the town. Still, the slight pause where he pretended to think about it was a nice touch.

"Reverend MacDonald has been the pastor out there for forty-nine years. He's ready to retire and he needs a very capable person to take charge of the congregation. I mentioned it to Daniel and he immediately recommended you."

*Of course he did*, Drake thought. *Why wouldn't he recommend the man some members of the church would like to see run out of town?*

The waiter brought his soup, but his hunger had dissipated

along with whatever initial enthusiasm he had momentarily experienced. He studied the soup until a thin film formed over the top of the broth.

He asked in a defeated voice, "When am I supposed to start?"

"June," Daniel said.

"June?!"

Heads turned in their direction again.

"Please keep your voice down," Daniel said.

"But why so soon? This seems like a bit of a rush."

"Reverend MacDonald's health is rapidly declining," Lang said. "He wishes to retire as soon as possible. It would be to everyone's benefit if you could be there as early as June 1st."

"Sounds like the decision's been made."

"No." Daniel shook his head. "It's entirely up to you. However," he shifted in his seat, "you should know that this is the only option the church will back you on."

So that was it. Daniel's implied threat, though softly conveyed, filled the entire room. They were telling him to move to Small Town, U.S.A. and spend his days preaching to farmers, or ranchers, or whatever they were out in Montana, or that was it. Or leave the church, he supposed. Then what? Go back to the law? Give up on his calling?

"Montana, huh?" He nodded. "Fine."

"Really," Daniel said, "in the long run, you'll see this is a great opportunity for you."

"I can't wait."

If Daniel caught the dejected tone in his voice, he decided to ignore it. He visibly relaxed. An invisible weight had come off his shoulders.

"I should tell you," Lang said, "that Reverend MacDonald would have preferred someone from the town itself to take over the church. Unfortunately, there wasn't anyone capable or qualified. I'm telling you this, Reverend Burroughs, because I want you to understand that Tanneheuk is a close-knit community, and there may be initial...reluctance...to an outsider coming in and taking over the congregation."

*Great.* This couldn't go smoothly. Why should it? It wasn't an opportunity, as Daniel labeled it. *It's my punishment*, he thought.

*I'm being banished.*

As if reading his mind, Lang said, "I'm sure Reverend MacDonald will work to ensure it's a smooth transition."

Drake could have sworn the man had a twinkle in his eye. The waiter arrived with their food. He noticed the untouched bowl of soup in front of Drake.

"Is everything alright?" he asked.

Drake motioned for him to take the bowl. He said, "I don't have much of an appetite after all. Please wrap this up for me, along with the sandwich."

He would take it with him and give it to a homeless person. At least someone would have an enjoyable lunch today.

# Chapter Three

Maryam jogged down the path, her hiking boots crunching the densely packed dirt and occasionally knocking loose an entrenched stone. Once, many years before, the path had been a gravel road that led up to the copper mine. Large rumbling trucks had traveled the road, belching smoke and moving tons of earth. After the mine closed and the road was no longer needed, years of rain washed most of the gravel away.

The forest grew steadily and encroached on the road until it now resembled a well-worn path. Maryam had taken to running the path three times a week after her speed training on the high school track had plateaued. She knew she needed to begin her training on uphill running, which would be a precursor to running on uneven terrain. It was a skill she planned to acquire in the very near future. She had the summer planned out and knew her goals for each month. With only four months left, she needed to stringently remain on schedule because every day counted.

Maryam was the product of biracial parents, which in other parts of the country might have caused her to grow up feeling ostracized. But in Tannehauk, racism was nonexistent. Still, Maryam did feel different from her peers. It just wasn't because of her race or the color of her skin.

Her hair chestnut hair held sun-bronzed streaks, and she had recently taken to wearing it boyishly short, not for looks but for convenience. Long hair was not conducive to running.

Maryam also had the long limbs and lean muscular structure of an athlete, which she had been since early childhood when she had decided on her lifetime goal. Once she made the decision (was it age six? seven?), she became active in all physical activities. She tried everything and stuck with not only the sports at which she excelled, but also the ones that didn't come as naturally. She refused to quit anything until she had at least achieved a level of proficiency that could be considered adequate.

Along with the hiking boots, she wore khaki shorts and a green camouflage print t-shirt. Strapped to her back was a dark green canvas backpack that contained a full plastic water bag that sloshed along with her stride. The water was for added weight to build up her speed and endurance. As she was near the end of her run, the drinking bottle she kept clipped to her belt was empty. She always timed her sips so the water lasted the duration of the run.

Maryam came to the end of the dirt path where the paved section of Lawson Road began, or ended, depending on your point of view. She slowed to a walk and took deep breaths while checking the stopwatch display on her wristwatch. She was pleased to discover she had shaved four seconds off her best time.

It wasn't always like that. Some days were better than others. But as long as she matched her previous running time, or better yet, beat it, she was happy.

On the days when she failed to match, when she actually performed worse, Maryam's mood remained dark until she was able to run again. She constantly pushed herself to do better. She had goals to meet.

She walked to where her old VW convertible with the rusted rear panel was parked. It was a faded orange color that may once have been red, but was too sun damaged now to tell for sure. Despite its dilapidated appearance, it ran reliably, and that was all Maryam cared about.

There were no friends in her life, and no boyfriend. She had classmates, neighbors, and acquaintances. That was all she wanted, and all she needed. She was too single-minded in the pursuit of her goal to care about frivolities.

She emptied the water out of the bag from her backpack on to the ground, and dropped it on the front passenger seat along with her drinking bottle. She checked her watch and decided she might be able to squeeze in a few hours of school. Not that she cared about that either, but her parents certainly did. They had already gone several rounds with her over the last few months about the number of days she had missed.

No one seemed to understand. Although it was her last year of high school, Maryam simply did not care. The day she had waited for was her eighteenth birthday, which had arrived the previous month. School was a waste of her time. Still, she went, or made the pretense of going, to keep up appearances and keep her family from worrying about her.

She got in the driver's seat and started the engine. It sounded like an amped up lawnmower, but it started on the first catch and got great gas mileage. What use would she have for something more cosmetically pleasing?

Maryam made a U-turn and headed back towards town. The temperature was on the cool side, in the low fifties, but she kept the top down. The sun was shining and the wind felt good on her sweaty skin. Her body temperature generally ran high, so she was normally comfortable in brisk weather.

She thought it was shaping up to be a pleasant day. She was on schedule and had acquired nearly everything she needed. In a town where her peers dreaded their eighteenth birthday, Maryam had craved it. She had marked off the days on the calendar until it arrived and brought with it the knowledge she was a step closer. A step closer to being chosen and fulfilling her destiny.

Slade Grayson

# May

Slade Grayson

# Chapter Four

With its spiky shape and shiny aluminum exterior, from a distance the structure resembled a Russian satellite that had broken orbit and crashed to Earth. As they drew closer, they saw it was a diner that once may have been gleaming and nouveau, but was now weather-beaten and dingy. Jonas decided to stop anyway for two reasons. One, because outside of one or two Mom and Pop gas stations, it was the first rest stop they had come across in the last forty minutes; and two, they needed to stop in order to relieve the built-up tension in the car. The four of them had argued over the past two days over who was to blame for the fiasco in Philly. But Jonas knew who was at fault: All of them.

He eased the Cadillac into the parking lot and parked underneath the paint-peeled road sign that said LAST CHANCE DINER. He parked lengthwise due to the moving trailer hitched to the rear bumper. He glanced up at the sign through the corner of his windshield. The sign was red with white letters and a neon border that formed the shape of an arrow, not coincidentally aimed at the aforementioned diner. It probably looked impressive lit up at night, but under the noonday sun, Jonas thought it appeared shabby and forlorn.

The Caddy was an El Dorado, a late 80's model with a dark blue frame and an oyster white leather interior. Despite a few worn spots in the seats and the sun-dulled paint job, the car was in excellent condition. With their constant traveling and accumulation of mileage, the car did not have its original motor or transmission. Most everything mechanical on the car had been replaced at one time or another, sometimes more than once. But Jonas kept the car clean and presentable. As he often told the kids, appearances count most.

He shut off the engine, got out, and stretched. He was fifty years old— a hard fifty— with squint lines around his eyes, a freckled scalp he shaved daily along with his face, a nose that had been broken more than once, and dull brown eyes that may as well have been bullet holes for all the warmth they exuded. Jonas wasn't particularly tall or short, but he was thick with a barrel chest, a gut to match, and meaty hands that looked big enough to squeeze the life out of a bull.

Jonas had the look, too, like he was always ready to throttle someone. It was not uncommon for a person to cross the street when they saw him coming. It was a look he could turn off simply by smiling. His smile reshaped his features and made him appear friendly and honest, two things he definitely was not.

He stretched his neck and arched his back to work the kinks out. There was a time when he could go days without sleep, drive for hours nonstop, and subsist solely on coffee and cigarettes. Now, six hours of driving was enough to cramp his muscles, and the coffee he had consumed an hour ago was eating through the lining of his stomach. He checked the trailer hitch and considered what he might order to eat. The passenger door opened.

"Gee, Dad," David said. "You couldn't find a more rundown grease pit to stop at? What do you think the special is here? Something with salmonella, I hope."

The sarcastic little shit was starting in already. David was Jonas's son from his first marriage, from the wife he had actually been in love with. A lifetime ago, it seemed, back when Jonas believed in love, commitment, honest work, and family values. Back when he was naive.

David had his mother's slight build and blond hair, but had inherited Jonas's eyes and caustic disposition. He was short with an elfin cast to his features, more traits from his mother. He resembled her in so many ways, which was why Jonas both loved and hated him.

Jonas lit a cigarette. "Are your brother and sister awake?"

"Yeah," David answered. "But they're pretending to be asleep."

He had his mother's smirk, too, goddamn him. Jonas put his

foot up on the trailer hitch and took a thoughtful drag on his cigarette. "Something bothering you?" he asked.

David said, "You know those two are doin' it, right? He sneaks out of our room, goes to her room, gives it to her once or twice, then sneaks back. He's like Santa Claus, except he gives her the same present every night."

"What the fuck's the difference? They're not really brother and sister."

David shrugged. "I don't know. They're still cousins. Kinda creepy, is all I'm saying."

"Let it go. He helps keep her in line."

"You mean like in Philly?"

Jonas felt the heat rise up his neck. He stifled the anger back down and turned away. There was a time when the kid never talked back to him and never questioned his decisions. Now it seemed like that was all he did. If Jonas yelled at him, he yelled right back.

*Kid.* Well, David was twenty-four, so technically he wasn't really a kid anymore. Still, Jonas called anyone younger than himself a kid, so David would always fit that criteria.

The back doors of the Caddy swung open in unison. Philo and Amber stepped out, looking groggy and stiff from sleep. Philo was Jonas's son from his second marriage. Although he hated his ex-wife with as much passion as he loved the memory of his deceased first wife, Jonas had a soft spot for the big, dumb kid.

Philo was three years younger than David, tall and broad with spiky black hair and almond-shaped eyes. His mother was a Vietnamese hooker Jonas had taken under his wing and attempted, unsuccessfully, to turn into a grifter like himself. Unfortunately, her whoring ways, much like her rampant drug use, were not so easily done away with, and Jonas had to dump her. He figured she probably went back to hooking, though he doubted she could make a living at it. She was such a lousy lay, Jonas figured her customers were probably always demanding their money back.

Philo was the only positive thing to come out of the experience. Truth be told, Jonas wasn't a hundred percent positive the kid was his. Not that it mattered; he loved the boy. He was stupid and loyal, like an overgrown slobbering puppy you could kick and it would still give you unconditional love. It would still lick the hand that beat it. How could you not love something like that?

Amber was his brother's daughter. Jonas had taken her in nine years ago, back when she was a sullen-faced fifteen year old and her father had gone to prison for killing her mother. She was thin with curly red hair, watery green eyes, and a smattering of freckles across her face. Jonas thought she neither resembled his brother nor, from what he remembered, her mother, so it wouldn't have shocked him if he were to learn his former sister-in-law had fooled around on his brother.

Amber was flat-chested, a fact she was incredibly self-conscious about because she tended to wear baggy shirts or, as now, overalls. They were all dressed casually today, as they usually were unless they had a con running. Jonas generally favored bowling shirts, jeans, and Timberlands, while Philo wore t-shirts, jeans, and tennis shoes. David matched his brother but wore a Hawaiian shirt instead of a t-shirt. Their casual attire hardly varied from day to day, except for the colors. Amber had a floral print t-shirt on underneath her denim overalls and flip-flops on her feet. Jonas thought with the red hair and freckles, she resembled Raggedy Ann.

"Are we stopping here?" Philo asked.

"No," David replied. "We're still moving and this is all a dream."

"I meant—"

"He knew what you meant." Jonas gave David a sharp look, then said, "Let's go in and get a bite to eat. We need to hash out our next move."

He dropped his cigarette and mashed it with his foot. The four of them walked across the near empty parking lot. Jonas half expected to see a closed sign in the window, but the place was open.

They stepped inside and were hit with the stale air of burnt grease and coffee that had sat too long. The tile floor was cracked and faded, and the chrome fixtures were years past shiny. A waitress stood behind the counter talking to the establishment's sole customer, an elderly man seated on the stool nearest the cash register.

The waitress was thick and pasty. Her hair was a tangle of tight gray curls and her uniform was a shapeless pale green polyester number. She might have been pretty thirty years ago, but time had left its indelible mark.

The man seated at the counter was probably old back when the diner first opened for business. He was stooped and slightly hunchbacked, and he wore a thick tweed suit, too warm for the seventy degree weather, but most likely comfortable on a man whose blood circulation wasn't quite as good as it once was. His suit hung on him the way a sheet would drape over a coat rack.

Jonas immediately smiled. "Howdy, ma'am," he said to the waitress. "Are y'all open for business?"

"Sure we are." The waitress smiled back. "You folks have a seat and I'll bring you some menus."

Jonas led the family to a corner booth as far from the counter as he could make it without appearing suspicious. He wanted privacy, but didn't want to look obvious about it. When they sat, Amber lit a cigarette and looked sulkily out the window.

"What's with you?" Jonas asked, but she ignored him.

"Dad, what's with the cornpone accent?" David said. "We're not in the South."

David sat next to him in the booth. Jonas resisted the urge to smack him on the back of the head.

"I want her to think we're from the South. Remember what I always taught you? The key is misdirection." Jonas said it slowly as if he was explaining it to an unruly child. Which, in a way, he was.

The waitress brought them four menus. Jonas glanced at it quickly. The menu was sticky and smudged, and the fare was strictly grilled and fried foods, about what he'd expected.

"Ma'am?" David said, "Y'all have grits here? I been hankerin' for some grits ever since we all left Loozeeana." He kept a dumb countrified smile on his face that made him look sincere rather than sarcastic.

"Nope, I'm sorry." Her name tag said she was Beth Ann. "We don't have grits. We have Cream of Wheat, though."

"Weelll, I'll just take a gander at the menu 'fore I decide."

Jonas glared at him, then ordered coffees all around. Amber piped up and said she'd rather have a Coke. The waitress nodded and left to fill their drink order. When she was far enough away, Jonas let David have the smack on the back of his head.

"Ow! What was that for?!"

"You know what that was for," he said in a low voice. "Knock off the shit."

David shrugged it off and looked at his menu.

Philo asked, "Do they have anything that isn't fried?"

He had a deep, wet voice as if he suffered from chronic sinusitis. In truth, he had been born with a harelip, and although it had been surgically corrected in his childhood, he still had a slight speech impediment and a thin, white scar on his upper lip. He was self-conscious about both.

"They don't have tuna melt on the menu?" David said, "What kind of diner doesn't serve a tuna melt?"

"I hate tuna fish," Philo said.

"Is that why Amber's always in such a bad mood?" David gave her a leer and a wink.

Amber said, "Fuck you." She spat it at him with pent-up venomous anger.

"Knock it off," Jonas hissed, "before I get up and leave the three of you."

That shut them up. The waitress came with their drinks. Everyone ordered hamburgers and fries, except Amber of course, who had to order a BLT to be different.

Jonas shook his head. Once the waitress was out of earshot, he said, "We're going to lay low for a couple of months. I've got something lined up in California for us. Something big. Big enough that maybe we can finally quit this bullshit and retire."

"Why wait?" David asked. "Let's get to California and get to it. Right? What are we doing out here in Moose Tracks, Idaho, or wherever the hell we are?"

"Montana," Jonas said, though he knew David really knew the state they were in. Sometimes he played into the kid's sardonic sense of humor, and then had the urge to smack himself on the back of the head.

"We can't get started until October at the earliest. That's when the right people will be in place. And I'm not gonna chance going out there early and fucking things up before we even get started."

"You don't trust us anymore." Maybe it was just his nasally

voice, but Philo sounded hurt.

"I'm not laying blame on anyone about what happened back East."

Which was not entirely true. He blamed Amber, although he still wasn't sure whether the girl had screwed things up on purpose or by accident. If it was on purpose, damned if he could figure out why. Jonas gave her a pointed look, but she kept her eyes on the window and played like she was irritated with everyone and everything.

"What we gotta do is like I said, lay low for a few months. We'll head to California at the end of September. In the meantime, we've stored up enough cash so we can live quietly." He looked at David. "And when I say quietly, I mean no nickel-and-dime scams or quick cons. None of that. We're not taking stupid chances, especially with heat on us already."

He looked at Philo and Amber. "We're gonna pick some small town and rent a place, maybe even get jobs. No stealing," he directed that at Philo, "and no shoplifting." That was directed at Amber, who rolled her eyes and stubbed out her cigarette in a scarred plastic ashtray.

"Okay," David said, "so we do the straight and narrow thing for a while. The dysfunctional Brady Bunch. Any ideas where?"

"Not yet," Jonas admitted. "We'll drive for a bit and the right place will come along. Sometimes we need a sign to point us in the right direction."

David smirked. "You're not getting religious on us, are you, Dad? Or were you talking about signs in a literal sense, like road signs?"

"I'm talking about signs from above," he replied earnestly. "Signs from the greatest con man of them all — God. If not for Him and all the bad shit He heaped on me in my youth, I might've gone legit."

Jonas held his coffee cup up, David and Philo lifted their cups and tapped them against his in a mock toast. Amber even joined in with her glass of soda. Tensions were eased and smiles made brief appearances around the table. They were beginning to feel like a family again. The waitress brought their food.

"Ma'am?" Jonas asked, "Does it ever get busy in here? Seems

awful quiet."

"Oh, sure it does," she said. "Usually at night. The truckers stop in 'cause we're open twenty-four hours. During the day, it's quiet, but business picks up after six generally."

He thought of asking how long she worked at the diner, but decided against it. One rule of con was, never engage someone in a long conversation unnecessarily. The more you talk, the greater the chance of letting something slip.

The burgers were burnt and the fries were limp and greasy. Jonas was thinking he should have ordered the BLT after all, when the front door opened. It caught him off guard because he usually watched the door and kept an eye on the parking lot. It was an old, ingrained habit that had not only saved him from several arrests, but also saved his life once when a former mark, from whom he had fleeced many thousands of dollars, had tracked him to an out of the way restaurant. The mark had come to kill him, but thanks to Jonas's habit of facing the door, and his usual choice of seats in close proximity to the back door, he was able to escape unharmed. But this time, he had slipped up and it irked him. It made him think that maybe, quite possibly, he was getting too old for the con man's life.

A blond-haired man with a neatly trimmed goatee entered. The late morning sun framed him in the doorway as he stopped to survey his surroundings, and when he stepped inside, it was as if he was stepping out of a ball of light. His hair glowed and dust motes in the air sparkled like stars. He was dressed in a dark blue work shirt, khaki pants, and tennis shoes, but he retained a formal air about himself. The only item that looked out of place was the black plastic wraparound sunglasses the man sported.

Jonas thought the sunglasses would suit someone with a rebellious persona, and he sensed more of a conformist vibe come off the man. Jonas had that talent; he could read people, simply look at them and instantly sum them up by the way they dressed, the way they carried themselves...their aura, if one believed in such things. Whatever it was, it was a gift he had, and it rarely failed him.

Jonas scoped him. He glanced out the front window and saw the man's car, an old silver Honda Civic with a smattering of road dust and, if he had to hazard a guess, New Jersey license plates.

Not a cop and not a Fed, Jonas concluded. Something white collar, but not a lot of money. His gut told him the blond man was harmless...but there was something there. A hesitation in the air as the world held its breath and waited for a universal shift in possibilities and probabilities.

The man took off his sunglasses and glanced in their direction. He produced a sociable smile, then turned it on the waitress as she came out of the kitchen.

"Hi," he said to her. "I was wondering if you could help me. I seem to be a little lost."

The waitress picked up a coffeepot and refilled the cup in front of the old man at the counter. She did it with practiced ease honed by years of performing the same duty.

"Where you tryin' to get to?"

His cheeks reddened slightly, though Jonas guessed it wasn't due to shyness. Rather, he suspected the man suffered from typical male embarrassment at having to ask for directions.

"I'm looking for a town called Tanneheuk?" His voice rose up at the end as if he was unsure of the name or unsure if the place actually existed.

"Oh, that's a nice little town," the waitress said with enough spontaneity to convince Jonas she meant it.

"Really? That's nice to hear," the man said. "I'm Reverend Drake Burroughs. I'm the new pastor for the church there. I'm looking forward to meeting everyone and getting to know the congregation."

Now *that* Jonas did not believe. His bullshit detector told him the man was not looking forward to his new post at all. It may have been nervousness or shyness, but Jonas had the impression the man would prefer to be somewhere else. He had a forced smile, combined with a perturbed manner he worked hard to conceal. He was quite successful at it, too, except for Jonas's ability to see behind a person's public mask.

"It's a small town," the waitress said. "Very quiet and cozy. The people are very nice."

"From everything I've heard, it sounds pleasant," the man said with as much conviction as a boy forced to recite why he loves summer school.

Jonas listened to the waitress give the man directions.

"Stay on this road, heading west. About three miles, the road splits. Stay to the right. If you go left, it'll take you back to the Interstate and you'll have to backtrack."

Reverend Burroughs said, "I've done that. I've gone down the other road, too, but it doesn't seem to go anywhere."

"You're not going far enough. Keep going towards the mountains. Once you come to the bridge, you're there. After the bridge, the road splits again. To the left is Lawson Road, which runs around the outskirts of the town and heads up into the mountains. Stay to the right and the road becomes Main Street. From there, you can make your way anywhere in town."

"You sound like you know it pretty well. Do you live out there?"

"Me? No." She smiled. "I go out there in June for the craft show they have. And there's an Autumn Festival in September a lot of us go to. They have a parade and everything."

"Thanks very much for your help." Burroughs nodded politely. He turned to leave, then turned back with an expression of puzzlement. "Why don't they put up a road sign directing people to the town?"

"Oh, the state keeps putting one up, but someone always takes it down. Been doing it for years. Folks figure it's a rite of passage for the teenagers."

The old man at the counter said, "Ain't no teenagers."

Jonas had forgotten about the old geezer. Now that he spoke up, he scrutinized him with the customary thoroughness he gave everyone. The man had tufts of cottony white hair that popped from beneath a worn Panama hat, and thick etched lines around his mouth and eyes. His skin was a deep brown that Jonas figured made him of Spanish descent, or more likely Native American. He guessed the geezer was between ninety and a hundred years old.

"Nope," the old man said again. "It ain't teenagers. It's the wildlife out there." He let out a laugh that sounded much like a cough, except for the mouthful of tiny yellow teeth that kept up the smile long after his body stopped shaking.

The waitress said, "Oh, hush up, Clem. This nice young man is gonna think you're simpleminded." She made a "tsk" sound and shook her head at the pastor, like, *What am I going to do with him?*

After Burroughs left and the waitress retreated back into the kitchen, Jonas said, "See? It's like I told you. Signs. We follow the signs."

"What signs, Dad?" Philo asked. "She said the teenagers keep taking the signs."

Dumb as dirt, but Jonas loved him.

"I don't mean signs literally, Philo. I'm talking about laying low for a few months and what happens? We hear this conversation about a nice small town called Tanneheuk. That's what I mean by a sign."

David said, "You're kidding, right? When you said lay low, I thought you were talking Seattle or San Diego. I didn't think you meant fucking Mayberry."

"I think it might be nice for a change," Amber said. "What names are we gonna use?"

"I'll be Billy Joe McCallister," David replied. "You'll be Bobby Sue. Philo, we'll call you Big Hungry Joe."

"Shut up," Jonas said. "We'll use our real names. We're gonna do everything legal and above board. I don't want any screw-ups. And you," he pointed to David, "and you," he pointed to Amber, "are gonna resist the urge to con, scam, steal, and shoplift. We're gonna be law abiding citizens for the next few months."

Philo, Jonas knew, did not have to be told. The kid would do as he was told. He was good like that. It was the other two that needed constant supervision.

"Hell," Jonas said, "we might even attend church." He relished the shocked look on his kids' faces.

Slade Grayson

# Chapter Five

Drake followed the directions the waitress had given him. He passed the turnoff for Lake Dulcet, Tanneheuk's metropolitan sister town. From his phone conversations with Reverend MacDonald, he knew that many of Tanneheuk's residents worked and shopped in the town of Lake Dulcet, which was more sprawling and populous, and it also had a mall, something that Tanneheuk lacked.

MacDonald had filled him in on the town, or at least gave him the abbreviated history. Tanneheuk was small, and quite content to stay that way. The town consistently resisted the opportunity to expand and become commercialized. All of its businesses, all stores and restaurants, were locally owned and were non-franchises. If you wanted a meal, there were a handful of eateries that could accommodate you. If you wanted a Big Mac or a bucket of the Colonel's chicken, you had to make the twenty minute drive to Lake Dulcet. Simple as that.

Years ago, Tanneheuk was supported financially by a copper mine. Once that dried up, the town relied on the exports of its local farms and the work provided in Lake Dulcet. Tourism was minimal, relegated to outsiders coming in to sample the fine home cooking of Tanneheuk's restaurants and the revenue generated by the bi-annual craft fair. But no outsiders stayed longer than a few hours unless they were visiting family. There were no hotels or motels in Tanneheuk.

In a voice that rustled like old parchment, Reverend MacDonald explained the town was a close-knit group. From time to time, new people settled in, but the townspeople were picky about whom they permitted to settle. MacDonald said there was a council of sorts who made the decision. He called them the "town elders," and told Drake not to worry: They had approved him to stay, sight unseen. Drake knew he should be relieved, but the idea of a town resistant to new inhabitants made him apprehensive. He knew it was a sign that he would have a difficult task of getting the congregation to accept him as their spiritual leader.

He came to the fork in the road and, as the waitress had directed, he stayed to the right. The engine of his battered Civic gave off a *chink-chink-chink* sound, and had done so for the last hundred miles. It had been his car since college, and he had purchased it used back then. The odometer had long ago passed the 200,000 mark, and he was sure it was only by the grace of God that the car still ran.

*We're almost there*, he thought. *Just hold together a little longer.* He sent a psychic message to the engine and tried to imbue it with positive thoughts, but knew it was silly. The car would either make it or it wouldn't.

He turned up the car radio. It was set on a station scan mode, and as he *chink-chink-chinked* down the road, headed for what appeared to be a valley nestled in a U-shaped mountain range, the radio suddenly locked on a station. Whereas earlier it had spewed forth static with intermittent bursts of hellfire preaching or twangy bluegrass music, it now blared Led Zeppelin in crystal clarity.

Once he recovered from his initial startlement at both the sudden clear signal and the loudness of the volume, he turned it down to an acceptable level. It was "Fool in the Rain." Drake nodded his head to the beat and drummed his fingers on the steering wheel. Upon closer inspection, the mountain range ahead had a croissant shape with small hills on the two edges leading up to bigger and bigger ridges until it peaked in the middle.

Drake knew the town was nestled down in the center, and could see now why it was so isolated. It was situated on a land that was naturally an enclave. Funny, though, that there wasn't a road sign with the town's name on it.

He traveled down the road, flanked on both sides by densely packed trees, as if nature, violated by the manmade path through its forest, would like nothing better than to cover its wound with scar tissue. The trees were thick and darkness was prominent between them. Rather than illuminated by the bright noonday sun, the forest appeared to be shielded from the light. The dense trees provided a tight canopy that blocked the sunlight. It gave him a foreboding sense of uneasiness, though he was hard-pressed to explain why.

He came to Fulman Bridge as the Led Zeppelin song on the radio faded into Pearl Jam's "Daughter." The bridge was narrow and low to the water, a concrete causeway with waist-high railings that traversed a fast moving mountain river. The water was a bottomless blue that sparkled like diamonds and reflected a rainbow of colors.

After the bridge, the road widened and came to another fork. He slowed to a stop. He remembered what the waitress had told him about staying to the right and the road becoming Main Street. He remembered, too, that Reverend MacDonald had said something about the road to the left was Lawson Road and that it ran around the town and ended in a gravel road. Drake turned the wheel to the right and was prepared to continue when he noticed something down Lawson Road. Well off to the side of the road, partially hidden in a patch of tall grass, was an animal carcass. The animal may once have been brown, but now was a bleached white frame. Its ribcage jutted up like broken teeth, sharp and angular and seemingly without a scrap of meat on them. In fact, there seemed to be very little meat left on the carcass except for pieces around the head and the hooves, which gave Drake the impression the body had been there for some time — long enough to be thoroughly picked over by carnivores.

Whatever it once was, it was big. There was something up near where the head would be, something that resembled... antlers? Could it once have been a moose? What could have killed a moose? A large truck, probably, or maybe it simply died from illness or old age. Drake didn't think there were any local carnivores big enough or ferocious enough to take down a full grown moose. Most likely its death could be attributed to natural causes.

He continued on, but wondered why his feelings of trepidation had increased. Perhaps the sight of the dead animal so soon after the ominous forest combined to increase the anxiety he naturally felt over his new position.

He drove on and as the waitress had described, the road did indeed become Main Street. He drove through the center of town and saw markets and stores, two restaurants, a diner, and a bar. One of the restaurants was located on a corner and had a patio with outside tables. The sign out front said CAFÉ ESTRELLITA. He passed a bookstore and several clothing shops, then came to the town's sole stop light.

Traffic was light. More people were on foot or on bicycles, and they all gave him curious looks. No one gawked, but Drake noticed people gave him a onceover and glanced at his license plates. While he waited for the light to change, from the corner of his eye, he saw three people exit a corner drugstore. They stepped out on the sidewalk and openly stared at him.

The man in front was tall and broad chested with a thick mane of silver hair pulled back into a ponytail. Sunlight glinted off his silver stubbled cheeks the way it would sparkle on a snowdrift. It matched a dangling silver necklace around his neck that made an obtuse triangle down his chest.

His two companions were women, one with short, spiked blonde hair, an upturned nose, and a sharp V of a waist. The other woman had a narrow face and shoulder length brown hair, with bangs that covered a generous forehead. The women kept slightly behind and diagonal to the man. All three wore untucked flannel shirts and jeans, although the blonde had her shirt tied under her chest, exposing her midriff.

Drake made eye contact with each of them and kept a friendly smile on his face. When they didn't return his smile, he gave them a short wave. They didn't react. He felt he was being studied, neither out of curiosity nor hostility. It was an assessment, but for what, he couldn't determine.

The light changed to green and he slowly accelerated through the intersection. As he headed up the street, he glanced in the rearview mirror and saw the trio still watching with stoic expressions. Then the blonde licked her lips, which lent the scene more sureality than it needed.

Drake shook his head and forced himself to mentally laugh it away. Just three locals checking out the stranger in town. That's all it was. Nothing more. He laughed out loud and thought about how he would tell his parents about it on the phone that evening when he called them.

His father wouldn't think much of it, but his mother had an appreciation for the theater of the absurd. She would surely find the whole scene funny. He also considered working it into his first sermon, something about the acceptance of strangers. Such were the thoughts that occupied his mind, but beneath was an underlying urge that threatened to break through to the surface. It was the urge to turn his car around, drive out of town, and not stop until he reached the East Coast.

He suppressed the urge and attempted to dispel it by holding it up to scrutiny, the way he might examine a disturbing nightmare in the light of day. Logical reasoning and his deep-rooted belief in the Lord generally tended to soothe his fears and discomfort, and today was no exception. He knew God had a plan for him, as He does for everyone, and Drake had faith in that plan.

Past the center of town, the shops and restaurants gave way to houses. Many were Victorian-style with wraparound porches and spacious backyards. Wind chimes were hanging from eaves and several houses had flagpoles in the front yard, the American flag billowing in the cool springtime breeze.

He came to another intersection, this one in the suburban section of town. Straight ahead, he knew from his conversation with Reverend MacDonald, was the Tanneheuk School — elementary, junior high, and high school — all set in a sprawling collective of one-story buildings within a hundred feet of each other. Further up was the town newspaper, and the local radio station that now streamed through his car speakers. The station was exclusively rock and roll and ran the gamut from the 1950s up to the present day. Pearl Jam gave way to the Stones, to Chuck Berry, and now to the Gin Blossoms.

Drake turned left at the intersection and the Victorian architecture became ranch-style homes. Three blocks up he spotted the church on the right. It was modest, albeit large, with a dark wood shell and beige trim. It resembled a meeting lodge more than a house of worship, with the exceptions of the large white cross on the steepled roof and the rows of stained glass windows along its sides. An equally modest sign out front near the street proclaimed it THE CHURCH OF GOD.

He turned into the parking lot and parked in a space on the side of the building within steps of the front door. He knew the office was in the back with a separate entrance, along with Reverend MacDonald's living quarters. Which reminded him: Where was he going to stay tonight? Sleep on the good Reverend's couch? Or was there an apartment complex he might have overlooked?

Farther out, there appeared to be farms. He hoped he wasn't expected to room with one of his parishioners and be forced to make small talk and pitch in with farm chores if his potential landlord turned out to be a Tanneheuk farmer. He liked people and liked socializing with his congregation, but running a church was time consuming and, at times, stressful. Stress he didn't mind, but he would prefer to deal with it the same way he prepared his sermons: with quiet reflection, undisturbed introspection, and prayer.

He checked himself in the rearview mirror, finger combed his hair, and took off his sunglasses. The goatee was new; he thought it made him look a bit older, maybe took some of the innocence out of his boyish features. It was neatly trimmed and due to his light complexion, near invisible. Drake had always had sparse facial hair and could go days without shaving before his stubble became noticeable. He had begun growing the goatee immediately after Daniel had told him of his new assignment. Another few weeks, maybe, and it would be properly filled in.

He got out of the car and stretched, then made his way around to the front door. The stiffness in his legs and back dissipated. He felt good now; the tension from earlier had melted away. He took in deep lungfuls of air and marveled at the sweet crispness of it. It smelled and tasted clean, and something about it changed his outlook. It washed over him and, as he entered the church, he was imbued with a sense of hope.

The inside of the building was spacious and well-lit, with a flowery scent Drake was familiar with, which came from a combination of burning candles and air freshener. Although none of the candles around the altar were lit, the scent still clung to the air. Far from cloying, however, it comforted him because it gave him a sense of familiarity.

The wine-red carpet was of commercial quality, thin, yet durable. A main aisle split the room with rows of pews on either side. The front altar was raised up a foot and had a podium with a microphone attachment, and speakers were mounted in the corners near the rafters. No organ or piano, though, which made him wonder if they went without music during the service or if the pastor played recorded music. Drake liked to begin and end a service with music. He thought it lent a soothing quality to the proceedings.

On the back wall, directly in the center, was a huge mounted wood cross. It was glossy with shellac, which gave it the appearance of having been flash frozen in ice. It was imposing and impressive, and as always, made him feel humble and full inside, as if his body was suddenly filled with a dense light that numbed all traces of self-doubt.

To the left, in an alcove of sorts, was a door. He assumed it led to the pastor's office and living quarters. He was prepared to walk over and knock on the door, announce his arrival and begin the formality of introductions and questions, etc., when the stained glass windows drew his gaze.

Stained glass was standard in churches, much as pews and crosses, but these were different. There were six, three on either side of the room. The two center ones were strictly multicolored glass windows, arranged in geometric patterns. The windows on either side of those, and directly across from each other, were pictures rendered in stained glass such as what Drake had seen in Catholic churches.

One window was a depiction of the crucifixion of Christ. It was a standard portrait, nothing he hadn't seen a thousand times before. The next was a depiction of Mary, mother of Jesus. Or at least, he thought it was Mary.

The stained glass portrait was slightly different from the many other artistic renderings Drake had seen. In this picture, Mary was darker skinned with somber colored robes that flowed about her. Missing was the ubiquitous halo that was always part of her portrait. There was a wildness to her; if Mary was generally portrayed as a virgin who became the mother of Christ, this Mary was an Earth mother who could inspire fear. Her gaze was cold, and depicted behind her was a purplish sky thick with silvery black clouds.

The window on the opposite side depicted a forest. Again, the effect was one of gloom rather than calmness. It was a forest thick with shadows, trees with interlocked branches, and massive trunks hundreds of years old. The depicted forest was one that remained isolated from modern civilization, a world unto itself where ancient primal laws still ruled and species long believed to be extinct still made their home.

All this Drake read from the Stygian darkness depicted around and between the trees in the picture. It reminded him of the forest he had passed on his way into town. He shivered involuntarily, and attributed it to the air conditioning.

The last window was the strangest of all. It was the picture of a wolf standing over two infants. The wolf was black with amber eyes, and rather than portrayed as a menacing figure to the infants, it appeared to be a protective figure. It stood over them in a fierce motherly way and projected a warning to any who might venture too close or wish to commit harm against the children.

Funny that he could get so much from a static picture. The stained glass portraits were the product of a talented artist. He made a mental note to ask Reverend MacDonald about their history. Perhaps the artist who created them was local.

"Romulus and Remus."

The voice startled him. Drake turned and saw a man several rows back, sitting on the back of a pew with his feet up on the seat. He hadn't heard the man enter, in fact hadn't heard him at all until he spoke.

"What?" Drake blushed like he had been caught in the act of doing something wrong.

The man said, "Romulus and Remus. The babies in the picture. That's who they are. They grew up to be the founders of Rome. Their mother was a wolf."

The man had long, jet-black hair that he wore combed back behind his ears. It nearly reached his shoulders, but curled up at the base of his neck instead. He wore a white cotton shirt with the sleeves cut off at the shoulders, jeans that were worn through at the knees, and a pair of moccasins.

"You were staring at that window. I thought you were curious about the picture."

"Oh," Drake said. "Uh, yeah...yeah, I suppose I was." He looked back at the stained glass window. "It's really quite striking. Seems odd, though."

The man stepped down from the pew. His movements were as fluid and limber as a yoga master's, yet there was a coil to his limbs as if his muscles were poised to react at the slightest provocation.

"How so?"

He walked up to Drake and cocked his head a degree. It reminded Drake of the way an animal might tilt its head if it was unsure of what to make of an oddity.

Drake replied, "I'm familiar with the story of Romulus and Remus. But it seems strange to have a myth like that represented on a church window."

The man let out a sharp bark of a laugh that startled Drake by its suddenness. He showed a lot of sharp-looking, white teeth.

"A myth? Funny that you describe it that way."

Drake shrugged. "How else would you describe the story of a wolf giving birth to two human babies?"

"Is it any more unbelievable than the story of a virgin giving birth to a demigod?"

"Jesus wasn't a demigod," Drake replied with a forced patience that concealed his indignance. "He was—"

The man stopped him with a wave of his hand. "He was the son of God. He *was* God. I know, Reverend. I'm familiar with your beliefs. And I apologize if it sounded as if I was making light of them. I meant no disrespect, as I'm sure you meant none when you callously described my beliefs as a myth."

That took him aback. It was a second before Drake found his voice. "I had no idea you believed in the story."

"Of course not. Why should you? Like most spiritual leaders, you believe yours is the one true religion and you dismiss everything else as fantasy."

"I apologize if I offended you."

The man laughed again, subdued this time. "No need to apologize, Reverend. I'm not offended."

He wasn't tall. In fact, he was nearly two inches shorter than

Drake. But he had the appearance of being tall. Something in the construction of his body, the lankiness of his torso, perhaps... Drake couldn't put his finger on it.

"I don't mean to pry, but I take it you're not a Christian?"

The man answered, "Not in the traditional sense," but didn't elaborate.

"Could you give me some insight into these stained glass pictures?"

The man nodded and seemed bemused. He pointed to the picture of the trees and said, "That one represents the Black Forest."

"Germany," Drake said. "What's the connection?"

"My people were driven out of Rome. Ironic because, as I said, they founded the city. They settled in an area known as Arcadia, but that didn't last either. From there, during the Dark Ages, two tribes emerged. One migrated to the area then known as Constantinople. The other tribe settled in the Black Forest. That's where my ancestors came from."

"And how did they end up here?"

Drake could see the man was pleased by the question. He had a vague smile on his lips, as if he savored the opportunity to talk about the history of his ancestors.

"They dwelled there for a long time in peace, but once again found themselves persecuted, as did the other tribe. They merged and sought sanctuary in France, but the French government was...reluctant, I suppose you could say, to offer them shelter. They struck a deal whereby France provided them with safe passage and guides to bring them first to Canada, then to here where they could have their own land that would remain isolated." The man shrugged. "At least for a little while."

"So this town is where your ancestors settled?"

He nodded. "Not just my ancestors, but also some of the French and Canadian people who came with them. They settled here. Some of my people chose to remain in Canada, and some chose to remain in Europe and go into hiding. But many came here and mixed with the Native Americans. The rest of the townspeople are descendants of pioneers who came west, looking to stake land claims, or descendants of the Native American tribes. And of course there are the others who have settled here over the years, newcomers such as yourself, whom we've permitted to make a home here."

"You make it sound like an exclusive club," Drake said. He intended for the comment to be lighthearted, but as he said it, he realized his tone lacked joviality. He briefly wondered if he still harbored bitterness about his reassignment to this small town far away from his friends and family.

But there was another factor at work. It was the man's effect on him, his bearing. Although the man acted polite and genial, Drake felt it was a front. He thought that beneath the man's humble facade was a smug elitist. When he looked at the man, Drake had the impression he was looking at a mask. He could almost peer beneath it, like he was looking through a dark tinted window and could subtly discern a shadow moving behind it. The mask, Drake thought, was his relaxed smile and easy voice. Whatever dwelled beneath the surface, however, was cold and calculating.

"It is an exclusive club, in a way," the man said. "We don't allow just anyone to stay in our town."

Drake searched the man's eyes to determine if he was serious. It was hard to tell because there were times during their conversation when he thought the man was secretly laughing at him. He didn't take it personally because the impression he had was that the man quietly laughed at everyone he encountered, as if he was the only one privy to a private joke. There was nothing in his actions that indicated such; it was an aura the man put out.

Drake shook his head. "I don't understand. You say 'we don't allow.' Are you on the town council?"

Again there was the tilt of his head. "Not exactly." He glanced around the church, appearing to be suddenly surprised to find himself in such a place. "I haven't been in here in years," he said. "Maybe I should come to service this weekend." He looked at Drake and winked. "See how you perform, if you're up to the task of spiritually guiding these people."

"I'm sorry, I don't mean to be rude," Drake said, "but who are you? You seem to know who I am..."

"You're Reverend Drake Burroughs, taking over for Reverend MacDonald. I'm one of the town elders."

"Well, I would very much like it if you came to my first

service," Drake said. He wanted to inquire about the man's name, and beyond that, ask what the function of a town elder was, but he had the feeling he was being led by the man's enigmatic dialogue. The man was being vague and mysterious so as to spark his curiosity, and the only reason for it, or so Drake believed, was for the man's own private amusement.

"No promises, Reverend."

There was a slight disappointment in the man's eyes that he hadn't asked the expected follow-up questions, and he felt a momentary flash of victory. Just as suddenly, he felt a twinge of guilt. As a spiritual leader, he knew he should be above juvenile mind games.

They both smiled at each other, a forced friendly grin that neither of them truly believed was authentic.

"I should go," the man said.

"Before you do that," Drake said, "could I ask you about the other window? The portrait of Mary is different than most depictions I've seen. I was wondering if you knew any background information on it." He pointed to the stained glass portrait of the fierce looking woman, and at the same time took childish revelry in the thought that the man hadn't succeeded in controlling the conversation.

"That's not Mary," he said. "It's a popular misconception. That woman is the mother of my people, the mother of Romulus and Remus. Her name was Lillith. The Christians adopted her look, watered it down, and used it for Mary, the mother of Jesus."

"I thought you said the mother of Romulus and Remus was a wolf."

"She was both."

Drake asked, "How can a woman be both human and a wolf?"

"I could ask you how a man could heal the sick, walk on water, and come back from the dead."

Before Drake could reply, the man turned and headed for the door. "I'll let you get settled in, Reverend. We'll talk again." Before he left, he turned and fixed Drake with a stare. "One more thing..."

Drake nearly laughed. It reminded him of one of those cop shows where you think the detective is about to leave, but stops at the door to drop a bombshell on the suspect.

"Tanneheuk is a beautiful little town. There's no poverty, no racism, and rarely any crime. We keep it that way by strict adherence to the town's laws. Reverend MacDonald and the sheriff will fill you in on all of that, I'm sure. If you have more questions, you can always ask me." He gave another half smile, half smirk. "Go with the flow here, Rev, and stick to the ways of the town. You'll have a happy life here if you do that."

"And if I do have questions, how can I reach you? Do you live nearby?"

"Oh, I'm around, Rev. I'm always around." The smile deepened and nearly reached his cold eyes before he turned and went out the door.

As he left, the open door let in a burst of afternoon sunshine making it appear that the man had been engulfed by the light. Only the swing of the shutting door proved the man had been there a moment before. Drake wondered, *What was all that about*?

# Chapter Six

Fern Wilde was a quarter Blackfoot Indian, a quarter Irish, a quarter French, a quarter Icelandic, and a hundred percent lazy according to her father. She was thirty-two and still lived in the finished basement of her parents' house. Although she worked three part-time jobs and could, if necessary, support herself, the truth was most of Fern's monthly earnings went to the purchase of copious amounts of marijuana. Also, Fern's mother did her laundry and prepared most of her meals. Cooking and laundry were two chores that Fern detested. So maybe Dad was partly right. Maybe Fern was a little lazy. But only when it came to the trivial things.

Fern was knowledgeable enough, and her parents certainly owned plenty of land, that if she so desired, she could grow her own marijuana and thereby save herself much of her hard-earned cash. But one of Fern's part-time jobs was town deputy to Sheriff Creel. The job consisted of driving around town a few nights a week and checking that the stores and businesses were locked and secure, ensuring teenagers were not congregating under the high school bleachers and sneaking beers, and on occasion driving Pete or Carl or any of the other regular patrons of Dennison's Bar home if they happened to consume one too many beers.

Her job as deputy never consisted of investigating or solving a real crime because, quite frankly, there was never a real crime in Tanneheuk. Well... almost never. The incidents that had occurred over the years — a few domestic disputes; a charge of assault; the time Tim and Martha McClenny's teenage son broke into the diner and cleaned out the till — those matters had been handled by people outside the sheriff's office. Those matters were resolved by the Tanneheuk town elders.

The point was, although Fern's job as town deputy was little more than a glorified neighborhood watch position, (hell, she performed her duties without wearing a sidearm), she thought growing marijuana would be a breach of her oath to uphold the law and honor the code of the sheriff's office. But smoking it? Surprisingly, that did not upset Fern's sensibilities in the least.

She had been a daily pot smoker since she was a teenager, shortly after the time when the Dodge Charger she had spent almost every waking moment restoring had slipped off the jack and crushed her left leg. The pain had been excruciating. Despite the expert job the surgeons did of removing the bone chips from her shredded leg muscle and resetting the bone so it would heal with minimal physical therapy, Fern had been left with chronic pain. Prescribed painkillers alleviated it, but also upset her stomach and left her with a disconnected feeling. So she smoked weed, threw away the pills, and felt fifty times better. Oh, and she still had the Charger. Drove it every day, in fact.

Now, fifteen years later, her leg still radiated a dull ache and she walked with a limp, but it was something she no longer took notice of. It had become ingrained, second nature to her daily existence, much like the perpetual buzz she cultivated from the weed.

Fern smoked a joint first thing in the morning upon waking, even before she got out of bed, which was coincidentally when her leg bothered her the most. She would dress, deliver the morning edition of the *Tanneheuk Sun* (her second part-time job), head home for a nap, wake again, and smoke another joint. Then shower, dress, eat, and head to KBLF, Tanneheuk's sole radio station, where she worked as a DJ (part-time job number three).

She covered the mid-afternoon to early evening shift four days a week, more if they needed her. While she played music and talked to her listeners, she would smoke another joint. After her shift, Fern made her nightly rounds in her official capacity as deputy, then headed home for a little television, yet another joint, and sleep. The next morning, like a digital loop, the whole process repeated itself. The only exception was those nights when she wasn't scheduled to work at the radio station. On those nights, she often showed up and spent time helping with office work, cutting commercials, or giving the custodian a hand with his work.

It was a small radio station in a small town; everyone pitched in on all the various work responsibilities whether it was part of their job or not. Besides, the bare-boned staff that manned the station, much like Fern herself, didn't have much of a social life to speak of outside of work.

She lay in bed and smoked the last vestiges of her joint and glanced occasionally at the clock. It read a few minutes past noon. Once her joint was down to a mere wisp of paper, she put out the smoldering ember in an empty Diet Dr. Pepper can on her bedside table. No ashtrays, for fear her mom would come across it during her regular housecleaning duties.

Yes, Mom and Dad didn't know about Fern's smoking habit. It was better that way. They were old-fashioned and would have been disdainful about it, preferring she stayed strung out on mass produced pharmaceuticals rather than utilize Mother Nature's method of pain alleviation. The illegality of it was probably the biggest problem they would have with her habit.

She got up and stretched, careful out of habit not to stretch her left leg lest it shoot forth a sharp pain that would puncture her gossamer narcotic cocoon. She felt warm and blissful, comfortable as she usually did, much like someone who was on the verge of falling into a deep sleep. It was the standard feeling she got from the marijuana: neither high nor low, just mellow.

Fern stood and stripped out of the cotton shorts and tank top she normally slept in. She allowed the clothes to pool onto the floor in a soft heap. It was laundry day and Mom would be down shortly to collect any odds and ends Fern had neglected to deliver to the hamper.

She padded to the bathroom, naked but for a pair of white socks, and stopped to regard herself in the full-length mirror mounted on her bathroom door. She studied herself in profile, then full on, and as usual was unimpressed with what she saw. She wasn't ugly, but she certainly couldn't be considered pretty either. Plain was what looked back at her from the mirror, and plain was how she would describe herself. Her face was just a little too long, her mouth a little too wide, nose a little too pointed, hazel eyes a little too dull, reddish-brown hair a little too listless, complexion a little too washed out...

It was as if when her DNA coalesced and the building blocks for her genetic structure began to form, one ingredient had been left out, a teaspoon of a secret spice that would have transformed the finished dish from bland to delicious.

Her body was too thin, and tall. Her breasts were little bigger than a pair of softballs. When she arched her back, not a lot, but slightly, her ribs were clearly outlined. In essence, she was built like the beanpole nickname she had been given back in high school.

*Better too skinny than too fat*, she told herself. She didn't work at staying thin. She just wasn't into food very much. Her mom would make lunch for her and there would be a dinner plate waiting for her when she got home, but Fern wasn't much of an eater. A typical day for her might be half a tomato sandwich for lunch, a few bites of chicken for dinner, and a couple of diet sodas spaced throughout the day. The rest of her meals generally were relegated to the trash bin or the family dog.

Fern didn't wear makeup, except occasionally lip balm during the bitter winter months. Had she deigned to apply lipstick and some eyeshadow, and paid a visit to the beauty salon to have her hair colored and styled, she could conceivably have raised her attractiveness a few notches, perhaps from average to cute. But a beautification regimen held as much interest for her as the prospect of moving out of her parents' house, which was zilch.

She looked herself over and gave her image a shrug. She used the toilet and brushed her teeth, then stood under the shower until her skin was mottled pink and red. She washed herself and shampooed her hair, and finished with a cold rinse that made her heart race.

Fern dried herself and dressed. Her underwear was ordinary, functional rather than showy. She owned several pairs of lacy silk bras and panties, but hadn't worn them in years. What was the point? Her sex life was nonexistent. She hadn't had sex in... Well, since the last time she wore the lacy underwear several years before.

Not that it bothered her. Fern had lost interest in sex. She found it not worth the trouble it entailed. She rarely masturbated anymore. She usually drifted off to sleep in the middle of the act. She didn't need sex. All she needed was her three part-time jobs and the monthly bag of pot she bought off her dealer.

She slipped on a pair of jeans and her khaki uniform shirt with the brown pockets, epaulets, and patches on the sleeves that read: TANNEHEUK SHERIFF'S DEPARTMENT. She pulled on a pair of navy blue socks and her brown lace-up boots with the heavy rubber soles.

Before she headed upstairs, Fern opened a dresser drawer and removed a locked metal box. She selected a key from one of the many that vied for space on her keyring, and unlocked it. Inside was a holstered nickel-plated .38 revolver with black rubber handgrips and a box of shells. More importantly, also inside the box was a clear plastic bag of marijuana and a square, flat cigarette case. She removed the case, shut the box, and locked it.

The cigarette case was chrome with inlaid green plastic designed to resemble marble. It was small, but it easily held twenty joints. She flicked the clasp with her thumb and it sprang open to reveal eleven rolled little beauties. It was enough for two more days before she would have to roll more.

She closed the case and slid it into her left pants pocket, then picked up the Zippo lighter from her bedside table and dropped it into her right pocket. Last, she grabbed her mirrored sunglasses off the dresser, gave herself a final check in the full-length mirror, and headed upstairs.

Mom was at the kitchen table, shuffling through index cards. Her mom was a big-boned woman with long, gray hair she kept tied in a ponytail. She wasn't quite fat, simply thick and fleshy. She had the appearance of being doughy, as if her body easily retained fluid. The steady stream of shapeless housedresses she wore did nothing to contradict the casual observer's estimation.

In truth, Fern's mother, Odette Wilde, was a large woman with big hands and big feet and the extra flesh that comes from aging and inactivity. Her face was jowly and appeared older than her fifty years, the result of decades of smoking. Even now, Fern's mother had a cigarette smoldering in one meaty hand while the other flipped through the index cards.

"Whatcha doin'?"

The question was perfunctory. Fern didn't really care what she was doing, but she knew her mother's feelings would be hurt if she didn't make an attempt to engage her in conversation before she left for work. Truthfully, her job at the radio station was what she cared most about in her life. If she could, she would stay at the station all day and night, and eat and sleep there. It was her sanctuary, her reason for getting up in the morning, (getting up at noon, anyway), her reason for drifting through the other mindless chores of the day. She lived for being on the air and playing music. If, for budgetary reasons, the station ever had to lay her off, she would offer to work there for free.

Her mother answered, "They're having a welcome lunch for the new church pastor the first weekend in June. Celia asked for volunteers to make the food. I said I'd make two pies for dessert. The meal is only for the church committee, their families, and the pastor. Two pies should be enough, don't you think?"

Fern shrugged, but her mom was still peering intently at her collection of dessert recipe cards. She didn't think her mother really expected an answer, and even if she did, she never paid heed to Fern's opinion anyway, so what was the point of asking?

"I was thinking apple pie." Her mom placed one card off to the side and dragged long on her cigarette. After a moment: "And a blueberry pie."

"Sounds good," Fern said.

*Ugh.* The apple was a good choice, but the blueberry pie always turned out to be a soggy mess. You would think her mother would have learned her lesson by now and retired that particular recipe.

Fern opened the refrigerator and took out the bag lunch her mother had prepared for her. She peeked inside and saw what appeared to be sliced turkey on rye bread with lettuce. Past experience told her there was also a thin coating of dark brown mustard, too.

There was a sliced apple in the bag, cut into quarters with the stem and seeds removed. The apple quarters were in a Ziploc baggie; they glistened red and gold. She decided she would probably eat the apple on the way to work, and maybe the sandwich later on her dinner break. She took a can of Diet Dr. Pepper for the drive.

"I'm fixing the rest of the leftover turkey for supper," her mom said, "with gravy and mashed sweet potatoes. I'll have a plate ready for you to heat up when you get home."

"'Kay." Fern knew she wouldn't be hungry, but at least the dog would eat well.

Perhaps sensing her thoughts, Jethro, their golden collie, ambled into the room. He moved to stand by her hand, his head an inch from her fingers as if he expected her to scratch behind his ears...or not, it really didn't matter to him. He was an older dog and had long outgrown the puppyish enthusiasm for being petted, but out of habit he still went through the motions due to years of repetitious behavior.

Fern, also out of habit, extended her hand and scratched Jethro's head. He wagged his tail lazily. She adjusted the red bandanna that he wore in lieu of a collar. When she was satisfied it was situated correctly, she gave Jethro a final double pat on his side. He sauntered off to the living room now that half of his daily goal was achieved. The other half would be completed later that evening when Fern returned home and scraped most of the contents of her supper plate into his dog dish. It was a continuous ritual that both of them engaged in with an indifferent aplomb.

Fern's mother placed the cigarette in her mouth, stood, then shuffled to the kitchen counter where she kept her two plastic recipe boxes. She coughed wetly, the same smoker's cough she had for as long as Fern could remember.

"Maybe you should come to the lunch, too."

"What lunch?"

"The lunch for the new pastor," her mother said with a tone of exasperation.

"I have to work."

Her mom gave her a pointed look. "I didn't tell you what day." She blew out a stream of smoke.

Fern wanted to disentangle herself from the conversation. She really wanted to get to the station and start preparing for her show.

"I thought you said it was the first weekend in June, or something."

"Yeah, but I didn't say what day." Her mom stubbed out her cigarette in an ashtray by the sink.

"What day?" Fern asked.

"First Sunday in June, after the service."

"I have to work."

"Fern," her mother said. "It wouldn't kill you to come to church with me and your father once in a while. And, it would be nice if you came to meet the new minister. He's single, you know."

*That won't last*, Fern thought. There were plenty of single, eligible women in town, and some not-so-single women, who would be figuratively chomping at the bit to make themselves noticed to the fresh infusion of a man into the community. She pictured the new reverend, whatever his name was, at the celebratory welcome lunch surrounded by drooling women who would mentally undress him with their eyes. *Probably fight over who gets to sit next to him*, she thought. It would serve them right if he turned out to be ugly and had poor hygiene. Not that it would make much difference; the town was so closed off that simply being new and/or different was enough of a turn-on to the bored women in Tanneheuk that he would still be the most popular person in town. At least for a little while, until his newness wore off.

"You wanna come and meet him?"

"I dunno. Maybe." Fern shrugged.

She didn't have the slightest desire to go to church, or meet a man for that matter. She was perfectly content with the rut her life had developed into.

"I gotta go." She headed out the side door before her mother had the chance to initiate one of her patented harangues about how Fern should meet someone and maybe get married. It was the standard speech her mother fell into, much as Fern's dad fell into his usual speech about how she should move out and get her own place.

She walked along the side of the house, down the driveway that stretched to the two-car garage. The garage was set in the back near the tree-lined woods that ran parallel to their backyard. Fern's parents actually owned a small portion of the undeveloped land behind their house, but like the other town residents, they never pushed the issue of who legally owned the land. It was understood that despite what land titles might say, the woods belonged to the elders.

Fern walked down the driveway to where her Charger was parked on the street in front of the house. The black Charger held a dull gleam under the afternoon sunlight. The paint needed to be retouched and a few rust spots needed to be sanded and buffed out. Fern had let it go for too long, although she did keep the engine tuned and timed to a Swiss watch-like precision. The upkeep of the outer appearance, which she used to be fastidious about, had declined over the years. She had even neglected to wash and wax the car for several months, as clearly evident by the fine coat of dust that was sprinkled over the car's frame.

She walked to her car and noticed a road-weary Cadillac with an attached moving trailer parked across the street in front of Mrs. Dallway's house. The back of the trailer was open and it appeared luggage was being transferred to the house. Next to the trailer was a blond-haired man with a slim build and an elfin face with a half-smile beneath dark sunglasses. He had his arms crossed as he regarded her.

"Nice," he said.

"'Scuse me?" Fern had her car door open and was in the process of leaning to get in when he had spoken to her. It caught her off guard.

"The car." He motioned with his chin. "Nice."

She sat down, the car door open and her feet still planted on the ground. She placed her lunch bag and soda on the passenger seat, then turned back to look at the man. He tilted his head down so that the sunglasses slid partly down his nose. He looked at her over the rims and his half smile became a full one.

He said, "Maybe you can take me for a ride sometime. In your car, I mean."

There was a snarkiness to his voice. Fern couldn't determine if it was intentional or if it was his natural manner of speaking. Whatever it was, it irritated her. And when she had her mellow pre-work buzz, the last thing she wanted was a minor irritation to burrow its way in and disrupt her harmonious balance.

She swung her legs in and closed the door. She started the engine, and as it roared to life, she rolled down her window and stole another glance at the man. He studied her with an unabashed openness that grated on her nerves. Fern put the car in drive and had her foot poised above the gas pedal when Mrs. Dallway's front door opened and another man stepped out. He was young, too, but that was the only trait he appeared to share with the blond man. He was big with dark hair, a slight Asian cast to his features, and a dumbfounded expression that made him appear newborn and innocent.

In a nasally voice, he said to the blond man, "Dad said to help bring the rest of the suitcases in."

The blond man frowned and said, "Thanks, Huey."

"My name's not Huey," the big man replied in a petulant tone.

Fern shook her head and drove away. She thought Mrs. Dallway must have strange relatives and wondered why no one in town had ever met them before.

As she headed to work, another idea edged around her mind and slowly wormed its way through the soft cloud that buffered her thoughts. She remembered Mrs. Dallway mentioning on more than one occasion about how big and empty her house felt now that her son was grown and out of the house, and the passing of her husband of forty-six years. She recalled Mrs. Dallway had talked of renting some of the rooms in her spacious house. *That must be it*, Fern decided. They were boarders. The only troubling thought was, Fern had assumed Mrs. Dallway would rent the rooms to locals. Those two men, however, were not from Tanneheuk. Which made them strangers. And, as Fern and most everyone else in town knew, strangers were often trouble.

# Chapter Seven

Jonas had begun to question his decision to lay low in Tanneheuk. Not the "lay low" part, but his choice of where. On the surface, the town appeared idyllic. The drive in through the woods and over the low concrete bridge had been both peaceful and aesthetically pleasing. Even the kids had stopped grumbling and squabbling, and had sat quietly and watched the passing scenery. The tension among them quelled, and they all settled into a calm peacefulness that was not quite happy, yet not quite melancholy. It was more of a comfortable medium that Jonas hoped would last, but his cynical side assured him it wouldn't.

Once they arrived in town, their prospects appeared promising. Jonas parked and the four of them got out to stretch and look around, check out the shop windows and get a feel for the locals. Jonas asked a passerby about lodgings, and was surprised to discover that Tanneheuk did not have a hotel or motel within town limits. The nearest place was a motor lodge all the way over in Lake Dulcet. There were two rooming houses, but both were full up for the foreseeable future. Jonas was about to order his three surly kids back into the car, when another passerby told him about a woman with three rooms for rent. Jonas inquired about directions, and after the man politely gave it to him, he was getting back into the Caddy when he caught a strange sight.

Across the street was a bakery. Through the large front window, he caught a tall, blond-haired man openly staring at him. Well, not just him, but at the four of them. The kids didn't notice. They piled back into the car, anxious to get wherever they were going so they could unpack and relax. But always vigilant and always on guard, Jonas noticed.

He stared back and expected the man to turn away or avert his eyes out of embarrassment as most people would do if they were blatantly caught staring. But the man didn't look away. He continued to stare until Jonas felt uncomfortable and got in the car.

It angered him that the man made him flinch that way. If not for his desire to remain "under the radar," as he clearly pointed out to the kids little more than an hour ago, he would have marched across the street, grabbed the guy by his throat, and said, "What the fuck is your problem?" He bet that would take the cockiness out of the bastard.

As they drove through the center of town, Jonas noticed the occasional cursory look, but once or twice someone openly stared. The impression he got was that the stares were not malignant in nature, but stemmed from a cautionary guardedness. Jonas's opinion, and this came from years of reading people, was that the stares originated from a place of protection similar to the way an animal would give you a guarded look if it thought you intended to trespass on its territory.

He shook it off and proceeded with the task at hand. He found the house in a quiet, picturesque neighborhood, parked the car, walked up to the door, and rang the doorbell. Mrs. Dallway, the white-haired senior citizen who owned the house, said that yes, she did have three bedrooms for rent, and that since her husband had "passed on" the previous winter, the idea of company certainly appealed to her.  But her intention had been to rent the rooms to some of the locals, you know, people she actually knew.

Jonas instantly turned on the charm and pressed her on it. He gave her a sob story about how he and his three children had lost their home in a combination fire and flood. Mrs. Dallway completely bought into it, not stopping to question how a fire and a flood could occur at the same time. She was still wavering, though, until Jonas stuck a fistful of cash into her hands. Good old hard currency was always the decisive persuader.

Things looked promising. The house was big and roomy, and the bedrooms were neat and orderly. It did have that old person combination smell of mothballs and liniment, but Mrs. Dallway kept herself confined to a few rooms. Jonas figured they could air the place out in a day or two.

The woman told him that they could have free run of the place as long as they respected her privacy and cleaned up after themselves. Oh, and no loud music after nine P.M., and no parties. No problem, Jonas assured her. He reminded himself that he would have to make sure the kids didn't pilfer the woman's jewelry and silverware.

His only concern? The house didn't have central AC, and with the approach of summer, he knew things might get a tad uncomfortable. Mrs. Dallway explained that the houses in Tanneheuk had been around for many years, many before central AC became de rigueur. Although the majority of the houses had upgraded over the years, or at least installed window units, Mrs. Dallway and her husband decided against it. They were never proponents of recirculated air, and were quite comfortable with ceiling and window fans.

"Besides," she told Jonas, "it never really gets that hot out here in the summer."

She did have a pool, which was a rarity in Tanneheuk. Only a dozen or so homes had pools due to the expense of installing one, and the lengthy application process one had to go through in order to get approval from the town to allow outside workers to come in and perform the labor (as there were no pool installers residing in Tanneheuk).

"But we simply had to have a pool," she told Jonas. "Mr. Dallway loved the water. I could hardly keep him out of it, even during the cold months."

Jonas half expected to look out in the backyard and see the old man's corpse floating in it.

So things were beginning to fall into place. Until David and Philo started arguing.

"What's the problem?" Jonas kept his voice low.

Philo said, "David was flirting with a woman that lives across the street. I think she's a cop."

"No, she's not." David looked at Jonas, like, *As usual, he's got it all wrong.* He said, "She's not a cop. She's a security guard, or something. She was wearing jeans, for chrissake."

Jonas looked at Philo. "What made you think she was a cop?"

"She had on a uniform shirt."

David said with a laugh, "Maybe she's a Girl Scout. And I was putting in an order for cookies."

"Philo, finish bringing in the bags. And get your lazy sister to help you."

Philo stalked off and mumbled something in his lispy way. Jonas knew it upset him when he criticized Amber, but the girl *was* lazy, and surly, and troublesome... He turned his attention back to David, first making sure the old woman was still out of earshot.

"You," he said, "Watch yourself."

"Come on, Dad, I was just talking to the girl. I didn't say anything inappropriate."

"I want a couple of months of peace and quiet. Don't fuck it up."

"How? By being friendly? Hey, what am I supposed to do while we're playing the straight and narrow game? I got news for you, Dad," he put his hand up to the side of his mouth like he intended to convey a confidential piece of information, "I don't think there's any escort services in this town. Unless you think the old lady is including erotic massages as part of the bed and board."

Jonas wanted to stay mad, but in spite of himself, he had to laugh at David's lewd comment. "You're an idiot," he told his son, still laughing.

They both laughed and Jonas put his hand on David's shoulder. It felt good sharing a laugh with his son. Over the last few weeks, much of their conversations had been stilted and forced. Or worse, it was a verbal war between David's sarcasm and Jonas's admonishments. It was the first time in quite a long while, that he had the urge to put his arm around David and give him a fatherly hug. But of course he didn't.

"So tell me about the broad across the street."

David shrugged. "I don't know. Just some Plain Jane on her way to work. I thought there was something sexy about her, in an ugly kind of way."

"She's ugly?" Jonas arched an eyebrow.

The kid usually only went for model types, and despite the fact that he was far from an Adonis, David usually scored with them. Maybe it was his confidence, or maybe they found his perpetual snarkiness attractive. Or maybe it was the wad of money he was willing to spend on them. It was hard to tell. But the fact was, the kid scored well outside his league.

"She's not really ugly. Just plain. Like Sandra Bullock after a five year prison stretch."

"Like I said, watch yourself."

But there was no force behind it this time. They brought the last of their luggage in and each set themselves up in the bedrooms that Jonas assigned them. He took the bedroom on the first floor, David and Philo took the middle one, and Amber took the last one at the end of the hall. Although he knew Philo would be spending his nights in Amber's bedroom, Philo would have to keep his things in David's room.

Jonas instructed both Philo and Amber on propriety and the importance of proper behavior in front of the landlady and anyone else they met. Amber gave him a disgusted look, which was nothing new, though he wasn't sure if the look meant she was unhappy that he knew about their relationship, or if she was pissed off that he lectured them on proper behavior. Philo took it well. As Jonas talked, Philo nodded his head and scrunched up his brow as if he was trying to memorize every word.

When Jonas finished, Philo said, "We won't let you down, Dad."

Jonas patted his shoulder to let him know he appreciated it. Things were looking up. Then the sheriff showed up.

Jonas didn't know it was the sheriff, at first. The mud-splattered jeep pulled up in front of the house and the Kris Kristofferson-looking cowboy got out. He watched through the front window as the man slipped a small notebook from his hip pocket and jotted down the license plate number of Jonas's Cadillac. It still didn't register that the man was a cop, not until he turned and headed up the front walkway. Jonas saw the gun and badge clipped to the man's belt.

Jonas found out the man was the part-time town sheriff. Full time, he was a carpenter. Mrs. Dallway was all over herself with friendly chatter. She offered him a glass of lemonade, which he humbly accepted. The sheriff smiled and made small talk with her as if she were a favorite aunt, but once he finished the lemonade, his demeanor turned official.

He told Jonas, "Let's step outside for a minute. I have one or two questions for ya."

The one or two questions, however, suddenly developed into a series, which made Jonas reassess the sheriff. He wasn't a country bumpkin who collected a paycheck for sipping lemonade with the senior citizens. He was the town's patriarchal figure, and he took the job seriously.

He asked Jonas about himself and his family, whether they had any outstanding warrants, what brought them to Tanneheuk, their intentions, how long they intended to stay...and on and on. Jonas answered appropriately, and hoped there weren't any warrants out for them. There shouldn't be...under their real names, anyway. He knew of half a dozen of their aliases that were wanted by various law enforcement agencies throughout the country, but there shouldn't be any black marks against their real name of Rafferty. Jonas never allowed the kids to carry more than one set of identification to avoid mishaps or lapses in judgment.

The point was, Jonas wasn't concerned (much) that Sheriff Creel might get a hit on the name Rafferty once he keyed it into the national database. What concerned him were the follow-up questions:

How long did they plan to stay? What led them to Tanneheuk anyway? Wouldn't they be more comfortable staying in Lake Dulcet? Were they planning on doing a lot of traveling in and out of town over the next several months?

And then the two questions Creel seemed particularly interested in: Did they plan to stay until late September? Jonas answered that most likely they would stay until October 1, but he would notify the sheriff should those plans change. He utilized his sincerest tone of voice.

The second question was, Creel wanted to know David, Philo, and Amber's ages. Creel didn't react to David and Amber's ages, but when he found out Philo was twenty-one, Jonas saw him stiffen. He could have sworn Creel paled a bit, wrote something in his battered notebook, flipped it closed, and slipped it into his hip pocket. Creel nodded his head like he had just received bad news, although Jonas couldn't figure out what difference his kids' ages made, and why Philo being twenty-one would produce such a deep frown on the sheriff's face. He waited for more, but the fire had gone out of Sheriff Creel.

Creel said in a subdued voice, "Let me know if ya decide to leave before late September."

"Sure, Sheriff."

Then he wanted to search the Caddy. He didn't say "search." He said, "Let's have a look at your car."

Jonas complied, though he was tempted to ask to see a warrant, or at least probable cause. But he kept his mouth shut and let the small town sheriff have his way. Creel looked under the front seat, opened the glove compartment and riffled through the paperwork he found inside — the registration, proof of insurance, and the original owner's manual. He looked in the backseat. He didn't find anything incriminating because Jonas was long past being an amateur.

Jonas asked, "Anything in particular you're looking for, Sheriff?"

"Oh," Creel answered with a noncommittal shrug, "just looking. Open the trunk for me, if ya don't mind."

Jonas felt the heat rise up from his chest to his head. Times like these, it was hard to keep up his hardworking, family-oriented, law-abiding everyman facade. He wanted to gut punch the sheriff, snatch his gun, and lock his country ass in the trunk of the Caddy. He'd let him snivel in there for a few hours until he decided the man had enough. Of course he didn't do any of that.

He put on a smile, said, "Sure," and unlocked the trunk.

It was empty, as was the moving trailer hitched to the bumper. All of their luggage had been moved into the house. He wondered if the sheriff was going to ask to look through their clothes, at which point Jonas would refuse because that would simply be too much. It would look unnatural if he didn't object to that.

But the sheriff made no mention of looking through their luggage. He tapped around the inside of the trunk and nodded his head. He didn't spot the hidden compartment behind the phony metal plate between the trunk and the back seat. If he did, and if he managed to find the hidden catch that opened it, he would have found the Rafferty family cache of guns, money, and stockpile of false identification papers, which included multiple driver's licenses, social security cards, and birth certificates for all of them, several names for each. All of them were relatively clean, except perhaps for an occasional misdemeanor offense.

Anytime one of their aliases was charged with a felony, Jonas destroyed all evidence of the name. It would be a hell of a thing to be pulled over for a traffic offense and have himself arrested on a felony charge because he had accidentally handed out the wrong set of credentials that morning.

The sheriff didn't find the cache, nor was Jonas terribly worried that he would. The hidden compartment was expertly concealed. If he had found it, well... Jonas would have dealt with that problem swiftly and efficiently. The sheriff shut the trunk and shut the trailer door.

He squinted up at the afternoon sun for a moment, said, "Got a few town rules to go over with ya."

"Okay." Jonas nodded solemnly. He took out his pack of cigarettes and offered one to Creel.

The sheriff said, "'Preciate it," and took one. He reached into his pocket for his Zippo, but Jonas already had his sleek gold lighter out, the one with the pinpoint flame.

Jonas lit the sheriff's cigarette, then his own. The two of them smoked in silence for a moment. They looked at the well-manicured lawns and the bright blue sky. They could easily have been neighbors standing on the front lawn, discussing the color of the grass or the frequency (or infrequency) of the seasonal rain.

"There are no cell phones or satellite phones allowed in the town limits," Creel said after a long pause. "Any calls ya make have to be landlines. So if you or your family has a cell phone or satellite phone, ya best turn it over to me now."

Jonas shook his head. "We don't."

Creel fixed him with stare. "Really? In this day and age, that seems a bit peculiar."

"That may be, Sheriff, but we don't have any portable phones. You're welcome to look for one, if you want."

Creel stared at him.

Jonas said, "In the past, when we've needed a phone, we usually pick up a disposable one. Or stop somewhere and send an e-mail. I have a laptop. Is that illegal in this town?"

"Nope. But if ya intend to use the Internet, you'll have to drive over to Lake Dulcet. There's no hook-up here in town."

"What's the deal, Sheriff? You trying to keep this town from entering the modern age?" Jonas tried to keep his tone jovial, but it came out sounding antagonistic. His anger had moved to a slow burn.

"Nope. We have many modern conveniences here. But this town is old-fashioned, and it wants to stay that way." The smoke from Creel's cigarette drifted up into his left eye and made it appear that he was squinting at Jonas. "If you're gonna have any problems complyin' with our rules, ya best say so now."

Jonas said, "Nope. No problem, Sheriff. I was just asking, is all."

"Okay, then. Rule number two is, if ya get a dog or a cat, keep it inside at night. If ya have to walk it at night—"

"There won't be any pets," Jonas said.

"In case ya change your mi—"

"We won't. My boy, Philo, is very allergic to animal hair. He can't be around them."

Creel nodded. "Rule number three. No huntin'. Fishin' is okay, but only in certain areas. Check with me first if ya decide ya want to go fishin'. Same thing with the woods. It's best to check with me if ya get the urge to go hikin' or climbin'. Much of the woods are privately owned, so check with—"

Jonas cut him off again. "We're not the outdoors type, but I promise you that we'll check in if things change. But they won't. My kids hate camping and fishing, and anything else that has to do with nature." Jonas grinned.

"Last rule. If you or your family has trouble with anyone in town, you immediately come to me. Do not, under any circumstances, take matters into your own hands. We clear?"

"As clear as a church bell on Sunday morning." Jonas turned his grin into a big shit-eating one despite the fact his fingers ached from wanting to knock the condescension out of Creel.

The sheriff nodded. His eyes searched Jonas for...what? Jonas wasn't sure. After several seconds of silence, though, Creel nodded as if he had come to a decision about something. He took a drag from his cigarette, then removed a battered leather wallet from his pocket. He handed Jonas a creased business card.

"My office number and home number is on there. Remember

what I said: Any trouble, call me day or night."

"Sure. Just not on a cell phone. Right?"

Creel nodded, but didn't acknowledge Jonas's weak attempt at a joke. Instead, he got in his jeep and drove away.

Jonas read the card. It said: "Sam Creel, Carpenter/Sheriff." It had to be a joke, right? He was both a carpenter and the sheriff, and he listed carpenter first on his business card?

What was with all those off-the-wall questions? And the town rules? Was he kidding? No cell phones, no Internet hook-up...

At first, Jonas thought the cowboy was fucking with him, or maybe purposely being difficult to get Jonas frustrated so he would pack up his family and leave. Maybe the town didn't like strangers, or maybe the sheriff didn't like Jonas. He couldn't see a reason for the latter because he had been cooperative and as personable as he could be under the circumstances.

No. Jonas's gut told him the sheriff had been on the level, which made the whole thing bizarre. What the hell was up with this town? Jonas shook his head. He had the urge to pack up the family and head immediately out of town. Maybe drive to the suddenly metropolitan-looking Lake Dulcet, or just plain head the fuck out of Montana. His instincts said move, find another hiding place for the summer.

Jonas fought the urge, just as he had fought the urge to unleash his mean, angry side on the sheriff. Just as he fought the urge to go inside the house and rip it apart, looking for the old lady's stash of money and jewelry. Just as he knew he would have to fight it every time she fell asleep in her favorite easy chair or went to the market to buy lemons for her lemonade. Just as he fought the urge to hatch a major scam on this two-bit, backwater, stuck in the 1970s town, and clean the yokels out of their government subsidiary payments and social security checks and farm produce profits. Just as he fought the urge to unleash the dark side of himself every time he had a run-in with a local cop like the sheriff, or any uniformed cop or state trooper in the past who had ever talked to him like he was a piece of shit, but he would stand there and smile and take it and say, "Yes, sir, officer, I sure do understand what you're telling me, you're the man in charge, yes sir..." and the whole time he wanted to get his shotgun out of the hidden compartment in the Caddy and fire it point blank into their stomach and watch that shocked look in their eyes when they realized before they died that their intestines were blown all over the concrete.

Yes, Jonas knew he repressed a great deal of rage, and that one day it would explode, probably at an inopportune time. He chuckled to himself and shook his head at his dark thoughts. He let the cigarette butt drop to the sidewalk and ground it out with his boot.

He decided to look on the bright side. No Internet here meant there was less chance of some busybody finding out the truth about the Rafferty family. The one thing Jonas craved for the next four to five months was, no trouble.

# Chapter Eight

Maryam ran for forty-five minutes through the woods, stopped and had a quick snack of a protein bar and sips from her water bottle, then jogged back to her starting point. She felt the strain on her ankles and calves from the uneven ground, mixed with her body's natural stiffness. When she landed on each step, she was careful to land on the balls of her feet and put her weight down in stages in order to ensure she didn't land in a rut and break anything. Her eyes were focused on the ground, on placing each foot down as firmly and evenly as possible. The run was nearly as mentally taxing as it was physically.

Maryam's timetable was on schedule: Next month would be endurance running over uneven terrain. She would begin making her forays farther and farther into the woods, up and down hills, over fallen trees, working her way closer and closer to the river. She would have to work it out on paper so the runs gradually grew longer. Mix in short runs so as to keep her muscle memory sharp, but not burn out her body.

The month after next, August, she would begin her night run training. September would bring a mishmash of running: running over rough terrain, endurance running, and night running. Once or twice (probably twice), she would do a complete night run to the river. Between now and then, she would also begin mapping the area and planning her routes.

Maryam had already decided on planning three separate routes.

More than that would make it too confusing; less than that left room for errors. And she couldn't have errors. Not when she was so close.

"Psst."

Maryam had reached the edge of the tree line and was headed for her car parked a few hundred feet away on the shoulder of Lawson Road when she heard the sound. She looked around.

The sun was high and the light filtered through the trees in golden arcs. It made the greens of the foliage brilliant in its hue. There was more than enough light to see by, unlike farther in where the canopies became dense and blocked the forest floor from illumination. Still, she couldn't spot the point of origin for the sound. Had she imagined it?

"Psst. Hey."

He was on her left, crouched down on his haunches by the base of a tree. He hadn't been there a minute ago, she was pretty sure, but maybe he had been behind the tree. Funny, too, that she hadn't spotted him a moment before when she had run by that same area. He stood out, not simply because he was naked, but because of his extreme paleness.

He was Caucasian; of that, there was no doubt. He was the whitest white man Maryam had ever seen, as white as an albino. His hair was white, too, and stuck out in tufts at all angles. Maryam wondered if a comb had ever touched the man's head.

"Whatcha doin'?" His voice was raspy, half growl and half whisper.

"Minding my own business." Her voice was steadier than she felt. She fought to keep the fear from rising up inside and taking control. "What are you doing?" she asked.

"Watchin' you, girlie-girl," he said. "Been watchin' you run. You like to run, doncha?"

Maryam shrugged. She remembered she still wore the water bag on her back and the straps were getting uncomfortable. Without taking her eyes off the man, she loosened the harness and slipped it off her. She let the weight of it carry across her shoulders and diagonally in front of her, down to the ground. She noticed the man didn't glance at the backpack. He kept his eyes steady on her.

"What do you want?" She used her tough voice. It made her sound confident, though she had begun to sweat again. This time, the sweat wasn't from physical exertion. She was sweating from the fear that clawed at her brain. She could let go of the strap and run full out for the car. She could...but she knew the man would catch her.

"Just want to talk. Nothin' wrong with that, is there?"

She shrugged again. The man stood up and took a step towards her. Her legs threatened to move of their own volition.

He must have sensed it because he smiled and said, "Don't get nervous, girlie-girl. I ain't gonna hurt you. If I wanted to hurt you, I would've already. I've had plenty of chances the last couple of weeks. I told you, I just want to talk."

"Talk about what?"

He stepped closer again, and again. His arms hung straight down at his sides, palms facing her, as if to say, *See? I don't have a weapon.* Except for the weapon God gave him. At that thought, she nearly burst out in an anxiety-fueled laugh.

"We can talk about whatever you want, girlie-girl. We can talk about the weather." He moved closer. "We can talk about why you run so much."

He was scrawny, but with a hard, stringy look to his thinness. His body was angular with edges that jutted here and there, but with a smoothness to it that made her think of a knobby stick worn down over the years by the elements. He had a light dusting of downy white hair on his arms, legs, and trunk, and a brambly patch on his groin. She glanced down quickly, unable to help herself from looking at his penis. It was stunted, but quite thicker than she would have guessed for a man his size. He was shorter than her.

"Is there something wrong with my wanting to run? I can run if I want," she said. "What does it matter to you? You people aren't supposed to be in this area this time of year anyway."

"We're not? Heh." He smiled and showed a set of white jagged-looking teeth. He was close enough now that he could reach out and touch her if he wished.

He said, "I go where I want to, girlie-girl. I don't follow the pack rules."

A rivulet of sweat ran down her back and neck. Her tank top, already damp with sweat from her run, clung to her more. She no longer thought of running. It was too late. He would catch her.

Beyond that, she didn't want to run. She shouldn't have to. She had more right to be here than he did.

"It don't matter if you follow the pack rules, but if you break them—"

"Then what?" He chuckled. "What if I break 'em? You gonna tell on me? The pack don't care if I break the rules, 'cause I ain't in the pack."

He was close enough that she could smell him. He had an earthy odor, one borne of living outdoors and bathing in mountain streams. She didn't find it objectionable; it was more disconcerting because she was so used to people who smelled of soap, deodorant, and perfume. A man's natural musk, combined with the scent of nature, was actually somewhat pleasing to her. *That* was the only thing she found pleasing about him. Everything else was creepy, from his whispery-choked voice to his bloodless features and cyclone hairstyle.

"What I do out here is my business." She spoke with a confident forcefulness she didn't feel. But her words gave her strength and she felt the anxiety melt away. "It doesn't matter if you're in the pack or not. You're still not supposed to be out here until late September. Being here violates the rules."

"You're feisty, aren't you?" He gave her a lopsided grin. "I like feisty." He sniffed. "You're menstruating, too."

It was meant to put her off balance, she was sure, but she let the comment slide by without acknowledgment.

"So why you runnin' so much?"

"That's my business." Maryam upended the backpack and opened the water bag inside. It dumped out on the ground. Some of it splashed on the man's legs and feet. He appeared not to notice.

"These woods belong to us half the year," she said, "and they belong to the pack the other half a year."

"I told you, girlie-girl, I ain't in the pack."

"You don't live in town, either."

"Nope. I live on my own. I mess with the pack, sometimes, but I'm not with 'em. Got that? I don't need a pack."

Now she understood. He was the Omega, the loner. The pack always had one, sometimes more than one, but always at least one. The reasons were unknown to her. Their ways were sketchily drawn to the townspeople. They preferred it that way — to live as enigmatically as possible.

"I once killed a bear," he said, like a kid bragging to his school chums. "Didn't have no help, neither. The pack killed one once. But the one I killed, I was all by myself."

"Good for you."

He chuckled again. "You don't believe, but that's okay. Don't make it any less true."

"I've gotta go." She took a step towards the small patch of field that lay between the tree line and her car.

The man matched her steps. He sniffed again.

"You smell fine."

Maryam didn't respond.

"You comin' back soon? Maybe next time, I'll run with you."

"Maybe," she said. When she was close enough to her car, she tossed the backpack into the backseat, followed by her empty water bottle that she unhooked from her belt. She glanced at him and saw him standing with his arms up and outstretched and his face pointed at the sun. He basked in the rays.

Out in the sunlight, he was less scary. Her nervousness faded. He didn't seem dangerous now, not like he did in the gloom of the forest. She still felt apprehensive, but it was more of a cautiousness, like what she might feel if she were unsure of an animal's potential for causing harm.

She thought, too, that if he had intended to attack her, he would have done so by now. *He would have gotten me in the woods*, she thought. *He could have gotten me earlier and I wouldn't have had time to react. He's just messing with me, trying to scare me.*

"When you comin' back?"

Maryam shrugged. "A few days. Maybe."

"My name's Merc," he said. "Short for Mercury."

She walked around to the driver's side door. He watched her with the same lopsided grin on his face. His eyes were very dark, two black pools in a sea of pale whiteness. He sniffed deeply.

"You sure do smell good, girlie-girl. I bet you taste good, too."

Maryam started the car. She resisted the urge to drive away too fast. She couldn't let him have the last word.

"You'll never find out," she said.

She didn't hear his response over the car engine, but she had the impression he said, "We'll see."

She put the car in gear, drove up the road a hundred feet, and made a wide U-turn that took her from one shoulder to another. As she headed back the way she came, Merc walked back into the woods. His pale figure was visible for a moment, then he disappeared into the shadows.

# Chapter Nine

Reverend Edgar MacDonald made a bad first impression on Drake, which was only surpassed by his bad second impression, and every impression thereafter. He was a cantankerous old man who would not have been out of place sitting in a badly lit bar with a bottle in front of him, railing against the injustices the world had heaped upon him. His white hair was very long and hung down between his shoulder blades in a long, thin ponytail, held together in multiple spots by brightly colored rubber bands. It made Drake think of an albino snake with bands of rainbow colors. The top of MacDonald's head was completely bald and marred by liver spots of varying sizes. MacDonald was also legally blind. A degenerative optic nerve condition had dimmed his vision.

"I can still make out shapes," he told Drake "But that's it." He shrugged. "Don't matter. What the hell is there to see anymore anyway?"

His voice was as dry and raspy as it had been on the phone, but what Drake found unsettling was the man's frequent use of profanity.

When Drake said, "Tanneheuk seems like a quaint little town," saying it to show MacDonald that he was open-minded and positive about his appointment to the church, MacDonald responded with, "It's a shithole. On the outside, it looks like fuckin' Utopia. But underneath, it's a shithole." Drake waited for him to elaborate, but MacDonald stared off into space.

The living quarters behind the church were spacious enough for one person. Two people might find it cozy, bordering on cramped. Drake was aware that Reverend MacDonald had been married for half a century. He asked if MacDonald and his wife had lived in the small apartment all that time, or if they had a house in town.

"No," MacDonald said, "we have a house. Had a house. I sold it after Shirley died. This apartment was only added onto the church six years ago when the place was rebuilt."

"The church was rebuilt?"

"Refurbished, I should've said. Modernized. Whatever the fuck you want to call it. They added this on for me. Now it's yours."

Drake looked around. There was a combination kitchen and dining area, living area, bathroom, and one bedroom. The rooms were furnished with pieces that were probably donated, as nothing appeared new. In fact, the furniture had a distinctive 60s and 70s feel, although it was all in showroom condition.

The den was actually the office MacDonald and his administrative assistant used for church business. Drake glanced into the open door and saw two desks, each with a computer monitor and telephone.

"One desk is yours. The other belongs to Celia, your secretary."

Drake pictured a pleasant old woman with eyeglasses attached to a chain around her neck, but MacDonald said, "She's a good kid. She just walked over to the school for a minute. She should be back soon."

"Is she a student at the high school?" Drake asked.

"What? No. Her sister is. Celia's older than that."

"Well, you called her a kid, so I naturally assumed she was a high school student who worked for you part-time."

"Reverend," MacDonald said, "at my age, everyone's a kid to me."

Drake smiled. "Can I ask how old you are?"

"Sure."

He waited a beat, then realized MacDonald's joke. "How old are you, sir?"

"Too old to fuckin' care. That's why I'm retiring."

Drake shook his head. Talking to Reverend MacDonald was like talking to a senior citizen version of Yosemite Sam with a gutter mouth.

MacDonald said, "Let's step outside for a minute. I want to smoke a cigar, and I make it a habit not to smoke indoors." He pronounced it as "ceegar."

They stepped out back and MacDonald immediately fired up a fat stogie.

"You smoke?"

"No," Drake answered.

"Me neither. Except for the occasional cigar." He puffed on it a minute, then moved his face in the direction of the sun. "Feels like a nice day."

"It is. I can't get over how blue the sky is. It's beautiful."

"Yeah, well, I wouldn't know, smartass."

"Oh, sorry," Drake said. "I didn't mean—"

"Relax, kid. I was just bustin' your balls. I ain't sensitive about bein' blind." He puffed on the cigar. "The place is yours," he said. "The apartment. I already moved out. Got a room with a nice family in town. Celia's family, matter of fact. They got a big house, extra bedrooms. I've always been close with her folks."

"I wondered what I was supposed to do about living arrangements."

"Wonder no more. You got an apartment in back of the church, rent-free. It's not much, but it's enough for you and any broads you decide to entertain."

"Well, I'm...I'm more interested in getting settled in and getting to know the parishioners, Reverend. I don't think I'll be entertaining, as you put it, for quite a while."

"Heh."

He puffed again and the cigar smoke clung to his face and Drake's. Drake fanned it away with his hand.

MacDonald said, "Knock off the reverend bullshit, will you? We're both reverends. You don't have to keep calling me that. Call me Edgar." He shrugged. "Besides, now that you're here, I'm just a parishioner myself."

"What do you mean?"

"What do I mean? I mean I'm retired. I don't have to do this shit anymore. I can spend my remaining days sittin' on the porch and smokin' cigars. The church is yours. Have fun."

"You're not...? Won't you be staying on for a little while?"

"What for? You can't handle it alone? Celia handles all the bookkeeping. All you have to do is write your sermon and deliver it once on Saturday and twice on Sunday. That's it. Occasionally, you drive over to Lake Dulcet and pay a visit to the hospital, or maybe make a housecall to one of the old farts here in town and spend an afternoon listenin' to them ramble about nothin'.'"

Drake had formulated a reply to MacDonald's rough remarks, when the woman came around the corner of the building. Drake's initial thought was, *I'm in trouble.*

She was a beautiful black woman with hair the color of bronze. It was an organized mess, long and curly, with light streaks that shone like polished brass. It surrounded her head in a halo of pipe curls that framed her oval face. She smiled at Drake and he felt a flutter in his stomach.

"Hi," she said.

She extended her hand and Drake shook it. It was warm and familiarly comfortable in his. Her hand in his felt as natural as if he had found a part of himself he had misplaced long ago, a part he hadn't been fully aware was missing, and now that it was back, it fit into himself with ease. It was a puzzle piece that made the picture complete. When he let go of her hand, it was akin to releasing an object that held heartfelt memories.

Drake wondered if she felt the same immediate connection between them, or if it was all on his side only. He searched her face, partially obscured by a pair of round, gold-framed glasses, and saw a twinkle in her hazel eyes. If they were indeed windows to her soul, Drake concluded she must have the purest and sweetest of hearts.

He introduced himself and Celia spoke a little about herself, mostly about her work duties and how she would help ease the transition from one pastor to another. Much of it Drake didn't catch; he was lost in her eyes and her smile, both of which gave him a warm tingle deep inside.

She wore a powder blue V-neck sweater, matching Capri pants, and sandals that displayed well-manicured, red-painted toes. Drake tried to focus on what she was saying, something about the qualities of the town and the congregation, the excitement of a new pastor, etc., but his attention was drawn to the gold toe ring on her left foot that matched the gold ring on her right thumb, the ample cleavage in the V of her sweater, the hourglass shape of her figure, the very white bra strap that peeked from beneath the edge of her sweater...

His eyes darted all over until he forced them to stay on her face. He blushed slightly at the thought that she might suspect the un-Christian things that flitted through his mind. At some point, MacDonald joined in the conversation. He asked about Celia's sister.

"I walked over to the high school and met with Mrs. Horvers." In an aside to Drake, Celia said, "She's the principal. My sister has missed a lot of school this year, and there's a question of whether she'll be able to graduate."

"That kid's always been a handful," MacDonald interjected.

"My parents have had enough," Celia said. "They refuse to try with her anymore. So I'm assuming the parental role." Her eyes went heavenward. "Not that it's doing any good. She won't listen to me, either."

"Maybe I can help," Drake said. "I've had experience in youth counseling. Maybe I could talk to her? Perhaps she's dealing with issues she doesn't feel comfortable talking about with her family."

He thought he might have pressed the issue a bit much. He wanted to impress Celia by playing the hero. If he could show her what a kind, considerate person he was, repair the rift in her family, he would shine in her eyes.

As soon as those thoughts took root, he immediately felt a wave of guilt. He was in town less than ninety minutes, and already he was working on seducing a member of his congregation? A woman who would be working with him at the church? What was wrong with him? He should desire to counsel Celia's sister because it was the right thing, the Christian thing to do, and it was part of his vocation.

He suddenly felt ashamed of himself and silently affirmed that he would work to help Celia and her family, and expect absolutely nothing in return, nor entertain the thought of making himself look good in her eyes. He would help the girl because that was what God wanted him to do.

"Thank you, Reverend. I will certainly try to get her to talk to you. Maybe you could help. She's very strong-willed, so it might be difficult to arrange something, but I'll see. She only needs to make up some assignments and maybe go to summer school, and then she can graduate."

"I'd be happy to help in any way I can."

"Great, you do that," MacDonald said. "In the meantime, I'm gonna get out of here."

"I'll drive him home," Celia told Drake. "Then I'll come back and assist you in getting settled in."

"The sheriff will probably stop by to make sure you understand the town rules," Macdonald said. "The main thing you gotta remember," he moved his cigar around in small jabs to illustrate his points, "is don't make waves. The town elders call the shots."

"What exactly are the town elders?"

"They're the... well, they're the assholes who run Tanneheuk. They have rules and we gotta follow them. That's all you really need to know. If you have any questions, ask the sheriff or ask Celia." He bent down and stubbed out his cigar on the concrete.

When he stood back up, he said, "Let's go, kid." He stuck his arm out and Celia took it. She walked him to the passenger side of her station wagon and opened the door for him.

"Wait!" Drake called out. "Aren't you coming back?"

"What for? All my stuff's moved out already."

Drake said, "That's it? You're done? You expect me to jump right in with no transition period?"

"Kid, you preached a sermon before?"

"Yes. Of course."

"So what the hell do you need from me? I did my time on the pulpit. Now it's your turn. I've earned my rest."

"But what about the congregation? Don't you want to say goodbye to them?"

MacDonald stood by the car door for a moment, his blind eyes fixed on a middle space between himself and Drake. He appeared to think about the question, then said, "Fuck 'em."

He slid into the passenger seat and let Celia close his door. She gave a quick knowing glance to Drake and went around to the driver's side. In that brief moment, he had shared something with her. He had begun to feel that he had arrived into a dreamlike world of absurdity, one that was a hair's breadth from the normal waking world, but that fell farther and farther away from reality the longer he stayed in it.

They drove away and Drake was left staring at the black scorch mark on the ground left by MacDonald's cigar.

# Chapter Ten

Fern pushed a button and the bluesy rock music of the Black Keys simultaneously filled her headphones and was broadcast out into the atmosphere and into the radios and stereos of the fine people of Tanneheuk. Man, she felt good. She leaned back in her chair and let the music wash over her. This is what she loved, what she lived for: playing music.

She had four songs loaded and ready to go, a quick break for an advertisement, then she planned to talk a little. She didn't know what about. Fern generally talked about whatever came into her mind, which was mostly the topic of music, but she would sometimes talk politics, cars, childhood memories, anything and everything. The show was an open format. She would take phone calls and let listeners join in. She had a core group of listeners, so the majority of the time the phone calls came from the same people.

She would talk, play music, play an occasional advertisement, more music, and so on. Some days, all she did was play music and forego the talk, only stopping to play an advertisement. The station, however, depended very little on commercials, as everyone in town was familiar with all the local businesses. Most of the station's funding came from donations and county tax dollars.

The radio station was small and didn't require much money for its operating costs. It was a single story building, the size of a two bedroom ranch house, which it actually had been many years prior.

Three people were more than sufficient to run the place, and many times it ran with fewer on hand.

Inspiration struck. Fern changed the order of music and brought the commercial up to run next. She would come back with a brief discussion of musical influences, a particular passion of hers. She loved discussing what bands inspired the current crop of artists, and rather than rely on what the bands themselves claimed as their influences, a thing she liked to do was play a few songs from a band and attempt to detect their influence from their sound. This was a topic she had covered in the past on her show and could be counted on to spark lively debates from her listeners.

After the break, she would announce today's topic and play another Black Keys song. Then she would play a Bad Company song and one from Mountain (probably "Mississippi Queen"), two definite influences she heard in their music. Maybe she would take it back further and play some blues. Maybe Muddy Waters and Robert Johnson.

After, she would take phone calls and let the listeners debate whether she was spot on or not. Fern never researched her topics. She tended to fly on her own wits and musical ear. She had a good ear, or so she believed, and her listeners more often than not agreed.

After the telephone debate, she would play a couple of the listeners' suggestions for bands they thought were an influence on the Black Keys. After the songs had run, Fern would agree (or not) with the choices, but she always left it up to the listeners to render the final verdict.

She was already thinking ahead to the next spotlight band. Probably Buckcherry, another favorite band of hers. She thought she heard AC/DC in their sound, for sure. Grand Funk Railroad? Iffy, but she would play it and let the listeners debate it. She felt the adrenaline-like surge gear up in her body that told her she was in for a stimulating couple of hours. She considered smoking her next joint early to enhance her enjoyment, and nearly had it out when the sheriff pulled into the parking lot.

The front window of the studio looked out on the mini-parking lot for the station. Fern usually kept the curtains open so she could look at the trees across the road and watch the sun set behind the mountain range. She wondered why the sheriff was paying her a visit, if she had somehow been derelict in her duties. She hoped he wasn't there to fire her, not that she could think of a reason for him doing so. But if that was the reason, it would dampen her enthusiasm for the remainder of her radio show.

Sheriff Creel stepped out of his jeep and walked to the front door of the station with his lanky stride. She slipped the cigarette case with her stash of joints back into the front pocket of her jeans and swiveled in her seat to look out the window of the control booth. She could see the reception area where Creel was now standing and talking to Myrna, the Program Director and General Manager of the station.

Fern took the opportunity to duck down and open the bottom desk drawer. Inside was a small mirror and, with a quick glance over her shoulder to ensure Creel was still engaged in conversation, she gave herself a quick appraisal.

Her fingers fussed with her hair, but it stayed lifeless. She finger-combed it anyway and wished she had blow-dried it or borrowed her mom's curling iron to give it a little bounce. Her eyes were a tad bloodshot, but that was normal for her. If Fern didn't look slightly buzzed, folks would wonder what was wrong.

She adjusted her clothes and checked her face. Her complexion was unblemished, although somewhat sallow. She wished she had thought to put on a touch of make-up before she left the house, but how was she supposed to know Creel would pay her a visit? She found a tube of cherry lip gloss and quickly applied it, and had just finished when Creel stepped into the room. He pantomimed a question: Was it okay to speak?

"Sure, Sheriff," she said, and slipped the lip gloss back in the drawer in such a way as to conceal it from him. Creel was twenty years older than her, and Fern had been in love with him ever since she was a child. She just didn't want him to know she was in love with him.

She said, "Let me take care of something first."

She set up two more commercials, which had been set for an hour away and would mean she would have to talk longer and/or play more music, not a problem for her in the least. She also loaded two more Black Keys songs in case the sheriff was inclined to talk for a while. She hoped he was.

"Fern," he nodded at her., "Sorry about disturbin' ya at work."

"Oh, that's alright, Sheriff. You're not disturbing me. What brings you by?"

*Please don't let it be because of some mistake I made or something I forgot to do on my rounds.*

If Creel had come by to correct her on something she had done, she would be mortified. Her mind raced over the possibilities. Her rounds were easy, but much of her nighttime hours were spent in a marijuana-induced fog.

"We got some new folks in town," the sheriff said. "In fact, they're staying across the street from your house."

"Yeah. I saw them. Talked to one of them. Young, blond-haired guy. He seemed kind of sleazy."

Creel smirked. "The one I talked to was older, shaved head and kind of hard looking. He acted friendly, but..."

"But what?"

He shook his head. "My gut tells me there's more going on there. They don't look like a typical family. And I don't like the way they showed up out of the blue. The elders won't like it much, either."

"Are they related to Mrs. Dallway?"

"Nope. I got the impression she's kind of anxious about them staying with her. Not sure why she agreed to it, but fact is, she did. So..."

"What should we do?"

"Nothin' yet," he said. "I'll run a background check on them and see what comes up. Plus, I'll run it by the elders. Well... I should say they'll run it by me, 'cause I know they're not gonna like strangers poppin' into town."

"Anything you want me to do," she resisted the urge to put her hand on his knee, "to help?"

"Naw. I'll take care of it. Just keep an eye on them and let me know if ya see anything suspicious."

Creel smiled at her in a way that to him was probably paternal, but it made her insides melt. She wondered if he ever thought of her in a way other than as a surrogate niece. (She refused to consider the possibility that he viewed their relationship as a surrogate father/daughter.)

His wife of twenty-five years had passed away two years ago

after a nasty battle with cancer. Creel had mourned her in his own way, which was to become more reticent than he already was. She had hoped he would open up at some point and talk about it, maybe talk about it with her. She wanted to help him ease the pain any way she could.

"Sure," she said. "I'll keep an eye on them. And let me know if there's anything else you need me to do." *Like come to your house and climb into your bed. I'll even wear one of your wife's old nightgowns, if you want.*

Actually, that was a callous thing to think. Fern had liked Sandy Creel, despite the fact she had been married to the man Fern had been in love with since she was eight years old. If she overlooked that, and she often did, Sandy had been a nice, pleasant woman, one of those people who never had a bad word to say to anyone, or about anyone, and generally seemed content with her lot in life. Which was why it was doubly tragic when she was diagnosed with an inoperable tumor. Folks shook their heads and spoke in hushed tones about how "unfair" it all was that someone so vibrant and alive could be suddenly struck down.

Fern agreed, although she had wondered why it was any more tragic than anyone else being diagnosed with a terminal illness. Still, she understood the sentiment. Sandy was the kind of woman who was everyone's sister, or everyone's mom. Everyone loved her. Even Fern, although not for the same reasons.

Fern loved Sandy because Sheriff Creel loved her. Sandy made him happy. When Sandy received her diagnosis, she immediately began to wither away, the way some people do when they discover their life expectancy has been reduced from years to months and they become deflated, as if a small tear has been made in their body and their life-force slowly seeps out into the universe. When Sandy was reduced to a hollowed out shell and mercifully died, Fern hurt not only for her, but mostly for Creel.

He said, "Well, I should let ya get back to work," and smiled again.

"Thanks for stopping by, Sheriff," she said. "You know, you can always come by. It doesn't always have to be work related. If you just want to, you know," she shrugged, "hang out or whatever."

Jeez, she sounded like a schoolgirl. She thought she may have blushed a little, too. If he noticed her slight embarrassment or the implications of her invitation, he was nice enough to ignore it. He stood up and touched her shoulder. It wasn't meant as anything more than a friendly gesture, but it still sent electricity through Fern's body.

"Maybe I will. I might come by and let ya teach me how to be a dee jay. You're so good at it and all. I listen to your show all the time, even sometimes when I'm sittin' at home. Ya play a lot of good music, Fern."

"Thanks," she said, and blushed unashamedly.

"I'd rather listen to your show than watch anything they put on the tee vee these days." He patted her shoulder. "Well, I'm off." Before he left the booth, he said, "Remember about keepin' an eye on your new neighbors. I don't want anything to happen where the elders would have to get involved. It's best to handle things ourselves without involving them. If we can."

"I'll watch them."

"Everything else okay?" he asked. "No trouble on your night rounds?"

"No. Everything's been quiet."

He nodded. "Good. That's good. Let's try to keep it that way."

He gave her a small wave and walked out. She watched him through the glass as he threaded his way past the reception area, tipping his head to Myrna in a good-bye gesture, and then he was out the front door.

"I love you," Fern said in a singsong voice.

Maybe she did. Her rational mind, when it functioned properly, told her it was simply a crush borne out of hero worship from the time when he saved her life. At other times, however, she thought it was more than that simply because the feelings had persisted all these years. She thought what had started off as a crush had grown and matured into love.

Fern was eight when she ran away from home. She had packed a shopping bag with a change of clothes, a pen and a blank notebook she intended to fill with the many adventures she would have on her travels, and two ham and cheese sandwiches with mustard, wrapped in wax paper. She also "borrowed" her dad's canteen, filled it with water, and had it slung over her shoulder by its long mesh strap. With the bag in hand and the canteen sloshing against her hipbone, she'd started off.

She wouldn't travel by road because her parents would quickly find her that way. Since she wasn't pretending to run away in order to procure sympathy or attention, but in fact really wished to leave home and find another place to live, being picked up on the road out of town was not what she desired.

Thinking back on it now, Fern couldn't recall what the cause was for her anger at her parents or her sudden desire to run away. It was one of those things that seemed of the utmost seriousness to an eight year old child, but years later was deemed too trivial to remember. All she could recall was that she had been angry at her parents and the thought of seeking out a new home far away had held a great appeal to her childhood self.

She proceeded into the woods and walked in the direction she believed was the way out of town. She walked for what may have been hours, but in truth was not that long, only appearing to be such to a young child alone in the woods. At one point, she sat down at the base of a tree and ate one of the sandwiches and sipped from the canteen. After what seemed to be an appropriate rest period, she stood and began walking again.

She walked some more, sometimes uphill, sometimes down, until her legs grew weary and she began to question her determination to run away. As the afternoon sun dipped down in the sky and the shadows of the trees lengthened, she started to have thoughts of turning back. Being out alone at night was suddenly a more daunting thought than it had been two hours before. Besides, her mom would be starting dinner soon and Fern usually helped her.

She was suddenly awash with homesickness and nearly emitted a sob. She turned to head back the way she had come, and faced a wolf. It was a young one with tawny fur and deep, dark eyes, not an adult but still as large as a full grown German shepherd. It stood so completely still that Fern wondered if what she was seeing was real. Unsure if she should move back a step or forward a step for fear of startling the animal, she made the quick decision to step to the left. Then the wolf growled menacingly and Fern lost all pretense of calmness.

She ran headlong into the woods and screamed. Or she might have screamed first and then ran. (Fern always remembered the order of events differently.) Her previously weary legs pumped with a renewed vigor as she tore past trees, over roots and rocks...

As young as it was, the wolf easily kept up. It snapped at her pant legs, leapt, and with a force greater than she would have expected, knocked her to the ground. Fern tumbled and came to rest on her back. The young wolf pounced on her and held her down with its two front legs.

Fern struggled, but the wolf was stronger than its small size indicated. She was outmatched, and all she could do once she recovered her wind was scream. The wolf leaned in, its snout inches from her face, and snarled. Drops of drool slipped from between its clenched fangs and spattered Fern's shirt.

A gunshot rang out and startled both of them. Fern turned and saw Creel, then just the town deputy, with a long-barreled shiny revolver pointed up in the air. He wore a gun in a holster on his hip like a Wild West gunfighter.

He pointed the huge revolver at the wolf and said, "Get off her or the next bullet goes into ya. It might not kill ya, but it'll sure hurt a helluva lot."

He was larger than life, like he had stepped full-blown from the pages of a Zane Grey novel. Back then, his hair was still mostly dark brown with strands of premature gray coming in. No beard yet, but he had a thick mustache that completed the gunfighter look.

The wolf didn't move, but it cowered slightly at Creel's words. No longer fierce, it cringed at the sight of the gun and acted as if it had understood everything he said. Actually, even back then, Fern knew the wolf understood. It wasn't a normal wolf; it was one of *them.*

"Stop!" another man yelled out as he ran up to Creel.

He was long and sinewy with straight black hair pulled back into a ponytail as thick as a horse's tail. His complexion was a reddish brown that contrasted sharply with his white cotton pullover and tan canvas pants.

"Don't shoot! She's just a child."

It wouldn't be until much later that Fern would realize the "child" the man referred to wasn't her; it was the wolf. Creel kept the gun aimed at the wolf, but Fern saw a hint of doubt flash over his features. Just as quickly, too, it was gone. His brow furrowed and, although it could probably be attributed to fanciful exaggeration that often colors one's childhood recollections, Fern swore she saw Creel's finger tighten on the trigger of his gun. He was preparing to shoot the young wolf.

The man with the ponytail said, "Luna! Go home!"

The wolf turned and with a sharp yelp that sounded not unlike a young child on the verge of a tantrum, ran into the woods. Once it was gone from sight, Fern managed to get shakily to her feet. She realized her face was wet. She had been unaware that she was crying. Creel put the large revolver back in its holster and walked to her. He picked her up easily in his arms.

"It's okay now, darlin'. It's all over. You're little Fern, aren't you? Ya know ya shouldn't be wanderin' in this part of the woods all alone like that."

All she could do was nod her head and sniff in a hiccupy way. She wiped her cheeks with the back of her hand and looked into Creel's warm, slate-colored eyes. He smiled reassuringly.

The ponytailed man said, "Luna's just a child. She doesn't know any better. However, as you know, she wasn't entirely in the wrong..."

Creel said, "I know."

He put Fern down and took her hand. They started down a worn dirt path. Fern took a last look at the ponytailed man behind them. She noticed how dark his eyes were, and the bright amber rings that encircled his pupils.

Creel guided her down the path that wove among log cabins. People were walking between them or moving into or out of the surrounding woods. Some stopped and stared at her, while others nodded at Creel and went about their business. Some Fern recognized from seeing them in town, but there were quite a few Fern had never seen before.

A naked man emerged from a stand of trees on their right and crossed their path. He passed by and headed directly for a cabin off to their left. Fern was quick to avert her eyes, but she monitored his destination with her peripheral vision. When she was sure he was inside the cabin, she resumed looking around. She noticed

Creel had paid the naked man no mind, as if it was a normal occurrence. Which it probably was out here. Because, although she had never visited this community up in the woods, Fern, much like everyone else who resided in Tanneheuk, knew these people who were a society unto themselves, yet were an integral part of the town.

They walked down the path and Fern tried not to return the looks she got. The people appeared not to notice Creel. He was a familiar sight, but Fern was openly gawked at by many of them. It was such a small community that everyone knew everyone else. It seemed to be comprised of maybe thirty cabins scattered around the forest and some a little ways up the mountain. Some of the cabins were huge, with two floors and a wide foundation. Some cabins were built directly into the side of the mountain, while others were built around trees, as if they had started off as small buildings, but had rooms added on over the years and the residents were reluctant to change the landscape.

At one cabin along the path, a feral boy of about three was chained in the front yard. He was small and thin, pale with white hair, and had a steel collar around his neck with an attached chain that ran around the base of a tree. He growled at her and thrust himself at them until the chain was taut. Every muscle in his naked body strained against his bonds as he tried desperately to get at them. Fern moved closer to Creel and looked away. She hoped by not making eye contact the boy would lose interest in her. But he still growled and snapped as they passed, and when she looked back at him, a horrific sight caused her to stop abruptly.

The boy's skin was rippling. It shifted and changed as if it was no longer solid, but had assumed liquid characteristics and could no longer retain its original shape. His brow bubbled and his face stretch. His neck bulged and thickened until it filled the steel collar that held it. Then the boy let out a gargled yell and his features shifted back to their original shape.

He sat down, hard, on the ground and clutched his throat where the collar had choked him. His interest in them had vanished, replaced by the sudden sharp pain he had experienced and his near-strangulation. The boy let out one last strangled cry and stared dejectedly at the ground.

The rest of her experience was a blur. She remembered

walking with Creel for a while on the path as it wound serpentine down the hillside until they reached his car. She remembered he drove her home and talked to her in a friendly and comforting way. She couldn't recall exactly what he said, but she remembered he tried to be funny, tried to keep it light so that she might come out of the shell-shocked state she had slipped into since the wolf attack.

At one point, she started to shake uncontrollably. Creel reached for her and slid her along the bench seat of the car so that she was up against his side. He put his arm around her and said, "It's alright, darlin'. Everything's gonna be alright. You'll see. Your parents are gonna be real happy to see ya."

From that time on, Deputy Creel, who in a few short years would become Sheriff Creel, was the bright shining knight of her heart. When the Charger slipped off the jack and crushed her leg, he had raced to her house, carried her to his patrol car, and sped with the lights on and the siren blaring to St. Mary's hospital in Lake Dulcet. He drove with one hand on the steering wheel and the other draped over the back of his seat, holding her hand as she cried out from the intense pain. He kept telling her to hold on, to squeeze his hand as hard as she wanted whenever the pain got too bad. She did, too. She squeezed it until she thought she might grind the bones of his hand to dust, that's how bad it was.

Creel got her to the hospital and talked to her nonstop to try and keep her mind off the white hot agony. When she woke up after the surgery, doped up on enough pain medication to put a herd of elephants to sleep, he was sitting in her room along with her parents. Her mom patted her hand and her father kissed her forehead, a decidedly uncharacteristic act for him. She met Creel's eyes. He gave her a smile and a wink, and from that point on, infatuation became love.

A persistent knock on the control booth glass brought her out of her reverie. Myrna knocked on the glass and motioned that they were broadcasting dead air. Fern whipped around in her chair and realized the commercials and songs had played while she had revisited her childhood and teenage years. She recovered instantly and at the same time wondered how long she had sat there after the music ran and her headphones had gone silent. Probably not that long judging by the relieved look on Myrna's face now that Fern was back on the microphone.

"Excuse the break," she said softly into the mike. "I wanted to give you time to digest that. The Black Keys are not a band you tap your foot to and forget about immediately once the next song begins to play. You experience them, the way you eat a five course meal, served to you one delicious dish after another, until your body is warm and full." She let that hang in the air a moment, then: "Now let's listen to some of their obvious influences."

Her hand went to the cigarette case in her pocket.

# Chapter Eleven

Creel thought the new pastor looked too young for the weighty role he was about to assume. They talked in the Reverend's new office, or MacDonald's old office, depending on how you looked at it. Creel gave him the verbal list of what was expected of a Tanneheuk resident.

Reverend Burroughs said, "Sheriff, I don't hunt or fish, and I've never been camping in my life, nor do I feel the urge to start now. I go hiking once in a while…"

The reverend sat in a high-backed burgundy leather chair behind an old, scarred oak desk. He was busily sorting through paperwork and a stack of file folders. He had a computer monitor on in front of him with what appeared to be an unfinished paragraph of text on the screen. Creel had the impression the man was a bit overwhelmed at the moment and was only half paying attention to what Creel was telling him. Celia was at her desk in the opposite corner of the room, typing on her computer and simultaneously talking in a low voice on her desk phone.

"I'm sorry, Sheriff," Burroughs said. "I'm trying to immerse myself in my new duties, and I have to prepare a sermon for Saturday. I thought I'd have time to ease into this position, but Reverend MacDonald essentially dropped me right into the deep end. I didn't expect him to retire five minutes after I arrived."

He said it good-naturedly, but Creel heard the tension in his voice.

"That's alright, Reverend. I know you're busy. And I know Reverend MacDonald already had several phone conversations with ya about our little town and some of its rules. But it's my job to make sure every newcomer is aware of how we do things out here. If ya want, I can come back..."

"What? Oh, no, that's not necessary." He looked up and made eye contact with Creel. "I'm sorry. I didn't even invite you to sit down. Please..." He motioned to a chair in front of his desk.

Creel took the offered chair and leaned his lanky frame down into it. He rested the boot of his right foot up on his left knee and examined the wall behind the reverend. The wall was one large bookcase filled with various theological texts, several versions of the Bible, a set of encyclopedias, and many other books that Creel was unfamiliar with. He assumed they were mostly religious in nature, although he spotted a few classics such as *Moby Dick* and *War and Peace*. There were too many to try and read all of the titles now, but Creel, who was an avid reader, decided he would pay another visit and possibly ask to borrow a few.

"As ya probably know, Reverend—"

"Please, call me Drake. I'm not a stickler for formalities."

Creel nodded. "Well, Drake, the important thing is that you're aware that the woods to the north and east of town are off-limits year round, and the woods to the south and west are off-limits only during the fall and winter. But check with me before ya enter any of those areas."

Drake said, "Okay, sure." His attention was focused on the computer screen. He typed two sentences, then said: "Wait. What?" He looked quizzically at Creel. "Why are the woods off-limits? Reverend MacDonald said much of it was private property, but am I to understand that someone owns all of the surrounding area around this town?"

"Well...in certain respects...yes. There's a community of people who live in those woods, and ya could say they own them. They have proprietary rights over the woods. And the town, too."

Creel shrugged as if the matter was not so unusual, and to him it wasn't. He had spent his whole life in Tanneheuk, and the ways of the town and the pact they had with the elders were second nature to him. He never questioned the why of things.

"The town elders," Drake said.

"That's right. Reverend MacDonald covered that with ya?"

Drake leaned back in his chair. "A little. But I have to admit,

I'm still unclear as to who they are."

"It's not really a big mystery. They're the descendants of the town founders. At one time, the town was strictly a settlement of their people, but in the 1800s, they allowed others to settle here. They made a pact with those people, and the pact is still in existence to this day."

"What do you mean by a pact?" Drake asked.

Creel shifted in his chair and crossed his other leg. He was trying not to appear uncomfortable, but the fact that he was hesitant in his answers, he knew, made him appear that way. He didn't want to hide anything, yet when it came to a newcomer, the best way to indoctrinate him/her into the ways of the pact was to ease them into it. Feed them small morsels of information until they became acclimated. Then he could give them the last two major revelations. By that time, the person was immune to surprise. Or at least more accepting of it.

"The townspeople have a pact with the elders. Basically, we live here with their permission. If we were to break the pact, well, we'd lose our home. And the town is very nice. You'll find that out for yourself once you've been here for a little while."

"Okay, but the pact is what exactly? I'm sorry," Drake said. "I'm still unclear about that."

"Like I said, we can't enter certain areas of the woods during spring and summer, and all of it is off-limits during the fall and winter. See, those people live off the land, so going into their, um, domain, could cause a disturbance. So it's best not to enter those areas at all unless you're absolutely sure of where ya are. And it would be best if ya cleared it with me first, too. Since ya weren't born and raised here, ya might not be able to tell what areas are safe."

Drake regarded him for a moment. "What would happen to me if I went into one of the areas I wasn't allowed? Would I be shot for trespassing?"

Creel couldn't tell if the young minister was being serious or attempting sarcasm. Whatever the case, it irritated him. He wanted to grab the reverend by his shirt and shake him until the smug look was wiped off his face. He wanted to shout, "*Just do what I tell ya, ya stupid bastard! There are worse things than being shot!*"

He controlled his impulses and said, "As I've tried to make clear, Reverend—"

"Call me Drake. Please."

Creel went on as if he hadn't heard him. "—we have a pact with these people, and it would be unwise to do anything to disturb that."

"You know, I met one of these elders."

"Oh, really?" Creel was interested. "Who was it?"

Drake described him.

"That's Roman. He's sort of the spokesman for their people. Their leader."

"Roman? Roman what?"

"That's it. Just Roman."

"Do they all have just one name? Like Cher? Or Charo?"

"Like Stendhal," Creel answered.

"Sheriff, I didn't realize you had a taste for classic literature. I love books, too. Do you read a lot?"

"Sure. Always have. Everything from classics to the modern stuff. Or did ya think I was just a dumb country constable?"

"What? No, of course not. I'm sorry, did I come off as condescending?"

"Nope. I'm just funnin' ya." Creel stood. "I best be on my way. I'm sure ya have a heap of work to get done before Saturday." He strode to the door and rested his hand on the knob. "Reverend, if ya have any more interactions with one of the elders, especially Roman, it's best to let me know about it. It's my job to keep things running smooth in Tanneheuk. And I take that job seriously."

"How can I tell who's an elder and who isn't?"

"You'll be able to tell the difference. The elders are pretty open about who they are. They act a certain way. I can't explain it better than that, but you'll see what I'm talking about." He nodded. "Good day, Reverend."

"Sheriff, please. You don't have to keep calling me Reverend. Call me Drake, and I'll call you...?"

"Sheriff will be just fine, Reverend. Call me Sheriff."

After Creel left, Drake noticed Celia was off the phone. "Was I rude to the sheriff?" he asked her. "I got the feeling I offended him in some way."

She shrugged. "I didn't hear the whole conversation, but I

didn't think you were rude."

She smiled at him and it gave him a warm feeling in his chest. He told himself to stay strong. He was new in town and he should be careful not to make any reckless decisions that could affect his career or livelihood. Celia worked for him and if he made a wrong move, there would be no going back. Sure, it seemed like the attraction between them was mutual, but maybe he was misreading the signals. Maybe her frequent smiles and shy glances were symptoms of her friendly disposition. If that was the case, and he made an overture to her that wasn't reciprocated...

It was a tricky situation and he needed to proceed with the utmost caution. One false move and his reputation in town could take a serious blow. Not to mention that it could put his job in jeopardy. He used the mental image of a sexual harassment lawsuit to dampen his attraction to her. It worked, temporarily at least.

She said, "Sheriff Creel is a very nice man, but he's always been a bit, um, tightly wound when it comes to maintaining order in Tanneheuk."

"Is it really that difficult a job? Everyone keeps telling me what a friendly town this is, a great place to live..."

"It is," she said. "It really is."

"But?"

Celia bit her lower lip and glanced away before she answered.

"My father is black," she said, "and my mother is white. They met when they were teenagers and fell instantly in love. And even though this was less than thirty years ago and you'd think such things would be more accepted, they still encountered racism. They were called horrible names, they were threatened, and they encountered prejudice at school and at work. They knew they couldn't go on like that, but they also knew they couldn't live without each other.

"My mother had a cousin who lived in Tanneheuk. They moved out here and found a town that harbored no prejudice or racism. They were accepted for who they were. Their skin color and the fact they were different races made no difference. They've never looked back and they're thankful every day for coming here. Their marriage is what I aspire mine to someday be like."

"I'm sure you'll be successful," Drake said, then couldn't help but ask: "Is there someone special in your life? I don't mean to pry. I was just, you know, wondering. Curious, really. Maybe 'curious' isn't the right word. As your pastor, of course I'd be interested in your happiness, as well as everyone else in our community."

He stumbled over his words as clumsily as a schoolboy. Worse, he felt himself blush.

"I'm not currently seeing anyone, Reverend," she said.

Was that a hint of red in her cheeks? Did he make her blush? It was wrong. He knew it was wrong. He was sliding down that slippery slope again, and this time, he might not be able to climb back up. He was new in Tanneheuk, hadn't yet delivered his first sermon, only knew three people in town, and she worked for him. Weren't those sufficient reasons to keep the relationship platonic?

Maybe once he was settled in for a few months, had become familiar with members of the congregation, gotten to know her, it would be a possibility that he could ask her out on a date. Take it very, very slow. Chaste, even. That would be acceptable. No one would be able to accuse him of impropriety.

"Well," he said, "I'm sure that, um, in time, that will be...rectified. You'll meet someone special."

"I have faith that I will, Reverend."

Did he imagine that twinkle in her eyes? She was flirting with him, wasn't she? *Lord, give me strength*, he thought. *I want to be improper. I so much want to be improper.*

Celia went back to typing on her computer with a hint of a smile still on her lips.

"I'm going to bring the rest of my belongings in from my car," he said.

"Oh?" She looked up. "Do you want some help?"

"No, that's okay."

He stood up and half stumbled to the door. He tried to conceal the fact that he was hurrying out of the room, but he still left abruptly. He walked down the short hallway, past the small kitchen, and out the back door.

He was struck once again by the sheer beauty of the landscape, the clean air and the sharp blue sky. He took in a deep lungful of air, and wondered how long before the newness of his home would wear off and he would miss the excitement of his former life in the big city. One thing he knew he would miss was the ocean.

Drake loved his weekly treks to the beach and swimming and surfing in the Atlantic. He was much too far away from either ocean now. He would have to ask Celia where the local swimming areas were. The river he had passed over on his way into town looked too tempestuous for anything less than a kayak. It was probably very cold, too, even in the summertime.

He turned to walk around the corner of the building to where his car was parked, and the hairs on the back of his neck suddenly stood at attention. In the past when he had heard about that sort of thing occurring, he had thought it merely an exaggeration on the part of the storyteller. In a novel when the author would describe a character that experienced the same thing, Drake would scoff and think it silly and cliché. Now he felt it and found himself startled by the feeling. More than a feeling, it was a physical sensation that caused him to automatically run his hand over the back of his neck to smooth down the phantom hairs.

Maybe it wasn't a true physical manifestation, but one of such psychic intensity that it caused a conditioned physical response. He looked around and tried to ascertain the origin of the feeling: Was someone staring at him? Did he step too close to a high voltage line? In many ways, it did feel like an electric current running around the outline of his body.

No, it wasn't that. His first instinct was correct. Someone was watching him. Behind the church, past the paved parking lot that ran completely around the building, was a narrow strip of grass that bordered between the pavement and the wooded areas that appeared to be predominant in Tanneheuk. He scanned the tree line and peered, as best he could from his vantage point, between the trees where the shadows were deepest. There...he could just make it out...a figure, standing, watching...

Who was it? Roman? Had he come back to engage him in more psychological sparring? But what was the point of spying on him? Drake's impression of Roman was that the man preferred face-to-face confrontation. No, this had to be someone else.

It wasn't necessarily something sinister. It could be someone strolling through the woods who happened to spot him as he came out of the back of the building. Maybe they wondered who he was, being that he was a newcomer and all.

*Newcomer.* Drake shook his head. He had already adopted their vernacular. Soon he would be spouting sentences with the words "town elders" and "pact" laced throughout, all parts of a normal, everyday conversation. He might even get used to the stuck-in-the-1950s feel of the town. No cell phones and no Internet? He had thought Reverend MacDonald was joking when he mentioned it in their first phone conversation, but the sheriff had verified it. Drake didn't mind the lack of a cell phone. He found them to be more of a nuisance than anything. But like most contemporary citizens, he had come to rely on the Internet for research and shopping.

He stood and stared. The figure was hidden in the shadows, but he could just about make her out. It was definitely a woman, though why or how he instantly knew that, he couldn't say. But it was a woman; he was sure of it. Watching him.

It was strange. He felt a connection across the void to this unknown, mostly unseen person. He wasn't a hundred percent sure she was there. It could be a trick of the light or a play of shadows.

Something down deep inside, something that didn't respond to logic or reason, told him that she was there. He felt her presence as clearly as if he was standing in a room with her. And he felt her eyes. An unspoken communication passed between them. He was lost as to what was said, but felt the stirrings of a primal instinct. His body, independent of his brain, wanted to respond. He had the urge to run to the woods, to run to her.

Then it was over. The connection was broken. The figure turned and moved back into the woods. There was a flash of white that he thought... No, it couldn't be, could it? Was she...? Was she naked?

No, it had to be an illusion. His mind playing tricks or the sun reflecting off beige-colored clothing. Still, it took every ounce of his willpower to stop himself from following her.

# Chapter Twelve

David sat in a wicker chair on the old lady's porch with his feet up on the white painted railing. It was late, probably after eleven, but he didn't feel like going inside and checking the time. The porch light was off so as not to attract bugs, but the street was well-lit enough that he wasn't sitting in total darkness. He nursed a bottle of beer and contemplated his options.

Dear old Dad had retired already, and Philo and Bimbo...oops, Amber, were probably on their second screw. David tried to wrap his head around that image. He likened it to a bear attempting to pedal a bicycle: a lot of grunting and effort, but the big dumb animal rarely gets anywhere.

Actually, David thought he might be wrong. There must be something to their relationship, otherwise Amber wouldn't put up with it. Philo, he was sure, was just happy to have someone interested in him, not to mention willing to have sex with him. It was Amber's motivation that puzzled him. Could she really be interested in his slowwitted half-brother? Of course, her past boyfriends weren't any better.

Boyfriends. That was funny. She had boyfriends the way David had girlfriends. With their lifestyle of constantly being on the move and living under false identities, none of them could carry on a real relationship that lasted more than a week. The majority of David's pick-ups were one night stands, and he had to admit, he preferred it that way. Actually, if truth be told, he preferred paying for sex. There was no work involved, no unnecessary conversation, no possibility of putting in the effort of picking a woman up, and once the act was over, they left. No muss, no fuss, no one fell in love, and no complications. It was perfect.

Was that the attraction between them? The convenience of it? It had to be. Philo wasn't a bad looking kid, he supposed. From a distance. He was big. Up top, anyway. David had seen him naked and to be frank, there wasn't much going on downstairs. As slight as he was, David had a much bigger package. There was no bragging here, but David had surprised women on many occasions by what he had concealed in his trousers. What he lacked in height and muscles, God had compensated him for in other ways.

As for Amber, David figured she was probably only good for one thing. And probably not all that much to speak of in that department. She came off as a bit of a cold fish, although...

Well, David had to admit there were one or two times he heard her and Philo going at it, and they sounded like they were enjoying themselves. Okay, let's be honest, he didn't "accidentally" overhear them. He purposely eavesdropped because he figured it would give him a laugh and possible ammunition for his patented insults.

He had been surprised at how vocal Amber was, and he had to admit, the dirty things she said kind of turned him on. It even made him consider the idea of seducing her, just to see what it would be like. He considered getting her drunk, using his skill at seduction he had practiced on many an intoxicated barfly, then giving her an angry fuck. Use her, abuse her, and snub her the next day. Oh, that would be sweet.

He couldn't do it. It would cause too much tension in their family dynamic, and once Dad found out, the shit would hit the fan. The way he favored Philo? David would probably be excommunicated from the Rafferty clan. Then what would he do? Get a real job? No fuckin' way. Plus, it would hurt Philo. Not about David getting kicked out of the family, but that David had taken advantage of Amber. Fucked his girl, so to speak. And though David would never cop to it, not out loud anyway, he kind of had a soft spot for the big idiot.

So no, he would never take a shot at seducing Amber. Now if the white trash bitch ever hurt Philo or dumped him? Yeah, he would definitely get some payback. He would fuck her, call her dirty names, make her fall in love with him, then never speak to her again, unless it had to do with some con they were running.

David hoped this next con, the big one Dad had talked about, was the last. He hoped to get a big enough cut that he could go off on his own, detach himself from his dysfunctional family and be self-sufficient. Enough money that he could run his own cons and maybe hire some professionals. David had ideas of his own. He was tired of taking orders from his father.

So Philo and Amber were screwing, or maybe they were asleep by now, the two of them drooling on their respective pillows. Dad was asleep early because he had been up for two days straight, driving. And the old lady who owned the house had turned in at eight o'clock.

David wasn't sure if that was her normal bedtime, if she was tired, or if she simply wanted to get away from them. All through dinner, despite Dad's attempts at being friendly and making polite conversation, the old woman acted nervous. Wary was a better word for it. David could tell she had second thoughts about letting them rent her rooms. But it was too late now. They were in.

The Raffertys were like a very bad infection: Once they secured a foothold in your system, you had a hell of a time getting rid of them. Normal treatment wouldn't do it. You had to resort to desperate measures. Even then, they had a habit of popping back up at inopportune times.

He smiled and sipped his beer. He liked the analogy. That was a good way to think of his family. Not something you want; something you catch and wish you could get rid of.

The street was quiet. Jeez. What, did everyone go to bed early around here? He might as well go to bed himself. The thought of spending the summer in this dead burg was almost as bad as a prison sentence. Almost.

He stood, stretched, and drank the remainder of his beer. He left the empty bottle on the railing. He figured the old woman could pick it up in the morning. A little exercise would be good for her. He turned to go in when the sound of the car caught his attention.

He looked up the street and saw the black Dodge Charger coming. It wasn't that the sound of the engine was loud. It was that everything else was so quiet, the sound stood out.

David smirked. Plain Jane coming home from work. Or maybe her boyfriend's house? Nah. He didn't get the impression she had a man. His dad had the gift of reading people. David had the gift of telling when a woman was sexually active or when she was in sexual hibernation. His read on Plain Jane was that she had been in a holding pattern for quite a while. For some reason, it intrigued him.

The car came up the road a little fast for a residential neighborhood. Not that he cared if she exceeded the speed limit. What he liked was that she didn't care.

The car pulled up to her house, turned into the driveway, backed out, and parked on the street in the opposite direction. She stepped out of the car and shut the door. David whistled. She looked around, unsure where the whistle came from. He thought she seemed a little loopy, like she was overtired or perhaps slightly drunk. Something about the way she moved and reacted to the whistle, like she was a half-second slow in reacting.

He whistled again and this time she homed in on the source. She looked in his direction and appeared surprised to see him standing on the porch. He waved for her to come over. She scrunched up her face in puzzlement. He chuckled at her expression. In a way, he found it kind of cute. Was she unsure of what he wanted, or unsure if he was talking to her? He motioned again.

She looked around as if she wanted to be sure he was talking to her and not someone behind or to the side of her. Then she looked back at him and took a tentative step forward.

*Come on, come on,* he thought. Boy, she was like a timid rabbit, not sure if she should accept a carrot from a stranger. *C'mere and maybe I'll show you my carrot.*

She walked across the street to him. He noticed her limp and tried to recall if she had been limping earlier that day. Maybe she'd twisted her ankle or something?

David stepped down from the porch and took a couple of steps towards her. He thought he would meet her part of the way.

"Hey," he said when he came within talking distance. They stood and faced each other on the walkway leading up to the old woman's house. She was taller than him so he had to look slightly up to make eye contact.

"Yeah?" she asked. "What do you want?"

He got a good look at her eyes and saw why she was acting a little dazed. She was stoned. Well, well, well. Plain Jane liked getting baked. That was interesting.

"Just wanted to say hi," he said.

She nodded. "Okay."

"So, how was your day? You just get finished with work?"

"Uh, yeah... Um, is there something you want?"

"No," he laughed. "What's with you? I'm just trying to be friendly."

"Oh. Okay." She nodded again and appeared unsure of what to say next.

"So? Your day? How was it?"

"It was...fine." She shrugged. "Look, I uh, I need to get to bed. I have to get up early."

She looked at him like she was trying to decipher a note written in an unfamiliar language. It was kind of...cute? He hated to admit it, but the plain-looking broad was beginning to grow on him.

"Okay," he said. "I didn't mean to disturb you."

"No, you weren't...you didn't disturb me."

"What happened to your leg?"

That took her by surprise, he could tell. There was a delayed reaction to his question, as all of her reactions seemed delayed. But once the words sank in, an expression of uneasiness crossed her features.

"What?"

"I saw you limping," he said. "I thought you might have hurt your leg."

"A long time ago."

"Oh." Then: "I guess it still hurts you, huh?"

"Yeah," she answered. "A little."

She was still trying to figure out some great puzzle or something. She kept looking at him like he was setting up some long and involved joke, and she was patiently waiting for him to deliver the punchline. He laughed.

"What's so funny?"

"Nothing," he said, though he knew she thought he was laughing at her. "It's just very hard to have a conversation with you. Trying to get more than two words out of you is like...is like trying to get a virgin out of her chastity belt."

"Oh." She shrugged again. "Well, like I said, it's late, so…"

"Yeah. Hey. You want to go out sometime?"

"What?"

"Out. You know, on a date? Like, me and you go out, we have a few drinks, go line-dancing or whatever you people do for fun around here. What do you say?"

"Um…"

Her expression was a mixture of confusion, disbelief, and suspicion. She either a) didn't trust him; b) didn't believe him; c) didn't understand him; or d) all of the above. David thought it was probably "d", which made him want to go out with her even more.

"I don't think so," she said.

"Why not?" Now he was the one experiencing disbelief. He had been turned down before, but by women who were much more attractive than this one.

"I don't think it's a good idea, that's all." She turned and limped back across the street and headed for her house.

He called after her, "Are you sure you don't want to go out with me?"

"Yeah," she replied without turning around.

"You mind if I ask you again, like tomorrow or the next day?"

"Do what you want," she said.

She walked up the driveway of her house, unlocked the side door and entered. The outside light over the door went out. He still stood there. Like a schmuck. Turned down by Plain Jane. He couldn't believe it.

The funny thing was, now he really wanted to go out with her. He was sort of playing around at first, but then got into it with her and decided what the hell, he would ask her out on a date. Her lack of interest fueled something inside himself. He was... Well, he had to admit it, he was smitten.

He shook his head and walked back up to the house. He smiled at himself. *Now I'll be obsessed with her until she agrees to go out with me. All because she wasn't interested. All because she turned me down. And I wasn't even serious. Was I?*

He noticed for the first time that it was much cooler out. He could even detect traces of his breath in the air. The temperature had dropped little by little after sundown. Fuckin' Montana.

When he reached the front step of the porch, he detected movement out of the corner of his eye. He turned his head sharply, quick enough to catch four animals running across the street. They were several houses down and came from the area between two houses and ran across the street to the yard between the opposite two houses. Then they were gone and David was left wondering what it was that he saw. They looked like, what…? Dogs? If they were dogs, they were big dogs.

It had happened so fast, he wasn't sure what they were. He was sure he hadn't imagined it, though. They were covered by the darkness between the houses and they moved fast. Very fast. Was it a pack of dogs running loose?

No, he thought it was something else. Not dogs. Too big to be dogs. But what? Coyotes? Wolves?

Nah, that was crazy. Four wolves running through a quiet town neighborhood and cutting between houses? Wolves wouldn't come this close to civilization. They stayed away from people. Right? Besides, wolves didn't get that big, did they?

Without admitting it to himself, he picked up his pace and headed inside the house. He wasn't scared of the mystery animals. It was just getting a little too cold outside and he wanted to get in and get warm. Yeah, that was the reason.

# June

Slade Grayson

# Chapter Thirteen

The rabbit was fast. Roman was faster. He had been chasing it more for sport than out of hunger, but the chase had stoked his appetite. When he eventually pounced on it and felt it squirm under his weight, he was salivating.

He held the rabbit firmly and felt it try to desperately move away despite the iron grip on its neck. Roman heard its heartbeat, could feel it as it thumped wildly inside its tiny chest cavity. The rabbit smelled of fear. It was a smell that appealed to Roman's basest instincts. Though he prided himself on his self-control, there were certain parts of himself that he could never keep in check. Nor, for that matter, would he want to.

He bit into the rabbit's torso and heard it emit a small squeak as his teeth ripped into its angora pelt. The coppery smell and taste of the blood enveloped his senses and stimulated him. He instantly had an erection.

The rabbit still moved, though not as much. It twitched as its nervous system and brain began its shutdown process. Roman burrowed his face into its body and worked to rip open its ribcage. The small bones snapped and his teeth tore into the sputtering heart. Warm blood covered his mouth and nose. There was no thinking now. His mouth moved of its own volition, on primal instinct rather than conscious thought. He tore at the meat and ate.

When little remained of the rabbit except bits of fur and gnawed bones, Roman walked to a nearby stream and dunked his face in the cool water. He drank greedily, then shook his face in the water to wash off the blood. Most of it came off, but two more shakes completed the job.

When he removed his face from the water and shook off the droplets that clung to him, a familiar scent caught his attention. He looked about and sniffed the air. He determined the point of origin based partly on the wind direction, and partly on what his gut told him. There was little thought involved; his brain knew what the scent was and where it came from. He followed the scent, tentatively at first, then in a more determined manner as it grew stronger. The anticipation urged him on, but he forced himself to be deliberate in his actions. The bloodlust had become something new, yet connected. The pulsation in his groin was still there, and he was eager for release.

He caught a glimpse of her yellow hair through a break in the trees. She noticed him, too, had probably sensed his approach for a while, but she pretended to be unaware of him. He knew what would come next: She was preparing to run. She loved taking him on a chase, loved to tease him. And he loved it, too.

She ran, and he followed. They ran until the passing trees were blurs of red and green and their lungs took in deep, long breaths. His legs pumped like pistons, the air around him became a swirl of intricate patterns comprised of smells, sounds, and colors that moved by fleetingly and left only trace impressions on his senses. He reveled in this glorious chase...until finally, he overtook her.

He caught her in the lower back, not hard, but with enough force to throw her off-balance and cause her to tumble to the ground. She came up in a crouch and faced him. The corners of her lips were drawn back in a silent snarl. She stared at him and waited...anxious...aroused...

He mounted her from behind and took her with an urgency that melted into tenderness. His thrusts became slower and rhythmic. Her hips moved in time to his. They moved that way for a while and he thought he would be content to never stop, to keep thrusting into her for hours and hours. Eventually, his weight on her took its toll and his own legs began to tremble from the exertion. He relaxed his control and orgasmed. Her body shuddered with her own orgasm a few seconds later, and they collapsed to the ground, spent. They lay together in a tangle of limbs. She nipped playfully at his shoulder and he nuzzled his face against hers.

He dozed for a while. When he woke, Salacia was back in her

human form. She rested on her elbows with her head back, her chin aimed at the sky, and her legs and toes pointed. The sun beamed down on her and cast her sleek frame in a golden aura. There was a smile of contentment on her lips, and her nipples were erect. Roman had the desire to reach out and touch them, but he realized his own form wasn't conducive. He sighed inwardly. He really didn't wish to change back yet, but since she had and he wanted to be able to communicate with her...

He closed his eyes and willed the transformation to occur. His claws and fangs retracted and his skeletal frame shifted. Bones moved, muscles shortened, and his nose and mouth pulled back to a human shape. Some of the fur withdrew beneath the skin, but much of it fell out in clumps. When his limbs reshaped themselves to human form, he brushed the loose fur off himself. The hair on his head lengthened. The ends went down and curled at the base of his neck and instinctually stopped. Roman could have willed his hair to grow longer, or to have stopped growing before that point, and after a few times, it would automatically stop at the same length. But the length he currently wore had been his style for many years, and he had no inclination to change it.

He smoothed his hair back and brushed it behind his ears, then shook off the few strands of fur that was still interwoven in the ends of his hair and that still remained on his body. He stretched and felt parts of his body still seeking, moving, shifting, changing. His skin still rippled in places that were borderline between wolf and man. Finally, the process was complete and he was human again.

The transformation took less than a minute and wasn't at all painful, but there was still an internal sensation that accompanied it that was uncomfortable. It was the feeling that his body was turned inside out, which, in some ways, he supposed it was. Still, despite the hundreds, maybe thousands of times, that he had effected the change from wolf to human, or human to wolf, there was still an uncomfortableness to it that made it seem as if reality had been ripped in half. It was hard to describe, almost impossible to explain to someone who had never experienced it. His fellow shapeshifters knew the feeling, had discussed it amongst themselves on many occasions, but it was one of those accepted things that came with their people — the lycanthropes, the werewolves. Besides, what was mere seconds of uncomfortableness in the grand scheme of things when they were able to live life as a human and a wolf? To them, "normal" humans were akin to beings who were born severely handicapped. To the elders, the humans were inferior beings.

He cleared his throat before he spoke. "Why did you change back?"

Salacia peeked at him from the corner of one eye. She kept her head tilted up to the sun. "Mmm. I like the feel of the sun on bare skin. I wanted to enjoy it."

There was a lilt to her voice he had always found engaging. When she smiled, she showed many of the long teeth that were indicative of those who were born shapeshifters. The ones infected with the lycanthrope virus— those few that survived— when they were in their human form, the casual observer could detect little evidence to suggest their true nature. The ones born with the virus, that were able to shapeshift from the time of infancy, had several traits in common. For one, their nails were sharper than a human's. Another trait was that their upper torso was noticeably longer than a human's. And third, their teeth were slightly longer and sharper, more fangish, than a human's. Roman, like Salacia, was born a shapeshifter. Therefore, the many traits she had, ones he found attractive, he had as well.

Roman stretched out on his back and basked in the sun with his hands folded behind his head. The weather was warm, but not uncomfortably so. He took in the sounds and smells around him. He heard Salacia breathing beside him, could hear her heartbeat if he listened closely. He could concentrate, focus his attention on just that one sound while simultaneously blocking out the multitude of sounds around him. He heard it now, steady, yet slightly elevated.

His own heartbeat increased due to his arousal for her, and he heard her own heartbeat quicken. Her scent filled his nostrils. It was a mixture of her usual flowery scent, combined with the dried sweat produced by their lovemaking. He smelled himself on her, which fanned his desire. He reached out and brushed a hand across her breasts. Her semi-erect nipples came to full attention.

"You never get enough, do you?"

"No," Roman replied. "And neither do you."

It was true. He smelled her arousal, the way the flow of her blood quickened, the rise of her heartbeat, the rapidness of her breath. He smelled the moistness between her legs and noted the subtle shift when she moved them slightly apart. She was ready for him.

Roman moved atop and slid into her with practiced ease. She arched her hips and with a sharp intake of breath, took him to the hilt.

She said in a thick voice, "We haven't done it this way in a long time. I was beginning to think you didn't want to look at my face when we fucked."

"That wasn't the reason," he said. "I prefer it the other way. It feels more natural to me." He paused. "But this way is good, too."

She smiled up at him, and he returned it. He nuzzled her neck as they moved in sync. He felt her tongue, moist yet sandpapery, as it flicked out on his shoulders, neck, and chest. He nibbled at her, gently so as to taste her, but not hard enough to break the skin or leave marks. She made a low sound as he nuzzled and nipped at her, and moved between her thighs, in and out. She emitted a succession of low growls of pleasure. It spurred him on in his desire for her.

She orgasmed first this time. He followed a minute later, then moved off and onto his back. They lay together and panted for air. Her hand sought his and clasped it. He turned to her and saw her breathing heavily, her eyes closed and a satisfied grin on her lips. He caught her earlobe between his teeth and gave it a playful tug. When she snorted in response, he let go and buried his face in her short blonde hair. It was normally spiky, but more so now that it was damp with sweat.

Another scent caught his attention. It was a familiar one, far away still, but moving in their general direction. Roman raised his head and sniffed the air. Salacia had also picked up on the scent.

"Father's looking for me," she said.

Roman looked for a glimpse of the large silver wolf. Or perhaps it was a barrel-chested man with a silver beard and matching long hair. He wasn't sure what form Mars, Salacia's father, was currently in. Salacia looked, too, but as they scanned the surrounding area, the scent slowly faded. Mars was moving away from them.

"He smelled you," she said. "He knows you're with me, so he doesn't want to disturb us."

"Then he approves?" Roman asked with a touch of lightness in his voice.

Salacia kissed the underside of his chin. "Of course. You know how he feels about you. He thinks of you like a son. He wants us to be together. Why wouldn't he want his daughter to be...?"

"To be what?"

"To be your mate. You've been the Alpha male for a while. The pack needs an Alpha female."

Roman scowled and moved away. He stood up briskly and brushed the dirt from his knees and elbows.

"What is it?" she asked.

"The pack has an Alpha female. Diana is the Alpha female."

"She's your sister," Salacia said. "She's not your mate. Once you choose a mate, that person becomes the Alpha female."

She sat up and moved into a cross-legged position. She tried to meet his eyes, but he kept them averted. He had his brow furrowed and a deep frown was etched on his face.

"You know I'm right, Roman. You have to pick a mate sooner or later. You have to reproduce. It's your duty to the pack. Your sons will become the future leaders. You must prepare for the next generation. In order to do that—"

"I'm aware of my duty to the pack," he said.

He fixed her with a cold stare that sent a sliver of fear through her. She knew he cared about her, maybe he even loved her, but there were times when she saw the stark coldness that was in him, when she knew he could be capable of anything if it meant it would serve his purposes. It was at those times that Salacia knew if Roman was given the choice of giving up his leadership of the pack or killing her, he would rip her throat out and never think twice about it. He might feel remorse later, but he would never question his choice.

He could be brutally cruel one minute, and completely loving and tender the next. It was the wolf part of him. Though he prided himself on his mastery over his animal side, Salacia knew the animal was always lurking right below the surface, ready to kill any perceivable threat to its existence or authority.

"Diana is the Alpha female," he said again. "I won't force her to step down."

"Step down and become a Beta like my father? Would that be so bad?" Salacia asked.

"She's earned her place."

"Earned it? She was born into it. And you've kept her there by your will alone. She certainly hasn't done anything to deserve respect. You make all the decisions. If not for you forcing her leadership down everyone's throat—"

"Enough!" He pointed a finger at her. "You," he said, "will watch your tongue and remember your place. Diana is the Alpha female. Don't ever question that."

The force of his will threatened to send her cowering. She drew her legs up and hugged her knees. She feared for a moment that he might strike her, such was his anger. He abruptly turned his back on her and contemplated the ground beneath his feet. When he turned back towards her, he had a hint of regret in his eyes. Regret for his outburst, or regret for the situation they were in, she couldn't tell.

"You...are special to me," he said. "Don't think I take that...take *you* for granted. I will find a way to work things out so we can be together."

"Is that why you insist on keeping our relationship a secret from the others? My father knows, but no one else. Is that why? Because of your sister?"

"Of course," he said. "There's never been two Alpha females. If I take a mate, in the eyes of the pack, she automatically usurps the current Alpha female. Diana is too special to me to simply cast her away."

"She doesn't have to be cast away," Salacia said. "That's my point. Being a Beta is just as good as—"

"Enough," he said again, though this time not as sharply. "Enough. I don't want to have this discussion now."

She nodded. The magic of the afternoon had been spoiled. She wanted to get some of it back, to get back to the intimacy they had shared just a few moments ago. Those times were rare because of Roman's normally closed off personality. The few times he let his guard down, let her inside, were the times she cherished. She wished and hoped that those times would become more frequent.

"So were you planning on walking back home like that?" His lip curled in an amused expression.

She smiled up at him, relieved now that the tension had eased. She stood up, stretched, brushed dirt off herself. Her back was filthy from the ground. She had trouble brushing off the middle area of her back, so she turned to him and said, "Little help?"

He smiled and brushed the dirt from her back, then let his hand fall to her buttocks. He rubbed both of them in turn, and gave her a swat. She laughed.

"Come on," he said. "I'll race you back."

They took positions next to each other and readied themselves. She closed her eyes and waited.

"Go," he said, and they both began their transformation.

Roman was faster. He was in his wolf form and running by the time Salacia's own transformation was complete. He was, and had always been, the fastest at the transformation. It was an inherent ability he had, one that others had challenged him on before. And he had always won. The shapeshifters who had a stronger wolf side than a human side, those members of the pack who were clearly more comfortable in their wolf form and who seemed out of place as a human — their human form as ill-fitting as a suit of clothes two sizes too small — even those shapeshifters couldn't transform as fast as Roman. He had beaten everyone who had ever challenged him. He was so fast and so natural at it, that the challenges had long ago ceased.

Her transformation complete, she ran after him. *I would do anything for him*, she thought. *If all he wants from me is sex, if it's only an affair and he never has the intention of making me his mate, well then, that's fine with me. Just as long as he lets me be with him.*

# Chapter Fourteen

He had her up against his desk, his arms around her, his mouth over hers. His hands moved over her body, stroking her back before sliding down to her hips. He kissed along her jawline and traced his lips down to the curve between her neck and shoulders.

Celia moaned. "Oh! Oh, Reverend!"

Drake pulled away and met her eyes. "Could you...could you not call me that when we're, you know...?"

"I'm sorry, Re... I'm sorry, Drake."

They were both flushed and breathing hard. She removed her glasses, placed them on the desk behind her, and resumed kissing him. He kissed her back with the same passion. He really, really wanted her.

They had flirted for weeks, and his banter, innocent and friendly at first, had been received positively. His flirtatious remarks had increased in boldness, and rather than pull away as he feared, Celia had lobbed her own in return. Soon, they were trading innuendo until the time came when one of them had to make a move. Drake felt since he was the man, it should fall to him to cross the line. By this time, he was sure his attentions would not be unwanted. He was right. For a small town girl, Celia sure knew how to kiss.

His hands slid down to her legs. She was half-sitting on his desk and he was pressed against her, between her thighs. He moved his hands up under her skirt and his palms caressed the silky smoothness of her legs. He lowered his head and kissed down her throat, down to her chest. He put his face in the bottom of the

V of her light pullover top, one that displayed plenty of cleavage. His lips kissed the valley between her breasts as his hands moved up her thighs, up, up to the elastic band of her panties.

"Oh! Drake! Oh!" Her voice was low and breathless. She wanted him. But then: "No! Wait. Stop. Stop, stop, stop," she said.

He had his fingers hooked in the waistband of her panties.

"What? What is it?" he asked. "What's wrong?"

"I can't... we can't..."

"Can't what? What's wrong, Celia?"

"We can't go any further. Not now. Not like this."

It had the effect of cold water being thrown on him. He instantly removed his hands from underneath her skirt and took a step back. He still burned with desire, the blood still rushed through his veins, but he felt a thin line of ice creep in. Had he gone too far? Was she about to accuse him of forcing himself on her? Taking advantage of her?

"I don't understand," he said. "Did I misunderstand? You know I like you. Don't you like me?"

"Yes. Yes, of course," she said. "I do like you, Reverend." She quickly added, "Drake," when she saw the pained look on his face. "It's just...it's a little fast, that's all."

"Oh." He straightened his clerical collar and attempted to smooth his shirt as best he could. He was very aware of the erection in his pants and figured she must be, too, but they both pretended not to notice.

"I'm sorry. I didn't mean to rush things."

"No, no, you weren't... It's not you. It's just... I'm a virgin. I'm saving myself for marriage."

"You're kidding," he said before he could catch himself. When he realized how it sounded, he added, "I mean, that's great. It's wonderful. That's a very admirable thing." He hoped she didn't catch the disappointment in his voice.

Marriage? What was he supposed to do? Marry her? He had only known her for a few weeks. They hadn't even gone out on a date. He couldn't consider marriage right now, not with his commitments to the church. Maybe in a year or two, or three... Even then, he didn't know her well enough to contemplate marriage this soon in their burgeoning relationship.

Yes, he knew how it sounded. He was prepared to have sex

with her on his desk, all while the church committee was outside arranging his welcome lunch. Yet, when the subject of marriage came up, he could think of a thousand excuses why the idea was premature. He was quick to decide that he didn't know her well enough to marry her, but he was ready to partake carnal knowledge of her with little forethought. He mentally berated himself for his weakness when it came to temptation.

Celia was suddenly self-conscious about her disheveled appearance. She moved off his desk and straightened her skirt and top, and used her fingers to fluff up the ringlets of her hair. She appeared to be too embarrassed to look him in the eye. He felt he should say something comforting.

"Maybe we should, uh, go out sometime?"

Her face brightened. "Sure. I would love to."

"Okay then." He nodded and thought, *Now what?*

They were going to go out on a date. A first date. But they had already made out. They had necked like two teenagers fumbling in the backseat of a car. His hands had explored her body, perhaps not as intimately as he had wished, but still... They had certainly moved beyond what proper etiquette dictated was appropriate behavior for a first date.

"Would you like to go out tonight?" she asked him.

"Okay. That sounds great. Uh...to be honest, I don't really know what there is to do around here. I've been preoccupied with writing sermons and getting settled in since I moved here. Maybe you could suggest something?"

"Sure."

She smiled at him in a way that should have made him feel good, but instead he felt a knot deep inside his gut. He was stuck now. He had to date her, otherwise she would think he was only interested in her in a physical sense. And although he did like her, and did have the desire to court her, the thought that their relationship could never progress beyond chaste kissing dampened his enthusiasm. He was ashamed to admit it, but his mind already contemplated the prospect of whether she would allow him to sleep with her if they got engaged. Engaged? Married? Would their relationship really go that far? What if they dated for a while and they found out they weren't compatible?

*Be honest,* Drake thought. *Those doubts you have about a sustained relationship with Celia stem more from your own screwed up self. Isn't that right? Sure, you like her. Sure, you find her physically attractive. Sure, you feel chemistry between the two of you.*

*But the question you really have is, Will you grow tired of her? She's sweet and kind and gentle — all traits you find appealing in a woman. But is it enough to sustain your interest? Will she be able to satisfy that part of you that you try desperately to restrain, that part of yourself that has an unquenchable desire to indulge in temptations of the flesh?*

It was much too soon to tell if she was the right woman for him, but deep down, Drake already knew the answer. She wouldn't be enough for him. The sad part was, he planned to pursue the relationship anyway.

He wanted to be wrong. He hoped God would give him the strength to control his physical desires. But even as he thought that, he sensed the beast in him, the ravenous creature that convinced him in the past to give in to temptation, strain mightily against its bonds. He silently prayed for the strength to keep it chained tightly inside himself. He wanted, with every fiber of his being, to live a righteous and moral life.

Drake and Celia composed themselves. She said, "They should be about ready to start the lunch. Are you ready to head outside?"

"In a minute," he said. "You go ahead, and I'll be right out." He smiled warmly at her. She really was a nice person. It was hard not to feel some sort of emotional attachment to her.

"I'll see you outside." She gave his hand a squeeze, then headed out of the office.

Drake waited until he heard the back door open and close. He sat down behind his desk and opened the bottom drawer. Back behind a stack of paperback Bibles was a half empty bottle of Jack Daniel's. It wasn't technically his bottle; Drake had come across it when he moved in. It was left behind by Reverend MacDonald, along with a smattering of other odds and ends the retired reverend must have decided he had no further use for. Whether the bottle was left intentionally, or if it was a test from God, Drake didn't know. He had placed the bottle so it was half hidden in the bottom of his desk. Why he didn't box it up with MacDonald's other forgotten belongings, or why he simply didn't pour it out, he couldn't say. Or maybe he knew the reason, but refused to acknowledge his weakness.

Whatever the case, he took the bottle out and uncapped it. He took a plastic drinking cup he used for water and poured himself three ounces. He downed it quickly before he could have second thoughts. It burned in his stomach for a moment, then spread its warmth throughout his body. He felt much better.

Drake wasn't an alcoholic; that wasn't it. In the past, he drank to relieve stress and unburden his mind. Where he had gone wrong was, he came to rely on it too much, until it blurred his decision-making capability. He wouldn't make the same mistake again, or so he told himself. He would only drink in moderation. Nothing wrong with that, was there?

He didn't wait for the voice in his head to answer, mainly because he was afraid he wouldn't like what it had to say. He placed the bottle back in its hidey-hole, stacked the Bibles in front of it, and washed out the plastic cup in the kitchen sink. He popped two breath mints into his mouth, straightened his black shirt and clerical collar one last time, and headed outside to enjoy the nice welcome lunch those kind people had arranged for him.

\*\*\*

Amber and Philo were shopping for clothes. Actually, Amber was helping Philo shop for clothes because when it came to picking things out for himself, the poor boy was clueless. For some reason, he could never remember his sizes and he was reluctant to try things on. If left on his own, he would purchase clothes that were either too big or too small.

And forget about fashion sense. Amber knew Philo's ideas about what matched and what colors looked good on him were far off the map of good taste. So she accompanied him to purchase a few items mostly because she didn't want him to be laughed at or made fun of later. Especially by that prick David.

They were in a small men's clothing shop in downtown Tanneheuk. Jonas had suggested they take the car and go to the mall in Lake Dulcet, but Amber didn't feel like traveling that far.

Slade Grayson

There were a handful of shops in Tanneheuk, and since she didn't need anything for herself, she thought they could probably find what few odds and ends Philo needed without a major road trip. He was very simple to shop for, really, as long as you could find a store that catered to the big and tall crowd. Today, all he needed was two pairs of jeans and some socks. Simple.

Not that Amber went shopping with him because she enjoyed the experience or because she actually cared about the big idiot. If anything, she liked Philo because he absolutely adored her. He had been lovestruck ever since they were kids. He would die for her, or so he had told her on many occasions. She found him to be stupid, naive, and...well...he was not the handsomest man she had ever met. But if she was going to be totally honest with herself, she had to admit she wasn't exactly a prized catch either.

She was kind of plain looking, bordering on ugly. She had an unpleasant disposition, no education or refinement, and her only two hobbies in life were smoking and sleeping. She enjoyed sex and had vigorously engaged in masturbation since puberty, until a few months ago when she had come to the realization that she didn't have to masturbate, not when Philo was willing to do anything to make her happy. Being naturally lazy, Amber decided she would allow him to do all the work, and she would lay back and enjoy. Sure, sometimes she had to return the favor, if only to keep him sexually enthralled to her.

It took a little instruction and a lot of patience from her to get him to learn all the things she liked, the things that gave her pleasure and would get her off. He was an eager student, however, and what he lacked in finesse, he more than made up for in enthusiasm and a willingness to do whatever it took to make her happy. His feelings didn't get hurt when she called him names and talked down to him. When she unleashed a verbal tirade against him, his sole objective was to find out why she was mad, and then do something to make her not mad. His happiness relied entirely on hers. The poor schmuck.

She slept with him every night and had him pleasure her, usually getting her off once or twice. Then she would direct him to use the bathroom and pleasure himself while she went to sleep. Or, every once in a while, she would take care of him, if only to show her appreciation for a particularly well done job or just to ensure that he remained in love with her. She didn't mind doing that for him once in a while. She wasn't completely selfish.

The only thing she insisted on was absolutely no kissing, unless he wanted to kiss her on the cheek...or some other place, if you got her drift. But the thought of kissing his big, wet, sloppy mouth made her cringe. That was one thing she couldn't stomach. It would be like French kissing a basset hound.

Philo had two pairs of jeans picked out, and despite his reluctance, had tried them on and showed them to Amber. She nodded her approval and told him yes, they fit. *Can we go now?*

But Philo wasn't done. He had a pack of athletic socks and now he was browsing through the shirts. Amber noticed he gravitated to the printed shirts with the loud designs— the Hawaiian shirts like David wore. She shook her head. His brother couldn't stand him, yet Philo wanted to emulate him. Pathetic.

"Don't look at those shirts," she told him. "If you need shirts, there are some nice ones over against the wall."

She pointed to a rack of western apparel. There was a row of cowboy-style shirts with snaps for buttons and piping around the chest. Philo looked presentable in those kinds of shirts. He looked okay in t-shirts, too, and flannel shirts. That was about it.

"But I want one of these," he said in his normally whiny, sulky voice.

"You'll look stupid in one of those shirts. Get one of the others."

"But David wears them. He doesn't look stupid."
*David's not built like a big stupid bull either.*

"Fine," she said. "You want people to laugh at you? You want to look like a hick? Then get one of those shirts."

She thought he might argue the point, and this time, she might actually let him win. She was tired of having to explain things to him over and over. Sometimes she felt like the mother of a dimwitted child.

*Fine*, she thought. *Get the ugly shirt. Look like a brick wall covered in ugly wallpaper. See what I care.*

But he didn't argue. He went and looked at the shirts she had pointed to. Huh. Maybe the idiot was learning after all. Maybe he was starting to grow up, and mature a little. Amber had a tinge of...

something.

Could it be pride? Pride in her big stupid child/love slave? Now that surprised her.

She told Philo she was stepping outside to smoke a cigarette and would be right back. She knew he would be a while; he had trouble making up his mind on what he wanted and what he liked. She imagined the inside of his brain as being a foggy place where thoughts got easily lost and ideas rarely ventured very far.

She walked outside the shop and lit a cigarette. She hoped Jonas appreciated this. It was another factor she considered when she agreed to take Philo shopping: the fact that Jonas would be indebted to her. So maybe when she asked to borrow the car to go to the neighboring town, he would be more likely to say yes. She needed a few hours away from all of them, especially Philo, who could be rather cloying.

Amber smoked her cigarette and glanced at her reflection in the store window. She wore her usual attire of overalls, t-shirt, and flip-flops. It worked for her, because let's face it, a designer gown would look as out of place on her as a tuxedo would look on Philo. So she stuck with what was comfortable.

She looked alright, she guessed. She checked out her butt. Was it getting a little fleshy? Her mom had acquired a big butt around her age. She wondered if she would follow suit. Ah, who cared? Philo would still want her, even if she got as big as a house.

She thought again about asking Jonas for the car. She could drive to the other town, maybe pick up some guy and scam a little money off him. She had a favorite trick: Go to a bar and find a half-drunk man. Not terribly hard to do. Then convince him to pay her for a sexual favor, like a blowjob in the men's room. She would get the money up front and run out on the guy when he had his pants down around his ankles. The scam had worked more times than Amber could remember. It was good for a quick fifty or a hundred bucks. Men were such suckers.

Boy, she was sick of this town. There was literally nothing to do. They didn't even have a movie theater. Goddamn town didn't have a McDonald's, either, and Amber was a person who enjoyed her McDonald's French fries. But she had been forced to go cold turkey since they arrived last month. Jonas had taken them out to eat many times, but they went to the places in town— the restaurant, the cafe, the diner. The food wasn't bad. In fact, it was actually quite good. But Amber didn't appreciate fine cuisine. As a child, she was raised on fast food, and when it came to eating, that was what she craved.

They often prepared meals at the house. Their landlady, Mrs. Dallway, would fix breakfast for them most mornings. For someone who had seemed unhappy to have them living with her at first, she had certainly come around. She had assumed the role of surrogate grandmother to all of them, most of it due to Jonas. He played the old woman like a harp. Most days, Amber thought Jonas had a stick up his ass, and thought, too, that he was slipping in his leadership role over the family as well as his role of master con artist, but she had to admit, he knew how to get people's trust and sympathy.

Anyway, Mrs. Dallway fixed breakfast, everyone fended for themselves for lunch, and dinner was usually Jonas's responsibility. He either took them out or prepared a meal for them. David cooked once in a while, generally something simple like spaghetti or meatloaf. As for Amber, she neither had the desire nor the inclination to cook for them. She spent most of her time in bed, or lounging by Mrs. Dallway's pool.

Mrs. Dallway had attempted to engage Amber in conversation a few times, but Amber's monosyllabic answers quickly discouraged that. David was polite and friendly to the old woman. To her face, anyway. Behind her back, he made faces and obscene gestures at her. Jonas was very warm and friendly, as the part that he played called for. As for Philo, Amber had the impression he actually enjoyed the attention the old woman lavished on him. She treated him like a big kid, which in many ways, he was. He had never had a real grandmother and could barely remember his mother. Naturally, he was starved for maternal affection.

They came around the corner, three of them, with an air of sovereignty. Although they were dressed like commoners— in jeans, moccasins, and loose pullover cotton shirts— they walked along the sidewalk as if they were rulers of all they surveyed.

Two were men. The one in front was a woman. She was strikingly beautiful. Her hair was long and flowing, and so dark it appeared to absorb light. Her skin tone was a dark tan, nearly brown, and tinged with red. She could have been Spanish or Native American, or possibly an amalgamation of both. She walked like a woman striding over the backs of her devoted male subjects. Amber immediately hated her.

The two men with her walked two steps behind and to the side of her in a triangular pattern. Amber had seen others in town do this. It was something the town elders would do. They walked in a flank formation with one person as point, a hierarchy of sorts. Amber wasn't sure how the ranking worked, but she noticed a few of the elders were leaders and the rest were followers.

They were a strange bunch. She had seen them walking through town on occasion, receiving deference from the townspeople like they truly were royalty of some kind. They walked through stores as if they owned them, and never paid for anything. If they wanted something, they simply took it. Although, to be fair, mostly what Amber saw them take was food and medicine. She wasn't sure where their clothing came from, but when they entered a restaurant, they were immediately seated, served, and treated like VIPs, even to the point that their meals were comped. The same for when they shopped for pharmaceuticals or hygiene products— they left the stores without paying for the items. Never had Amber seen anyone raise an objection to their behavior, nor argue the point.

One night, after they witnessed a group of elders walk out of the diner without paying for their meals, Jonas had made the comment that it was similar to the power the Nazis had in Central Europe during World War II. The major difference, he said, was the elders weren't rounding up people for concentration camps. At least not yet, anyway.

They walked in Amber's direction, headed straight for her as a matter of fact, and appeared not to have any intention of changing direction or walking around her. As if they expected Amber to move out of the way. Well, they were in for a surprise. Amber wasn't some cowering townie.

She stood her ground and glared defiantly at them. They walked up to her and stopped at the last possible moment, until Amber thought they might actually walk over her. She stood so close to the dark haired woman, she could clearly see the honey-yellow circles around the pupils of the woman's eyes. Not honey-yellow, exactly. The color was the same as her name— Amber. It was kind of funny, in a strange otherworldly coincidental kind of way.

The woman said, "Move."

Amber dragged on her cigarette and stood her ground. The two men behind the woman bristled. One man was short and thin with a long blond Mohawk that waved to and fro in the light breeze. The other man had flame red hair streaked with white and a matching scraggly beard. He appeared to be much older than the other two. Lines showed in his face like battle scars.

Amber wanted, in every fiber of her being, to blow smoke in the woman's face and tell her, "You move." But instead, she stepped to the right and allowed them to pass. Something told her not to confront them, that things would go very badly for her if she did. She tried to convince herself it was because of Jonas's warnings about keeping a low profile and staying out of trouble, but that wasn't really it. Her ability to read people, honed by years of living with a master con artist like Jonas, told her that these people were not to be trifled with. They exuded a danger that was palpable.

She let them pass and watched the dark-haired woman walk by. Her hips twitched in her skintight jeans and her breasts, unencumbered by a bra, bounced in her cotton shirt. Amber watched her with disdain. Even without her regal bearing, she would have hated the woman. Amber hated all beautiful women.

They continued down the sidewalk and turned to cross the street. Amber saw the two men take the lead and cross a step ahead of the woman, blocking her on either side from potential harm. Once they were across, the men moved back into formation, two steps behind her. They turned a corner and were gone from sight.

Amber shook her head. Weird.

Slade Grayson

# Chapter Fifteen

The aroma of spareribs cooked slowly over an industrial-sized barbecue grill filled the air. Jonas savored the delicious smells that wafted over him. Sure, maybe cooking over charcoal was a carcinogenic, but it sure tasted damn good.

Jonas wasn't invited to the church luncheon. Not that he hadn't crashed a social function or two in the past, but in such a small community as this one, it was hard to blend in and pretend to belong. He tagged along with Mrs. Dallway, who was a member of the church committee and who had been invited to attend. Jonas had wrangled an invitation by planting minute subliminal suggestions in her head. It wasn't terribly difficult; the old woman had become a den mother to him and his brood, and she enjoyed helping them become acclimated to their new home.

So why did Jonas want to come? He wasn't sure, really, other than maybe he was tired of spending time with his ungrateful and surly kids. He was tired of watching Amber never lift a finger around the house, spending all her time sunning herself by the pool and never getting tan, but rather, becoming more and more freckled. Tired of watching Philo mope around behind her. Tired of listening to David's caustic remarks and insults, and his increasingly bigger and bolder ideas about how they could fleece the local rubes out of their life savings. Most of all, Jonas was tired of sitting around and doing nothing.

Because as much as he laid down the law to the kids about how they needed to maintain a low profile, Jonas was more bored than all of them. How could he not be? He was stupid to think he could live a quiet, honest lifestyle and not go stir-crazy. He was, deep down, a shark. Did he really believe he could be content living with minnows?

To distract himself from his boredom, he finagled an invitation to the church lunch given to officially welcome the new pastor. David had to tag along, too. He saw the little shit now, standing in line with his paper plate, waiting for his free meal.

He stood between two middle-aged women. Jonas saw him talking to them, back and forth, with a practiced ease. He had the women giggling. Jonas could only imagine what line of bullshit he was laying down. But the kid always did have a way with the ladies. He came across as witty and flirtatious, but not leering, like someone's prized son home from college and sucking up to his parents' friends. He was quite good at it, Jonas had to admit.

There were three rows of picnic tables set parallel to the food serving lines. One line was for the cold dishes: potato salad, macaroni salad, etc. There were also hot dishes, such as the baked beans and corn on the cob, set in platters over burners to keep them warm. The next line was the dessert line, which had all its dishes covered with tin foil until folks finished stuffing themselves with the main courses. Jonas's information from Mrs. Dallway was that there were plenty of pies to be had, and slices of watermelon to go with it.

The third line led to the two big grills that pumped out fire and smoke and flash-seared the meat thrown on top of its crosshatch bars. One had the spareribs that tempted Jonas's appetite and had enticed David to stand in line for. The other grill was filled with hamburgers and hotdogs. It was all food that Jonas ate, but he didn't enjoy cookout food. He liked his food hot, or at least with a semblance of warmth, but his experience with cookout food was that the food never stayed hot from the grill. It could be smoking with heat, come directly off the burning coals, and when Jonas would sit down to take a bite of his hamburger or chicken leg, it would be cold. It just never retained the heat of the grill. He wasn't sure why. Maybe it was linked to eating outdoors, or possibly there was a weird thermodynamic loophole that caused charcoal-cooked meat to go cold faster than normal. He didn't know.

So he decided to take a seat and wait for the dessert table to open up, at which time he planned to put a serious dent in the number of pies that were offered. Not to mention a few healthy slices of watermelon.

He lit up a cigarette and took a drag, his elbows on the table and his arms steepled in front of him. The woman next to him, one of those churchgoing prudes with a permanent sour lemon look on her pinched face, made a disgusted sound.

He turned to her and said, "Get over it, lady."

If he wanted to smoke, goddammit, he was going to smoke. If the woman didn't like it, she could move her chunky ass. Which, as it turns out, she did, but not before she gave Jonas a steely look of utter contempt. He quelled the urge to flip her off. Instead, he took a sip of punch.

Punch. He couldn't believe it. He had thought...hoped anyway, that there would be beer served at the picnic. But of course there wasn't, because this was a church picnic, and everyone knows church people don't imbibe. *Yeah, right.*

David got his helping of ribs, and Jonas saw him say something to the cook. In response to whatever he said, the cook shook his head "no." Jonas put it together: David was asking for two helpings. The cook pointed at the line of people behind David, probably telling him that he would have to serve those people first before seconds would be offered. David talked some more.

Jonas saw him working his gift, could actually see his son utilize the gifts that Jonas had passed down to him, both verbally and genetically. Because some of it had to be inherited. You couldn't get as good at it as David without some of it being encoded into your DNA. Jonas wasn't that good of a teacher.

And, since he was being honest, Jonas knew David was more naturally adept at being a con artist than he was. If he wanted to, and if he could shake his weakness for quick scores, David could be a master at the con. Unfortunately, he was too lazy to put in the time and effort. He liked the quick buck, probably more than he liked the quick lay.

The cook put a second helping of ribs on David's plate. David smiled and said something to the cook, who laughed in response and shrugged. That was how gifted David was. He could convince people to do what he wanted, and leave them feeling like he had done them a favor.

Jonas smoked his cigarette and scanned the crowd. The turnout was bigger than he thought it would be. When Mrs. Dallway mentioned a church committee lunch, he had pictured a group of twenty people sitting around a circular table and saying grace before digging into a platter of finger sandwiches. The church committee, apparently, was quite large in Tanneheuk. Everyone brought their spouses and children, too. Young children scampered underfoot and teenagers sulked together in groups, while their parents did their best to ignore them.

One thing stood out to Jonas, although he couldn't be sure if he should attach any significance to it. At least half of the older teens who were present had leg injuries. Several were on crutches or had canes, some with knee braces or leg braces. Not all of them were like that. There were some teenagers who were perfectly fit and healthy. But the number of disabled ones seemed to Jonas to be inordinately high.

Maybe the kids out here were accident prone. Still...

He supposed it could be nothing. Perhaps he was reading too much into it. Maybe it was connected to some rite of passage, like when the kids reached a certain age, their peers required them to leap from a high point into the local watering hole. Or they went off-roading and drove recklessly, as teenagers are apt to do. There could be a dozen reasons for the injuries, but something about it seemed odd. The percentages were much too high for the small group that was afflicted.

Another thing he noticed, and he wasn't sure why it stood out to him, was the disparity of the ages in the community. The ratio of children compared to the number of adults was much lower than he would have expected. There were plenty of people aged twenty-five and up, but the number of children appeared low. It was as if at some point in the past, the townspeople had made an agreement to cut down on their procreation. There were still babies being born, but Jonas would have guessed the number to have been higher than what was represented at the picnic.

Obviously, he knew that not every child in town was present. That wasn't the basis for why he questioned the low number of adolescents. Jonas had witnessed it all over town, too.

Whenever he went to the store, or out to eat, or just wandered the downtown area, he saw plenty of middle-aged residents and senior citizens, a smaller group of twenty-somethings, and then as the ages grew younger, the number of people dwindled. It was strange. Also, now that he thought about it, there were many twenty year olds with limps or leg injuries, some even with prosthetics. There was something to his line of thought. He wasn't being paranoid after all.

He didn't know how it all added up, but he was sure there was something to it now. Jonas, a master at keeping secrets, was adept at spotting when someone else was hiding something. He suddenly realized the town was keeping one helluva secret. He wondered what it was, and if he could cash in on it somehow.

***

Maryam didn't want to be here. It was a waste of her time. Couldn't they see that? She should be training right now. She was down to less than four months. Every single day counted. Maryam's parents had insisted she accompany them to the church luncheon. Not for them, but for her sister. It would mean a great deal to her sister, they said. Maryam acquiesced, but with the stipulation that she wouldn't stay more than an hour. She had calisthenics to do, plus she needed to inventory her equipment. She also intended to head out to the end of Lawson Road. Not to run, but to scout the location for signs of Merc.

She hadn't seen him since their first meeting, although she had kept a wary eye out for him. In fact, after their initial meeting, the first few times she ran, she had trouble. She couldn't concentrate and nearly lost her footing several times because she continually checked behind her to see if he was there, following or waiting to attack. She still wasn't sure if he was a friend or foe. Unfortunately, when it came to those people, Maryam knew that none of them could be counted on as a friend. All of them must be viewed as a potential threat.

She wandered behind her parents as they made the rounds along the tables. They stopped occasionally, made small talk, and sampled the homemade dishes. It was all an incredible waste of time. As far as she was concerned, everything that was not part of her training schedule could fit into the category of time-waster.

She hated being forced to mingle with people she cared very little for, which was almost everyone. It was enough to drive Maryam to do something rash. Like overturn a table, perhaps. She wouldn't, though, mainly out of consideration for her sister, who was one of the few she cared about.

Her sister was talking to an older woman, the two of them smiling easily. They were joined by a third person, the new young minister her sister was always going on about. Maryam studied him. She tried to see what her sister saw in him, but never having spoken to him, it was hard to see the attraction.

She knew Celia was attracted to him, not simply because she spoke so often about him, although that was a major tipoff. Maryam could tell her sister was attracted to him by the way she looked at him, and the way she looked when she spoke about him: She positively glowed. Maryam watched her now, the way her eyes sparkled as he spoke, the way she couldn't keep from looking at him. Yeah, her sister had it bad.

Maryam couldn't see it. Sure, he was cute, she supposed. He had a shy smile and a boyish countenance. But nothing that would elicit a "Where have you been all my life?" look like what Celia was giving him now. Celia saw them and waved them over.

"Mom, Dad, you remember Reverend Burroughs," Celia said.

"Good to see you again, Mr. Brooks, Mrs. Brooks," the minister said.

He shook their hands, and stuck it out to shake Maryam's. She considered ignoring him, but Celia said, "My sister, Maryam." Now she was forced to shake his hand.

He smiled at her and said, "Nice to meet you, Maryam. Celia's told me a lot about you."

She found his grip to be too firm. A sign of overcompensation. He feared being thought of as a weak person. Maryam returned the firm handshake, and added a little extra pressure just for spite. She hoped for a reaction, but the man's eyes gave away nothing.

He kept his brotherly smile and said, "How is everything, Maryam?"

She nearly laughed in his face. Like he really cared! He had no clue who she was. If he did, he wouldn't have asked such a stupid question. How was she? She was behind schedule in her training. She had a strange albino shapeshifter watching her run and making veiled threats. (At least, she thought they were threats. It might have been his way of flirting.) And she still had to make arrangements with the other members of her age group in order to cement the fact that she would be chosen for the hunt.

"I'm fine," she answered with a hint of disgust in her voice. How was she doing? God, what a stupid question.

"You graduated this year, didn't you?" the minister asked.

Before she could respond, her mother said, "Barely."

The minister looked from her to her mother, then back at Celia, who appeared to be the most uncomfortable.

Maryam realized Celia was slightly embarrassed by her family. Not that she was naturally ashamed of them, rather, she wasn't ready for the man she was infatuated with to see that they were far from the picturesque family that only exists in old movies and 1950's television shows. Maryam's family was very dysfunctional, and actually, Maryam was mostly to blame for it.

When Celia was young, the family had been close-knit and loving. It was when Maryam came along that the dynamic changed. Not at first, mind you. Maryam was a happy, well-adjusted child. It was when she chose her path in life, decided on her ultimate destiny… That was when the tension in the family began.

Her parents couldn't accept it. They couldn't accept what she wanted to do and what she wanted to be. Celia had been excused from the drawing because of her asthma. Her parents didn't have to go through the years of anxiety and worry that accompany a Tanneheuk resident's eighteenth birthday. They were excused, and felt blessed even when others in the town were jealous and envious, sometimes even spiteful. But it was hard to take the petty comments of others seriously when you were secure in the knowledge that your child would not be chosen.

Then Maryam came along. She was healthy. There was nothing wrong with her, nothing that would excuse her from the drawing. What really disturbed her parents was that Maryam *wanted* to be picked. She told them it was her destiny to be chosen. She had been telling them that for years now, yet still they refused to believe it, refused to accept it, refused to discuss it. Maryam grew so frustrated, she no longer communicated with them at all. In her mind, she compared it to trying to convince a group of atheists that you want to dedicate your life to God. You either had the calling or you didn't, and no amount of explanation or debate would change anyone's mind.

"I graduated," Maryam said. "That's all that matters, isn't it?"

Actually, she really didn't graduate. Not in the traditional sense. The school principal, Mrs. Horvers, simply passed her through. The thinking was, *What difference would it make?* Everyone knew Maryam would not be going on to college, nor would she be entering the workforce. Maryam's goals were not a secret among her teachers and classmates, which was why they all thought her to be insane.

Maryam's mom ignored the remark. She smiled and fawned over the minister. Maryam imagined her mother was already planning Celia's wedding. She looked at her father and saw the approval in his eyes. It overshadowed the pain that was normally there.

She was suddenly overcome with a poignant tenderness for him. She truly did love him, but why couldn't he understand? Once she accomplished her goal, he would never have to worry about her again. Isn't that what all loving parents want? Her father shouldn't be afraid for her, and he shouldn't fight with her. He should help her to fulfill her destiny.

But the constant look of worry that he wore... At times, like now, it hurt her deep inside. She wanted to reach out and touch his face. She wanted to ease his anxiety and pain. She wanted to say—

"Have you tried any of the food, Reverend?" Maryam's mother asked.

It cut off the flow of empathy she had briefly experienced and Maryam reverted to her sullen self. The gaps in the wall she had erected around herself were never open for very long.

"No, I haven't had the chance yet. But I'm looking forward to it," Reverend Burroughs replied. "It all looks and smells delicious."

And then the two of them engaged in more useless prattle, with Maryam's father and sister chiming in. Maryam stood, her face a blank mask, and waited, waited, waited for this damnable waste of time to be over.

\*\*\*

Fern also thought it was all a waste of time, though not for the same reasons. She simply saw no reason why she should attend the luncheon. So why did she come? Three reasons: her mother nagged her about it for weeks; her father had to work and it would have meant her mother would have to go by herself; and she knew there was a better than average chance Sheriff Creel would stop by. Which was the main reason she agreed to come along, if truth be told.

Fern's mother, Odette, knew everyone and knew their health status. She asked about spouses and family members who had been or were presently ill, and asked each person specific questions that pertained to such. Fern was amazed; her mother rarely left the house except to go to the store or to church, yet she knew intimate details about whether someone's cousin suffered from gout, or if someone's uncle was incontinent. Her mother possessed the skill of gathering and remembering every minor health fact about her neighbors, fellow church members, and their families.

She saw him from the corner of her eye. He was sitting at one of the tables with his father, a plate of spareribs in front of him and a generous amount of barbecue sauce on his fingers. Much to her displeasure, he spotted her. He quickly wiped off his fingers on a wad of napkins, stood up, and made his way over to her. The whole time Fern thought, *I don't need this right now. Why can't he leave me alone?*

David said, "Hey. What do you know? You do go other places besides work."

Fern shrugged and tried to ignore him. Her mother had been talking to Rita Beardsley and Mrs. Dallway, but they stopped when David approached. They were more interested in what transpired between the two of them than in whatever gossip they had previously been exchanging. Fern felt their eyes on her, which added to her overall discomfort. David appeared oblivious.

"The food's pretty good," he said. "You want me to get you a plate?"

"No."

*Oh, why won't he just go away?* He would wait up for her at night sometimes when she returned from work, then attempt to engage her in conversation. He tried to engage her all the time, in fact, and kept asking her out on dates. She would put him off, make excuses or just plain tell him no, which didn't discourage him in the least. The next time she saw him, he would smile and shrug, and invariably he would ask her out again.

"What's wrong?" he asked. "You're not hungry? Come on, let me get you a plate of ribs. The cook likes me. He'll give you an extra helping if I tell him to." He flashed her a smile that vacillated between a friendly grin and a leer. Somehow, he made it look almost charming.

"No," she said again, and because she felt her mother's stare, she added: "Thank you."

"No problem. Can I get you something to drink at least?"

It was increasingly hard for her to be rude, especially in front of her mother and neighbors. He was being too nice and polite. Still, she didn't want him to get the impression he was making any headway with her.

"I'm fine," she said.

"What about you lovely young ladies?" he said to the others.

Fern had the urge to roll her eyes, but the girlish laughter of her mother surprised her. Even Mrs. Beardsley and Mrs. Dallway blushed like two shy schoolgirls. Was it possible that they actually liked him?

They each asked for a soda, except for Fern, who would not be swayed. Maybe the older women were easily charmed by him, but she still thought he was obnoxious and sleazy.

When David left to get their refreshments, Odette put her hand on Fern's arm and said, "He seems like a nice young man."

Now Fern did roll her eyes.

Mrs. Dallway said, "And he's certainly smitten with you, Fern. He's asked me all sorts of questions about you."

*I'll bet*, she thought, and wondered what he was really up to. She had no illusions about herself, therefore, she couldn't convince herself David was really interested in her. There must be an ulterior motive.

Odette said, "You should go out with him."

"I don't want to go out with him, Mom."

"He's very nice," Mrs. Dallway said. "He's always very

considerate towards me, asks me how I'm doing..."

It didn't match up to the picture Fern had in her head. Her impression of him was much different. Her belief was that what they were seeing was an act...and not a very good one.

To her, his politeness came across as too fake. There was a hint of smarminess to everything he said.

He came back with their sodas and handed them out. He said to Fern, "I brought you one anyway."

She opened her mouth to refuse it, but the can he handed to her was Diet Dr. Pepper. He gave her a look, like, *See? I've been paying attention.*

"Thank you," she said. She had to admit, she was impressed in spite of herself. The man was definitely observant.

He flirted a bit with the women with one eye on Fern the whole time. He was working to get her to like him, and despite his obvious intentions, it was beginning to work. The fact that he wanted her to like him caused her, against her better judgment, to soften towards him.

She didn't want to. She had fully intended on remaining cold towards him. But he was just so damn ingratiating! How could she possibly stay indifferent?

Mrs. Dallway said, "David is so nice. You know what he did for me? The other day, I found him examining some of my jewelry. He told me he had the idea to make a list of the valuables I have in the house in case of a break-in. He was worried about my valuables being stolen."

David shrugged. "Well, I'm just a cautious fellow by nature. Wouldn't want you to get cleaned out, Mrs. Dallway. There's a lot of criminals out there."

She said to the others, "I told him how we don't have to worry about crime here in Tanneheuk. But the boy is still worried. He asked me if he could take my gold and silver pieces to a jeweler in Lake Dulcet and have them appraised."

"I would feel better about it if I knew that your jewelry was accounted for and insured. That's all. Oh, and that antique silverware you have up in the trunk in the attic. I should have that appraised, too."

"Isn't he sweet?"

"You're the sweet one, Mrs. Dallway. You've been like a..." his eyes welled up, "...a grandmother to me," he said. "I'd never forgive myself if something happened to your precious belongings and keepsakes."

The three older women were melting in his presence, but Fern saw through his charade. How could the others not see it? He seemed to enjoy being blatantly phony. And even more, enjoyed that most people couldn't tell.

*So, is that why he likes me?* She wondered if that was the sole reason, or did he see her as a challenge? Did he just want to fool her the way he was fooling everyone else? Or was he simply trying to bed her? If so, the idea was not as unattractive as she originally thought. She was as much a sucker for flattery as anyone else, even when it was an act.

*I might play along,* Fern thought. *But I'm still not going to sleep with him.*

"After I make my rounds tonight," Fern told him, "I'm going to stop by Dennison's Bar."

"Okay," he said.

"I'm saying..." This was harder than she thought. "I'll be there tonight at the end of my shift. Around eleven. If you're there at the same time..."

"Oh," he said. Then, with a smile, "Ohhh."

She already regretted her decision, especially when she saw the smug expression on his face. Like he won something.

"Hey, that's great," he said. "I'll be there. Definitely."

If he winked at her, she decided she would call the whole thing off. But he must have sensed her uncertainty because he refrained from further outward signs of delight.

They drank their sodas and made small talk, even Fern, which seemed to surprise her mother almost as much as it did her. She was doing this for Creel, she told herself. She was going to get close to David in order to keep an eye on him and his family, as requested of her.

That's what she kept telling herself because the truth was too scary to contemplate: She was starting to like David.

\*\*\*

Drake was introduced to some of Celia's friends. Somehow, without his knowing it, he had become her unofficial boyfriend. Or maybe it was official, because she was certainly treating him that way. The way she smiled at him and touched his arm when she laughed, the way she stayed by his side when he moved among the people and greeted them, the way she was easily calling him "Drake" now, rather than "Reverend."

It was comfortable between them. He liked that and he liked her. Part of him enjoyed the familiarity, the closeness of being a couple. It was the other part, however...

There was a wildness inside himself, a part that bristled at being tied down to one woman. He felt it shift deep down in his soul whenever she smiled at him or touched him. It growled threats of rebellion when he imagined the progression of his budding relationship with Celia. It was as if he was attempting to place a collar on an untamed animal.

He felt good around her, and without question he wanted to sleep with her. The idea of being tied to her for the foreseeable future, that was the part that gave him a claustrophobic sense of suffocation. Luckily, the rebellious part of him was minute. He was able to push it down, muzzle it, so he could appreciate what he had: a great girl who had burgeoning feelings for him.

He had sampled the food and shared much of it with Celia (they had already begun to act like a couple). It was all delicious, and the people were more than friendly. He was complimented on his sermons, which bolstered his ego, but more than that, it strengthened his confidence.

Writing and delivering sermons was a tricky thing. You wanted to deliver a message without being didactic, and you wanted to be entertaining without offending anyone. Drake tried to be informative, engaging, and humorous, all while working to get a simple message across. He worked hard to keep the interest of the young members of the congregation, but not alienate the older members in the process.

"Where's Reverend MacDonald? Didn't he want to come?" he asked Celia when they finally had a moment alone.

The retired minister had been unusually reclusive since Drake's first day in town. He hadn't even bothered to show up for any of the services.

Celia said, "Don't take it personally. He rarely comes out of his room. When he does, it's either to eat or to sit on the porch. I think his vision has become much worse, and he's feeling badly about it."

"I'll pay him a visit. Maybe tomorrow."

Celia's friends, Drake couldn't remember their names (Lacy and Susan? Stacy and Luanne? Something like that...) came back and chattered eagerly with her. Her friends looked alike, except one had blonde hair and the other brown, and they dressed similarly in hippie skirts, tank tops, sandals, and an abundance of jangling bracelets.

Drake was struck suddenly by how young she was. Although she was mature and intelligent, around her girlfriends she regressed to a teenage level. He wondered which one was the real Celia: the serious girl with morals who assumed a parental role with her younger sister and worked to help support her family, or the infantile magpie who whispered in her friends' ears and giggled with them over juvenile jokes. He had the urge to distance himself from the three of them lest someone see them together and think that he, too, was immature.

"We should go tonight," one of Celia's friends said.

Drake didn't hear the beginning of the conversation, as he was trying to think of a way to politely extricate himself from the group.

Her other friend said, "Come on, it'll be fun."

"Maybe," Celia said and turned to Drake. "What do you think?"

"About what?"

"Dennison's Bar is having karaoke tonight. What do you think?"

"Sounds like fun," he said. "You should go."

"No, I mean, what do you think about coming with us?"

*Oh, no.* What did he think? What did he think about going to a bar and making a fool of himself by singing off-key and probably overindulging in alcohol? Because of course they wouldn't be satisfied unless he got up on stage and sang. He could already picture the three of them practically forcing him to do it, not being satisfied until he made a complete idiot out of himself in front of the drunken crowd. And he would be tempted to drink, as well. He foresaw himself giving in to temptation and having one too many. And word would quickly spread around town about the new minister and the unseemly way he conducted himself.

"I... I don't think that's really my type of thing."

"Please?" Celia touched his arm. "You'll have a lot of fun. I promise."

The other two joined in. "Come with us, Reverend. You'll have a blast. It's always a lot of fun."

They talked over each other, their voices melded into one until his resolve melted and he was willing to agree to anything, as long as they would just shut up.

"Okay," he practically shouted, then in a subdued tone, "Okay."

Celia and her cohorts didn't pick up on his irritation. They were distracted by their victory at getting him to agree to go. He forced a smile and attempted to appear to be looking forward to it, but inside he groaned to himself and tried to think of an excuse to avoid going.

As the women fell back into chattering amongst themselves, Drake quietly slipped away. He walked around and shook hands with everyone. He thanked them for coming and for making him feel welcome. He picked up a ginger ale and sipped it, and secretly wished he could duck back into his office and take another shot of the Jack Daniel's.

His skin began to tingle. The air was charged, as if moments from a lightning storm. He glanced at his arm and half expected to see the hairs standing up. He saw her then, and jumped slightly, like he had experienced an electric shock. He thought, *Wow*, and he may have mouthed the word, too. He couldn't be sure.

She was beautiful and dark and mysterious and sexy. God, yes, she was sexy. Her hair was as black as a moonless night, and her dark eyes with amber rings burned holes in him. She stood only a few feet from him, openly staring at him. Drake looked her up and down and thought: *Without a doubt, that body is made for sin.*

He had never seen her before, yet he had a strangely familiar sense that he had. He knew her somehow, or thought he did. The part of him that refused to be tamed, that constantly threatened to rebel against the shackles of his discipline — it knew her. It stirred inside himself and waited, tense and coiled.

To say he wanted her was an understatement. He wanted her the way his lungs wanted air. He barely registered the two men with her — one with a blond Mohawk and the other with white-streaked red hair and a beard. Before any of them spoke, he knew they were town elders.

"Hello, Reverend," she said.

Her voice was as smooth and silky as poured cream. She had the barest hint of an accent, as if English was not her native tongue, but she had spoken it for so long, the remnants of her old language were worn away to a vague impression. Drake was struck, too, by her eyes. They were the same as Roman's, which meant they had to be related somehow.

"Yes, hello," he said, and strained to keep his voice even.

He instinctively stuck his hand out and she took it. He was surprised he didn't receive a shock when they touched, such was the electricity between them. Her hand was incredibly warm, as if a low flame burned within her. He felt the heat not only in his own hand, but up his arm and into his chest and head. He found that he was having difficulty forming a coherent thought.

"Welcome to Tanneheuk," she said. "How do you like our little town?"

"Uh, well, it's quite nice, actually."

He reluctantly let go of her hand, and immediately missed the warmth of it. He forced himself to look at her companions. He nodded a hello, but they stared back impassively. The man with the Mohawk stared through him, but the red-haired man had a sneer to his mien, as if he had been forced to swallow something distasteful.

"I'm Diana," the woman said. "These are my companions, Apollo and Sol."

Apollo was the red-haired man and Sol was the man with the blond Mohawk. Before Drake could offer his hand, Diana told them, "Go help yourselves to some food."

Sol moved away immediately on command, but Apollo hesitated a moment.

"He won't like this," he said.

"Go." Her voice was soft, yet commanding.

She had the self-assurance of a field general, someone who was accustomed to being obeyed. He had not thought it possible, but Drake's attraction to her intensified.

Once Apollo had stormed off, Drake said, "Your friend seems a bit on edge."

"He's fine. Sometimes my family can be overprotective."

"Oh, you're related?"

"In a way," she said. "We're all connected."

He sensed a hidden meaning in her words, but he let it pass without comment. He was more curious about something else.

"Have we met?" he asked. "Or have you come to one of my services? Because I feel as if I've seen you before."

"You have seen me," she said. "The day you arrived. I was in the woods. I've seen you several times after that, but I'm not sure if you were aware of me those times."

"The woods? I remember... I remember thinking there was someone there, but..."

She waited.

"That was you? I thought maybe I imagined it. Why were you...were you...?" In a low voice, he asked, "Naked?"

"I was."

The back of his neck was suddenly moist.

She said, "I sensed you that day. I felt you come into town, just as you felt me watching you."

He wanted to ask questions, but his throat refused to work. Those eyes of hers, the way she stared into his soul... He was in a dream that he didn't want to wake up from. On the contrary, he wanted to dive deeper into it to see the dream to its inevitable conclusion. The conclusion here being that he desperately wanted to have sex with her.

Diana said, "You feel it, too, don't you? Feel what's going to happen between us? I won't rush it. I'll wait, patiently, until you're ready. You'll come to me. You'll resist at first, but eventually you'll come. You have to. It's too strong between us."

Drake wanted a drink. He wanted to feel the whiskey slide down his throat and begin the slow burn from his stomach into his chest and throat. He wanted the whiskey to drown out his inhibitions and muzzle the voice in his head that constantly prattled on and on about being good, being strong, being moral...

"We'll see each other again," she said.

When she walked by him, she leaned in close. They were the same height and their faces matched up perfectly. She tilted her head and sniffed his neck, then moved her nose up to his hair and sniffed there, too. She moved away from his line of sight and he stood transfixed. He still felt her breath on his neck and the slight brush of her nose against his skin and hair. Her scent stayed with him. It was the scent of pine needles and wildflowers, with an earthy undertone that made him picture the forest after a heavy rain.

He stood and blinked, and worked hard to clear her from his mind.

"Yowza, that was one hot number," a voice said.

Drake turned his head and saw a short blond-haired man leering at Diana as she walked away. "Excuse me?"

"That Indian princess that just sniffed you like a dog sniffing a bone. She's hot. What is she? Is she an Indian? Or Spanish? She looks like she could be both. I bet that's an interesting combo, huh?"

Drake asked, "Who are you?"

"David Rafferty," he said. "Just moved to town a few weeks ago, and I gotta tell you, I haven't seen much Grade A prime like what was just talking to you. You know what I mean? Maybe I should've been a pastor."

"You're being incredibly rude."

"Whoa, easy, Rev. I'm not saying anything bad. I was paying you a compliment. That's all. Keep your collar on."

"Are you purposely saying things to get a reaction?"

David shrugged. "Nah, not really. Well, maybe... I don't know. I do think she's hot, though."

Drake had enough of the conversation and David's salacious comments. He turned to leave.

"Watch yourself, Rev," David said, "The pretty black chick you were talking to earlier looks upset about your new girlfriend. Good luck explaining that one."

Drake saw Celia looking at him. She was still with her friends, who had apparently not noticed what had transpired between him and Diana. But Celia had seen it, and even though she was laughing and talking with her friends, he could still see the hurt in her eyes when her gaze met his. Drake felt guilty for wanting Diana, but he wanted her nonetheless.

# Chapter Sixteen

"How many?"

Creel answered, "We're at maybe a pool of twenty people. That's if ya up the age limit."

"We should increase the age to twenty-five. We'll have to do it sooner or later anyway."

"It's..." Creel shook his head. "It's too big of a jump. It won't go over well."

Roman spread his hands. "What would you have us do? The pool shrinks every year."

They were sitting in the main room of Roman's cabin. Creel was sunk low in an old recliner. Bits of white woolly stuffing poked out through the threadbare tweed upholstery, but the chair was still as comfortable as a pair of well-worn shoes. Roman sat across from him on an equally frayed couch. He sat in a cross-legged position with his bare feet tucked under each leg, dressed in his familiar garb of old jeans and a loose cotton pullover. The cotton top had eyelets so it could be secured with a leather thong or cloth twine, but the eyelets were bare and the shirt hung open loosely.

The rest of the cabin was sparsely furnished. There was a table and a set of four chairs in the far corner of the room next to the kitchen, and a few lamps, both electric and kerosene, scattered about. Half the cabins were wired for electricity, but the portable generators that powered them were usually only used during the winter. Most of the time, the light came from candles or the kerosene lamps, and heat was provided by fireplaces and wood-burning stoves. All of them, however, were outfitted with running water. Creel wondered what they did before, if they carried water back and forth from the river. That was long before his time, though.

"It's not as if I want this," Roman said. "If it were entirely up to me, I would do away with the whole tradition."

Creel leaned forward. "What are ya sayin'? Are ya sayin' ya might do away with the whole thing?"

Roman shook his head. "I'm saying if it was entirely up to me, I would. But I have the pack to consider. Many of them won't give up the old ways that easily."

"But you're their leader. They'll do whatever ya tell them."

"That's true." He said it matter-of-factly, without a hint of arrogance. "But part of my leadership is deciding not only what is good for my pack, but what their needs and wants are. And at this point in time, many of them are not ready to break from tradition."

Creel wanted to argue the point further, but he knew it wouldn't do any good. Roman never took advice from an outsider. Why should he? He rarely took advice from his own people.

"Pass the word around," Roman said, "that everyone must stop maiming themselves or their children."

"I don't understand."

"Don't pretend to be oblivious, Sheriff. You know what's happening. It's bad enough that the birth rate has drastically gone down, but the so-called 'accidents' that seem to afflict the teenagers... Really, it's an insult to my intelligence."

"Ya can't blame people for—"

"I'm not blaming anyone. I'm just saying I expect it to stop. If it doesn't, instead of twenty-five, we might raise the age limit to thirty. Perhaps older."

Roman turned his head sharply and appeared to read something in the air. Creel wondered at how one moment he could be as regal in his bearing as an emperor, then just as suddenly he would react to something on a primal level. The poise would be stripped away and all that remained was pure animal instinct.

Roman said, "One of our new arrivals. We named him Picus. He's waiting outside to talk to me."

"Ya got a new member of the pack?"

"It's rare, but it happens. Their pack may disband or simply die off. Or the pack is hunted down and killed, such as what happened to many of our kind in Russia after the fall of the Soviet Union. They find themselves alone. Sometimes they hear about us and travel many miles to ask for a place here. A few we've turned down over the years, but not many, because not many make it this far. It's a dangerous world out there for us as well as anyone else. More so because we're greatly outnumbered."

*But in this little community,* Creel thought, *you don't feel the danger because your people have all the power. You, Roman, as the Alpha male of the pack, have all the power. I wish it wasn't so, but it is.*

"Do ya want to invite him in?"

"He can wait."

Creel nodded and sipped his water. It was cold enough to make the inside of his mouth tingle, and tasted clean and fresh. It was the only thing he was offered to drink when he came to visit. It was the only thing he ever saw them drink.

"Tell the people to start having children again. I'll work to eliminate the yearly hunt. I agree that it no longer serves a purpose."

Creel was surprised at Roman's concessionary statement. But just when he thought he scored a victory, Roman said, "However, it won't happen this year. Or next. In fact, it will probably take ten years. That's the best I can do. And, that's only if the people stop maiming themselves or their children. That's my decision."

Creel agreed to it because what else could he do? He knew the townspeople would be upset by the conditions, but it was his job to sell it to them. He kept the peace, that was his duty, and keeping the peace meant making compromises and sacrifices. A few more years of sacrifices. Ten at the most. They should be happy with that.

Creel would make them see that what they had in Tanneheuk was worth protecting, worth sacrificing for, and if necessary, worth dying for. He would surely lay down his life for the good of the town. He wouldn't ask them to do anything he wouldn't do himself.

Roman stood and Creel took it as his cue that their informal meeting was at an end. He put his glass down on the scarred table in front of the couch and walked with Roman to the door. His boots reverberated loudly on the wood floor.

The floor of Roman's cabin, much like the others Creel had been in, was sanded and polished to a smooth glossy surface. He could roll on the floor naked (not that he had the desire to do such) and not worry about catching a splinter.

When they stepped outside, Creel saw the man who waited for Roman. He stood in the shade of the trees with his head down. He had a twitchy way about him, his head and hands jerking involuntarily. His brown hair was unkempt, and he had a patchy beard that gave him an unwashed appearance. His twitch became more pronounced when Roman's fixed stare settled upon him. Creel had seen Roman use the stare before, always on his subordinates. Not quite an intimidation tactic, rather, it was Roman's display of power over them.

"What did you want to see me about, Picus?" Roman asked.

Picus answered in a guttural voice. To Creel, it sounded like a series of nonsense words mixed with growls, but Roman understood him and replied in the same language.

"It's Russian," he told Creel. "Picus understands English, but he's not yet comfortable speaking it."

Creel nodded. There were a few Russian immigrants in the pack. Roman would have picked up the language from them, or perhaps from his father, Jove. Creel remembered the man was fluent in many languages.

The two conversed for several minutes. Creel didn't bother to pay attention or attempt to understand what they were talking about. He studied their body language. Picus kept his head bowed and refused to make eye contact with Roman. Roman kept his stare on him and placed his hands on Picus' shoulders.

It could have been misinterpreted as a show of brotherly affection, but Creel knew it was another display of Roman's dominance. He had been around the pack enough to recognize the behavior patterns: hands on their back or shoulders meant dominance of one over the other. If they were in wolf form, Roman or one of the Beta wolves would sometimes place their paws on the back of the subordinate wolves. The Alpha female, Diana, dominated most of the male wolves, with the exception of her brother, Roman.

When Roman and Picus finished talking, Picus slipped away with nary a backward glance or a word to Creel.

"He's skittish," Roman remarked. "Which is understandable after what he's been through. He finds it hard to trust anyone. Even us. I've tried to explain to him what we have here. I don't know what the Russian word for Utopia is, but I think I made my meaning clear to him. It'll take time for him to adjust."

"Utopia?" Creel asked. "Ya really feel that strongly about the pact?"

"Of course. You don't?"

Creel shrugged. "In some ways. In other ways, I think things could be better."

Roman smiled mirthlessly. "You surprise me, Sheriff. You should be the biggest advocate of our pact. Hasn't it worked well for us these past several hundred years?"

"That's a matter of opinion, I suppose."

Roman turned and studied him. Creel felt the dominant stare, but it failed to have the same effect on him as it did the others. He stood his ground and stared back. If Roman was taken aback, he didn't show it.

He asked, "You're no longer happy here?"

"Happy is a relative term. I don't know what I am. Maybe I'm just tired."

"Let me ask you, Sheriff: When was the last time you had to arrest someone for breaking and entering? Or for assault and battery? When was the last time you had to investigate a serious crime? Or had to worry about a gang war or a drive-by shooting? Things are pretty good in Tanneheuk comparatively speaking. Compared to the rest of the world, really. Am I wrong?"

"I get your point, but—"

"No rapes, no murders, no drug wars, no terrorist bombings... everyone gets along. There's no poverty and no racism. Is that not Utopia? My pack keeps this town protected, and all we ask for is one thing."

"One thing." Creel smirked. "Ya make it sound small."

"It is small, in the grand scheme of things." Roman put his

hand on Creel's shoulder. "Give it time, Sheriff. I'll phase it out. But it won't happen quickly. In the meantime, keep the peace. Do your duty."

"I always do."

Roman took his hand away. They stood and watched members of the pack come and go between their cabins and into the surrounding woods. Creel had known most of them since he was very young, or since they were very young. Many wore the usual ensemble of what Creel called modern Native American mixed with thrift shop Bohemian chic: sandals or moccasins, hippie skirts and tank tops or simple cotton dresses on the women; jeans and cotton pullovers or flannel shirts on the men, most with the sleeves cut off. Some walked naked unashamedly.

"You haven't mentioned the newcomers. I assume they passed your background check."

"They seem to be clean," Creel responded. "You want them gone? Because it'll mean one less for the pool."

"No. Let them stay. This town needs newcomers once in a while."

A strong breeze came through the trees and tousled Creel's hair. It had a bite to it that made him think of the transition from winter to spring rather than early June. He had noticed it when they were sitting in Roman's cabin. The windows had been open, as they generally were through most of the year except for the most bitterly cold of winter days. The breeze had blown through the room and Creel had thought how fresh and clean everything felt up here, more so than down in town.

"Another mild summer...." Creel could only recall a handful of uncomfortably hot days over the years.

"Not this year."

"What do ya mean?" He wasn't sure if Roman was being figurative or literal.

"The heat's coming," Roman said. "Not for a few weeks, but it's coming. We're more attuned to that sort of thing. That's how I know. The heat is coming."

Creel nodded, still unsure if there was a double meaning to Roman's words.

# Chapter Seventeen

After what seemed to be an eternity, Maryam was able to get away from her parents. She drove fast to the end of Lawson Road, parked, and changed into her running gear. She changed clothes out in the open without a hint of modesty. Even if there had been someone around to see her, it wouldn't have made a difference. Maryam was long past the time of her life when she felt self-conscious.

She pulled on two pairs of thick boot socks, then her new pair of hiking shoes with thick, rugged soles and leather padding around the ankles. Her intention was to break them in now so they would be worn and comfortable by September. The extra socks would help stretch them out and provide protection from blisters, although she knew she would be getting some anyway. Blisters were inevitable, but she was prepared for the discomfort that would come. It would be temporary, like most other things in life.

She took two bottles of water that she acquired at the church picnic and poured them into her drinking bottle, then clipped it to her belt. Her movements were quick, yet precise, like she was late for an appointment, but didn't want to move too hastily lest she forget something important.

Before she got out of the car, she strapped ankle weights to her legs. It was a new tactic she was trying. The idea was that the added weights would increase the difficulty of her run and therefore increase her endurance level.

As she always did, she left the keys in the ignition of her car. Much like everyone else in town, Maryam never considered the possibility of theft.

She walked towards the woods and scanned the surrounding trees, but saw nothing. No sign of Merc, or anything else for that matter. The woods were unnaturally quiet, but it didn't give her pause. She knew from experience that it was sometimes like that. A quiet stillness would descend over the trees and Maryam would imagine that she was the only living being left in the world. The idea was not unappealing. To her, humans were a cancer. She thought the Earth would be better off without them.

She started with a light jog, moving with practiced ease over the now familiar terrain. She imagined herself as the wind; she floated over the grass and dirt, up over exposed tree roots and rocks and gullies. She moved with swiftness and grace. She was as fast and agile as an animal, as a wolf. But she would have to be faster and more agile than a wolf in order for her to fulfill her destiny.

It didn't take her long to work up a light sweat. She wasn't concerned with her time today, so she opted to not utilize the stopwatch function on her watch. She glanced at it and saw it was a little after three. Her plan was to run for an hour, then run back.

A flash of white from the corner of her vision caught her attention. She turned her head to look, quickly so as not to lose track of where she was running. The terrain could be treacherous at times, and one misstep could cause a broken limb. Maryam couldn't afford that, not when she was so close to her goal.

She failed to see what it was. Possibly it was an optical effect, a beam of sunlight, perhaps, bouncing off the flora. It could simply have been a mote in her eye.

It was the knot in the pit of her stomach, however, that told her it was more than that. It was *him*.

She saw it again, this time on her right, diagonally behind her, but keeping pace. She didn't turn her head this time. She needed her full attention on running, especially since she instinctively picked up her speed. She refused to admit to herself she was scared, but her body knew better. It automatically shifted to "flight" mode.

He was there, to the side and periodically behind her, a. white wolf. Beautiful, if it wasn't so damn frightening.

Maryam's anger grew in proportion to her physical exertion.

The harder she ran, the angrier she became at the fact that he was scaring her. If she had a weapon, a knife, or better yet a gun, she would have stopped and made a stand. The worst part was, she had a weapon in her car, a commando-style knife with a black razor-edged double-sided blade and a hollow handle that contained matches, fishing tackle, and most importantly, a glow-in-the-dark compass. The knife had been purchased via mail order (as hunting supplies were noticeably lacking in the shops of Tanneheuk), and Maryam had planned to begin carrying it on her runs in order to grow accustomed to its presence.

The compass was the primary reason for the purchase of the knife, as well as the knife itself. She thought it a good idea to plan for every contingency, such as the fact that she might get caught. If she had the money or the resources, she might very well have purchased a gun. But no, that wouldn't do either. A gun was strictly prohibited and could disqualify her from what she hoped to accomplish. The knife was prohibited, but her intention was not to use it on her pursuers. Not unless she was caught by them, in which case she had lost anyway, and what would it matter then?

The point was, she had left the knife in the glove compartment of her car because she hadn't intended to start carrying it until she began her night running. Now she wished she had it on her. She wouldn't be penalized if she used it against Merc in self-defense.

Her run became steeper as the terrain turned more vertical. Her legs pumped like steel pistons. But still, he was with her. She couldn't gain distance on him. Worse, she had the sense he was playing with her, that he could overtake her if he wished. She felt, or perhaps she imagined, his breath on the back of her legs.

Why did she pick today to wear the ankle weights? She couldn't stop to take them off. He was too close. His jaws snapped on the heel of her shoe, just enough to cause her to lose her balance and tumble to the ground. She rolled with the impact, a move she had practiced many times, just in case. She made her body as round as possible and rolled on the ground until the momentum had dissipated. She came up in a crouch and braced for his attack. Although she was defenseless and no match for him, she would fight him to the end. She would use her hands and her teeth. She would punch, scratch, tear...

Merc was still on all fours, but he had reverted to human form. He shook off the excess strands of white fur that still clung to him, the way a dog would shake off water. He stood up straight. Maryam could see the muscles in his legs shift and rearrange themselves, as if his body was unsure of what form it was supposed to settle on. When he stood, his frame aligned itself and the moving muscles settled into place. He stood over her and gritted his teeth in what her first impression told her was a grimace. She realized he was smiling at her.

"You'll have to run better than that, girlie-girl," he said in his whispery growl, "if you want to outrun the pack."

Maryam tensed. Now would be the time for him to attack. Instead, he turned and bounded away. As he ran, his body shifted and contorted again, transforming in reverse from human back to wolf.

Maryam was transfixed; never before had she seen one of them change, either from wolf to human or human to wolf. She wasn't horrified by the sight, rather, Maryam nearly broke down in tears at the absolute beauty of it. Even the word "beauty" was insufficient. It was an epiphany for her.

When her shaky legs were able to hold her, she stood and collected herself. Her water bottle had come unhooked and lay a few feet away. She retrieved it, brushed the top off, and took two unsteady sips. Her hands shook.

Her shoe, the one Merc had bitten, had deep gouges in them from his fangs. Not deep enough to completely puncture the leather, but deep enough to be noticeable. Maryam didn't care. She brushed herself off, checked herself for bruises and scrapes— nothing serious, she concluded— and walked back the way she had come. Her mind replayed over and over the sight of Merc transforming into a wolf. Eventually, the tears came.

*Please, God*, she thought. *I want this. I want this so bad. Please.*

# Chapter Eighteen

It was karaoke night at Dennison's Bar. David Rafferty thought Fern must be fucking with him. It was the only explanation he could come up with — that she set him up. No way the chick who played all that cool music on the local radio station would really want to meet at a bar that was featuring a karaoke event.

Maybe she didn't know. He told himself that maybe she had forgotten what night it was, or maybe the karaoke was a new weekend feature. Surely the chick who'd devoted an hour the previous night to the music of The Clash would not be interested in karaoke. Right?

Or maybe she played a joke on him. Maybe she was on her way home right now, laughing about the practical joke she played, how she had convinced him to wait at the bar and listen to the local yokels murder old top 40 hits with their off-key renditions. Or maybe it was David's own fault for arriving early.

Fern had told him around eleven, and he had arrived a little after ten. The place was livelier than he would have thought, or from what he remembered the last (and only) time he had paid a visit. That was a month ago, and all he recalled from that particular visit was a group of morose guys staring at a boxing match on the surprisingly small TV set up above the bar. The group was so listless, they didn't cheer either of the fighters, and appeared neither happy nor sad at who won the bout. David had gulped down his beer and gotten the hell out of there, worried that the dullness might be catching.

The place was alive tonight, though. There was a crowd this

time, made up of men and women, many of whom David recognized from seeing around town: shopkeepers and waitresses, housewives and farmers. There were couples and groups of friends. It was a diverse bunch compared to the handful of heavy drinkers David had been witness to previously.

Perhaps that was the reason for the karaoke? To bring in a better crowd? If that was the case, it certainly seemed to be working. Too bad no one could sing. Even the mix of women in the place failed to contain a truly stand out singer. The singers ranged from barely tolerable to downright awful. It could be a *Twilight Zone* episode, where a guy visits a small town and finds that everyone is inexplicably tone deaf.

Not that he could do any better. David knew he couldn't sing, but you didn't see him up on the makeshift stage pretending that he could. The crowd didn't seem to care whether the others could sing. Everyone who went up there, no matter how terrible they were, received a generous amount of applause and verbal encouragement. Which added to David's assumption that everyone in town was indeed tone deaf.

But no, that wasn't really it. What it was, was that the crowd all knew each other and were simply having fun by attempting to sing favorite old songs, and then clapping for each other's effort whether it was successful or not (most often not). That was the reason for the crowd's enthusiasm: neighborliness. That, and the consumption of large amounts of alcohol.

A stringy-haired blonde was currently on stage singing a mangled version of No Doubt's "Don't Speak." David thought he could hear dogs howling in the background. He swiveled on the bar stool and looked out over the crowd. He expected to see laughing, or at least snickering, but was surprised to see the audience laughing *with* the singer rather than at her.

She knew she couldn't sing, but she was having fun anyway, and the crowd was with her. It was weird. David was used to making fun of people who made fools of themselves. The idea that people could laugh at themselves without humiliation, and that others would be supportive of them instead of trying to tear them down, was an alien concept.

Somehow, he wasn't sure how it happened, but he found himself joining in the crowd's enthusiasm. Sure, she was bad, but so was the guy before her, and probably the person after her. So what? She was laughing, and David had to admit, there was something infectious in the air that made the fun contagious. He found himself, God help him, smiling. When the song was over and the girl took a theatrical bow, he clapped along with the audience.

He sipped his beer and waited for the next performer. The bar's owner, a ruddy-faced older guy named Cal, stood off to the side by the karaoke equipment and watched the performances while his manager, a big-boned woman named Doris, worked the machine and helped the patrons pick their songs. She called for the next person to come up. The pretty light-skinned black chick David had seen earlier at the church picnic detached herself from a group back in the corner and weaved through the crowd to the front. The group contained the two girls she had been with at the church picnic, along with some new faces, both male and female. The minister was there, too, dressed in casual clothes.

*Well, well, well...*

David figured the minister must have done some fancy verbal footwork to get the black chick to forgive him eyefucking the raven-haired chick who had sniffed his head and neck. David had taken notice of the way the minister had looked at her. It wasn't anywhere close to the way he looked at the black chick. He looked at the black chick, like, *"Hey, I like you. I want to buy you flowers."* The way he had looked at the raven-haired chick was more like, *"I'd cut off my right arm for the chance to fuck you."*

David liked the black chick. She had an hourglass figure, which he kind of dug. Actually, he liked a healthy set of breasts on any woman, but the curve at her waist that accentuated her extra round hips really set off the whole package. It was to his taste, which made his attraction to Fern even more of a mystery. She was nothing like what he usually went for. Even when he chased after skinny broads, they generally had a stunningly pretty face. Fern was average, and built like a straw. A straw without the ridged bendy part.

The only thing he could figure was, he found her indifference to him to be a challenge. But if that was truly the case, then why was he looking forward to her showing up? It must be one of those freak of nature things, like when you see a hot chick with an ordinary schmuck of a guy. Only, David was the hot chick in this relationship. That particular thought bothered him so much, he downed the rest of his beer and quickly asked for another.

The music started. David recognized the opening notes. It was Sarah McLachlan's "Building a Mystery." Surprise, surprise, the black chick sang it well. David had to admit, she had a nice voice.

The crowd got into it, too, he noticed. They were quiet and paying attention. The rowdiness subsided. Everyone had the consensus that they were witness to something special and didn't want to miss a second of it.

The black chick...what was her name? They announced her name right before the beginning of her performance. Selena? No, that wasn't right. Celia? That might be it. Anyway, she sang the hell out of the song. David was digging it. It wasn't his type of music, but he liked the fact that she sang in the right key, and he liked the way she was singing to one person. She moved her eyes around the crowd, and sometimes closed them, but inevitably she would look at the minister. Especially the line where she sang, *"You're so beautiful, a beautiful fucked-up man."* When she sang it, her eyes stayed locked on the minister.

*What a lucky bastard*, David thought. Here was this attractive, obviously smitten woman singing to him, and he had the raven-haired hottie sniffing him over like he was a delectable treat. David considered the idea of becoming a minister.

Not a real one, because he didn't believe in God and he certainly didn't have the calling to do charitable work. He just wanted to wear the uniform. Plus, he could easily think of a dozen schemes to con money from people if he was a minister. And he wouldn't really have to fake it. From what he understood, he could easily become ordained over the Internet. All it took was a couple of clicks of the mouse, maybe pay a small fee.

Man, the fun he could have... But enough of that. He was missing the performance.

She went through the whole song and never missed a beat nor strayed off-key. David wasn't saying that she could make a career out of singing, but she certainly was better than any other amateur he had seen. She sang it with emotion, too, like she was ready to strip off her clothes and offer herself up to the minister. Now *that* would have been a show.

When she finished, David half expected the guy to run up to the stage and stick his tongue down her throat. He was giving her a look, like, *Your chastity will not be safe for much longer*. The look she returned said she was willing to give it up.

*Ah, young love*, David thought.

Then his date walked in and the sarcastic thoughts he had in his head suddenly felt inappropriate and kind of...mean. *Ugh*. David hoped he wasn't falling in love. And he certainly hoped he wasn't growing a conscience. That was a career killer in his profession.

Whatever he felt, and he wasn't ready to admit love so soon in the relationship – or ever, for that matter – he certainly had an affection for the Plain Jane broad. She met his eyes soon after she walked in the place, and she began the trek across the unusually crowded bar. People greeted and spoke to her as she made her way over, and he could tell by the stiffness of her carriage and the uneasiness in her eyes that she wasn't used to talking to people face-to-face.

It was funny, really. She talked effortlessly over the radio, yet in person, she was introverted. Or maybe it wasn't shyness so much as she was uncomfortable talking one-on-one.

She came to the bar and took the stool next to his — the one that he had to keep telling people was "taken," and then received a dirty look like the people didn't believe him. She took the stool and without looking at him, ordered a beer from the bartender.

The bartender, a younger version of the owner, probably his son, put a Heineken in front of her. "Hey, Fern. How's your folks?"

She nodded while taking a thirsty sip, then answered, "They're just fine, Lloyd. How's things here?"

"Pretty good. Dad's karaoke idea went over well, as you can see." He paused to wipe away several wet glass rings on the bar. "You gonna do a song, Fern?"

"Don't think so. I don't sing them…"

"You just play 'em," he finished for her. "Right?"

She nodded again, and took another healthy swig. David was preparing to ask if they wanted to be alone when Lloyd was called to the other end of the bar to fill a large drink order.

David said, "You two are friendly. You a regular in here?"

"I stop in here at the end of my shift to see if anyone needs a ride home." She still hadn't looked at him. She peered intently at the label on her beer as if it was an unknown object and she found the intricate pattern and colors to be fascinating. "Also, we dated a long time ago. Back in high school."

She picked at the edge of the label with the corner of her fingernail and peeled a strip off. David nodded his head. He wanted to ask a follow-up question, actually more than one, but he got the sense it was a sore subject. Normally, he would ask anyway, just dive right in. Tear down the psychic walls, see what was behind them, make himself at home inside the other person's head until he had them right where he wanted them and could make them do whatever he wanted.

But he didn't do that this time. Which worried him a little.

"Who's next?" Doris's voice boomed over the sound system. "Who wants to try a song? Come on, don't be shy. We're all friends here."

After the last performance, the crowd's enthusiasm had waned. Perhaps they knew they couldn't top Celia's song, so why make a fool of themselves and ruin the memory of the last, and best, performance?

"You want me to sing another song?"

The crowd groaned at Doris. David hadn't heard her sing; he had arrived afterwards. But the talk of the place was that she was by far the worst of the evening. No one, it seemed, wanted a replay.

"Well, come on," she said. "If you don't want me to sing again, get off your lazy butts and get up here. Somebody better get up here soon...or else."

The crowd chattered at once, a mixture of groans, hoots, and verbal pleas for Doris to not subject them to another wildly off-key performance.

Doris said, "Alright, since I don't see anyone else volunteering, I'm gonna have to sing another one. Something with high notes."

Before the collective groans and pleadings grew in volume, one voice was heard above the others.

"Doris? We've got a singer right here."

David, along with everyone else in the place, turned his

attention to the back of the room. It was the black chick, Celia, who made the offer. She was pointing to the minister, who was unaware that she was volunteering him. The minister looked around to see who she meant, then with a shocked expression realized she meant him. He immediately put his hands up and vigorously shook his head no. His cheeks went red, and as the crowd called to him to go up on stage, they grew redder.

Up on stage, Doris said, "Reverend? You want to come up and treat us to a song?"

The crowd waved him on and became more vocal in their encouragement, but the reverend had no intention of moving from his spot. He laughed out of embarrassment, which stoked the crowd to further encouragement. They really wanted him to sing now.

"Come on up here, Reverend. Come up and treat us to a song," Doris said.

David saw Celia take his hand and pull him through the audience to the stage. People laughed and clapped him on the back as he was half-led, half-dragged up front. He still shook his head no, but he was laughing steadily, like he might go through with it.

"Folks," Doris said, "give Reverend Burroughs a nice hand for coming up."

The audience applauded him as he climbed up on stage. Celia went to the side where Doris was now flipping through the song menu. David saw Burroughs had a drink in his hand. It could have been soda, but intuition told him it was something slightly stronger. He wasn't drunk, but the good reverend had certainly imbibed a little today. Not enough to where he slurred his words or had trouble being steady on his feet, but a little.

Burroughs said into the microphone, "You folks don't really want me to sing. Really, I can't sing."

David heard the nervousness in his voice. Someone in the audience yelled out, "Come on, Rev! Belt one out!"

Burroughs laughed and handed his drink to someone in the front of the crowd. He was loosening up now; the humor of the situation overrode his anxiety. And by their conspiratorial giggles, David knew Doris and Celia had picked out a song for him to sing.

The music started. There was a brief lull while everyone waited to recognize the song from the handful of notes. The realization hit everyone at once: It was "Lovin', Touchin', Squeezin'" by Journey.

Reverend Burroughs read along with the lyrics as the song played. He talked rather than sang, but as the song continued and the crowd egged him on, he began to sing the words. He was awful, as he had tried to warn the audience he would be, but his willingness to commit himself to the performance, added with the obvious fun he was having, made up for his lack of talent.

Plus, and David had to grudgingly admit it, the reverend had a great stage presence. He had a natural and magnetic charisma that demanded the audience's attention — a talent that certainly attested to why he was well regarded as a minister. Or so David had been told. Personally, he had never stepped foot inside a church in his life, nor did he foresee that changing in the future. But he had heard other people talk about the new town minister, and the consensus was that he was gifted at delivering a sermon.

David thought it a waste of an ability. Anyone with the power to enthrall a group of people ought to capitalize on it, either through show business or grifting. David didn't see much difference between the two occupations.

The song continued and Burroughs got more into it. He used the stage to his benefit, prowling it like a true rock star. The crowd was in his hands now. David looked off to the side and saw Celia's eyes locked on Burroughs. She was glowing. David smirked.

When he came to the "Na Na" part of the song, Reverend Burroughs got the audience to sing along. Even David found himself singing with them. He looked at Fern and saw she was caught up in it, smiling and singing, too. Their eyes met and he felt... something. Something new. Something different.

He wasn't sure what it was, but his original estimation of her changed. She wasn't plain. She was kind of cute. How could he have ever thought she was plain looking?

When Burroughs finished, the audience enthusiastically applauded. David found himself clapping, too.

Burroughs said into the microphone, "You folks are way too kind. I hope I didn't hurt your ears too much."

The audience was adamant that he hadn't.

"You're being too kind, and I thank you."

They cheered him to do another song.

"No, I better not. I wouldn't want to subject you to more torture."

The audience urged him on, but Reverend Burroughs laughed and said, "I'll save it for the weekend service." He left the stage and David thought, *What a waste of a naturally gifted con man.*

He turned back to Fern and said, "You want to get out of here?"

She shrugged. "And go where?"

David thought for a moment. "Can I drive your car?"

# Chapter Nineteen

They were flush with exuberance, the five of them in Celia's car. Celia drove and Drake had the passenger seat next to her. Celia's friends were in the back: Lacy, Susan, and Susan's boyfriend, Delroy, a lanky guy with a crew cut and adult acne. Lacy and Celia were talking excitedly about Drake's performance, not about how bad his singing was, but by his ability to engage the audience and get them to join in. They told him how funny he had been, how impressed they were at the ease he had shown in winning over the crowd. People seemed to naturally like him.

Drake shrugged it off and displayed humility, but inside he glowed at the compliments. He enjoyed being the center of attention.

In the back seat, Susan and Delroy talked about Delroy's kid sister, Charlotte, who had been depressed and sullen the past year. Drake hadn't heard any of the details, focused as he was on Lacy and Celia's adulation. He thought he might ask them about the girl, maybe suggest that he could counsel her, but his mind was all over the place. He'd had a few shots before Celia had picked him up, and had two drinks while they were at the bar, so he was feeling lightheaded.

Not drunk, though. He was not drunk, nor would he get drunk. Although he had relaxed his commitment to never touching alcohol again, he would certainly never drink to excess. In fact, to make up for the several drinks he had consumed today, he would purposely go the next two weeks without drinking. No, make it three weeks. He made a new, firmer commitment to himself.

Celia found his hand in the dark on the seat next to her and intertwined her fingers with his. It made his heart beat faster, the fact that no one else could see them holding hands. Like they were two teenagers hiding their romance.

They dropped Susan and Delroy off first. Delroy patted Drake's shoulder when he got out. Susan was all giggles and hugs with the women; she was a little loud from the evening's festivities, but not obnoxiously so. They left them at Susan's place, a house she shared with her mom and brother.

Delroy made a pretense of walking to his car and preparing to head home, but Drake thought it was mainly for his benefit: They didn't want the minister to know that Delroy would be spending the night with Susan. Drake smiled to himself. Did people think he was so naive as to believe they didn't engage in premarital sex? Still, he appreciated the fact that they cared what he thought about them.

They drove on. He had the urge to look out the back window and see if Delroy followed Susan inside the house, or if they were still making a show of saying goodnight next to Delroy's car. He had the urge, but he didn't look.

He was disappointed when Celia pulled into the church parking lot. He had hoped (desired?) they would drop Lacy off first. Then he would have invited Celia inside. Just for a few minutes, of course. Maybe few kisses, a little touching... Who knows where the evening would have led to? But Lacy was still in the car, chattering away about next week's craft show and all the baking she was doing with her friends.

"Fresh pies all weekend," she said. "We make a lot of money. But boy, the work involved!"

Drake half listened. He tried to think of an excuse for Celia to come back after she dropped Lacy off. Or a reason for Lacy to take Celia's car home and... But no, that wouldn't look right.

He said, "Well...," and couldn't think of anything to come after that.

Celia said, "I had fun tonight. Thanks for coming out with us."

Her eyes sparkled and her mouth looked ripe for kissing. Lacy ruined the moment by saying, "Yeah. It was a blast. We should do this more often."

Her head was next to the back of his seat so that she practically shouted in his ear. As it was, he got a whiff of her margarita-soaked breath.

Drake smiled and said goodnight. Before he reluctantly got out of the car, Celia squeezed his hand and gave him a look. He read the message in her eyes. She said that she wished she could stay too, but...

*Wouldn't the world be a much simpler place if the word "but" didn't exist?* Drake thought to himself. He returned the hand squeeze and got out.

Celia wiggled her fingers at him through the car window as she drove away. Lacy motioned goodbye with a drunken schoolgirl exaggerated wave. He could hear her voice still going as the car sped away. He shook his head and turned to the front door. He didn't have the key. He had the ring with the key to the back door and his car key, but he had neglected to bring the ring that held the front door key.

He generally used the back door, but Celia had dropped him off in front because the parking lot was well lit. The back was shaded from the parking lot lights and the lights on the church were aimed towards the front. Drake walked around the side of the building and headed for the back. He entered the shadow world between light and dark, the light cast from the front of the building made the darkness in the back appear particularly dense. When he fumbled for the lock on the back door, he sensed a presence to his right. It was Diana, completely nude, her bronze-skinned body aglow from the light of the full moon.

Drake stared at the apparition before him and wondered if it was real or the product of an alcohol-induced hallucination. She moved closer and parts of her were revealed: round breasts with reddish brown nipples, a long torso and thinly curved waist, hair as dark as midnight, and eyes that sparkled like twin flames in the night. He caught sight of the dark patch of hair between her thighs before he quickly averted his eyes.

"Won't you invite me in?" she asked.

"I..." His mouth was dry. "I don't think that would be a good idea."

"You know it's going to happen, Reverend. Sooner or later, it's going to happen. The connection between us is too strong. I can feel your presence. I've felt it since the day you came to Tanneheuk. And I know you feel mine."

He swallowed. He had the urge to reach out and... No, it was best not to contemplate such things. Was she real? She looked unearthly, like an elemental product of a union between the forest and the moon.

Diana stepped closer and he took in her scent, the same scent he had picked up on at the picnic. It made him think of rain on lush trees, bathing in mountain streams, and sleeping under the stars. It made him feel as if he was in the presence of something primal.

"Don't fight it," she said, her voice little more than a whisper. "It's too strong to fight. Give in and let it happen."

She took another step closer and he put his hand up in a "stop" gesture.

"Wait. We can't... can't... I don't know what you expect from me, but this...isn't right."

"Of course it's right." Her lips were very red and glistened with wetness. "It's too strong to not be right. You feel me, like I feel the quickening of your heartbeat, the flush of your skin, the throb between your legs."

It was true, everything she said. He had an erection.

"Don't fight it," Diana said. "Invite me in. We don't have to talk. We don't have to think."

Drake closed his eyes. When he opened them again, his eyes were like steel.

"You need to leave. Now." His voice was steady and sure. He summoned the inner strength from deep in his soul where his unshakeable faith resided. When he spoke, his voice was filled with the confident resolve he only displayed during his sermons. It was the same resolve his congregation was privy to when he preached.

"I'll go." Diana nodded sadly. "I'll go because I know it's only a matter of time before it happens. You'll have to come to me next time. All you have to do," she spaced out the words so each one resonated in his head, "is come to me." Then she was gone, moving back into the shadows, into the night.

Drake managed to open the lock on the door and get inside. He closed and locked the door behind him, though he doubted she would be back. He believed her when she said she would wait for him to come to her.

He walked directly to his office, took the Jack Daniel's out of its hiding spot, and drank a healthy portion without the benefit of a glass. His hands didn't shake as he had thought they might. But inside he was trembling. He felt cracks form in the foundation of his soul.

# Chapter Twenty

Fern laughed, which was a strange feeling for her because she rarely laughed. The joint she was smoking may have had something to do with it, but more likely it was the company. David made her laugh. She had to admit, she found him funny.

He drove her car, which was another odd feeling because she never, ever, no exception, allowed anyone to drive her Dodge Charger. Not her parents. Not her boyfriends, what few there had been. She would have allowed Sheriff Creel to drive it — "drive it" being a metaphor for several things — but he had never shown an interest in it (again, another metaphor).

But she wasn't pining for Creel for a change. She was too busy having fun with David.

She was in the passenger seat, taking an occasional hit off her joint. She had offered it to David, but he declined, saying it wasn't his thing. He didn't seem to mind if she smoked, however. He wasn't judgmental that way. She liked that.

She smoked her joint and let David handle her car. It was a bit much for him, a little too much horsepower, too much Detroit steel. He kept to the speed limit and took each turn slow, but he lacked the control she had over the metal beast. The car seemed a hair's breadth away from breaking off like a runaway horse. She had years of experience driving the Charger, so maybe if she took that into consideration, he wasn't doing so bad after all.

They were driving around Lawson Road heading in the

direction away from town. He was in the middle of a story that made her smile and occasionally elicited a laugh.

"So I tell Philo to stop worrying, Dad's not going to find out. Meanwhile, the hooker's standing outside waiting for one of us to get out of the car because we can only go one at a time. He swore up and down that it wasn't really a hooker, that I was playing a joke on him."

"Who did he think the woman was?" Fern asked.

"He thought it was someone I knew, like we were driving along and I happened to spot some woman friend of mine, walking along 42nd Street, eleven-thirty at night. Philo claimed she was too well dressed to be a hooker."

In an aside to Fern, he said, "She was dressed conservatively, I have to admit. But still, eleven-thirty on 42nd Street? Anyway, when he finally realized it was a real hooker, he got really upset. I tried to calm him down, but he was acting like our dad was going to have a CSI team go over the car and, you know, find traces of DNA. I was like, Philo, it's just a blowj...uh, it's just oral sex. You know?"

Fern nodded and took another hit off her joint. "So what happened?"

"So Philo stood outside while I... Well, you know. He refused his turn, so I paid for myself. And I had to borrow the money from him, too, 'cause I was a little short at the time."

Fern giggled.

"The whole ride home, Philo's looking over the interior of the car with practically a microscope, looking to see if there was any evidence that a hooker had been in it. He bitched and moaned the whole way home." David did an imitation of his brother's whiny lisp: "I didn't want any part of that, but I ended up paying for it. Ith's not fair."

The imitation was close to being cruel, but Fern smiled anyway. All big brothers picked on their younger ones. Right?

"Did your father find out?"

"No. I was a little concerned that Philo would rat me out, but he kept his mouth shut. I guess he figured if he told on me, I'd never pay him back the money I borrowed."

"Did you?"

His impish grin. "Well, no. But I will one day... Maybe."

Fern laughed.

David came to an abrupt stop. Fern looked out the windshield and expected to see something blocking the road. The Charger's headlights pierced the darkness ahead, but caught nothing in its stare except for Fulman Bridge.

"Why'd you stop?"

"Uh...this may sound a little weird, but..."

"But what?"

"I have trouble driving over water."

Fern looked at him to see if he was joking. The frown on his face told her otherwise. "Really? Why?"

"Ah, I don't know. It's weird, right? I can drive through tunnels, but when I come to a bridge, I don't know. I have trouble. It's like...it's like I feel myself drawn to the edge, like the water's pulling me in or something." He looked at her. "Weird, right?"

Fern shrugged. "A little."

David looked out the back window, then out both sides. "Guess I'll turn her around and we can head back. Man, it gets dark out here. Like we're at the edge of the world. You know?"

Fern said, "Switch places with me. I'll drive over the bridge. I want to show you something."

"You sure? I don't mind driving back."

But she was already sliding across the seat to him. She could have gotten out and walked around to the driver's door. It would have been easier and she wouldn't have had to straddle the Hurst shifter in the middle. But it was too late; David slid over and helped her move over top of him.

He took hold of her hips and moved her up and over. Her butt rubbed over his crotch and she thought maybe... No, scratch that. She was pretty sure that something definitely pressed up against her as she moved over top of him. It was either an erection, or a pack of Lifesavers with a mind of its own.

So he was physically attracted to her. It wasn't an act he was putting on. He couldn't fake an erection, she was pretty sure. At least, not one that came on him so quick. She had the urge to linger on him, maybe rub her backside on his lap a bit. But it was too uncomfortable and she suddenly felt awkward and self-conscious.

She moved into the driver's seat and when he was settled in the passenger side, she proceeded forward. David kept his eyes off the road or the dark rushing water under the bridge.

"What's with the radio?" He was turning the knobs, but nothing came out the speakers.

"It doesn't work," she said. "I never bothered to get it fixed because I don't listen to the radio when I'm not working. If I'm not the one playing the music, I'm not interested in listening to it."

"The other DJs don't play anything worthwhile?"

"No, not really. Not unless they're borrowing from my playlist. Which they do a lot." She paused. "The tape player works. And there's a stack of tapes in the glove compartment."

"A tape player? Holy shit! You've got an 8-track?!' He laughed. 'I can't believe it. I didn't think those things existed anymore. Where did you manage to find one of those? And 8-track tapes?"

He had the tapes out of the glove compartment. Fern heard the dull thunk of the thick tapes as David looked them over.

"I have more at the house. I just keep a couple in the car for road trips."

"Where did you find these? I see it's all seventies stuff, which I'm not really into, but hey, I won't judge." He smirked.

"Of course it's seventies music," she said. "What else would be on an 8-track tape?"

"Good point. But tell me the story of why there's an 8-track player in your car."

"It was there when I got it and I never thought about taking it out. I don't think the car would look right with a modern stereo system. The 8-track gives it character."

He smirked again. "Yeah, if the character is a 1970s burnout."

She hit his shoulder in a playful manner. "You pick out a tape?"

"Yeah." He slid the tape in and ELO's "Strange Magic" blasted over the speakers. He turned it down.

"Sorry. Didn't mean to kill your eardrums."

"We're over the bridge, by the way."

From the corner of her eye, she saw him let out a quiet sigh of relief.

"Wow," she said softly. "Bridges really do bother you."

"Yeah," he said. "Don't tell anyone, okay? Nobody knows. Not even my family."

There was a wistful tone to his voice that struck a chord inside her. She was seeing a new side to him, and it was strikingly similar to a side of herself. The side that feels alone in the world and not able to open up to anyone because... because there wasn't anyone to open up to. Until now.

Maybe she was getting ahead of herself. As funny, and occasionally as emotionally touching, as she found David, she still didn't trust him.

"I bought a box of 8-track tapes at a flea market a few years ago," she said.

"John Denver, Allman Brothers, Elton John..." He put the tapes back in the glove compartment. "What, no Elvis?"

"I have one back at my house. I'll bring it next time."

He gave her a sly look. "So you're saying there's going to be a next time?"

"Maybe."

David, still with his sly smile, nodded. His old obnoxious cockiness was coming through again. She turned off onto a dirt road partially hidden by the trees and the domineering darkness. Although the turnoff was hidden, she knew the location of the dirt road from equal parts memory and instinct.

The road was narrow, yet smooth, and covered by overhanging tree branches that gave it the sense that they were traveling through a tunnel of foliage. The headlights cut through the gloom to a point, but it was Fern's knowledge of the road — more of a path, really — that enabled her to navigate it.

David said, "So are you taking me somewhere private so we can make out? Or is this some kind of *Deliverance* set-up?"

"Nervous?"

"A little."

She made another turn, this time entirely on instinct because the break in the trees was invisible in the dark, and the nose of the car took a sudden dip as they went down an incline. Fern braked and put the car in park.

The headlights cast out onto a still body of water. They were parked in front of a small lake. Fern cut the headlights. It was a cloudless night, and the moonlight transformed the water into thousands of diamonds sprinkled over black velvet.

David said, "Very nice," but not in his normal sarcastic way.

It gave Fern a warm feeling inside, like she had shown him a private side to herself and she was glad he reacted appropriately.

They got out silently, stood in front of her car, and watched the calm water. The air was cool; she resisted the urge to shiver. She thought he might use it as an excuse to put his arm around her, and she wasn't ready for that.

She had never been into sex. Not that she didn't have the desire or the drive for it, she just wasn't very good at it. She was clumsy and awkward, and had never been able to orgasm, not even when she masturbated, which was an infrequent thing. One boyfriend had told her that she wasn't doing it right and hadn't had the right lover. He bragged he would be able to make her orgasm. But his method, or lack thereof, didn't change anything. She thought maybe she was frigid, or there was something psychologically wrong. Or maybe it was the excessive marijuana smoking she did. Whatever the case, she rarely masturbated anymore and she hardly ever thought about sex.

She doubted if she slept with David that anything would be different. One thing she could say about him, though, was that none of her previous boyfriends had been able to make her laugh like he did. That was a disturbing thought, both because she was already thinking of David in a "boyfriend" context, and also because she was considering the possibility of sleeping with him.

How had this happened so fast? When did she go from not liking him and not trusting him to considering him as boyfriend material? He was shorter than her, for one, sarcastic, and of dubious moral character. He was nothing like Sheriff Creel. So what did she see in him? She wasn't sure. But there was *something*.

She felt his hand move tentatively against hers. His fingers slowly worked their way around until he was holding her hand. She didn't take his in return; she let it hang slack and allowed him to hold it. But after a minute, she felt uncomfortable in the fact that she was purposely not responding to him, as if she was being rude somehow, and she clasped his hand in return. He didn't react, but she could sense the wave of satisfaction that rolled off him.

David looked at her and said, "So what do you think?"

"About what?"

"You want to make out for a little while?"

She couldn't be sure, but she thought she might have blushed.

She pulled her hand from his and said, "That was a weird thing to ask."

"How come?"

"How come? Because you're not supposed to ask someone, a girl, if she wants to make out. You...you either know, or you don't know."

"Okay, I get that. But what if the guy doesn't know?"

"Um, you know," she said, "you go to kiss her, and uh, see if she pulls away."

He reached up, pulled her face down to his, and planted one on her. She was shocked at first...then embarrassed...then indignant... Then she kissed him back.

After a moment, he pulled back and looked deep into her eyes. She tried to read what was going on behind his eyes, but couldn't guess at what he was thinking.

He licked his lips. "Cherry lipstick?"

"Lip gloss," she said.

"Nice. So... You want to make out for a little while?"

"Okay," she said.

Slade Grayson

# Chapter Twenty-One

The flames threw sparks in the air that resembled fireflies. Children ran around the campfire, some in wolf form, others in human. They laughed and chased each other, playing a game that only they understood.

Roman was watching the children. He was unaware that Salacia studied him, so she was able to observe him in an unguarded moment. He smiled at the children's antics. He truly loved kids, especially since they were a rarity in their pack. Most of the shapeshifters had difficulty conceiving, and when they did, seldom did the child make it through to its birth. Most often, the woman miscarried several months into her pregnancy.

No one knew why it was difficult for the shapeshifters to procreate. It had something to do with their unusual body chemistry and make-up, and possibly because they were a closed community of sorts, but the matter had never been scientifically studied. It was just a fact of their existence. So when one of their clan did become pregnant, and the child lived long enough to be born, it was a celebrated occasion. Children were prized and treated as special gifts. Salacia knew that Roman prized the children more than anyone. After all, they were the future of the pack.

Unfortunately, the pack had dwindled over the years. It was simple math: With fewer and fewer children being born, the pack would eventually face extinction. They had decreased in numbers, from five hundred at the beginning of their settlement, to ninety-eight adults and nine children currently. That number would drop even further, and Salacia knew Roman worried about the eventuality.

Not that there was much that he could do about it. He couldn't control their biology, nor could he recruit new members. Although they welcomed refugees from all over the world, they received very few of them. Their pack was too hard to find, which was what they preferred. Secrecy had always been their main survival method.

Roman encouraged new members be brought in, and he encouraged each of the women to continue trying for children no matter how many times they miscarried. Salacia had not yet become pregnant, although her sex life with Roman was quite active. But she was sure it was only a matter of time. She didn't doubt that she would get pregnant one day, when the time was right, and she was sure she would produce several children for him. Much of her beliefs were probably due to her love for Roman and wishful thinking, but it didn't dampen her ardor or belief that she would eventually conceive.

He was lost in the capering of the children. His eyes followed them as they ran around the campfire, between the trees and cabins. Salacia imagined him watching their own children. Would he have the same wistful smile? Or would he join in the frolicking?

An adult wolf, thick and muscular with a white streak in its red fur, appeared from the shadows of the trees. As it walked towards Roman, its body shook and transformed into human form until it walked upright. It was Apollo, one of the shapeshifters that Roman assigned to watch over Diana.

Fully in human form, Apollo brushed off the remaining strands of fur that still clung to his body as he traveled the last few feet to where Roman waited. Apollo leaned in and, in a hushed tone, said something to him. Salacia was too far back to hear what it was, but she distinctly heard Diana's name. She saw, too, Roman stiffen at what he said.

Roman said something in return. Apollo nodded and moved off, transformed back into wolf form, and moved into the dark of the trees. Roman walked in the opposite direction. Salacia followed quietly and stayed downwind.

Instinct told her that Roman would not appreciate her company. She suspected he would be angry if he knew she was following him, but her curiosity overrode her concern, especially because she sensed Roman's anger had something to do with his sister.

As he approached his cabin, Salacia circumambulated his route. She slipped her sandals off and moved barefoot through the woods until she was on the opposite side. She walked carefully along the side to the edge of an open window. It was Diana's bedroom; the room partially lit by a kerosene lamp set on low.

Salacia peered over the edge of the windowsill. The bedroom was awash in a soft, warm glow of red and gold. Diana was in her bed, a simple wooden frame with a rope net base set low to the floor. It held a single mattress. The bed was handmade, like most of the furniture in Roman's cabin. Nothing was new or store bought. If it wasn't crafted by hand by someone in the pack, then it was donated by the townspeople.

Diana was swathed in a thick comforter with only her head and the toes of her right foot peeking out. She was asleep, or at least pretended to be. Salacia had the sense she was really awake, but had her eyes closed and feigned sleep.

Roman's voice, harsh and angry, came from elsewhere in the cabin. Salacia thought Diana's body tensed under the comforter at the sound of his voice.

Roman came in the room and yelled, "Diana!"

"Mmm?" She stirred under the comforter and stretched, still keeping with the act that she had been asleep.

Salacia moved as far away from the window as she could without losing sight of what was happening in the room. She feared that Roman or Diana might catch her scent, but the wind was on the opposite side of the cabin and she made sure to breathe as silently as possible.

"Where did you go?" Roman's voice was hard as steel.

"What do you mean?" Diana said. "I've been here asleep."

"Don't lie to me. You purposely left your escorts. And I've told you repeatedly not to do that."

Diana raised up on her elbows and met his glare. "I'm not a prisoner, brother," she said. "Don't treat me as one."

"No, you're not a prisoner. You're an important member of this pack. And there are protocols you must abide by in order to enjoy the privileges your position affords."

"Privileges." She spat the word back at him. "I can't go anywhere without your bodyguards following. You get angry if I become too friendly with anyone in the pack, and you've made it clear you don't approve of me talking to the townspeople."

"We have to be careful," he said. "Everything we do—"

"Careful? That isn't what this is about. It's about our father. You're worried ab—"

He cut her off. "You're right. I'm worried it will be found out. I'm worried you'll let it out somehow. You're unstable. You have been ever since..."

They stared at each other, no longer angry, but lost in a mutual memory. Salacia tried to make sense of what they were talking about, but it was like trying to make sense of a jigsaw puzzle with most of the pieces missing. Did it have something to do with Jove, Roman and Diana's father?

Everyone in the pack knew of the troubled last years of Jove's life, as he had never recovered from the loss of his wife, who'd died giving birth to Diana. He turned into a hollowed-out shell over the years, prone to melancholic moods and an occasional unpredictable violent outburst over some imagined slight. Roman had been taking over the leadership role of the pack for some time, until the time came when Jove mysteriously stepped down and abandoned them all. Roman had received word from him that he relayed to the others, that Jove had decided to live off on his own. And then the day came when they received the news, again through Roman, that Jove had died. No details.

Everyone accepted Roman's word. Truth be told, the pack knew Jove had been psychologically and emotionally impaired for years, and when he left, there was a general feeling of acceptance... and maybe a little relief.

Roman could now fully take on the leadership role of the Alpha. It was a role that suited him, one he was literally born for.

Roman broke the silence. "Going off on your own without your escorts, it has nothing to do with what happened with our father. It has to do with the new minister."

"I don't know what you mean."

"Don't lie to me!" he shouted. "You think I don't know? You think I don't know you've been sniffing around him since he came to town? You think I don't know you're in heat? I can smell it!"

Diana turned her face away, either out of embarrassment or anger, Salacia couldn't be sure.

"What would you have me do?" Diana asked softly.

"Stay away from them," Roman answered. "Stay away from *him*. We don't mix with their kind."

"I can't help it," she said, her voice still low, as if the words pained her. "I can't stop myself. There's something about him. He's not like the other humans. There's something special about him. I can feel it down deep inside myself. Something draws me to him."

"You're just in heat," Roman said. "That's all it is."

"No," she said firmly. "It's more than that. I'm telling you there's something about him that makes me...respond."

Roman made a disgusted sound. "A human? He's nothing. He's weak. You could have any member of the pack."

"You wouldn't allow that. You don't want me to be with anyone else."

"What is that supposed to mean?" His voice no longer had the inflection of anger. It was cold now, as hard and as sharp as a jagged chunk of ice.

"You don't want me to be with anyone else because you can't..."

"I can't what?" He stared at her.

She looked away. Her hair fell across her face and shadowed her features. Roman waited with his fists clenched.

When she didn't respond, he shouted, "I can't what?!" and ripped the comforter off her. He took a step as if he intended to strike her, but the sight of her naked body stopped him.

Diana pushed herself back against the wall until she was in a half-sitting, half-lying position. She was braced on her elbows, her knees raised up in twin arches, the soles of her feet flat against the mattress.

"You can't have what you really want," she said. "You want what father had, everything he had, including me. But it wouldn't be accepted. Not in our culture, or any other."

Roman's jaw was set tight and his face flushed red with anger. But there was more at work than simple anger. There was desire in his eyes, as well. Salacia knew his looks and how they corresponded to his emotions. She had been on the receiving end of that particular look many times, minus the barely restrained rage.

"Come and take what you want, brother," Diana said. "No one else will ever be good enough for me in your eyes because you want me."

She moved her head so her hair fell to the side and exposed her neck. It was a gesture of subservience, a sign of vulnerability, but the power in the room had shifted. By exposing her throat and offering her body up to Roman, Salacia knew that Diana had gained dominion over him. Or perhaps she always held such sway, but Salacia had never been witness to it before.

"Come, brother," Diana said. "Come take what you want. Prove you're a greater Alpha than our father."

For a moment, Salacia thought he would. She heard his quick breathing and sensed the rapid heartbeat, the fire that raced through him...

He grabbed Diana's ankle and yanked her towards him. His other hand went to her throat. He was bent over her, his arm pinning her to the bed. Salacia saw a flash of fear cross Diana's face. But Roman abruptly released her, turned, and stormed out of the bedroom.

Salacia stood frozen, then quickly recovered her senses. She had to get far away from the cabin. If Roman knew that she...

No, that couldn't happen. He couldn't know what she witnessed.

She hurried into the woods, trying to put distance between herself and the cabin. She stripped as she ran and prepared to shapeshift. She spotted him as he came out the front door, far away but still visible. Like all shapeshifters, Salacia's night vision was exceptional.

Roman sniffed the air before looking in her direction. They made eye contact. Roman was simultaneously running and tearing at his clothes. Salacia ran away from him and began her transformation. Roman was in full wolf form when he pounced on her back. She was in mid-change. Despite her fear, she marveled at how fast he could shapeshift.

He was on her, his front legs pressed on her back and his pelvis thrusting at her. She continued her transformation until she was in full wolf form and they melded together like two custom-fitted pieces. Roman thrust at her...urgent...savage...

She had thought he was angry, that he knew she had spied on him, and she thought he ran at her to hurt her. Maybe even kill her. But that wasn't it. He needed her to unleash his pent-up anger and frustration. But was she merely an outlet for him? Or was she a substitute for his sister?

# Chapter Twenty-Two

Reverend MacDonald sat hunched in a rocking chair on the porch of Celia's house when Drake arrived. He had called ahead and asked if he could come over and visit with MacDonald, who replied gruffly, "What the hell for?"

Drake told him over the phone that he wanted to ask questions about the town, specifically the town elders. MacDonald was quiet for a moment. Drake thought he might tell him no or make an excuse, but MacDonald agreed and told him to come over.

Drake parked in front and walked up to the house. MacDonald was framed in the glow of the morning sun. He looked older than Drake remembered, and frail, as if the daylight caused him pain.

MacDonald said, "You're still driving that same old shitbox. I can hear it coming a mile away."

Drake shrugged, then realized his gesture was pointless. MacDonald couldn't see it. He said, "Well, as much as I'd like a new car, my finances won't allow it right now."

He took the matching rocker next to MacDonald and studied the old minister. He still had the same hard, unfocused stare, but everything about him appeared shrunken. Retirement had deflated him. Or maybe, Drake considered, he was slowly fading from existence. His hold on life had loosened with the onset of retirement, and now he was in the process of slipping away into the ether.

MacDonald wore a tweed jacket over a flannel shirt and

corduroy pants. The attire looked too warm for the mild summer morning, but he didn't appear uncomfortable.

MacDonald said, "You can use my bike, if you want. It's in their garage." He hooked a thumb to the left to motion to the Brooks' garage. "Hell, I can't use it anymore. I haven't been able to ride in years, since before the missus died. You might as well get some use out of it."

Drake nodded. "Thank you, Reverend."

A bicycle would come in handy. He could use it to get around town when the weather was nice. It would probably add life to his car if he only used it for out-of-town errands.

MacDonald reached into his inside coat pocket and removed a half-smoked cigar. "So what did you want to talk to me about?" He placed the cigar in his mouth. His hand went to his side pocket and came out with a lighter.

"I want to know more about the elders."

"Christ," MacDonald muttered as he fired up his stogie.

"There's one…" Drake said. "Her name's Diana."

MacDonald groaned. "That one's trouble. More trouble than her brother, Roman."

"Trouble, how?"

"Okay, look, this is a long fuckin' story," MacDonald said. "You sure you want to hear it?"

"Yes, of course." If it gave him insight into the mysterious elders who held the town enthralled, he certainly wanted to hear it.

"I came here a long time ago, back when I was a punk kid and running from the law."

"You were a criminal?"

"Yeah. Petty shit. It wasn't like I was Al Capone or anything."

Reverend MacDonald's swearing had always been disconcerting, but now that Drake knew of his illustrious past, it contextually made sense. Still, the man had been a minister, and a minister saying "shit" and "fuck" was off-putting, to say the least.

"I came out here to hide out. I stumbled onto this town by accident. It was a different world then, but the town was pretty much the same as it is now. Only, there were different people in it. And different elders. He paused to suck on his cigar. "Roman's grandfather was in charge. A big, burly guy. He was the one who decided to let me stay here. He saw my potential, I guess you could say. It was him who arranged for me to stay with the town minister and his family. I was barely out of my teens. He figured the reverend would be a good influence on me, and obviously..." He shrugged, as if to say, *"You see how I turned out."*

"When Roman's grandfather died, his father, Jove, took over. He was different. Erratic. You never knew what he was gonna do. One minute, he could be a really nice guy. The next, he was acting bugfuck crazy. Most of the time, he walked around in a fog."

"What do you mean?"

"You know, like a depressed teenager. Poor me, and all that. He was nuts, or maybe just extremely moody. They say he never got over his wife dying. Medication probably could've helped him. The sheriff liked him, though. Those two were close friends. Creel never saw the craziness, for some reason. Or maybe he overlooked it, I don't fuckin' know."

"Then he died and Roman took over?" Drake asked.

"Yep. And that prick's been calling the shots ever since. You asked about his sister? Stay away from her. I've never said two words to her, but from what I've seen, back when I could see, and from what I've heard, she's as nutty as her old man was."

"She didn't seem crazy. Just...intense."

What could he say to MacDonald? That Diana had propositioned him twice? That she had showed up at the church naked and essentially offered herself up to him as a sexual feast? If he told him that, he would also have to admit that he had been a hair's breadth away from taking her up on her offer. He would have to admit that he was up most of the night (in more ways than one) thinking about her luscious body.

It was more than her body. More than her sensuality. The attraction between them was palpable. He was a piece of steel and Diana was the magnet.

MacDonald chuckled. "She don't seem crazy, kid, 'cause you got the hots for her. Even a blind man like me can see that. But believe me, she is. It runs in that family. Too much inbreeding, if you ask me."

Drake hadn't seen signs of inbreeding in the elders, but he asked anyway.

"It's a closed community," MacDonald answered. "What do

you think happens? Maybe it's not mothers and sons or fathers and daughters hooking up, but most of them are blood cousins in some way or other." He shrugged. "I wouldn't be surprised if Roman was throwing it to his sister. That prick acts like he's a modern day Caligula."

"I still don't understand why these so-called elders hold so much power in Tanneheuk, or why the townspeople treat them like...like a conquering army. Do they own the land the town is built on? If they do, why do they live up in the woods away from it?"

"Not on paper, but the town belongs to them. They've lived here longer than anybody, and they choose who lives here and who doesn't. The town is like...it's like a herd of cattle. And the elders protect the herd from anything that can potentially hurt it."

Drake shook his head. The whole thing was strange, and he had the feeling there was more to it, but no one would give him the final piece of the puzzle.

"Look," MacDonald said, "it's not a bad town. You could have a pretty happy life here. Just don't rock the boat. Keep away from the elders, especially Roman and his nutty sister. Get yourself a nice girl. Like Celia. I know she's sweet on you and she's a good kid. You couldn't do better than her."

"I understand what you're saying, but—"

"But nothing. Don't ask so many questions and don't rock the boat. That's my only advice. And my last advice."

They sat in silence. Drake thought he had been admonished, but beneath that he sensed MacDonald had been on the verge of telling him something. It was obvious, however, that the old man was done talking about it. For now, anyway.

MacDonald said, "Lead me to the garage and I'll show you the bike."

He reached out a tentative hand and found Drake's shoulder. They both stood and Drake led him to the edge of the porch.

"Let me know when I should step down so I don't fall and bust my ass."

"Right here," Drake said.

They stepped off the porch and walked to the garage door. When they stopped, MacDonald dropped his hand. Drake lifted the door and peered inside.

"Under the tarp," MacDonald said.

It didn't register right away until he pulled the tarp back and saw the black and chrome beast before him.

"This?" Drake said, "I thought you were giving me a bicycle. This is...this is a motorcycle."

"It's a Harley. And I can't ride it anymore. I got no one to will it to, so you use it. Unless you don't think you're man enough."

In the dim light of the garage, with the sunlight streaming in and bouncing crazily off the chrome, the motorcycle beckoned to him the way Diana beckoned. It said, *Come and ride me. Come and make me yours.*" It was the same voice Drake heard in his head the previous night when he had looked deep into Diana's eyes.

"Well?"

Drake answered, "I'm man enough."

# July

Slade Grayson

# Chapter Twenty-Three

In July, Roman's prediction to Sheriff Creel came true. Tanneheuk was hit by a heatwave unlike anything it had previously experienced. Temperatures regularly topped a hundred. Those that had air conditioning in their homes stayed inside. Those that didn't stayed in front of their electric fans or visited neighbors who had air conditioners. At night, the temperature dipped; it was still hot, but bearable. During the days, the heat was brutal.

The heat caused anger and violence to erupt among the shapeshifters. Several times, members of the pack had to be forcibly restrained from ripping into each other. There was much grumbling and outbursts of aggression, but only one killing. Roman's position as Alpha male was challenged by Camus, a slightly younger shapeshifter who lusted after Diana more than he desired Roman's leadership role. Although normally Roman would have used the force of his personality to dominate any would-be usurpers, he had allowed the matter to escalate to violence.

Roman and Camus squared off, surrounded by a circle of older members of the pack. The fight was quick and bloody, but Roman sustained very little damage to himself. He tore into Camus. He used his fangs and claws, and when he had subjugated Camus and everyone believed the fight was finished, Roman continued to tear into him. He killed the younger shapeshifter, then transformed back to human.

He stood over the body, naked and covered in blood, and announced like a primal barbarian god, "If anyone else wants to challenge my rule, step forward now and I will show you the same mercy I showed him."

No one stepped forward, and although many were horrified at Roman's savagery, deep down many were impressed at the ferocity he used to defend his authority. His position as Alpha male would be secure for many years to come. Even Salacia, who was shocked at the bloody carnage that Roman caused, found herself aroused and hoped that he would take her in the woods that evening.

\*\*\*

Maryam cut back on her training. She feared that she might burn herself out or cause herself heat exhaustion. She still ran, but for much shorter distances, and she consumed plenty of water and took salt tablets. For the entire month of July, she didn't see Mercury once. She thought maybe he had moved on, but somehow, she doubted it. She suspected he was biding his time and would show himself again.

\*\*\*

Passions also ran high throughout the town. Fern and David's relationship was consummated. Fern experienced her first orgasm. She knew it was an orgasm because the intensity of it caused her to cry afterwards.

Thereafter, she slept with David every night. He would wait on Mrs. Dallway's porch for her to come home. Then she would sneak him into the house down to her basement apartment. They would have sex (she couldn't bring herself to call it "make love" – too sappy). They'd sleep for a few hours. Then she would help him sneak back out, careful that her parents didn't see.

Neither of them mentioned the "L" word, but their affection for each other was apparent. They took to calling each other pet names, and prided themselves on how sickly sweet they could make them. It was a silly lover's game, but it made both of them smile.

\*\*\*

The heatwave caused tempers to flare among the Raffertys. David was exempt because he was hardly around, now that he spent much of his free time with Fern — much to Jonas's consternation. Jonas wasn't happy about the relationship. He thought David messing with the town deputy was like a kid playing with matches next to a dynamite factory.

However, it kept the sarcastic little shit occupied. He wasn't sitting around and stirring up shit as he was usually prone to do. And Jonas had met the girl. She was a little spacey, which he knew was the result of her frequent pot smoking (David had admitted it to him). Other than that, she seemed harmless. Jonas didn't believe she possessed a cop's mind, *i.e.* she didn't suspect everyone of criminal behavior.

Still, he thought the relationship held the potential for trouble. What if David let the wrong thing slip? He was smart and incredibly gifted in the art of the con, but he was also cocky and arrogant, too. Sometimes he forgot that being smart didn't necessarily equate to everyone else being stupid.

As for Philo and Amber, Jonas had given up on trying to convince them to get jobs. Amber was too lazy, and Philo followed her lead in everything she did. Her main occupation was sunning herself next to Mrs. Dallway's pool and having Philo bring her cold drinks and cigarettes. With the heatwave and the lack of air conditioning in the house, Amber had taken to wearing a bikini all the time, even to the breakfast and dinner table. When Jonas commented that he thought it inappropriate, the little bitch commented that maybe he needed to get laid. He could swear, too, that she was trying to tempt him to make a pass at her.

It made him angry instead. Angry enough that he slapped her. Then she went crying to Philo, who came out of his room and tried to decide if he was mad at his father or if he was upset that Jonas had allowed himself to be provoked. Ultimately, Philo decided he wanted to mediate peace. Jonas went along with it, but all the while he contemplated ways to get rid of Amber, either before they left town in the fall, or shortly thereafter.

Mrs. Dallway picked up on the tension in the house and took to staying in her room. She would occasionally come out for meals or to visit with neighbors or her children, but she was quiet around the Raffertys. She no longer seemed enamored of the "poor family who had lost their home."

Jonas understood. He didn't want to be around his family much either. He took to going out often, driving to Lake Dulcet and spending the day in town. He even frequented the diner where he and his family had first heard about Tanneheuk. He struck up conversations with Beth Ann when she was working, and Clem, the old man who appeared to be a permanent fixture at the counter. On Saturdays, to get out of the house, Jonas began to attend church.

***

Drake rode his newly acquired Harley Davidson around town, up and down Lawson Road, up to the Interstate, and anywhere else his fancy struck. The first day, the bike felt awkward, but the next time he rode, it became an extension of his body. It felt right, like a missing appendage had been reattached and now he was whole. He loved riding the Harley; he reveled in it.

He took to dressing in more motorcycle riding conducive clothing: black boots and black denim pants. He still wore his black shirt and white clerical collar when he rode, and part of him enjoyed the looks he received from townspeople and elders alike. He started thinking of himself differently, even contemplated getting his ear pierced or getting a tattoo. Something to complete his new "rebel priest" look.

He decided against it. Drake thought he was probably pushing the boundaries of what he could get away with as it was, and he didn't want to alienate members of his congregation or lose their respect. The motorcycle and bike attire were enough...for now.

Diana still tempted him. He saw her through his window at night, standing at the edge of the woods, naked usually. She would stand there for a few minutes, seemingly aware that he was watching her. She waited long enough to let him decide if he would go to her. When she had decided he wasn't, she would melt back into the shadows and be gone, and Drake would be left with a near-sleepless night. He would agonize over whether he should have given into temptation, and would wonder how long he would be able not to.

He saw her in town often, too, more than before, as if she was suddenly everywhere. He would be sitting in the town diner or browsing in the bookstore and he would think of her. Magically, she would appear. She would walk past the front window of the restaurant or shop, wherever Drake happened to be. His eyes would follow her as she walked out of sight, always flanked by her two escorts. The only time she was alone, or so he believed, was when she appeared to him at night.

It was funny how she appeared when his thoughts of her were the strongest. Was she psychic? Or was it that her close proximity triggered something inside him? He often thought of her throughout the day, but when she was nearby, his thoughts were the most vivid. He was a receiver and she emitted an unbearably strong signal.

As Drake's obsession with Diana grew, his relationship with Celia became distant. They went out on dates, but on his part it was perfunctory. They kissed still, but their relationship was chaste now compared to what it had been. He went through the motions, but his mind was always elsewhere. It was always on *her*.

One night, he gave in. It was a particularly hot night. He had the air conditioner turned up high, until the windows of his bedroom were thick with condensation. But still, he sweated. He couldn't cool off. A cold shower, ice water, still he burned inside. The heat came from within him, and he knew there was only one thing that would release it. One thing that would quench the fire.

The clock on his nightstand read a little after two. He threw off the damp sheet and ran his fingers through his sweat-slicked hair. The air conditioner hummed, but the coldness didn't touch him. He walked to the back door. His hand hesitated on the lock, then he threw back the bolt and opened it. He stepped outside clad only in his boxers. The night air was stifling. It hit him like a blast furnace, but he was already burning. In bare feet, he crossed the warm pavement to the woods. He didn't see her, but she was nearby. He felt her, felt the buzz in the air that told him she was close.

She appeared from the dark of the trees, a night apparition, naked and beautiful. Her lips were slightly parted, poised in the act of asking a question, but she waited for him to speak first.

"I can't fight it," he said. His voice was hoarse with desire. He sounded like a drug addict who has decided he can't live with sobriety any longer.

"I know," she said.

"I want you. I must have you."

"I know," she said.

"I can't go on without having you."

"I know."

She came to him. Her movements were slow and dreamlike. She reached out and touched him. They embraced. A sigh came from the depth of his soul, the shudder of relief from a drowning man who has decided to give up and not fight the current anymore. Drake was lost and he didn't care. He let the current take him.

# August

Slade Grayson

# Chapter Twenty-Four

July passed and took the heatwave with it. It was still hot, but seasonably so. The temperature rarely topped ninety, and it cooled off at night. The town relaxed. The pressure had dissipated, as if the air had been let out of a balloon. People resumed their daily existence, embarrassed by the short tempers they had displayed the previous month.

Fresh from the shower, Fern padded from the bathroom to her bed. She had a blue flannel robe wrapped around her, but it added little insulation from the cool dampness of the basement. David faced away from her, on his side, asleep.

Usually he left after she returned from delivering newspapers, but he had been asleep and she found she didn't want to wake him. She should have made him leave at 6:30 when her father left for work. She decided to let him sleep while she showered. She had smoked a joint while the water heated up, then brushed her teeth, shaved her legs, and bathed.

Now it was 7:30 and she knew her mother would be moving around upstairs. Plus, if he left now, there was a chance a neighbor might spot him skulking away. And wouldn't that be an interesting question she would have to answer once word got back to her mother?

Fern would kick him out. Just not yet. She slipped under the thick comforter, moving slowly and deliberately so as not to wake him. He turned suddenly and grabbed her.

"Gotcha!"

She laughed and put her arms around him. He buried his face

in her neck.

"You smell nice." His voice was muffled.

"Fresh from the shower."

"Yeah, I might have to get me one of those. I probably smell like..." He moved his face away and made a show of sniffing his arms and chest. "Sex," he said.

"I like it," she said.

He took her in his arms again. "Me, too."

"What's on your mind?"

"Just you, Cinnamon Roll." He slipped a hand inside her robe.

"Don't start anything you're not willing to finish, Sugar Plum," she said.

"Don't worry about me. I'll finish." His hand moved up to her breast and his thumb brushed lightly over her nipple.

She inhaled sharply at the sensation. It was funny to her how one of his hands could make her body melt. She kissed him deeply and let her tongue entwine his.

Fern heard footsteps coming down the basement steps. It had the effect of a bucket of ice water being thrown on her. David had a look of surprise, but also a tiny smirk, like he enjoyed the idea of being discovered in Fern's bed. She shoved him under the thick comforter.

"What—"

Fern shushed him and pushed him down so his head was next to her hip, then attempted to arrange the comforter so his shape was hidden.

"It's dark under here," he said.

She stuck a hand over his mouth and quickly scanned the room. An empty condom wrapper on the night table. She snatched it and shoved it under her pillow. David mumbled something.

"Sshh!"

Where were his shoes? Under the bed. He always placed them neatly under the bed. His clothes? Folded on the chair. God, he was so neat.

Her mother was at the door. Fern arched a leg up, the one opposite David, so it formed a tent of sorts under the covers, the better to conceal him.

Her mother walked in.

"Oh, you're awake," Odette said. She had a laundry basket

half-filled with dirty clothes under one arm. "I'm doing a load of laundry." She picked up various articles of clothing as she walked around the room. She headed for the chair that held David's clothes.

"Those are clean!" Fern said a bit shrilly.

Odette stopped. "Okay." She frowned and gave Fern a look. "Are you feeling all right?"

"Sure. Fine. Why?"

Odette shook her head. "Since you're up early, do you want some breakfast?"

Breakfast? Was she kidding? All Fern wanted was for her mother to go away so she could sneak David out of the house.

"No. I'm not hungry. I'm going to nap for a little while."

Very slowly, she felt David's hand slide up her leg. Oh, God, what was he up to?

"Are you sure? You seem like you're wide awake."

David's hand moved up to the upper part of her thigh, then to her pubic area. His fingers tickled her and traced circles. She moved her hand to stop him, but he restrained her with his free hand. Meanwhile, his other hand worked closer and closer until his finger began to trace the lips of her vagina.

"I'm not hungry, Mom." Her voice sounded shaky.

"Oh, Fern!" her mother exclaimed.

"What?"

She wanted him to stop, but he had her pinned with his leg and free hand. The only way she could stop him would be to struggle, and that would raise suspicions from her mother.

Odette said, "Look at these dirty dishes. Why did you let them build up like this? You know it'll attract bugs." She was referring to the tiny sink in the little kitchenette area across from the bedroom.

Odette ran the water in the sink. Her back was now to Fern, but she was still there within eyesight. And David wasn't stopping. He was enjoying himself under the covers.

He slipped a finger inside her and Fern stifled a gasp. She looked at her mom, who was obliviously adding liquid soap to the sink of hot water.

"Honestly, Fern, I don't know how many times I've told you

not to let the dishes pile up like this."

"It's fine, Mom. Just leave it."

David moved under the covers. He was now between her legs. Fern looked to see if her mother noticed the movement, but Odette still had her back to them, her attention focused on the dishes.

"You know, your father and I just had a talk about you and how you're still irresponsible. He wants you to move out. He says you're never going to grow up if we don't force you to."

She was washing the dishes. *God, this can't be happening.*

Fern let out an affirmative sound, unsure if her mother had asked her a question. She heard her mother talking, but only half of the words were getting through. Fern was more focused on David's fingers.

David removed his finger, the one that he had been stroking inside her. Fern nearly let out a sigh of relief. Now his mouth and tongue were working on her. *Oh, no*, she thought. *Oh, no. Not that.* That was something he was especially talented at.

She arched her other leg and looked to see if any part of him was visible. The middle of the bed, between her legs, looked like a lump of sheets and blankets, but that's all it looked like. No way could her mother suspect there was a man under there performing cunnilingus on her daughter. Unless Fern happened to give it away, which she nearly did by moaning. She controlled it at the last minute. Unfortunately, she couldn't seem to control her breathing, which had become significantly more rapid.

Her mother was still talking as she soaped up the dishes, rinsed them, and placed them on the plastic rack next to the sink.

"It's your father's opinion," Odette rambled, "that I do too much for you."

And so forth. At one point, her mother may have made the suggestion that she wanted to fix Fern up with someone, but she barely heard it. Her attention was all on David and his talented tongue. He had let go of her hand — she was beyond the point of putting up a fight — and had slipped it, along with his other hand, under her buttocks. He used them to raise her up slightly so he had better access. Fern had one hand up over her head, clutching the bedpost. Her other hand rested on the side of David's face and petted him like a loyal pet.

Odette asked her a question.

"Uh, huh," Fern answered, not sure what she'd just agreed to. She periodically threw in an affirmative sound or words to make her mother think she was listening, like, "Yeah." "I know." "I guess." "Okay." And so on.

Meanwhile, David was steadily pushing her to the brink of orgasm, then he would slow down or change what he was doing. She would come back from the edge, only to be pushed right back up there again by him. He seemed to have a precognitive ability to determine how close she was, and he used it to drive her up and down the ecstasy scale.

Her mother still talked and still washed dishes. David had slowed down. He now worked at a languid pace. Her body was taut from the expectation of an orgasm, but now that he had changed his rhythm, she felt frustration boil up inside her. Frustration that he was teasing her, and frustration that her mother was still in the next room.

Odette washed the last dish, dried her hands, and added the small hand towel to the laundry basket. Meanwhile, David took Fern's clitoris gently between his teeth and stroked it with his tongue. Fern bit off the involuntary moan that escaped her, but it still caught her mother's attention.

"What?" her mother asked

"Nothing, Mom. Would you leave now and let me get some sleep?"

"Are you feeling okay? You look flushed."

"I'm fine! I just want to be left alone!"

Her mother picked up the laundry basket and stomped out of the room. Her feelings were hurt; Fern would have to apologize later. All because David thought he was being clev— *Oh, God.*

He had released her clitoris and was now licking it with long, steady strokes. He pulled his hands from beneath her. One hand moved up to her breasts and worked back and forth between them, rubbing and lightly pinching her nipples. With his other hand, he inserted a finger into her vagina while another finger tickled the area between her vagina and anus. The combined effect sent her into overdrive.

She dug the heels of her feet into the small of his back, grabbed onto the bedposts with both hands, and let the orgasm wash over her body. She emitted a moan that started off low and gradually increased in pitch, until she thought she might scream.

She wanted to scream. She wanted to scream David's name. She wanted to run upstairs, go up to the attic, push open the small window up there and step out onto the roof, naked, and scream David's name to the whole neighborhood...the whole town. Hell, she wanted to scream it out to the world.

She didn't, of course. She swallowed the yell, although her mouth remained open in a silent scream. Wave after wave hit her until finally, it was over and she lay panting on the bed.

David poked his head out. "Wow. Your whole body raised up on that one, Apple Dumpling. I thought you were going to levitate off the bed, like something out of *The Exorcist*."

"You...," she panted, "asshole." She looked down and saw him smiling up at her, his mouth and chin glistening wet.

She closed her eyes and tried not to grin, but it came anyway. David chuckled and hopped out of bed. She heard him head for the bathroom. She opened one eye long enough to catch a glimpse of him in his jockey underwear. She closed her eye and gradually brought her breathing back to normal. Her heart still raced, but she felt that slow down. She heard David gargling in the bathroom, the toilet flush, and the water in the sink running. Then he was back in bed with her.

She opened her eyes and peered at him. He was on his side, braced up on an elbow, and looking at her.

"What?" she said with a lazy laugh.

"I'm just checking you out...Fernandiaz."

She gave him a look.

"I looked through your wallet while you were in the shower." He shrugged. "I was bored. Couldn't help it."

She gave him a playful shove. "Jerk."

"What's the big deal? I like Fernandiaz. It's a nice name."

"I was never crazy about it. That's why I shortened it," she said. "I'm not crazy about Fern, either, but..." Now it was her turn to shrug.

"I thought it was a joke when I first got to know you, you know, like your parents thought 'Fern Wilde' was funny. Fern Wilde, wild fern, something like that. But Fernandiaz Wilde? That's kind of cool."

"I think *you're* kind of cool, Peach Pie."

They kissed for a moment, passionately, like teenagers. When they pulled apart, Fern stretched over him and opened the drawer on her nightstand. She brought out a silver ankh on a chain.

"Ooh, jewelry," David said.

Fern placed it around his neck and hooked the clasp. She hoped he wouldn't make a joke or a sarcastic comment. She meant it to be a gesture of endearment, but sometimes David could be insensitive when she made a tentative step towards anything that gave their relationship legitimacy.

He didn't this time. Maybe he saw something in her eyes.

"What's this?" he asked.

"Just wear it for me." She turned it so it caught the light, then patted it down against his chest. "It looks good on you."

"You know what else looks good on me, Plum Pudding?"

"Me," she laughed. She pushed him onto his back and mounted him.

\*\*\*

Drake sat at his desk and typed notes for the weekend sermons. Since the start of his affair with Diana, his sermons had become more "fire and brimstone." Once, he preached about love and understanding, forgiveness and tolerance. Now his sermons were "wrath of God" based. He preached abstinence, self-control, and sacrifice. He preached damnation for nonbelievers.

The more he gave in to temptations of the flesh and debased himself, the stronger the content of his sermons. His religious fervor increased in proportion to the shame he felt over his inability to stay away from Diana. His passion infected his weekend sermons.

Consequently, his sermons became more and more popular. Drake had record turnouts. The pews were filled and people stood lined along the walls to watch him preach. Some of them came twice, on both Saturday and Sunday, despite the fact he preached the same sermon on both days. It was unreal.

He couldn't explain it, except that possibly they found his zeal inspiring. He would look out at the crowd at times, especially when he was deep into his Old Testament God, fire from the sky, floods and plagues talk...or lately, when he found himself inexplicably obsessed with Revelations and the end of the world...and he would look out into the eyes of his congregation and see rapturous attention. They hung on his every word.

He always ended on a note of hope. If they gave themselves wholly to God, if they trusted in the Lord, then they were saved. They would be safe.

As Drake's weekend services grew in popularity, so too did he begin receiving requests for individual counseling. Every week he had two or three members of his congregation coming to see him. It was funny; when he first came to town, no one was interested in what the new minister had to say, but now he had to book appointments well in advance. He was in demand.

When he met with his congregation, however, they had very little to say. Drake felt they were holding back, that they were troubled by something and needed spiritual advice, but none of them would open up. They made excuses or talked about innocuous things. He wondered if it was because they still thought of him as an outsider.

His appointments were generally from middle-aged members of the church, those that had teenage children. It appeared to be a common link. They would talk about their marriage and their children, would ask questions about God and how they could strengthen their faith. Still, Drake saw something behind their eyes. The members of his congregation were deeply troubled. They needed guidance, but were too afraid to open up. Drake was frustrated and felt helpless at the same time.

In the meantime, Diana came to him every other night. She would appear at the edge of the woods, and at first, he would join her and they would make love outside, loudly and passionately. But then he invited her into his room, and that became their routine.

She preferred sex on the floor rather than the bed, so he would strip off his sheets and blanket and lay them out with pillows scattered about. They would make love all night. Diana was insatiable, and so too, it seemed, was he. He couldn't get enough of her.

They would go again and again, until he thought he couldn't

possibly go anymore, before she urged him on to greater heights. The next day, he would be spent. He moved through his daily routine like a sleepwalker, sometimes plagued by strange fevers that came and went and left him burning up one minute, and afflicted with chills the next.

It was as if Diana had infected him in both body and soul. And just as his body returned to a semblance of normality and he felt physically better, it would be time to be with her again and the process would repeat itself. Like now. He felt fine now, awake and rested, but later that evening, she would come to him again. Tomorrow, he would plod through his daily existence, tired, dazed, and sporadically feverish. He couldn't break the cycle because the sex between them was unlike anything he had ever known. It was transcendent.

He was bothered by other things. They had unprotected sex. When he asked about the possibility of pregnancy, she laughed and assured him it was "nothing to worry about." He took it to mean that she was on birth control, or physically unable to conceive, but he didn't ask any follow-up questions. He should, but he knew it wouldn't really matter. Whenever she was around, he was incapable of rational thought. Still, he worried about disease.

He hesitantly broached the subject once. She replied, with an enigmatic smile, that he needn't worry about that. She said she was healthier than any woman he had ever known, and that her people were not susceptible to most diseases or viruses. "Her people." As if she was of a different species. He found it odd, but didn't question it.

Also, there were scratches. Diana preferred to be taken from behind and on all fours, but when they did engage in the missionary position (Drake's preferred way), she would wrap her legs around him and clutch at his back with her hands. Her nails raked his back and left red scratches. They were shallow, but occasionally drew blood and itched terribly for several hours before they faded. Drake checked Diana's nails several times, but they appeared to be short and not overly sharp. She seemed amused by this, and by Drake's confusion over how she kept scratching him.

"Sometimes in the throes of passion, I lose control," Diana

said, as if that explained how her short nails could scratch him so easily.

Drake sat at his desk and tried to concentrate on constructing his weekend sermon, but really all he thought about was her, about seeing her later that night and the things they would do. They were more than just passionate. Sometimes they acted like rabid animals with each other. They even bit each other on occasion. Not in an aggressive way, but playful. Not hard enough to break the skin, although they left plenty of bruises — mostly on him. Diana didn't bruise as easily, or perhaps her bruises simply healed quicker.

He opened his desk drawer and removed the bottle of whiskey. It wasn't the same one. He had finished that bottle long ago. This was number... Well, he hadn't kept count.

He twisted off the cap, briefly savored the aroma, then took a healthy swallow. He drank directly from the bottle, having long ago given up the pretense of needing a glass, and let the warm liquid set fire to his stomach while it simultaneously steadied his nerves. He took another before placing the bottle back in its hiding spot. From another drawer, he removed an open pack of breath mints. He took two and put them in his mouth. It might not cover all of the alcohol on his breath, but it would be enough to pass a cursory inspection.

He stood and walked to the bathroom. He examined his reflection in the mirror, and had trouble maintaining eye contact with himself. For one thing, he looked terrible. His eyes were bloodshot, his goatee (which had filled in after months of growing it), was straggly and hadn't been trimmed in weeks. He needed a haircut, too, and about twenty hours of uninterrupted sleep. And to quit drinking.

It wasn't his tired and haunted look that made him turn away from his reflection; it was the overriding guilt. He couldn't go on like this, he decided. It was enough. He was going to crack, if he didn't completely fall apart first.

He needed to stay away from her. That's all there was to it. He needed to kick the habit — cold turkey. He needed to be strong.

Drake walked briskly into the church area and knelt down in front of the altar. He clasped his hands together firmly and bowed his head. Although the church was empty, he kept his prayer silent.

He prayed for strength and guidance. He prayed for deliverance from temptation and the cold black emptiness he felt growing in his soul. He prayed, most of all, for a sign of what he should do.

He prayed: *Please, God. Please help me. Please help me overcome this. Tell me what to do. Show me. Give me something, a sign, anything.*

"Drake."

That voice, seductive and alluring... Why would God do this to him?

He looked behind him. Diana stood twenty feet away, dressed in a floral print shirt with billowy sleeves and a plunging neckline that displayed her cleavage. The shirt was tied below her breasts so her midriff was exposed. Her hips were poured into tight bell-bottom jeans. On her feet, she wore sandals. If there had been a flower in her hair, it would have completed the provocative "flower child" look.

She asked, "What are you doing, my love?"

"Why are you here, now?"

"I couldn't wait until tonight." She moved her fingers up and down the neckline of her shirt, rubbing both the cloth and the luscious skin underneath.

"You shouldn't be here now." His voice was thick.

"Why not, my love?"

She moved to him and extended her hand. Without thought, he took it and she pulled him to his feet. The electricity between them was undeniable. Although they had made love scores of times, the attraction between them had not diminished. Drake wanted her now as much as he had the first time.

She said, "Come with me and meet my people. Live with us, with me, in my home in the woods."

"But what about my home here? My church?"

"Leave it behind," she said.

He stared at her lips, full and dark over shiny white teeth. He had the urge to kiss her, as he did all the times he was within touching distance of her.

"Leave the church? But they need me. This is my calling."

She smiled. "Your calling is to be with me. You feel it, don't you?"

"I feel the chemistry between us, sure, but—"

"Not chemistry. More than that. With my people, we are each destined to be with one person. When we mate, we mate for life. It's primal, more than a feeling. When we meet the person we're destined to be with, we know it. There's no question, no doubt." Her eyes were locked on his. "I knew it the moment I first saw you. Even from a distance, I knew it. You are my mate. And you knew it, too."

Drake nodded.

"Say it," she said.

"I am your mate," he said.

"And I am yours."

He could have denied it, he supposed, but not to her. She was telling the truth. He felt it. He had always felt it.

"Come back with me. Leave this world behind. My people will accept you, once they see we're meant to be together. It doesn't happen often that an outsider is allowed in, but it will in your case. They'll accept you in time, and in time you'll be one of us."

His mind was jumbled. He wanted a drink, and he wanted her. Yet, he also wanted salvation. Was this his sign? Was this what God wanted for him?

He took her in his arms and buried his face in her hair, in her neck, inhaling her scent. He ran his hands up under her shirt. It came untied and her breasts hung unencumbered. He caressed them, then brought his lips down and kissed them. He kissed her nipples and lightly circled them with his tongue. She put her head back and clutched his hair with her hands. A low moan ran up through her and escaped from her parted lips.

She pulled his face up to meet hers, kissed him, then lifted herself and wrapped her legs around his waist. His erection strained against his pants. He walked her to the raised platform at the front of the church, the one that he stood on every Saturday and Sunday and preached morality to his congregation. He leaned her down so his weight was on top of her. His hands moved over her body while his mouth covered hers with passionate kisses.

It was the cross that stopped him. The big wood cross mounted on the wall behind the platform. He happened to glance up and when he saw it, he froze. The sunlight filtered through the stained glass window and dappled the shiny veneer of the cross. It glowed in the sun like an accusatory glare.

"We can't do this," he said.

"Of course we can."

Her hand slid between their bodies, down inside his jeans. Her fingers encircled his erection. Her hand was warm; the heat spread throughout his groin. He was fast losing his self-restraint.

"Not here," he told her. "We can't do this here. Let's go somewhere else."

"Of course, my love."

They stood and rearranged their clothes. It was awkward for him, as if they had been caught doing something wrong, but when he checked her expression to see if she was angry, she had a soft understanding smile.

"I'm sorry. It's just—"

"Sshh." She put a finger to his lips. "It's all right. We can go somewhere else. I would never refuse you anything, my love."

He nodded, while part of his brain analyzed the implications of that. Was it a double entendre? Sometimes it seemed that everything Diana said had a sexual undertone to it.

She followed him into his living quarters. He opened a closet and brought out a large wool blanket. He handed it to her.

"You know of a place we can go?" he asked. "Somewhere secluded where we won't be seen?"

She nodded. "Of course."

"Okay." He stripped off his black shirt and clerical collar, then rummaged in the closet for a casual shirt to wear. He selected a short-sleeve, dark blue button-down shirt. He felt Diana's hands on his bare back. Her fingers traced the ridges of the scratches she had given him the last time they were together. She kissed each one. Goosebumps broke out across his flesh. She did that every time they were together. After they had finished making love, and if she had raked his back with her nails, she would roll him over onto his stomach, then kiss and lick each scratch. It was both soothing and erotic.

Drake pulled away and put on his shirt. Up on the top shelf of the closet were two motorcycle helmets. He handed one to her.

"I don't need a helmet," she said.

"You should wear one."

"For safety? Or because you're afraid someone will see us

together?"

"Both," he admitted. "I'm not ready to make our relationship public."

"As you wish, my love."

"So where to?"

"Take the road out of town, past the bridge," Diana said. "I'll give you directions from there."

# Chapter Twenty-Five

Creel wanted a cigarette. The shapeshifters hated cigarettes. Something about the smell they found offensive. Cigar and pipe tobacco smoke they could tolerate, but not cigarettes. It irritated their heightened sense of smell. Consequently, Creel would have to wait until his meeting was over to smoke.

He met with Mars, Mars's daughter Salacia, and Mars's woman, Flora. They were in Creel's office — part jail and sheriff's office, part carpenter's office. Creel conducted all of his business out of the first floor of a building in downtown Tanneheuk. The upper two floors were apartments that housed some of the town's single residents, and one or two childless married couples.

Creel's office/jail was simply a room with a cluttered desk, phone, and a long outdated computer and printer. Creel had never upgraded his system because, quite frankly, he never saw the need to. Most of the customers to his carpentry business were repeat clients. He did have a fax machine in the office, but that was for the sheriff's half of his profession.

Along with his one room office was a small jail cell; another room held a bathroom. In all of Creel's years as sheriff, the jail cell had never been used. Creel wasn't sure if the lock on it would still work, nor was he entirely sure he knew where the key was.

Mars and his two companions had refused the offer to sit, so Creel stood as well. He was surprised when Mars contacted him and requested a meeting. Most times, Creel met only with Roman.

If he met with any of the others, it was usually by Creel's request. But more surprising than Mars wanting to meet with him was the reason for it.

"How long have ya known about this?" Creel asked.

Mars had just dropped the bombshell on him that Roman, and possibly his sister, Diana, may have been responsible for the death of their father.

Mars said, "Salacia overheard Roman and Diana talking many weeks ago. She kept it to herself until recently. She felt she had to tell someone, so naturally she came to me."

Creel glanced at Salacia as Mars answered. The girl looked haunted. Creel had heard the rumor that she was secretly Roman's woman. He could see from her expression that it was true, just as he could see that it was tearing her up inside to betray him.

It bothered Mars, too, but he concealed it better. He stood with his arms crossed over his broad chest. His silver ponytail swung freely behind him as he looked back and forth between Creel and his daughter.

"What made ya come forward with this?" Creel asked her. "If it bothered ya, I don't understand why ya waited."

"I tried to forget about it," Salacia answered in a small voice. "I didn't want to do anything that would cause trouble for the pack."

Creel thought it was more than that. She didn't want to betray her lover... and something else. She was not telling the whole story about what she heard and saw. But maybe she thought whatever she was keeping to herself was incidental.

"You understand, I'm sure, the difficult position this puts us in," Mars said.

He did. It could cause a civil war among the shapeshifter pack. Many would side with Roman. The older ones, the ones who had been loyal to Jove, would rebel. Many of the older shapeshifters saw Roman as an upstart, while the younger ones worshipped him. Discord among the pack would mean trouble for the townspeople.

Part of Creel wanted him to denounce Roman for patricide. Jove had been Creel's friend, and although Creel had heard the stories of Jove's manic mood swings and violent outbursts, he had never personally witnessed any of it. Therefore, he was reluctant to believe it. Like any loyal friend, he didn't want to believe the bad things about what his friend supposedly did. He preferred to think such incidents were exaggerated or falsified due to the malicious machinations of others.

However, part of Creel also knew that the stories were probably true. He had seen his friend act out of character at times. It was why, when he heard Jove had left the pack and later died, Creel wasn't shocked by the news. He had believed his friend had descended into madness and subsequently taken his own life.

The news that Roman may have killed Jove incensed Creel. He wanted to drive straight to Roman's cabin and give him a taste of the double-barreled shotgun he kept in his jeep.

Instead, Creel said, "We should keep this between us."

After all, it was the only thing they could do. As much as Creel wanted to confront Roman, and if the story turned out to be true, seek retribution, the end result would not be worth it. The safety of the town was Creel's priority, and a rift among the shapeshifters could jeopardize that.

He looked to Mars and saw he agreed. It pained him, Creel knew, because Mars had been Jove's Beta before he had been Roman's. He had also been friends with Jove almost as long as Creel. But Mars was practical, too. He didn't want a civil war, especially one that he probably couldn't win. There were more shapeshifters closer to Roman's age, and who shared his ideals, than those who remained loyal to Jove's memory. In the long run, Roman would ultimately be victorious and would retain his Alpha position. All others would be killed or exiled.

Salacia had a look of relief on her face. Creel understood; she *wanted* them to decide to keep the matter quiet. It absolved her of her guilt. If she had kept what she overheard to herself, it would have eaten her up inside. Telling her father wasn't much of an option, either, because she didn't want to stab her lover in the back. Now that she made the difficult decision to tell, and Mars and Creel agreed to bury it, she was free to move on, straight back to her lover's arms. Creel wondered how Mars felt knowing that the man who may have murdered his best friend had been sticking it to his daughter for months.

"So we're all in agreement then?" Creel asked.

Mars ran a hand over his stubbled chin and nodded. Salacia nodded without the reluctance her father showed. Creel looked to

Flora, who stared back flatly. She didn't need to nod; she sided with Mars on everything.

Flora was a strange one. Her mousy brown hair hung limp over an expansive forehead. She wasn't pretty, and she wasn't ugly. She was... severe, was the best way Creel could think to describe her. She looked like the most humorless person in the world. Creel had never seen her smile, nor heard her make a witty remark or laugh. In fact, Creel couldn't be sure he had ever heard her speak. She was simply there, a separate and loyal appendage for Mars.

They left his office without further discussion. Really, what more could they say about it? Creel knew that as much as it bothered them — meaning him, Mars, and Salacia, because it didn't appear to affect Flora at all — they all knew their best option was to bury it. Creel wondered how long it would take before the secret burst from its shallow grave and bit all of them in the ass.

***

Jonas stood at the front picture window and watched David slink his way along the side of the house across the street, then emerge into the midday sunlight and walk nonchalantly across to the Dallway house.

He entered through the front door and Jonas said, "How long you planning to ride that train?"

"Good morning to you, too, Dad."

That smug look, like he had just pulled off the crime of the century.

"I'm serious. How long you planning on stringing her along?"

David answered, "I'm just having fun. What's the problem?"

"Well, for one thing, besides her radio job and newspaper route, that woman is fifty percent of this town's police force."

Jonas followed him into the kitchen where David rummaged through the refrigerator. He took out packages of ham and cheese and a jar of gourmet mustard.

"It's no big deal. We're just hanging out. Casual. That's all." He opened the jar, looked inside, and made a face. "Is Amber eating my mustard again? You know, I buy this stuff 'cause I like it. If she wants some, why can't—"

"David."

He looked at Jonas, like, *What?*

"Stick to the subject. Where are you planning on taking this relationship with the town deputy?"

"Dad, relax." He pulled a loaf of pumpernickel bread down from the top of the refrigerator and began construction on two sandwiches. He lavished a generous amount of mustard on four slices of bread.

"It's like this," David said. "I'm just having fun. That's all. I mean, come on. Have you seen her? She's too plain for me. She's Olive Oyl. Do I look like Popeye?"

Jonas said, "Just having fun, huh?"

"Yeah."

"What's this?" He pointed to the silver ankh that dangled around David's neck.

"Ah, it's something I picked up somewhere. It came in a box of caramel popcorn, I think."

"She gave it to you?"

"Oh, uh, yeah. I guess." He shrugged. "Why? What's the difference?" He piled ham and slices of Swiss cheese on the bread.

"What does it mean when a woman gives a man a piece of jewelry?"

David replied, "It means she's getting the best lay of her life. Heh, heh. Am I right?"

He put his hand up for Jonas to give him a "high five." Jonas simply stared at him. David put his hand down and shrugged.

"Well anyway, what's your point?"

"You know that when a woman gives you something to wear, like a piece of jewelry, it's a sign of commitment. So stop giving me a line of bullshit about how you're just having fun."

"Okay, look. Maybe she sees it as something more. I don't know. But me? No. Not even close."

He stacked the sandwiches and deftly cut them into halves. He arranged them on a paper plate, then licked mustard off the edge of his finger. He looked at Jonas.

"I mean, she's got a limp. What, I'm supposed to be seen in public with a chick that has a limp? Where am I gonna take her?

To the Special Olympics?"

Jonas said, "I get it, smart guy. You don't care about her."

"Right. I'm just tapping it. I'm not gonna marry it."

"But she's falling for you. Or haven't you been able to tell? When we first moved in, she didn't give a shit about her appearance. Now I see her, she's dressing nicer. She's got her hair styled..."

David had a faraway look in his eyes. "Yeah. She's got, like, little waves in her hair. And she wears make-up now. Not a lot, but more than she used to. I noticed that, but..."

Jonas nodded. "She's emotionally involved. So now you're stuck. You have to keep up the act or else you risk her running to her boss, the sheriff."

"What's he going to do? He already did a background check on us a couple of months ago and we came up clean."

Jonas fought the urge to smack David's forehead.

"Think. This is a small town and the only law here is the sheriff and your little fuck buddy. You screw her over, there's no telling what she'll do. Or her boss."

"Dad, relax. I got this." He picked up the plate of sandwiches and walked into the living room.

The living room furniture could be classified as antique, though in reality they were simply hand-me-downs from Mrs. Dallway's parents, and grandparents before them, that had been well cared for. She had an ornate old rug, several chairs, a couch that had its cushions sealed in plastic, and a very old, elaborately designed coffee table. Mrs. Dallway stipulated to them when they first moved in to not walk on the rug with their shoes on, and to never place anything, besides perhaps a book or magazine, on the coffee table.

"Where's Mrs. Doubtfire?" David's nickname for the old lady.

"Visiting neighbors," Jonas answered.

David proceeded to walk on the rug in his tennis shoes, plopped onto the couch with a resounding hiss of air escaping from the plastic, and dropped the sandwich plate on the coffee table. David, along with the rest of them, only abided by Mrs. Dallway's rules when she was home. He put his feet up on the table, placed the plate in his lap, and took a healthy bite of his sandwich. Jonas stared at him.

With his mouth full, David said, "Dad, relax." He swallowed. "I know what I'm doing. I could play a superhot heiress like a pinball machine. You think I can't play a small town, Plain Jane pothead? Relax. I got this."

Jonas shook his head and thought, *Famous last words.*

\*\*\*

Drake sat on the blanket on the ground and pulled on his boots. Diana, dressed in his shirt and nothing else, was curled up beside him, her knees pulled up and her head resting on one arm. She watched him with a satisfied smile on her lips. He glanced down at her and couldn't help but grin.

"What?"

"Nothing," she said. "I just enjoy watching you."

After they had crossed Fulman Bridge, Diana directed him to turn onto a dirt road nearly hidden between clumps of overgrown grass. They stayed on it for a quarter mile, until she told him to stop. He pulled off into a flat clearing. They spread out the blanket and made love in the sunlight. Diana was more vigorous than usual, and much more vocal. Her cries of passion became screams at the end.

Drake leaned down and kissed her. When he pulled back, she asked, "Will you come back with me?"

"I can't give up the church."

"Of course you can."

"What I meant was, I don't want to give up the church." He saw the disappointment in her eyes, so he quickly added, "That doesn't mean we can't make our relationship public."

He would have to have a very uncomfortable conversation with Celia, but he knew it was time to do that anyway. It was time to come clean.

Diana sat up and folded her legs under her. "We can't be together publicly if you're not one of us. You have to join my people."

"I don't understand. You make it sound like you're a member of an exclusive club. Why can't we—"

Diana's expression stopped him. She turned her head and

stared off into the distance. She was suddenly alert to something, but Drake saw and heard nothing outside of the normal sounds of nature.

What was it? A car coming? An animal? All was quiet. They may as well have been the last two people on Earth.

She stood, briskly unbuttoned and removed his shirt, then handed it to him.

"You have to go," she said. "Quickly."

"Why? What is it?"

"Just go." She stared off at the same unspecified point. "Now."

"Why aren't you getting dressed?" he asked as he pulled on his shirt.

"You must trust me," she said. "Don't ask questions now. Just do as I say. Get on the motorcycle and go back to the church. Don't stop for anything. I'll be there tonight and I'll explain everything."

She looked at him. He stared into her eyes, those amber-ringed bottomless pools that always threatened to pull him down into their depths.

"*Now*," she said.

He moved without argument. It may have been her tone of voice that told him he was suddenly in a dire situation. More likely, however, it was the way her eyes narrowed. Drake suddenly found himself staring into the eyes of something very dangerous.

He picked up his helmet, put it on, and slung himself on the Harley. He gave her a final look, but her attention was focused elsewhere. She was poised, like a predator sifting through invisible air currents for signs of its quarry.

He rode off. He cautiously navigated the dirt road, took the turns slow, and avoided the deep ruts that marred his path. His mind was awash with questions, but they would have to wait until later.

From the corner of his eye, he caught a flash of gold in the sunlight. It moved behind the trees and kept pace with him. An animal. A fast one.

It was a wolf with blond fur, big, muscular. It easily kept pace with him, then slowly closed the distance. Suddenly, it turned to cut across diagonally towards him. It leaped in the air and Drake braced himself for the impact. A dark mass caught the wolf in midair and knocked it from its trajectory.

Drake stopped and looked back at the two animals— for that was what the second thing was. A wolf, black as midnight, smaller than the other, but apparently more ferocious. The black wolf ripped into the larger blond one. Drake was stunned by its savagery. He was mere feet from the main road, but he was transfixed by the spectacle before him.

The blond wolf never had a chance. Perhaps it was due to the surprise attack of the black one, or perhaps the smaller wolf was fighting a more desperate battle— it wanted the victory more. Whatever the case, the blond wolf was unable to regain its footing. The black wolf had its jaws clamped on the blond wolf's throat. Its teeth cut into the flesh of the larger wolf. Blood seeped between the black wolf's jaws.

The blond wolf struggled, but it couldn't overcome the leverage of the smaller one. Its flailing limbs became less frantic, until the animal stopped struggling altogether. Gradually, it was still.

The black wolf kept its jaws on the throat of the blond wolf until long after the wolf was clearly dead. Blood had gushed down the blond wolf's body and pooled underneath it. The blood gave its fur the appearance of being rusty and black. Drake was captivated by the sight...until the black wolf released its teeth from the dead wolf's throat.

When it pulled back, bits of gore dripped from the wolf's mouth. A jagged hole was left in the dead wolf's throat. It stared lifelessly up from the ground, up at the sky and to whatever animal deity it had pleaded to in its last moments.

He should pull away now, he knew. He should gun the motor, pull out on to the main road and not stop until he made it to the center of town. But he couldn't. He had to watch the black wolf, because... because deep down he knew.

It was crazy. Insane. It went against everything he believed in, and everything he believed possible. But he knew. What was worse, he had always known. The black wolf looked up at him. Those amber-ringed eyes. Even with her blood soaked snout, those eyes were still beautiful, still hypnotic.

There was a crack inside his head, an echoing boom like the

sound of a glacier sheared in half. It was the crack in the foundation of reality, the break-up of his staunch beliefs and faith, of everything he had ever learned, believed, and known. A curtain was lifted on Drake's world. He suddenly saw all the dark ugliness that existed beyond the veil of his own reality. He saw the ungodliness around him, and realized now that he had let himself become mired. Worse, he had enjoyed it.

He broke the gaze of the beautiful black wolf and roared away, out on to the main road. He took the turn too fast and nearly lost control of the bike, but miraculously, he kept it upright. He sped back to town like a man who had just escaped the gaping maw of Hell.

# Chapter Twenty-Six

Thirty minutes into her run, Maryam spotted him. She wasn't looking for him. In fact, she had stopped watching for Merc a few weeks prior. But today, he reappeared as if he had never gone away.

He followed behind her as she ran. She increased her speed, and he matched it. She had the impression he was teasing her, that he could easily overtake her if he wished. He was waiting for the right time, she thought, or maybe he simply savored the chase.

They entered an uphill clearing. She sensed he was about to make his move. He had increased his speed and was now only a few feet behind her. Maryam reached into the pocket of her shorts. Her fingers closed over the small canister. When Merc was close enough that she felt his breath on the back of her legs, she whipped around and squirted mace in his eyes.

He stumbled and fell, and simultaneously let out a howl of pain. Maryam stood ready, panting, the mace still clutched tightly in her hand. Merc rolled on the ground and rubbed his face on his two front paws. His howls slowly evolved into yells of anger and pain as his body shook and rippled back into human form.

Merc was on his knees. He rubbed his eyes with the heels of his palms. His eyes and the skin around them were an angry red. Water leaked from his nose and eyes, and he was unable to staunch the flow. His yells stopped and he glared at her through bloodshot eyes.

His yells had been horrific. Merc yelled in the same strange guttural whisper he spoke in, which made it sound like a man screaming and gargling at the same time. It was such an ugly sound that Maryam had to fight to keep from running away. But the yells stopped and she was able to regain her steely composure. She crouched down, grabbed him by his hair, and held the can of mace inches from his eyes.

She said sharply, "Don't move. Don't struggle. You try to fight me and I'll give you another shot of this."

"I wasn't gonna do nothin' to you," he said through gritted teeth. "I was just playin'."

"I'm not playing!" she screamed in his face. "This is my life! You hear me?!"

"I hear you, girlie-girl," he said in his choked whisper.

"I've been waiting for this my whole life. I've been planning it for years. I've trained. I've sacrificed. And now that I'm this close, I'm not going to let a sick little fuck like you ruin it for me."

"Ruin what?"

She released his hair, stood, and backed away several steps. She kept the mace steady in front of her. Despite the physical pain in his eyes mixed now with hatred, Merc didn't move.

"I'm going to run next month," she said. "And I'm going to win. When I do, your people will have to give me what I want."

"What do you want?" he spat it at her with venom in his voice.

"To be one of you."

The hate in his eyes turned to amusement. "One of us? You think it's that easy? You'll never be one of us."

"We'll see. But in the meantime, you keep away from me. You come near me again, you chase me, and the next time I'll use more than mace. I swear, the next time you come near me, I'll kill you. You hear me, you sick fuck?"

"I hear you, girlie-girl. Next time? I won't be playin' neither. Next time, I'm comin' for blood. It won't be quick. I'll eat you little bits at a time."

Maryam backed away. She took her steps carefully, fearful she might stumble and fall. She thought he might make a surprise attack on her now. He watched her, but didn't move. Then he shifted back to wolf form. Maryam waited. She thought now was the time that he would run at her.

He turned and ran in the opposite direction. Maryam lowered the mace, her hand shaking. She thought it was from fear, but realized her adrenaline was pumping in overdrive and was making her feel unsteady. She barked a mental command to herself to calm down, told her heart and lungs to slow. She took deep breaths and cleared her mind. This was nothing. The real fight was coming.

***

Creel knocked on the door and Fern's father answered.

"Sheriff," he said with a nod.

"Hello, George. I need to speak with Fern for a minute."

George Wilde held the front door open and stood to the side so Creel could enter. Creel passed through a small foyer and entered the Wilde's living room. The room was dark except for the light coming from the television. George had the evening news on. The smell of dinner, either in the process of being prepared or having recently been consumed, drifted in from the kitchen.

George called out, "Odette, tell Fern the sheriff's here." He sat in his worn Lazy Boy recliner and asked, "You want some coffee? Odette just made a pot. Or maybe a beer?"

"No thanks, George."

Creel sat on the couch. George stared at the TV. The sound was turned down too low to hear what was being said, but George stared at the screen like he could understand every word that came out of the newscaster's mouth.

Creel looked at George in the half-light. He was a short, ruddy-faced bald man with a prominent potbelly and a perpetual look of disgust, as if the whole world had disappointed him and he thought he deserved better.

Odette stuck her head in from the kitchen. "Fern's on her way up, Sheriff. You want some coffee?"

"No thanks, Odette." He smiled genially at her.

"Okay. Let me know if you change your mind. I've got some leftover blueberry pie, too."

"I'm not staying that long. Maybe next time."

Odette nodded and returned to the kitchen.

"How're things at the plant, George?"

"There's talk of layoffs. I got a bunch of deadbeats working under me, but they'll probably keep them and let me go. That's how things go over there."

Creel didn't think he had ever heard George utter a single positive statement the whole time he had known him. He figured the plant probably would lay George off, but not based on who did or didn't do more work. Usually, when George was laid off from a job, it was due to his constant negativity. However, he always seemed to land on his feet. He had always been able to find another job right away and maintained steady employment until his new supervisors got sick of his constant complaining and "poor me" attitude.

Fern entered the room and Creel nearly did a double take. Her hair had stylish waves to it that gave it the illusion of being thicker and fuller. She wore make-up, too, he noticed. Not a lot, just enough to bring out color in her cheeks and lips. A little eyeliner, too. She was dressed nicely, not in her regular uniform shirt, jeans, and Timberlands. Today she wore a red silk shirt, dark navy pants, and a pair of flats. Creel was speechless.

Fortunately, Fern's father spoke up. "Take the trash out to the curb before you go out, Fern."

"Were ya on your way out?" Creel asked.

"In a little bit," she said.

"Can ya step outside with me for a minute? I need to talk to ya"

"Sure, Sheriff."

"Don't forget the garbage," George reminded her.

Creel looked at Fern, but her face showed no reaction to her father. He felt embarrassed for her, and a little sad because he knew Fern was at an age now when she no longer expected kind words or affection from her dad. If her father ever said anything nice to her, Creel thought Fern probably wouldn't know how to react. Like a dog growing up with an abusive owner who is suddenly treated with kindness.

Not that George physically abused Fern. His abuse was limited to insensitive remarks and generally ignoring her the rest of the time. If he had ever tried to physically abuse her, Creel knew he would have raced over and...

Well, he wouldn't have killed George. Maybe just pistol-whipped him.

He followed Fern outside and helped her move the trashcans from the side of the house out to the curb. The sun was setting low and the streetlights had come on. When they were finished, Creel said, "I stopped by the radio station. They said ya had the night off."

"Yeah, but I'll still make my rounds later, though."

"Oh, I wasn't worried about that."

She had her usual glassy look. Creel wondered if she still took painkillers for her leg, but he had never asked. He figured it was none of his business, really.

"The reason I needed to talk to you was..." His eyes fell on the exposed part of skin on her upper chest that her shirt, in its generously scooped neckline, saw fit to display. "...that I wanted to ask if ya ever learned anything about the Raffertys." She had a light scattering of freckles on the area above her breasts. Creel forced himself to look away.

"What about them?"

"Remember at the beginning of the summer I asked ya to keep an eye on them and let me know if ya saw anything suspicious? I know you're dating one of the Rafferty boys, so..."

"Yeah," she said. "David. I'm dating David Rafferty."

"Well, I don't mean to pry. I'm just following up." He shuffled his feet and stuck his hands in his pockets.

"Um..." she shrugged. "There's not much to say. His family doesn't...they don't really do much. So I can't say they've done anything wrong."

"None of 'em work, right?"

Fern thought for a moment, then shook her head.

"Where do they get their money from?"

"Um...David said something about an insurance settlement. I think David's brother collects disability of some kind. And the father is retired military, I think."

It all sounded vague, much like the answers Jonas had provided on the several occasions Creel had visited him over the past few months. Each time Creel talked to him, Jonas became more cocky. It had gotten to the point where Creel didn't trust himself alone with the man. He was afraid he might step outside the official guidelines of his office and hit him.

"Keep me posted. Okay, Fern?"

"Sure, Sheriff. Of course I will."

"Okay."

He looked at her and noticed she appeared as uncomfortable as he felt. She must hate the fact that besides everyone in town gossiping about her and the outsider, that now her boss and longtime friend was questioning her about it.

"Well..." He didn't know how to end the conversation on a positive note, so he leaned over and kissed her on the forehead. "Ya look nice," he said. "Have fun on your date."

There was a funny look in her eyes. Embarrassment? No. He thought maybe she was touched by his gesture. He felt something, too. A lump in his throat.

It was ludicrous, he knew, and he desperately wanted a cigarette. He gave her a wave and climbed in his jeep. As Creel drove away, he saw her in his rearview mirror. Fern stood on the curb and stared after him.

# Chapter Twenty-Seven

Celia used her key when no one answered her knock. All the lights were off, but she knew Drake was home. His car and motorcycle were both parked in back.

She walked through the kitchen and turned on the lights as she went. She looked in the office and called his name. His helmet was on the floor next to his desk, dropped as if he had been in the middle of something and it had slipped, forgotten, from his fingertips.

His desk drawer was open. She called his name again, then walked down the hallway to his bedroom. It was empty, as were the other rooms. She went to the door that separated his apartment from the church. She tried the knob; it was unlocked. Celia gave it a tentative knock and opened it.

The church was dark like the other rooms and appeared to be empty. She was about to turn and leave when she heard a rustling sound. She knew instantly it was him, there in the dark. She sensed his presence. Why wouldn't he answer?

"Drake?" Concern permeated her voice. "Are you okay? Please answer me."

There was a row of light switches next to the door. Celia flicked on the first one. The room was softly lit by an outer row of overhead lights. Drake was a few feet away, his back to the wall under the wood cross. He had his knees drawn up to his chest. An empty bottle of Jack Daniel's was on its side on the floor next to him. Celia rushed to him.

"Are you okay? What's wrong?" She crouched down next to

him and examined his face.

Drake's eyes were open, but he stared off into nothingness. She didn't think he was hurt, but his vacant stare and bloodless complexion made her think he was in shock.

"Drake, what is it? What happened?"

He reeked of alcohol, but didn't appear to be drunk. She touched his face and he flinched, then he looked at her and appeared surprised to see her there.

"What's happened?" she asked.

There was fear in his eyes, and something else: shock.

"I'll get help," she said.

His hand clamped on her arm.

"Don't. Don't go," he said. "Don't leave me here. Pull me out of the darkness."

"Oh...oh, baby," she said "It's okay."

She pulled him to her and cradled his head on her chest. She held him tight and stroked his hair.

"Sshh," she said, "It's okay, baby. It's okay. Please, just tell me what happened."

Even as she said the words, she knew. But she needed to hear him say it.

He shook his head. "I can't," he said. "I'm in Hell. I let Satan lead me down into the abyss, and now I'm lost. I'm surrounded by darkness."

"Tell me," she whispered soothingly.

"Demons," he said. "Everywhere, there's demons. All around me."

He had witnessed it. Creel and MacDonald had wanted to indoctrinate him slowly. They had been afraid Drake couldn't handle it if he was immersed too quickly. In the past, they had found that outsiders weren't able to accept the town's secret if exposed to it too fast or too soon. It was best to let them acclimate. Move in, make friends, grow comfortable... Then they would be fed portions of the secret bit by bit, until it seemed as natural to them as the birds in the sky or the grass underfoot. Expose them too quickly and you risked *this*.

"It'll be okay, baby," she whispered in his ear. "I swear it will." Celia stood. "Come on." She pulled him unsteadily to his feet. "Let's get you cleaned up. I have to make some phone calls and then, I promise, you'll understand everything."

\*\*\*

They were parked at their favorite spot, the one in the woods next to the water that Fern had showed him two months before. It had become their spot now, and they often went there after a date. Or sometimes they went there directly, made out or had sex before heading back to Fern's place.

Tonight, they had gone out to dinner first. Although Fern had been seen with David in public several times since the start of their relationship, she still felt awkward and uncomfortable. She had the paranoid belief that everyone was watching them, that she was being judged by the other townspeople.

Except it couldn't really be considered paranoid because Fern often caught them — the service staff or other patrons — openly staring at her and David. Perhaps it was only curiosity due to the fact that Fern rarely had a relationship that lasted long enough for her to be seen in public with someone. Or perhaps the curiosity stemmed from the fact that David was an outsider. No matter the reason behind it, Fern imagined everyone around her was passing judgment on her and her new boyfriend.

Tonight, they ate dinner in town and put up with the cursory looks and the spate of whispers behind their backs, or at least Fern did, because David never paid attention to that. After dinner, they stopped for a beer at Dennison's, which turned into three. Instead of going back to Fern's bedroom, as she had wanted to do, they went to their place in the woods.

Fern had to drive over Fulman's Bridge. David still couldn't do it because of his phobia. Fern parked in their alcove off the dirt road, and they climbed in the backseat and had fumbling, clumsy sex that made them both laugh.

When they were done, they dressed and gave each other sly looks. While Fern pulled on her pants, David grabbed her and took her onto his lap. She laughed and squirmed, her pants only pulled up to her knees.

"Give me a kiss, Apple Pie," he said.

She brought her lips down to his and kissed him. There was a rush of warmth in her chest, as if a miniature sun had replaced her heart and instead of blood flowing through her veins, it was heat. It spread through her limbs and up to her head, and when it reached the top, she felt a surge of giddiness and thought:

*This is what it's like. This is what it feels like to be in love. I finally know now what I've been missing.*

She nearly cried from both happiness and the fleeting thought that it might not last. But she didn't cry. She rested her head on David's shoulder and enjoyed the fullness she had inside herself.

They sat like that for a while, her on his lap, head on his shoulder, his arms around her, the 8-track playing John Denver's "Annie's Song".

David said, "Candy Cane, I hate to spoil the moment, but I gotta pee."

Fern kissed his cheek. "Go pee, Tomato Plant."

"Nice one." He smiled.

She slipped off his lap and finished dressing. David already had his pants on. He pulled on his shoes and stepped out of the car, bare-chested. He walked around the front and moved behind a cluster of trees.

Fern hooked her bra, slipped on her shirt, and buttoned it. It startled her when David rushed back. He practically threw himself into the front seat.

"Shit," he panted. He turned off the 8-track.

"What happened?"

"It's stupid," he laughed. "I was walking back and I tripped on something. A dead animal."

"What kind of animal?"

"A big one. Jesus." He laughed and shook his head. "Like a really big dog. On steroids."

An icy fist closed over Fern's gut. She put on her shoes and climbed out of the backseat. She reached past David to the glove compartment and brought out a flashlight.

"Show me," she said. God, she wanted a joint.

David put on his shirt, then led her to the spot. When her flashlight beam fell on it, David said, "That is one big dog."

*Oh, Jesus.* "It's not a dog."

"Is it, uh...a wolf?"

Fern didn't know who it was, since there were a good number

of blond-haired shapeshifters in the pack. But she knew it was one of them, and she knew by the torn throat that it did not die accidentally.

She heard David say, "Oh, shit."

Fern cast her flashlight beam around the area where David was looking. They were surrounded by a circle of wolves. The forms began to ripple and flow. They transformed into human, with Roman taking the lead and stepping forward towards them. He shook off the remaining hair from his body and stepped to where the dead wolf lay.

"It's Sol," he said, looking down at the fallen shapeshifter.

Fern looked to David to see how he was taking it all in, whether he was scared shitless or shocked by what he had witnessed.

His eyes were wide and his mouth hung open, but he didn't appear traumatized or even afraid. He said, "Oh, man, that was the coolest fuckin' thing I've ever seen!"

# Chapter Twenty-Eight

Jonas walked into the kitchen and nearly ran into Amber, who was leaning against the counter and drinking one of the beers she kept stashed in the back of the refrigerator. She usually kept two stuck behind a head of lettuce and one inside a Tupperware container with AMBER written on the lid. Mrs. Dallway didn't approve of alcohol, but she either never noticed the not-terribly-well-concealed beer, or she had given up on trying to enforce her puritanical rules.

When Jonas walked in, he flipped on the light and stopped short before he bumped into her. Amber wore a ratty pink bathrobe, and nothing else. The robe hung open, and although she tied it when she saw Jonas, he thought there was a moment of hesitation. Like she wanted him to get a look at her body.

What kind of game was this? Was she really trying to run one on him? The old seduction bit, get him hot and bothered by showing him the goods? Make him want her so she could wrap him around her finger like she did to Philo?

Jonas wasn't interested. Forget the fact that she may or may not be blood related (probably not), Jonas in no conceivable way found her attractive. Neither her scrawny, flat-chested body nor her tight Raggedy Ann curls. And even if she had been physically attractive, even if she possessed the legendary beauty of Helen of Troy, Jonas still wouldn't fall into her trap.

He wasn't a mark; he was a con man.

He opened the refrigerator, took out a container of orange juice, and poured himself a glass. Her eyes were on him. He made sure to not look at her and not look at her body.

"You're up late," she said.

"You got something on your mind?"

"Been thinking..."

*Here it comes*, Jonas thought.

"About striking out on my own." She threw her head back and guzzled the rest of her beer.

"That's not a bad idea," he said. "You want me to drop you off at a bus station? Or you planning on buying yourself a car?"

"I thought we'd get a car."

"Who the fuck is we?" he asked, although he already knew the answer.

She gave him a look like she had been waiting to spring this on him.

"Philo. He's coming with me."

"The hell he is."

"I think he is. Dad."

Jonas slammed his glass down on the counter hard enough to cause juice to slosh over the side. He took a step towards her. She didn't react, but he saw a quick flash of fear in her eyes. Deep down, he felt a twinge of enjoyment at that.

"That boy is staying with me," he said. "You're free to go off and do whatever the hell you want, but you're not taking my son with you."

"Think so?"

She crumpled the beer can and tossed it into the trash. There was a separate can for recycling aluminum, but Amber could never be bothered with trivialities such as recycling. The fact that she threw the can in the trash rather than leaving it on the kitchen counter was, in itself, a minor miracle.

"He wants to come with me," she said. "Can you blame him?"

"Listen to me—"

"No, you listen." She had her courage back. "He's coming with me," she said, "and if you want to make sure he's well taken care of, you'll count off some of our hard-earned money you been holding on to." She put her hand on her hip. "Unless you think you can talk him out of it. But I don't think you can give Philo what I give him." She let her hand slip down off her hip so it grazed the area between her thighs. "You don't have the equipment for it.

Dad."

She walked out of the kitchen, and Jonas seriously contemplated the thought of killing her.

\*\*\*

David asked Fern:

"So is everyone in town a werewolf? Are you one?"

She shook her head, which was a shame because he thought that would have been so cool. The idea that he might have been fucking a werewolf for the past month... Man, that would have been awesome.

The one that had introduced himself as Roman — David had the impression he was the leader of the pack — was talking to a red-haired man with a thick red beard streaked with white. The others in the group had carried off the dead wolf's (werewolf's?) body. David wasn't certain where they went.

All of them were naked, except for David and Fern. They appeared comfortable that way, which David found odd. The women weren't self-conscious in front of him or the other men, and the guys stood around nonchalantly with their dongs swinging in the breeze. Like it was perfectly natural. Which, maybe it was.

David checked to see if Fern was looking at Roman's equipment or his red and white bearded companion. She wasn't. She stared at the ground, lost inside herself. It wasn't the first time she had mentally drifted away, but generally she only got that way after a joint or two. Which reminded him...

Fern hadn't smoked one in a while. Maybe that was why she seemed distant. Maybe she was really craving a joint, or maybe her leg was hurting her. It usually went hand-in-hand with her, he had discovered. It could be that, he supposed, or maybe this situation was particularly upsetting to her. But she had grown up in Tanneheuk, so why would being around werewolves bother her?

The red and white bearded one finished talking to Roman and moved off into the woods in the same direction as the others. Roman turned and strode towards them.

Fern had started her Charger and had the headlights on. Roman and his companions hadn't needed the light. Even in human form, Roman said their night vision, like their other senses, was far superior to an ordinary human. But Fern had wanted to check out the body of the wolf. She had acted concerned that they might blame the wolf's death on her or David, but Roman had assured her that wasn't the case.

"We know who did this," he had said, then sniffed the air. "The scent is unmistakable."

It didn't appear to put Fern at ease, however. David hadn't been concerned they would be blamed, or attacked for that matter. He was too engrossed in the whole concept that werewolves actually existed.

As if he had read David's mind, Roman said, "We prefer to be called shapeshifters. Newcomers always say werewolves, but that's limiting. Our people turn into wolves, but there are others in other parts of the world who turn into different animals."

"I saw a black guy in your group," David said. "No offense, but he's a wolf, too?"

"Liber. Yes, he's one of us."

"But shouldn't he turn into an African animal, like a zebra or lion?"

"It doesn't work that way," Roman replied.

The headlights lit up his naked body. His eyes and teeth gleamed in the artificial light. He looked like a young god standing before mortals.

David tried not to glance down at... Ah hell, he couldn't help himself.

*Jeez,* he thought, *are all the werewolf guys built like that? Did that come from being a werewolf... shapeshifter... whatever?*

"It's a virus that gives us our ability," Roman explained. "Some of us have inherited the virus from our parents. Others acquired it later in life. It changes the body's genetic makeup, allows us to control our bodies on a cellular level. Whatever animal we turn into is determined by what strain of the virus we have. My pack are all wolves."

"If you bite me, does that mean I turn into a werewolf?"

"Shapeshifter," Roman corrected.

"Yeah. Shapeshifter."

"Possibly, but most likely not. As I said, it's a virus. One that usually kills a person because their body can't handle the metamorphosis. Only one in a hundred, at most, survives the process. Otherwise," he spread his hands, "the world would be filled with shapeshifters."

"Yeah. Makes sense," David said. "How many are there of you?"

"Here, there are ninety-eight of us in this pack. Ninety-seven now. In the world? I wouldn't know. Not as many as there once was."

David glanced at Fern from the corner of his eye. She still appeared to be lost in her thoughts. There, but not there. Then a thought struck him.

"Hey, if there's werewolves—"

"Shapeshifters."

"Whatever...shapeshifters...does that mean vampires are real, too?"

Roman made a sound of disgust, a look of annoyance on his face.

"I prefer not to discuss that Euro-trash."

"Wait, so you're saying...? Holy shit! Vampires are real?!"

"Very distant cousins. A mutated strain of the virus that we have. But again," he held up his hand, "I would prefer not to discuss them."

"This is so fuckin' awesome," David said. "Really. I can't begin to tell you—"

"We should go," Fern said.

She had been quiet for so long, her voice actually startled him. Roman, however, seemed unaffected.

Roman said, "I have an internal matter to deal with. But if you're interested in learning more about my people, come up to our cabins. Tomorrow, if you want."

He turned and moved out of the light. David watched his body change, melt and flow, until he was walking on four legs and was covered in fur. It happened so quickly that David's eyes were scarcely able to follow it. He had been looking at a man and, in the matter of a few blinks of his eyes, he was looking at a wolf. Amazing.

The wolf, Roman, entered the dark of the woods. David shook

his head.

"This is so cool. Why didn't you tell me about this?"

He looked into her eyes for the first time since Roman and his friends had shown up. There was something there. Not fear. Something else.

"What's wrong, Pineapple Cake?"

"I don't like those people."

She walked to the driver's side of her car. David noticed her limp was more pronounced.

"Your leg bothering you?"

"Yeah. But that's not the problem."

She got into the car. David slid into the passenger seat just as Fern lit up a joint. The strong aroma instantly filled the interior. Fern took two long, deep drags and exhaled one after another. David nearly caught a buzz from it.

"What's the problem?" he asked. "They don't seem like bad people, you know, except for whoever killed the yellow-haired one. But Roman seemed to know who did it, so..." He shrugged.

"I didn't tell you about them," she said, "because I like to pretend they don't exist."

Her voice had a dreamy quality, as if she was drained. He would have thought high, but the marijuana couldn't have hit her system that fast. As soon as Roman and his cohorts had made their appearance, Fern had acted like the life had been sucked out of her.

"What's wrong?"

"Don't get involved with them, David. I've never liked them. None of them."

"Roman doesn't seem so bad. A little full of himself, maybe, but—"

"I don't like them."

"But don't you think it's cool that they're werewolves?"

"Shapeshifters."

"Whatever."

"Cool? Not especially."

"Yeah? Why not?" David said, "They get along with you guys. Right?"

She took another deep drag and looked out her window. She was quiet so long, he started to think she had forgotten he asked her a question. She said,

"If a cat gives a mouse permission to live in the same room with it, do you think the mouse would ever be comfortable living with the cat?"

She turned her head to him. Her eyes were dull and lifeless.

"I don't know. I suppose not."

"That's why I don't like them. And that's why I'm not happy they have free run over the town I grew up in. I'm a mouse surrounded by cats."

He didn't know what, if anything, he could say to that. He shrugged noncommittally.

"Don't get involved with them," she said. "Sometimes they let humans hang around them, like mascots. Don't do it. Okay?"

"Sure."

Even as he agreed, he knew it was a lie. How could he not talk to Roman again? How could he not know more about those people? To find out these beings existed, and then pretend otherwise...

He couldn't do it. He had to see more.

Slade Grayson

# Chapter Twenty-Nine

It had to be a dream. It couldn't be real. Drake would wake up soon and find out the events of the past day were all a manifestation of nerves, lack of sleep, and guilt over his affair with Diana. Except that would be too easy.

He had showered and changed his clothes. He shaved, too, though he didn't need to. He dressed in his black shirt and clerical collar because it gave him comfort in its familiarity. When he came out of his room, Sheriff Creel and Reverend MacDonald were there. Celia had brewed a pot of coffee and all of them had steaming cups in front of them. Drake sat and Celia poured him a cup. He had the impression they had something weighty to unload on him. He wasn't disappointed.

"Werewolves?"

"Shapeshifters is the more politically correct term," Creel told him.

"What's the difference? The only thing they turn into, according to you, is wolves. So isn't werewolves an accurate term?"

Creel said, "They feel that the name werewolf distinguishes them from the other were-animals in the world, and they prefer to not have that distinction. So call them shapeshifters."

Drake stared at him. Then he let out a laugh, shook his head, crossed his arms on the table, and put his head face down on them.

"I can't believe we're having this conversation. All of you are insane." He looked up at Creel. "Tell me this is all a bad joke. I'm on some reality show and you're filming this with hidden cameras."

Creel sat across from him with his back to the wall. He fixed Drake with a look like he really didn't care if Drake believed him or not.

Drake knew Creel didn't like him. He always had the same sour-faced expression whenever he was forced to deal with Drake. He saw the disapproving smirk, too, when Creel noticed his black jeans and motorcycle boots.

"It's no joke, son," MacDonald said. "You know it ain't. You musta seen something with your own eyes. Am I right?"

"I don't know what I saw."

"Yeah, you do. The sooner you admit it to yourself, the better it'll all be. Believe me. I went through the same thing many years ago myself. Once I accepted it, life got a little easier."

"Tell him the rest," Celia said.

"Tell me what?"

"The shapeshifters...the pack..." Creel said. "They protect this town. They decide who lives here and who don't. Those that do live here, they get the security of knowing that they're free from crime, poverty, racism and such. The shapeshifters protect the town. They keep it safe. They've done it for generations upon generations."

"But there's a price," Celia said.

"Of course," Drake said. "There always is. What's the price here?"

MacDonald shook his head. "I hated this. I hated this from the start. But there was nothin' I could do. Everyone said to not make waves. Even my wife. Tradition, they said."

"What? What tradition?"

"The shapeshifters have a tradition," Creel said. "Payment for their protection. It was started way back when by the Blackfoot Indians that used to worship them as gods. They would offer a yearly sacrifice, some captured member of a rival tribe. Maybe some white man headed out west who got lost along the way. 'Course, when they didn't have a prisoner to use, they'd sacrifice one of their own. Just once a year."

Drake's mouth suddenly turned very dry and he had a sinking

sensation in his gut. "What are you saying? You offer them human sacrifices?"

Creel answered, "They call it a hunt. They like the chase, the kill. Once a year, in September, the beginning of fall."

"And you allow this to happen? In this day and age, you allow ritual murder by...by a bunch of...of monsters?"

Creel looked down at his coffee. For the first time since he met him, Drake had the impression Creel wasn't feeling superior anymore. He acted embarrassed, and a little ashamed.

"Ya don't understand," he told Drake. "It's easy to look at it from an outsider's point of view, but we live here. Most of us grew up here. When ya grow up with certain traditions, it becomes an accepted way of doing things."

"You're committing murder, is what you're doing. They are not people. They are demons. Monsters. They are not of God."

"There's more," Celia said. "Years ago, people started..." She cleared her throat. "They..."

"They started maiming their kids so they couldn't run," MacDonald finished. "I'm sure you've probably noticed the number of young people in town with leg injuries, and the accident prone teenagers. If they can't run, they can't be picked for the hunt."

"Oh dear God."

Drake stood up suddenly and the room tilted a bit. He thought he might fall, but he regained his balance and staggered away from the table. He made it to the sink and held on to the edge. He concentrated on his breathing and stared at the slow drip of the faucet until his head cleared.

He whispered, "What are you people doing?"

"Ya have to understand, Reverend," Creel said. "It's not like we approve of it. Hell, I been tryin' to change the system for years. But it's a pact between them and the town, and it goes back so far... It can't just change overnight. It takes time."

Drake turned back to face him. "Time? You're killing people! Every year! And letting parents maim their children!"

"It sucks, I know," MacDonald said. "But in this case, I gotta agree with the sheriff. I tried to get them to change, too. It takes time."

"Time's up," Drake said. They all looked at him.

Drake read their faces. Creel suddenly seemed weak and ineffectual. Drake's original impression was of a smug country sheriff who thought he knew it all and looked down on everyone else. Now, all Drake saw was a figurehead, a lackey for Roman and his demonic shapeshifters.

He had thought MacDonald was a crusty small town minister, perhaps a step or two away from senility. But MacDonald was just some former petty thief who found a niche for himself in Tanneheuk, and had now given up on everything because he had lost his wife, eyesight, and his ministry.

Celia was another story. She looked at him with an expression he thought at first was sympathy, but now realized was hope. She *wanted* him to know about the town's dirty secret. She wanted him to be outraged. She wanted him to take a stand against it.

"We have a pact," Creel said. "But Roman is working to change things. Given time—"

"No," Drake said. "No more time. This ends now."

"Look here. Ya can't just—"

"No, you look, Sheriff. No more murder. No more maiming our children. This isn't just a crime. This... This goes against God. No more of it."

Celia asked, "What should we do?"

"This is what we're going to do. Sheriff, tomorrow I want you to take me up to where these people live. I'm going to tell Roman the pact is over. No more yearly hunt."

He expected Creel to argue with him, but Creel stared at his coffee. He nodded his head slightly, but didn't meet Drake's eyes. All the fight had gone out of him.

MacDonald said to Creel, "You gotta admit, the kid's got balls."

# Chapter Thirty

Diana had vanished. When Roman had returned the previous night, he discovered that she had slipped back to the cabin while he and the others had been preoccupied with Sol's body. She had packed some of her belongings and left.

Some of the others had witnessed her heading east, but Roman thought that was probably a ruse. Most likely, Diana would circle around and head west. She knew they would be looking for her. He could find her, track her down as easily as any other prey. Her scent was still strong. He had the urge to follow her, to run her down, to...

He shook it off. He would let her run for a while, until eventually she decided to come back. She had to because, after all, where else could she go? Where else would she be accepted? Even if she found another pack to take her in, she wouldn't be an Alpha. She wouldn't be royalty. She would be a commoner, most likely relegated to being someone's mate. He knew Diana wouldn't stand for that.

Even with the anger many of the pack members felt over her killing of Sol, she was still the Alpha female. She had nothing to fear, not even from Sol's family, outside of some grumblings perhaps. No one dared retaliate against her. The only person Diana had to fear retribution from was Roman. That was why she had disappeared. But she would eventually return. He was sure of that.

It was midmorning and Roman had been surprised by an unexpected visit. David had parked at the base of the pack's settlement and walked up the long, winding dirt road that led to their cabins. Roman was made aware of his arrival by some of the other pack members. Strangers were always regarded with suspicion and caution, so Roman knew David was on his way. His enhanced hearing had caught the unfamiliar sound of the car, and he smelled David's recognizable scent: a combination of Mennen Speed Stick and too much cologne.

Roman was surprised at how quickly David had taken him up on his offer. It was a pleasant surprise though, because for some unfathomable reason, Roman liked him. There was just one thing about him Roman found annoying:

"So if werewolves, sorry, shapeshifters exist," David said, after Roman had given him a brief tour and introduced him to some of the others, "and vampires exist, what about zombies?"

"I've never encountered one," Roman answered. "I would think that if they do exist, it's probably not the way you imagined."

"Okay. Okay, what about ghosts? Do they exist?"

"I've never experienced one."

"Aliens?"

"I really wouldn't know," Roman said, sounding a bit exasperated now. "How would I know that?"

David shrugged. "I don't know. I figured you would know all that stuff cause, you know, you're a—"

"Don't say werewolf."

"I wasn't. I was gonna say shapeshifter."

They sat inside Roman's cabin, the same front room that Roman had his talks with Sheriff Creel. The windows were open and a warm breeze flowed crossways through the room. Roman inhaled the smells. He wanted to be out running now, perhaps hunting something to eat. But he wanted to humor his guest a bit, too.

David said, "You have to understand, this is really crazy for me. I mean, I watch movies and read books, and all along I thought it was all make-believe. To find out people like you are real..." He laughed and shook his head. "It's like discovering a whole new world."

"If you have questions about my people," Roman said, "I'll answer them. But don't ask me questions regarding the existence of other creatures or life forms."

"Okay. Sorry. Umm..." David bit his lower lip. "Okay, what

about the changing part? Does it hurt?"

"No."

"Okay, uh, when you turn into a wolf, do you keep your human brain? Or do you think like a wolf?"

Roman smiled. "My intellect, as well as the others of my kind, remains the same in both forms."

"Cool. So like, you're not overcome with an animal-rage or impulse or anything?"

"Hmm." *How to explain this?* "Not exactly," Roman said. "Shapeshifters are not quite human, not quite wolf. We straddle a fine line between both worlds. Some of my people are closer to the wolf side than the human. You can see it when they're in human form. The wolf is always close to the surface. You see it in their eyes, the constant growth of facial hair, the way they move and react. The wolf is right below the surface, straining to come out. We try to teach them mastery over their wolf side, but some find it difficult."

"What about you?" David sat back in his chair. "Do you have control over your wolf side?"

"I have perfect control over both sides, wolf and human."

"Nice." David nodded. "What do you guys eat? Like raw meat, or do you cook stuff?"

"We enjoy hunting wild game from time to time, and often we'll eat it fresh. But mostly we prepare our food and store it for the winter. Or we go into town and eat. The townspeople are generous in giving us things, if we need them."

David's eyes took in the room. He looked up at the huge wooden beams that ran overhead. Roman could tell he was trying to think of something clever to ask.

"So you guys can only be killed by silver bullets, right?"

Roman laughed. "An interesting legend, but no. An ordinary bullet would do the trick, although we are much harder to kill than an ordinary human."

"Why's that?"

"We heal faster," Roman answered. "Our immune systems are enhanced, as are our healing abilities. You must understand, to transform the body into the form of a wolf means that we have control over ourselves down to the cellular level. So a cut or a puncture wound, our bodies can heal that almost instantaneously."

"Wow. So you guys are like invincible?"

"No, not quite. We still get injured. Any injury to our hearts or brains is potentially life-threatening. We also age slower than a human. Not so much when we're younger, but once we reach adulthood, the aging process slows down."

"How old are you?"

Roman said. "Probably twice the number you think I am."

"Cool," David said. "And you're sure I can't join your group?"

"Pack, not group, and if I were you," Roman replied, "I wouldn't risk it. I don't think you'd survive the virus."

"Too bad." David brightened. "Hey, what about Frankenstein's monster? Was that real?"

*Not this again.* "I highly doubt it."

"What about fairies? And I don't mean the homo kind, I mean the kind with wings and pointed ears."

Roman groaned and rubbed his eyes with the palms of his hands. He was starting to regret befriending this human.

A strange, yet familiar scent caught his attention. He jerked his head up sharply.

"What?" David looked around. "What's the matter?"

"Someone's coming," Roman said. "The sheriff. And someone else." Roman stood and walked to the door. "I'll be back in a moment."

David said, "Yeah, uh, I should probably wait here. The sheriff doesn't like me very much."

Roman walked outside in time to see Sheriff Creel and Reverend Burroughs coming up the dirt path. The sheriff was dressed in his standard jeans and denim shirt, with a wide brimmed cowboy hat on his head and a gun clipped to his belt. Burroughs looked different from the last time Roman had seen him. He was dressed in his black minister's uniform and white collar, but Roman noticed he was wearing black jeans and boots. Not the look of a typical small town minister.

There was something else different about him, too, Roman noticed. He walked with a purpose, with determination. When Roman had first met him last May, he had the sense of a man who was unsure of his place in the world. Now, he walked towards Roman as if he was the newly appointed constable of Tanneheuk

— God's peace officer coming to lay down the law.

"Sheriff. And Reverend," Roman said in greeting. "To what do I owe the honor of this unexpected visit?"

Creel opened his mouth to answer, but Burroughs cut him off.

"We've come to tell you that the ritualistic murders of the townspeople's children are going to stop."

The statement took Roman by such surprise, all he could think to do was stare openmouthed at the young reverend. Then he recovered and laughed. "Oh, really?" To Creel, he said, "Ritualistic murders? What's our idealistic friend referring to, Sheriff?"

"No more hunts, is what he's saying," Creel said. "We told him last night about the town's yearly tribute to the pack."

"Reverend, I see you decided against taking my advice about not making waves."

"Besides being against the law," Burroughs said, "it's barbaric and it goes against God."

"God?" Roman walked towards him. "You speak to me about God? Look around you, Reverend. You're surrounded by gods."

Burroughs glanced around and took in the veiled threat. There were others coming to and from their cabins in the midst of their normal morning chores and activities. Some milled about, curious about what Roman and the two humans were talking about. For the most part, they pretended to ignore them because they knew Roman would signal them if he wanted them to be involved in the discussion. Still, Roman knew his voice was heard to all within earshot.

"Don't talk to me about your deity, Reverend. You are in the presence of something much greater than the myths and fables your Bible talks about. A word from me, and my people would tear you limb from limb."

He stepped forward until he was eye-to-eye with Burroughs. The man was using sheer force of will to keep fear and doubt from crumbling his new persona. It was admirable in a way, but Roman would not let a human come to his home and dictate what he could and couldn't do. Especially not a human that his sister had been—

He clenched his fists and suppressed a growl. Burroughs saw something in Roman's eyes, something that made him take a step back. His face was impassive, but Roman saw uncertainty flicker behind his eyes. If Roman attacked him, Burroughs was unsure whether Creel would come to his aid.

"You're an outsider, Reverend. This town belongs to us. I agree that the hunt is outdated, and perhaps a bit barbaric, but it's tradition. One that will change...eventually. Not this year, however. So accept the fact."

"Or else?" Burroughs asked with a tone in his voice that grated on Roman.

"What will you do?" Roman said, "No one here will come to your aid. You're alone."

"I'm not alone. I have the Lord on my side. I'll take that over your army of demons."

"Demons?" Roman laughed. "You're quite humorous, Reverend. What a quaint notion you have. God and the Devil, angels and demons... It all fits into a perfect little box, doesn't it? Anything you don't understand or that doesn't comply with your ancient text, must be of the Devil. Correct? And what am I? Am I Satan, Reverend?"

Burroughs smiled tightly. "No, Roman, you're just a lowly demon scrounging for a piece of God's creation. But God has sent me here for a reason. I'm here to stop your darkness from spreading."

Roman tried to stare him down, but the soft spoken minister he had previously encountered was replaced by something new. Roman was looking at a man who had stared into the abyss, and had come away with steel for a spine. He thought he should rip his throat out now before the matter went any further.

It was like an infection; it should be cut out before it could spread. But Creel was there.

Roman looked at Creel to see what his stance was, but the sheriff refused to look at either of them. He stared at the ground and shuffled his feet. What was this? Roman wondered. Was Creel really going against him? Was he breaking the pact between Roman's people and the town? Roman asked him.

"Well," Creel said, "it's just that, as ya know, I've thought for a while that the hunt should be stopped. You and I talked about it."

"You..." Roman had the urge to scream at both of them. But it wouldn't do to easily lose his composure in front of his people. He brought his voice down to a lower register. "You come up here and think you can dictate demands to me? The hunt will continue until I say otherwise. Nothing in this town will change until I say it does. Believe me, Reverend," Roman fixed him with a cold stare, "it would be nothing for me, or one of my pack, to make you disappear. Or perhaps you might become the subject of our next hunt."

"There is no hunt," Burroughs said.

Roman looked at Creel. "You are still welcome up here. But not *him*. Do not bring him back up here. If I see him again away from the town, either alone or otherwise, I will personally eat him."

That comment got to Burroughs. Roman saw it in the man's eyes, although he didn't visibly react. It gave Roman a slight sense of satisfaction anyway.

"Sheriff, next month, the first day of Autumn, you will conduct your selection and we will have our hunt," Roman said. "I don't want to hear anything else about it."

He turned and walked purposefully back to his cabin. Neither man responded, nor did he expect them to.

Slade Grayson

# Chapter Thirty-One

Maryam took a second inventory, then a third. She was meticulous to a fault. She had to be if she wanted to successfully complete her objective. She went through her checklist: two belt-clip water bottles; a glow-in-the-dark compass; a water bottle filled with red pepper; a double-edged, hollow-handled dagger; a full can of mace; thirty empty plastic jars with screw top lids.

The empty jars wouldn't be used the night of her run, rather, their purpose was for the morning before. She would have plenty of time to fill them up beforehand. Also, the knife and the can of mace were (she hoped) not to be used at all. If she did, it would be considered cheating and she would be disqualified. Which meant that even if she completed the run, they would still kill her. She had to complete the run on her own merit without resorting to weaponry. Her intention was to have them with her, just in case. If she was losing, if there was no doubt that she wasn't going to complete the run and they were going to catch her before she reached the river, she would use the dagger and the mace. If she was going to die, then she had no compunction about hurting any of them. Obviously, she hoped it didn't come to that.

The time was coming. Maryam felt it in the air, like an electric current that hummed below the surface of her everyday life. It had been there for years, she knew, the electricity sparking off her internal clock as the years, then months, then weeks, counted down. Soon it would be days, and then hours...

She felt the gears turning and the resonance increasing, like a tuning fork coming closer to her ears. She felt it all around her and in everything she did. The hum grew and the hands on the clocks clicked louder and louder.

In a matter of only a few weeks, events would converge. She was ready. More than ready. She was anxious. Maryam saw herself as a live wire in search of an outlet. She would run. She had to run.

Lately, she had the crazy urge to drive up to the pack's settlement and challenge them. Screw the date and screw the protocols. She wanted to lay down the challenge right now.

She couldn't. Everything had to be by the book and according to the rules of the pact. She could bend the rules, but outright breaking them was out of the question. When she won, and she was positive she would, there could be no question about it, no doubt.

She had it all planned, down to the last detail. Nothing could go wrong, and nothing would go wrong. She had a plan. She would be picked, she would run, and she would win. Then she would become one of them.

\*\*\*

Her mother was giving her shit about David. Again. Fern was in the living room by the big picture window, waiting for David to pick her up and drive her to her shift at the radio station. David used her car on a regular basis. Not that Fern minded, but it added fuel to her mother's dislike for him. Odette's opinion was that David was a "user," interested only in what he could get out of Fern.

"He's too slick," Odette said loudly from the adjoining kitchen, "in everything he says and does. When he talks to me, it feels like he's putting on an act. I don't trust him, Fern, and neither should you."

"Uh huh." Fern had given up on arguing with her about him, and had taken to periodically muttering acknowledgements whenever her mother started in on one of her anti-David rants.

She didn't have to wait in the living room. She could sit in the kitchen where her mother was constructing two fresh pies, and listen for the distinctive rumble of her Charger. But she chose not to because she wanted to put literal distance between herself and her mom to accompany the figurative distance she felt in her heart.

While her mother greased and floured two pans and mixed pie filling, she kept up a loud (so Fern could hear her clearly in the next room) running commentary about what was wrong with Fern's boyfriend and how Fern could do so much better if she applied herself. Odette even brought up Fern's past boyfriends and listed how they were better than David and more suitable for Fern.

Which was funny in one of those ways that wouldn't make you laugh, because Odette had never approved of any of Fern's old boyfriends either. Odette's revisionist opinion that Fern's previous boyfriends had all been fine, upstanding citizens was yet another example of her sanctimoniousness. Truth was, Odette had never approved of any of Fern's choices in regards to men, jobs, or anything, until after they were gone or Fern had moved on to something new. Then Odette would criticize Fern's next choice by comparing it unfavorably to the last one, and conveniently forget that she had criticized that one as well.

"He doesn't work," Odette said. "None of his family works, far as I can tell. All he does is sponge off you."

That wasn't really true. David had never asked for money, and Fern hardly ever paid when the two of them went out. It wasn't as if he was borrowing money or using Fern's credit cards. Okay, he had started regularly borrowing her car, and he rarely replaced the gas he used, but that wasn't the same as sponging off her, was it?

"Honestly, Fern, I don't know what you see in him."

Fern thought, *He likes me. He makes me feel good about myself. He makes me laugh. And, oh yeah, he's good in bed.* In fact, his skills at oral sex were unsurpassed. Fern considered telling her mother that.

She thought about saying: *You want to know what I see in him, Mom? He can eat pussy like nobody else. In fact, if eating pussy was an Olympic sport, David would win the gold. I don't know about you, Mom. I don't know when the last time, if ever, Dad took a trip down south, but if a man could use his tongue on you and make you cum so hard you practically have an out-of-body experience... Well, you'd probably let him drive your car whenever he wanted, and you wouldn't give a shit about whether he replaced the gas he used.*

She should say all that to her mother, but of course she

wouldn't. She imagined the reaction if she did: the shocked silence, the wide-eyed look of surprise on her mother's face, the sputter as her mother attempted to formulate a response. The thought of it made Fern giggle.

"What about that cute Reverend Burroughs? There's a rumor that he's dating Celia Brooks, but that might just be town gossip. If you want, Fern, I could invite him for dinner one night."

"Uh huh," Fern said absently.

Odette stuck her head in the doorway. "You want me to invite him?"

"What? Oh...no, Mom. Sorry, I didn't hear what you said. I'm already dating someone."

She turned back to the picture window. Where was he? She wished he would hurry up and get here so she could get out of this god-awful conversation. As her mother went back to her pie preparations, Jethro ambled in the room and walked languidly to where Fern stood. She scratched behind his ears and habitually straightened the red bandanna that was tied around his neck.

Then she heard the telltale rumble of her car's exhaust, the growl it made, like a dragon on the prowl for a fresh virgin to feast upon. It gave her a little shiver of excitement when she heard it, similar to the shiver she felt when David touched her. The Charger came into view and turned into the driveway. David beeped the horn once. It was another source of contention for Odette.

"Why does he have to do that?" Odette asked her. "Why can't he come to the door like a gentleman?"

*Because he's not a gentleman*, Fern thought, which was what made him so good at...certain things. Fern went into the kitchen and got her bag lunch from the refrigerator. She also took two diet Dr. Peppers, said "Bye, Mom," and had her hand on the doorknob when she noticed Jethro still watching her.

"I'm taking Jethro with us," she said to her mother.

She motioned for the dog to follow, and he did. Her mother said something, but Fern was already out the door. She was sure it was more disparaging remarks, so what did it matter?

Fern opened the passenger door of her car and pushed the seat down so Jethro could climb into the back. He got in with practiced ease and put his front paws up on the back of David's seat. He sniffed David's hair.

"Hey, big guy," David said and reached behind to pet him. Content with his greeting, Jethro sat down on the backseat and looked out the window. Fern got in, handed one of the sodas to David, and kissed him.

"How are ya, Cherries Jubilee?"

"Much better now, Strawberry Cheesecake," she said.

They kissed again and Fern shut her door. David backed out of the driveway and headed for the radio station.

"I thought Jethro might enjoy the ride. Just bring him back after you drop me off. My mom's home."

"I'll keep him with me," David said. "Me and the old boy can hang out together while you're doing your work thing. If that's cool."

She shrugged. "Sure."

David liked Jethro. More importantly, Jethro liked David. Fern took it as a sign. Animals and small children seemed to like him. She thought that was evidence that he was inherently a good person.

"So what have you been doing the past few hours?" Fern asked.

"Running a couple of errands. Nothing exciting."

An evasive answer, which Fern instinctively didn't like. She wouldn't press it. It was too nice a day to spoil the mood with a stupid argument. Still it nagged at her a little. Did he go against her wishes and go see Roman? She hoped not. She would almost prefer it if he was cheating on her.

"What's the subject of your show today?" He reached over and playfully squeezed her knee.

"Probably a spotlight on Eric Clapton. All the different bands he was in, then his solo stuff. You want me to open that for you?" She motioned to the soda balanced between his knees.

"No, not right now. I'll drink it later."

Fern opened hers and sipped from the can. She focused on the taste and the small bubbles that fizzed in her mouth. It was an attempt to not think about the sudden gnawing in her stomach that told her David was keeping something from her. Before she could stop it, fear that he might be leaving soon crept into her head. He hadn't mentioned it, but the unbidden thought was there just the same. She couldn't help it. For whatever reason, Fern suddenly thought that her time with David would be ending soon. She had the urge to cry, but she swallowed it down and mustered a smile for her boyfriend.

***

Night had fallen and Drake was alone in his office. The sheriff had dropped him off hours before and Drake had spent the time planning his next move. He surely wasn't going to let the matter drop, nor was he going to let himself be threatened by Roman.

He was in his office. Celia had left an hour before. The radio was on and tuned to the town's station. Fern Wilde was still on the air. It was after eight and Drake knew from experience that she usually ended her show between eight or nine, sometimes ten if she was on a roll. Tonight, she was strangely quiet. She was playing more music than usual and not taking as many phone calls from her loyal listeners. Not that Drake was intimately familiar with the inner workings of the local DJ's schedule and show format, but it was a small town, and like any small town, it was hard not to be aware of everyone else's business.

"Layla" came through the small speaker set up on Drake's desk. He sat back, put his feet up on the corner of the desk, and considered the sermon he intended to deliver the following weekend. He knew the message he wanted to get across. It was going to take all of his oratory talent, energy, and faith to turn these people around and bring the town up into the light where it belonged. He had faith he could do it — faith in himself and in God.

Creel had been strangely quiet, both on the drive to the shapeshifters' settlement and on the ride back. Drake had attempted to draw him into conversation several times, at least to get a sense of where Creel stood, if he planned to side with Roman or not. But Creel had remained tight-lipped. He responded with one word answers and kept his gaze averted. Drake didn't know what to make of it. Was Creel angry? Upset? Ashamed?

Drake didn't waste time worrying about it. Creel should be ashamed for allowing things to go on as long as he did. That was going to change, with or without his help. Drake was going to sway the town away from Roman's evil grasp and bring the entire congregation to the glory of God. His next sermon would be the first volley in his attack.

There was a tap at the back door. Creel? No, he had a forceful knock. It couldn't be Celia either because Drake had told her not to knock anymore. MacDonald had given her a key when she worked for him, and although she hadn't used it since Drake's arrival, he had told her he wanted her to use it again. He trusted her, fully and completely.

He went to the back door and hesitated with his hand on the knob. Was it Roman? No, if Roman was coming for him, he probably wouldn't knock. Drake pushed aside the small curtain that covered the window of the door. He froze at the sight of her, but quickly recovered and opened the door. He didn't say anything, although he had the impression she expected him to. She was still beautiful, but she looked worn and disheveled. Her bare feet were crusted with dirt and the man's shirt and jeans she wore were several sizes too big.

He wondered what had happened to her and felt a flash of sympathy and desire spark deep inside. He stamped it down immediately and said in a voice devoid of emotion, "What do you want?"

"Aren't you going to invite me in?"

He opened the door wider and stepped back. Diana entered, trailing a whisper of her natural forest scent. The scent normally would have aroused him, but now that he knew the terrible truth about her, the scent was more alien than anything else.

She entered the kitchen and leaned back against the counter. Drake shut the door and regarded her. There was an awkward silence between them.

"There's tension now," she said, "but not like before. Not sexual." She smiled bittersweetly.

"What do you want, Diana?"

"Shelter," she said

"You'll have to find that with your own kind."

"You'll throw me out into the cold?"

She flashed her eyes at him. She was trying to bait him, but he refused to play along. He stared at her and waited for her to get to the point.

She shrugged and said, "I can't go home. Roman..." She shrugged again. "Sorry. I must look awful. I borrowed these clothes off someone's line."

"Why can't you go home, Diana? Aren't you one of the leaders of those...your people?"

"I don't fear them. It's Roman. He won't be happy with what I've done, with the fact that I killed a member of the pack to save the life of a human." Her eyes were steady on his.

"Did Roman send him to kill me?" Drake asked. "Why? Until yesterday, I was clueless about what you people were."

"Roman warned me to stay away from you. I didn't, so... I don't know. Maybe he sent Sol to kill you to punish me. Or maybe Sol did that of his own accord. It makes more sense that way. If Roman wants someone dead, he doesn't send someone else to do it. He kills them himself. It's one of the reasons he merits so much respect from the pack."

"Still, you're his sister."

"Yes, and as a female, I don't have the same authority that he commands. Although the pack would never attempt to hurt me, Roman might. He would never try to kill me, but he would want to punish me for killing Sol. He would take great delight in punishing me...hurting me...degrading me."

"Go ask for his forgiveness, Diana," Drake said. "Or go somewhere else. But you can't stay here."

"Why not?" She gave him a look of defiance.

"Because this is a place of worship. A place of God. Your kind doesn't belong here."

"My kind? What is my kind? Doesn't your God accept everyone?"

Drake said, "Not the spawn of Lucifer."

She laughed, a sharp bark of laughter that sounded on the verge hysteria. She moved away from the counter and Drake stepped back.

"You're afraid of me? You think I'd hurt you, after what I did to protect you?"

"I don't know what you would or wouldn't do." He intended to say it without an ounce of emotion, but it still came out with a melancholic tone.

"You think I'm a devil? I'm evil?"

"You're not a devil," he said. "You're the spawn of the devil, from many generations ago. Lucifer created demons and they mated with humans. You're the offspring of that. God didn't create you. The devil did."

Her eyes watered as the words struck deeply, and for a brief moment he felt sympathy for her and regret at what he had said. He quickly shut the door on that train of thought before it could take root. He thought of God and his beliefs, his faith, and he was once again like stone inside.

"You..." Her voice shook and her bottom lip quivered ever so slightly. "You love me. I know you do. I've felt it, in the way you've held me, the way you've kissed me. I've seen it in your eyes."

"I don't love you."

"Yes, you do. You do."

"I don't."

"Say it," she said. "Say you love me. You do love me. Now say it."

"I don't love you, Diana."

"You're lying. You're lying to me and to yourself. Be true to yourself, Drake. Admit that you love me."

"I don't—"

"Admit it!" she screamed.

He said each word with controlled deliberation: "I don't love you. You are an abomination in the eyes of God. I could never love an abomination."

She let out a yell and slapped him. Her nails raked the side of his face. It happened so quickly, her movements so fast, that he barely registered what happened until she shoved past him and ran out the back door.

He closed it behind her. His legs were wobbly and his hands shook from a combination of adrenaline and shock. At that brief moment when she had lunged at him and slapped his face, Drake had seen a glimpse of the wolf. Her face had elongated and her teeth appeared sharper, just for an instant, before it reverted back to human.

It was fleeting, like an animal pressing its face against a fogged up window of a house before turning and running back into the darkness. Drake had to admit, it had been a terrifying sight.

After he secured the lock on the door, Drake went to the bathroom and examined his face in the mirror. There were three scratches that ran down his left cheek. Droplets of blood beaded up along the cuts, and a few seeped out to run thin lines down to his jaw line. The scratches were thin, as if made with a razor blade.

*Those were her nails*, he thought. *Her claws.*

He took a handful of cotton balls from the cabinet under the sink and brought out a bottle of hydrogen peroxide. He soaked one of the cotton balls and gingerly touched it to the top scratch. It burned. He grimaced at the pain, but he kept applying it, on one after another. He let the peroxide soak into the cuts, then dropped the spent cotton and applied peroxide to a fresh one, until he had a wad of pink-stained cotton balls in his sink. He had nearly covered every inch of all three scratches when he looked closely in the mirror. The peroxide was bubbling along the thin lines.

*Clean*, he thought. *Make it clean. Wipe away all the filth from her and make it clean. This is my penance for losing my way, for floundering. God will make me clean again.*

# September

Slade Grayson

# Chapter Thirty-Two

Amber emptied Mrs. Dallway's jewelry box into a pillowcase, then went to the closet and pulled down the second jewelry box that was tucked up on the shelf among the folded sweaters. She emptied the contents of that box, too. Rings, watches, earrings, and necklaces clinked together and coalesced into a mass of gold and silver.

Amber had sent Philo up to the attic to collect the silverware. She instructed him not to take the box, but simply dump it into a pillowcase like she was doing. The silverware wouldn't be sold as a set, it would be sold to be melted down. It might be traced otherwise — the same reason she passed on taking Mrs. Dallway's credit cards. Amber, despite her many flaws, had no intention of making the same rookie mistakes. She liked to think that she learned from her past missteps.

She found some tens and twenties in Mrs. Dallway's nightstand drawer. The money was next to the old woman's handful of ointment tubes, an assortment of Hollywood gossip magazines, and the plastic cup she kept her dentures in. She hadn't tried to hide the cash. Frankly, she probably didn't think her boarders would rob her. But Amber didn't give a damn about betraying anyone's trust. She was skipping out with Philo. Jonas and dickhead David could take the heat for this one. Amber needed as much capital as she could get her thieving hands on.

There was still the matter of hitting Jonas up for money and a ride to the bus station over in Lake Dulcet. Amber would pack the jewelry and silverware in her suitcase, along with any other valuables she could carry. Jonas was supposed to be back soon. Her plan was to get him to drive her and Philo to the station, hopefully long before the old woman got back from visiting her weasel-faced son and his dumpy wife.

Amber pictured herself on a bus with Philo, miles and miles away when Mrs. Dallway came home and discovered her jewelry and loose cash was missing. She would call the sheriff, and Jonas and David would have a lot of explaining to do.

She smiled with a cold satisfaction at the thought. Nobody deserved it more than those two. David with his sarcastic quips and I'm-better-than-you attitude, and Jonas with his disdainful looks and sneer of contempt. She had tried to entice him into fucking her.

She'd thought that if she could get Jonas into bed at least once, the guilt and self-loathing he would experience afterwards would make him pliable. She could get more money from him, maybe even the car. But Jonas wouldn't take the cheese, so to speak.

Amber had even tried to seduce Mrs. Dallway's son, partly out of boredom and partly because she had the idea she might use it to blackmail him later. He, like Jonas, also wouldn't take the cheese.

When he came to visit his mother, either alone or with his pudgy pig-nosed wife, Amber would walk by him in her bikini and throw him looks. He would stare at her, his eyes roaming up and down her pale exposed skin. Amber would smile at him, wink, shift her legs so she sat with them slightly apart, absently scratch her upper thigh...

He would get flustered, but he wouldn't approach her. Not even when Amber was able to orchestrate it so it was just the two of them alone in a room. The weasel would make a useless comment about the weather, and Amber would nearly groan in frustration. Eventually, she gave up and thereafter ignored him when he visited. Sometimes men were just too goddamn stupid to take what was being shoved in their faces.

Philo came in the room with a jangling pillowcase.

"What do you want me to do with this?" he asked in his wet, lispy voice that used to grate on her nerves, but now was only a minor source of irritation, like background static that she had learned to tune out.

"Put it in my suitcase, but pack it tight so it doesn't move around and make noise."

He nodded, but didn't move. He stared at the floor. Amber knew this move. He had a question, but was hesitant to ask.

"What?"

"I was just..."

"What?"

There was a sharpness to her voice. What the hell did the retard want?

"Um, why aren't we going with Dad to California? He's got a big job lined up for us. We been waitin' on it all this time, so..."

*Because I can't take anymore of him and his smug, blond-headed son,* she thought. *Bad enough I'm stuck with a big ugly retard like you.*

"I told you, we need to get out on our own. I don't believe there really is a big job. If there was, we wouldn't be sitting around here for months and months."

"But Dad said—"

"Dad's a con man, remember? You can't trust anything he says."

"Dad wouldn't lie to me," Philo said querulously.

"Whatever. Just do what I tell you."

She had the desire to slap him across his face, a couple of times, hard enough to raise a red welt on his cheek. Her hand itched for it, such that she felt a phantom sting on her palm like she had actually struck him.

He turned suddenly, with the quick abruptness of a child who had failed to get his way, and nearly walked headlong into Mrs. Dallway. Amber swore to herself. She had been so engrossed in her own thoughts and arguing with Philo, that she hadn't heard the old woman come home.

Mrs. Dallway looked at the both of them and the pillowcases clutched in their hands with a confused expression as she tried to make sense of what she was seeing. Philo dropped the pillowcase. It landed with a clatter. Mrs. Dallway stooped and picked it up while Amber and Philo stared.

Like Philo, Amber was frozen in surprise. Her mind raced while she tried to think of an excuse, a plausible story, a believable explanation. Nothing came.

Mrs. Dallway picked up the pillowcase and peered inside. "My silverware?"

Her eyes shifted back and forth between Philo and Amber. She trembled and her lips moved anxiously. Amber thought she looked like a woman who had just received horrifying news, which in a way she had. She received the news that her mind had shielded from her: that her boarders were a bunch of criminals. She turned and hurried from the room.

Philo stood transfixed.

Amber shouted at him, "Stop her!"

She hurried to the hall and saw Mrs. Dallway rushing for the stairs, Philo lumbering behind her. Amber figured she was going to go downstairs and call the sheriff. Or maybe she was going to run outside and yell to the neighbors, "They're robbing me!"

"Stop her, Philo. Do something right for once in your idiot life."

They reached the stairs and Philo reached out one meaty hand to grab Mrs. Dallway. His fingers missed the top of her shoulder, and his hand hit her between her shoulder blades in one mighty swipe. Mrs. Dallway was knocked forward, just a step, but it was enough. She let out an, "Oh!" before she tumbled down the stairs. Amber heard the sickening thuds as the woman fell, then a quiet stillness.

*This did not just happen*, she told herself. *It has to be a dream. Please let it be a dream.*

Amber would have prayed if she believed in that sort of thing. She waited to wake up from the obvious nightmare she was having.

Philo still stood at the top of the stairs, silent and staring down. Amber walked slowly up behind him. She didn't want to look, but what choice did she have? She had to see the damage for herself so that she could somehow formulate a plan of action. The body was splayed out at the bottom of the stairs in the same position as that of a carelessly tossed rag doll.

"She fell," Philo said.

"No shit."

Amber wondered what she was going to do now. Call an ambulance? She couldn't do that, obviously. Not that it mattered. The twisted body, the head set at an unnatural angle, it was clear Mrs. Dallway was dead.

"I didn't mean for her to fall. I was tryin' to grab her." He sounded on the verge of tears.

"Just shut up for a minute and let me think."

What could they do? They could take the woman's car and get the hell out. Get to the next town and get on a bus or a train. Let Jonas deal with the mess and/or fallout. Serve the asshole right.

"Okay, listen," she said.

Philo seemed not to have heard her.

"Philo. Philo!"

His eyes focused on her.

"Go back in her bedroom and get the two pillowcases of stuff, and pack them in my suitcase. Don't worry about packing them tight. Just pack them. Then get the bedspread off her bed and bring it to me."

He stared at her.

"You got that?" *You stupid fuck.*

He nodded and shambled off back down the hall. Amber decided then and there that at the first opportunity, she was going to leave his ass somewhere. She would take all his money and every valuable item he possessed, which wasn't much to tell the truth, and abandon him on the side of the road. Or maybe in a cheap motel room. Or at a restaurant after a really big meal and a killer bar tab, and she would pretend to go to the bathroom, but instead she would keep walking out the door to the car and go, and leave him stuck in a dire situation. Kind of like the situation she was in now.

She went down the stairs and stood over the body, and moaned. But wait, no. Amber hadn't moaned. The moan came from the body. Oh, shit, the old woman was still alive.

This was good, right? She was alive, so it wasn't murder. She could call for help and say Mrs. Dallway tripped and fell down the stairs.

It wasn't a great story. In fact, it was pretty flimsy. After all, the woman lived in the same house for what, fifty years? And she never fell down the stairs before, so why today did she suddenly become clumsy? And what if she regained consciousness? It would become robbery and attempted murder.

The old woman moaned again. Amber slowly knelt, until her

left knee was resting on Mrs. Dallway's throat. She kept going until her entire weight pressed down on the old woman. Her hands twitched for a moment, then nothing. No sound. No struggle. It was surprisingly quick and easy, and Amber thought, *That wasn't so hard.*

She stood up just as Jonas walked in the front door. He saw the body and Amber standing over it, and said, "You stinkin' bitch. What the fuck did you do?"

\*\*\*

David said, "I still can't figure out how this happened."

Jonas shook his head. What was the little shit going on about now?

They were in a patch of woods a hundred yards from a dirt road David had showed them. He had directed Jonas to it, past Fulman Bridge, and when Jonas asked him how he knew about it because it was semi-invisible from the main road, David was evasive. He mumbled something about Fern showing it to him.

It figured. Jonas knew David couldn't have found it on his own, because he couldn't cross the bridge on his own. Jonas knew about David's phobia of driving over water, though he didn't let David know he knew. Someone had to take him there and show it to him.

Even disregarding the bridge phobia, the dirt road was too well-concealed. You couldn't see it by simply driving by. Which was good because Jonas, David, and Amber had come out to bury a body.

Jonas said, "How many times we gonna go over this? Philo knocked her down the stairs."

He and David dug the grave, while Amber held two flashlight beams on the spot. She had been strangely quiet. Jonas had expected her to complain: Complain about having to help, complain that it was Philo's fault, complain that it wasn't hers. Except it was.

"No, I know how Granny died," David said. "What I'm saying is, I don't understand how this happened." He stopped and leaned on his shovel. The flashlight beam caught the thin sheen of perspiration on his face.

"I mean, I was having a nice day. I dropped my...I dropped

Fern off at work. I stopped and had a sandwich at the diner. A good one. Slices of turkey in a pita bread, with lettuce and tomato. Big glob of mayo. Pretty good. Then I decide to stop off at the house for a quick shower. Next thing you know, I'm burying a body in the woods."

Jonas stopped and lit a cigarette off the one in his mouth. He flicked the near-finished one into the hole, then stuck the fresh one in his mouth. He had been chain-smoking since he had arrived home and discovered what happened.

Each cigarette he finished, he let the smoldering butt drop on the ground. He didn't care about traces of DNA or evidence that could link him to the body. Once it was discovered that the old woman was missing, Jonas and the rest of them were sunk. So what did it matter?

People would automatically suspect foul play. Descriptions of Jonas and his family would be spread out all over the country. It was over for them as far as flying under the radar. All because of her.

David had resumed digging. Jonas joined him, surreptitiously observing Amber. She was responsible for this. She had messed it all up for them, just as she had done in the past.

"Couldn't Philo have come along and helped?" David asked.

Jonas said, "Just dig. He's where he's supposed to be."

Back at the house, a forlorn figure, staring at the wall. Jonas figured bringing him would be a mistake. Philo needed to calm down and put distance between himself and what happened. Also, there was another reason Jonas didn't want him here. An idea he had.

Jonas and David dug the grave with two shovels they took from Mrs. Dallway's garage. Jonas dug and thought about Amber: She wasn't his niece. She wasn't his blood. She was the offspring of his brother's cheating wife, and all she had ever done was cause problems for him and his two sons.

"That's good enough," Jonas said. He tossed his shovel to the side and stepped out of the grave.

David groaned. "Thank God." He tossed his shovel next to Jonas's and stepped out. He looked at his hands. "Great. I've got blisters. I told you I wasn't cut out for manual labor. Why did we have to dig such a big hole anyway?"

"Because."

"Oh, well that explains everything."

Jonas waved to Amber to follow them. He said, "Keep the light on us, not the hole." *Stupid bitch.*

They walked to the car. Jonas unlocked the trunk of the Caddy and opened it. The body was wrapped in a sheet and the thick comforter Philo had stripped from the woman's bed.

Jonas took the top half of the body and yanked it from the trunk. Ash from his cigarette dropped like confetti onto the comforter, but he took minor notice of it. His mind was preoccupied with the next step, and the one after, and the one after, and so on until he reached his goal.

He followed all the different paths in his head like a maze. He hit dead ends and blocked passageways. He backtracked, tried another path, until finally he saw the way clear.

"You gonna help me," he said to David, "or stand there with your mouth hangin' open?"

David said, "My hands hurt," but he stepped forward anyway and took Mrs. Dallway's legs.

They carried the body to the grave, dropped it unceremoniously on the edge, and Jonas rolled it in. He lit another cigarette and dropped the old one on top of the body. He smoked and contemplated the situation, shook his head and smoked some more. He stood there for a while, dimly aware of David huffing to catch his breath and Amber holding the flashlights on the corpse.

"Could we just bury her and get out of here?" Amber said. "This is creepy enough without us standing around."

David snickered. "It's funny you talking about what's creepy. With your personality, I could rent you out to haunt a house."

"Oh, fuck you, David! Okay?! Fuck you!"

"No, fuck you. If it wasn't for you, we wouldn't be in this mess. Now we got a murder rap on our heads. You know what that means? It means cops, state police, Feds, newspapers… We just went from being con artists to armed and fuckin' dangerous." He said, "And they'll fuckin' travel to the goddamn Amazon if they have to in order to extradite us."

Jonas was surprised at the anger in the kid's voice. He had been the sarcastic prick for so long, Jonas had forgotten about the other side of him.

"It wasn't my fault!" Amber yelled.

"No. It never is," David said.

"It wasn't. It was your retarded brother's fault."

"If he's retarded, and you're fucking him, what does that make you?"

"Fuck you."

"Not even with Philo's dick."

Jonas smoked. Then he began to laugh. It started as a low chuckle, then grew into a deep belly laugh. Amber and David looked at him as if they thought he might have lost his hold on sanity, which maybe he had, but he still couldn't help but laugh.

It was funny. The whole mess was funny.

He flicked his cigarette in the open grave and laughed. David smiled, and broke into a chuckle. Soon, he was laughing, too, and Amber as well. The three of them laughed until they couldn't stand up straight. Jonas had tears in his eyes and his sides ached.

The laughter subsided and they took deep breaths. The occasional remnants of a laugh came through, but for the most part it had subsided. Jonas casually picked up one of the shovels, swung it in a wide arc, and brought the flat end against the back of Amber's head. He did it quick and forceful, a swing for the fences like he had been swinging a bat against a fastball.

The shovel made a sickening thud against her skull. The impact rang along the long wood handle, up into his arms. Amber dropped the flashlights and fell face first into the hole. She landed on top of Mrs. Dallway's body and was still.

"Jesus, Dad!" David gasped.

Jonas stepped into the hole and brought the shovel up over his head, back behind his shoulders, and brought it down again and again on the back of Amber's skull. If the first blow hadn't killed her, if it had only stunned her, then these blows would certainly do the trick. He particularly thought the last blow had caved in the back of her head.

He stepped out, lit a cigarette, and began to shovel dirt on top of the bodies. David stared at him.

"You planning on helping me?"

David picked up the other shovel, slowly and carefully, like he was attempting to snatch food from a lion's den. Jonas realized the kid probably wondered if he was next.

"It had to be done," he said. "She was trouble. We're better off without her around to fuck up the works. Understand?" When he didn't get a reply, he asked again: "Do you understand?"

"Yeah."

They filled in the hole, then walked back to the car.

Jonas said, "When we get back, we're gonna tell Philo that she ran off. Got it? He'll be upset, but he'll get over it. Deep down, he knows what she is. What she was. He'll believe that she ran out on us."

"Yeah," David said, then quietly, "Jesus."

They walked to the trunk. Jonas opened it again and placed the shovel inside. David did the same, along with one of the flashlights he had picked up from where Amber had dropped them. The other was in his hand.

Jonas rolled his shoulders. He felt the tightness in his back, up into his neck. He wanted to stand under a hot shower and let the water beat on him, let the heat soak into his body and wash away the soreness. Wash away everything. He also planned to take a handful of painkillers when they got back. He couldn't afford to lay up for a day or two with a stiff and sore body. They were going to have to move — fast and soon. David stared at him as if he was no longer sure who Jonas was.

"It's over and done. There's no going back, so let it go," Jonas said.

"The woman was an accident, Dad. But Amber—"

"Amber was a cancer. She was killing our family. She had to be dealt with."

"But—"

"Let it go."

Jonas took the flashlight from him and shined it into the deep recesses of the trunk. He reached in and felt for the latch that secured the panel to the false back. He found it and heard the telltale heavy click as the panel came loose. Jonas removed it.

He pulled out a dark green plastic tarp that was stuffed inside the small compartment and unwrapped it. Inside were several bundles of cash, all hundreds, and a manila envelope filled with fake driver's licenses, birth certificates, Social Security cards, and several passports. There was also a thick rolled up sheet of bubble wrap.

Jonas slowly unrolled the bubble wrap. Spaced apart inside was a revolver, two Glocks, and a sawed-off shotgun. He handed the revolver to David.

"It's loaded," he told him.

David took it, a bit reluctantly Jonas thought. He put the two Glocks in the waistband of his pants, stuck a bundle of cash in his pocket, and wrapped up the remaining money and false identity papers back in the tarp. He reached deep into the compartment and brought out several boxes of ammo. He handed one to David, stuffed the folded tarp back into the compartment, and replaced the panel. It clicked into place. Jonas shined the flashlight along the seams; the panel appeared flush against the back of the trunk.

"The shotgun's going under the front seat. One of the Glocks is going in the glove compartment. I'll keep the other one with me. I don't trust Philo with one, so we'll have to look out for him. Understand?"

"What's with the hardware?" David asked. "What's the plan now? Rob banks? Go on a shooting spree?"

"Kid, I don't know about you, but I'm not planning on spending the rest of my life behind bars." Jonas pulled one of the Glocks from his waistband and held it up sideways, barrel pointing up at the night sky. "This is what's going to keep us out of prison. I'm gonna shoot anybody who gets in our way. They're gonna be looking for us, and I'm not going to go quietly. Got me?"

David stared at him.

"Look, nothing's changed," Jonas said. "We're going to wrap up things here and head west like we planned. We'll probably do something to change our appearance, definitely change our names, get another car along the way. But if some state trooper tries to pull us over somewhere, or someone comes stumbling along and figures out who we are or what we did, I'm gonna put a bullet in their head. And that goes for that shitkicker sheriff and your deputy girlfriend. Got me? We're gonna hang out two more days, then hit the road. So keep it together and keep up appearances. 'Cause I got no problem killing anybody...*anybody*...that might try to send me to prison. Understand?"

The kid was quiet so long Jonas started to wonder if he even heard what he was asked. But David answered after a long moment.

"Yeah, Dad. I understand."

# Chapter Thirty-Three

The scent came in spurts from all over the area. It was heavier in some spots and lighter in others. There was a line of urine, too, that encircled the area where Diana had marked her territory. It smelled fresh. Roman deduced that she was marking it regularly.

Diana was camped far up along the mountain ridge on the west side of Tanneheuk. He wondered why she hadn't kept going into another state, or north to Canada. At first, he thought she might be reluctant to leave, that maybe her plan was to stay away for a short period of time before she came back and begged for Roman's forgiveness. He was her family, after all, and they were her people. Maybe she couldn't leave them as easily as she had initially thought.

Another thought took root in Roman's head. Perhaps she stayed close to Tanneheuk because of *him*. The thought caused a white hot flash of anger to erupt in his mind.

Roman had tracked her in his wolf form. It was easier to travel the distance over the rocky terrain in his four-legged body. Although he could have tracked her in his human form, his senses were slightly more acute as a wolf. The wolf body was designed better when it came to the utilization of the five senses.

Here, he found the spot where Diana had eaten dinner — a beaver, if he wasn't mistaken. Her scent was heavy at the spot next to the mountain stream where she bathed every day. There were a few other spots where her scent lingered stronger than others. She was all over and the scent filled his head with a warm familiarity. He would never admit it, but he truly missed her.

Diana possessed a calming influence on him and was always a perfect sounding board when he needed to think through a difficult matter. By the same token, she was also able to stir up anger and conflict with him just as easily. In either case, he missed her and missed the passion that she could evoke from him.

Cut out of the side of the mountain by thousands of years of exposure to the elements, mostly hidden in the dark of the night, was a shallow cave. Roman thought it had once been a wolf den, and after that perhaps a shelter for a bear. It was abandoned several hundred years before when the wolves and bears migrated out of the area due to the influx of the shapeshifters.

Wolves, bears, and coyotes generally wouldn't live in the same proximity as shapeshifters. They sensed shapeshifters as something odd and scary, something not to be easily identified as friend or foe. Perhaps the wolves and coyotes feared that they might be replaced by the strangely similar, yet higher evolved, life forms. The bears lived in peace with the wolves, but were known to be antagonistic of shapeshifters (and vice versa) as were the lynx and mountain lions. But bears generally had enough intelligence to decide to move on rather than risk confrontation. Whatever the case, the shallow cave had long ago been abandoned. Until now.

Roman shifted back to human form, shook off the few strands of hair that still clung to him, and walked two-legged to the entrance. It was almost big enough to stand up in, and only three feet deep, but it would provide adequate cover from the rain. Diana was in the process of changing back to human. She was wrapped in a blanket and had probably been asleep when she sensed his approach. She came out of the cave, stood, and wrapped the thin blanket around her naked body.

Roman took in her scent, the smell of wet grass and mountain lakes. Something else, something new, underlaid her natural scent. Roman couldn't decipher it.

They regarded each other. The night was cool and a breeze ruffled Roman's hair. He smoothed it back, a reflex gesture at best because he barely noticed the wind or the damp earth under his bare feet, or anything else besides the sight of his sister in front of him.

He tore his eyes away from her and glanced inside her makeshift den. Cans of food were stacked against the back wall, perhaps twenty in all, and a neat stack of empty cans next to it. Most of it was vegetables and canned fruit. Roman took notice of several cans of corned beef hash. Not that she needed it. He was sure she hunted for her meat. He didn't see any bones, but she most likely buried those, as she would eventually do with the empty cans.

A pile of clothes was near the area where she had been sleeping. Some items he recognized as hers, and others he didn't, various items she probably scavenged from somewhere. A few more blankets, threadbare ones that probably wouldn't keep her warm in the coming winter unless she planned to stay in wolf form.

"Are you ready to come back?" he asked.

Diana stared at him with a haughty, defiant expression. He smiled in spite of himself. He had wanted to play the role of the displeased, yet benevolent ruler. His plan was to allow her to come back. He would feign anger and disappointment in her actions, then once he determined she had spent a sufficient amount of time wallowing in her shame, he would grant her absolution.

But he spoiled it by smiling. Or rather, she spoiled it when she stood before him with a bearing that proclaimed she was a queen and a look that said she would challenge anyone who dared to question her royal lineage. It was so...so like her. He realized now how much he had truly missed her looks, her expressions, her very presence. He couldn't possibly stay angry at her, even in the face of her relationship with the minister, or the fact that she killed one of her own people to protect him.

Roman had missed her. He couldn't help himself. He had to smile now that she was there in front of him, as regal as ever.

"I'm not going back," she said. "I'm fine here."

Roman made a show of looking around. He didn't try to hide the small sneer of his lip that said he found her living conditions distasteful. He wanted her to know how far she had fallen, in his opinion.

"Not quite befitting an Alpha female, wouldn't you say?"

She didn't answer. Her chest rose and fell beneath the blanket. Her breathing was quick, a sign that she was anxious.

"Leave your rags and food scraps. Come home. Eventually,

everything will be as it was. They'll forgive you in time. You're the Alpha. They don't have a choice."

"And you?"

"You're my sister. Of course I'll forgive you. In time."

"Why did you order Sol to kill him?"

Roman let out a yell of exasperation. "You want forgiveness?!" he shouted. "Then don't speak to me of your human lover!"

"I didn't ask for forgiveness," she said calmly. "Nor have I asked for you to find me and offer me the chance to come back. I simply asked why you ordered Sol to kill him."

Roman huffed and turned away. He had the urge to change to wolf form and leave her. Why should he deign to answer her? He needn't answer to anyone. He was the Alpha male, the ruler, the emperor of a pack of gods.

"You want to know why?" he said suddenly and whipped back to face her. "Because it was an embarrassment. Because I told you repeatedly to stay away from him, and you repeatedly defied me. Because you couldn't control yourself and you degraded yourself by continuing to..." His throat tightened and cut off his words. He willed himself to relax. "I told Sol that if he found the two of you together, that he should wait until he was alone, and then make sure it was the last tryst the two of you shared. I didn't specifically say to kill him."

"What did you think Sol would do?" she asked. "Did you think he would have a talk with him? You knew Sol was a killer. You knew what he would probably do. Sol was always cold and emotionless when it came to the humans. He referred to them as cattle."

"I didn't know Sol would try to kill him."

"You might lie to the humans, brother," Diana said. "And you might lie to our people. But don't you dare lie to me."

His face flushed.

"Tell me the truth," she said.

"Fine," he said through gritted teeth. "I ordered Sol to kill him. I would have done it myself. I wanted to do it myself. But I knew if it was me, you would never forgive me."

"But why? Just to hurt me?"

"No, my sister." He stepped close to her. Her scent was thick in his nostrils, and again he smelled something different. Something different...yet not.

"It was not my intention to hurt you. It was my intention to save you from yourself. Can't you see? Can't you see what you were doing to yourself? To us?"

Diana laughed bitterly. "You sound more like a jealous husband than a sibling. But then, that's what it's really all about. Isn't it, brother?"

"Don't speak those words to me again," he said, his voice as hard and unyielding as iron. The anger flared up in him, along with another feeling that he loathed to acknowledge. It was lust.

"Do you deny that you want me?"

"Yes," he answered.

"Your body betrays you."

It was true. His loins stirred and his heart rate increased. He grew hard. The fact that she was right, that he did indeed desire her, only made him angrier. Roman slapped her. Her head snapped to the side. She returned a look of contempt. He backhand slapped her and she lost her composure. She beat at his face and head with the flats of her palms until he caught her arms.

Diana tried to break free. Her teeth were bared and she fought with all her strength. Roman struggled to hold her. He managed to push her back against the rock wall next to the cave entrance. He released her left arm, but his other held her right arm up as if they were engaged in a dance. Roman rubbed his head against hers, then down along her neck and chest. He bunted his nose against her and made snuffling sounds. His erection rubbed against her thighs.

Diana thrashed at him with the fist of her free hand, but she fought against an unstoppable force. He hardly felt her blows. She was beating against years of lust and desire; she may as well have battled the wind or the rain. It was coming, and nothing could be done to stop it.

Roman lifted her leg up and thrust himself between her thighs. Diana screamed, "No! No!"

He smelled it again, the familiar (yet not) scent that mixed with her natural body odor. With her vagina exposed, it came stronger. Suddenly, he identified the smell. Roman released her and stepped back. The lust was wiped away as quickly as his faded erection. He

Slade Grayson

stared at her in horror.

"You...you're..."

"What, brother?" she asked. She panted for breath. Parts of her body were mottled red from where he had grabbed and pressed against her.

"What have you done?" His voice was filled with disgust.

"What's wrong? Don't you want me anymore?"

"You're *pregnant*?" The word spit from his mouth.

"Yes. I'm carrying his child."

No longer did he see the beautiful woman that aroused his passion and desire, nor did he see his sister standing before him. He saw an unclean creature, something dirty and defiled.

"You goddamn gutter whore," he said. "You would allow that to happen? Allow yourself to be impregnated by a human?"

"Yes! I'm pregnant! Not by a human, but by a man. A man, brother. He's given me something you haven't been able to give Salacia."

Roman growled. "Watch. Your. Tongue."

"It's true, isn't it? How many times have you been with her? And still, she's barren. Maybe the world will be spared your offspring. Maybe my child will one day lead the pack."

He took two steps towards her, ready to strike. His only thought was to hurt her, make her bleed, put his hands around her traitorous throat and squeeze.

Diana must have sensed his intent because she began to change. Her body shook and rippled, teeth, claws, and snout extended. Roman changed too, and although Diana had begun before him, he still completed his transformation first. He was still the fastest at releasing his wolf side. Even faster than her.

He lunged at her. Diana attempted to defend herself, but she was caught in the intermediate stage of not human, not wolf. Roman had the advantage. His teeth tore at her. Warm blood covered his snout. The coppery smell and taste of it drove him into a frenzy. Diana's claws raked his chest and stomach as he ripped at her with his teeth.

His fury had unleashed his full animal side, and although the rational part of his mind was subverted, there was still a dim corner in the recesses of his brain that registered what was happening. It noted that Diana's transformation was completed, and also that as frenetically as she fought, she was still going to lose. Roman's quicker change worked in his favor, but it was also the fact that he had given himself over totally to his primal instincts. There was no quarter in him, no mercy.

They ripped and tore at each other for an eternity, or so it seemed to him. Diana was ferocious; her teeth clamped on his right foreleg down to the bone. Her claws sliced through his flesh. But Roman felt very little of it. He was caught up in a blood frenzy.

She put up a mighty effort. A lesser person would have succumbed. Even enveloped by anger and hatred, he retained a shred of admiration for her. But he was Roman, the Alpha male. He had defended his leadership countless times. He had total mastery over both his wolf side and human side. He would bow before no one, not even her.

Diana's efforts weakened with her blood loss, while Roman's remained constant. She slowed down, her guard dropped. He instinctually utilized her tactical mistakes against her, and slipped in and caught her throat in his teeth.

She struggled, but it was no use. Roman was locked on. He pushed her down until he was on top. He released his jaws for a split second so he could move in and go deeper. He was in far enough now to cut off her breathing.

He let go when she stopped struggling and her body was limp. He looked down at her lifeless form and experienced regret. It wasn't too late to undo it. She hadn't been dead long enough to stay that way.

The shapeshifter virus worked hard to repair her wounds, just as it worked hard to repair his own. Soon, her respiratory system would kick back in. Her heart and lungs would start back up. Any brain damage she had incurred from the lack of oxygen would be repaired by the healing properties of the virus.

Roman already felt his wounds closing. If he wanted her to remain dead, he would have to ensure her brain damage was irreversible. The only way to do that, without a weapon, was to keep her heart and lungs from restarting.

All of this flowed through his mind in the span of a second. In the next second, he came to the conclusion that Diana would have to remain dead. If she came back, she would never cease trying to kill him. Their fight had cost her the unborn child; he was sure she had miscarried from the severe wounds he had inflicted. That was something the virus couldn't repair. She would hate him. She would want him dead, especially since he had decided that the minister would have to die now.

The decision had been made when he discovered Diana was pregnant. That was something that could never happen again. His bloodline would not be soiled with the minister's children.

No, Diana had to die. His people could not have a king and queen who continuously fought and tried to kill each other. It would breed dissent, and the pack needed order at all times. Better that Diana never returned to them. Better that she simply disappeared. Like their father.

With tears streaming from his eyes, he bent his head down and slowly, methodically, tore out Diana's throat.

# Chapter Thirty-Four

The next morning, Fern stopped by the sheriff's office. When she had arrived home the previous evening, there was a note from her mother taped to her door. The note said Sheriff Creel wanted to see her after she completed her morning paper route. Odette worded the note in a terse script as if it had been barked at her like an order.

Fern figured it wasn't anything serious or the sheriff would have called for her at the radio station during her shift. Still, it was early in the morning, much earlier than the sheriff's usual office hours, so when she opened the door to his office, it was not without trepidation.

Creel was behind his desk with a calculator and a folder of receipts in front of him. The desktop lamp cast it in a pool of gold that washed up on Creel's features. Fern's first impression was one of dreariness.

Her second impression was that Creel had been up all night. His shirt was rumpled and his normally combed hair hung limp over his forehead. His eyes were sunken, or had the appearance of such due to the thick, black half-moons that underlined them. Creel appeared not to have had a restful night in quite a while.

"Mornin', Fern," he said. "Come on in and sit down. Sorry to ask ya to stop by so early. I know ya usually head home and catch a few hours of shuteye."

"That's okay, Sheriff." She sat in the stiff backed wooden chair across from him.

Creel looked at a receipt from the file in front of him, keyed a figure on the calculator, then typed in a notation on his computer. There was a stack of similar folders next to the open one and a full ashtray behind it. Fern had seen him perform this chore in the past, though usually at a later hour. Creel was meticulous about his records and bookkeeping in regards to his carpentry business. He once told her it was the only way he could earn a profit working with a limited client base. He had to keep track of every expenditure.

"Why'd you want to see me?" she asked.

Creel closed the file and pushed it aside. Fern saw the deep lines in his face, as if he had aged a decade in the past few weeks. She wondered what weighed so heavily on him.

He pushed up his glasses and rubbed his bloodshot eyes. He asked tiredly, "How's everything?"

"Okay." She shrugged.

Actually, everything was not okay. David had cancelled on her last night. He had called her at the station and begged off on seeing her after her shift. He complained of a migraine, which was a first for Fern. She had never heard a man use the excuse of a headache to get out of a date, especially when there was guaranteed sex at the end of it.

It was the first time he had cancelled on her, the first night they had spent apart since the night they first slept together. Fern felt the loss; her bed had never felt emptier, nor could she shake the sense of abandonment. She also took notice that he hadn't called her a corny nickname, not even when she called him "Mango Muffin." She expected him to return the serve, or at least chuckle over her originality. Instead, he said he would call her the next day and hung up.

Just like that. Like they were a casual thing. Like they hadn't spent all those nights together. Like they weren't in love.

Creel asked, "Everything okay between you and the Rafferty boy?"

"Sure," Fern lied. "I guess."

She wouldn't tell him about her fears that David was drifting away, either because he had grown tired of her or tired of the town. (Probably both, she thought.) She wouldn't tell Creel partly because she was afraid he would say, "I told ya so."

"You're old enough to fend for yourself, I know," Creel said.

"But I still try to look out for ya."

"I know, Sheriff."

"I just want ya to be careful with him. I still don't trust that family."

Fern waited for him to continue. She figured he hadn't asked her to his office at such an ungodly hour to give her dating advice. Creel lit a cigarette. He took his time with it, reluctant to broach the difficult subject.

"You been keepin' your gun cleaned and oiled?"

"Sure," she answered.

"When was the last time ya did some target practice?"

"Been a while. Why?"

"I'm thinking ya should get a little practice in. Maybe later today, if ya can."

"What's going on, Sheriff?"

"There's trouble coming, I think," he said. "The reverend's got the town stirred up."

"I've heard."

Fern was well aware of Reverend Burroughs's vitriolic sermons against the elders. Not that he called them elders, or even shapeshifters. In his sermons, Burroughs called them "demons and "servants of the devil." She didn't attend his services, but her mother never missed them, sometimes going both Saturday and Sunday, and she would fill Fern in on what she missed. Odette's eyes would gleam as she spoke of the sermon. His words were infectious, and not only Odette had gotten caught up in them, but the townspeople were catching the same fervor.

The consensus all over town was that the reverend was right. Everyone talked about it and everyone agreed. They saw him as a prophet who brought them a message from God. Fern was surprised at how the townspeople, seemingly resigned and apathetic before, had quickly rallied behind a radical idea: Don't obey the elders and to hell with the pact. Secretly, Fern was behind the idea, but the way it caught on so quickly was still surprising.

"The reverend's got them all convinced not to honor the hunt this year, which is stirrin' up trouble at the elders' settlement," Creel told her. "Also, there's been incidents in town."

"Like?"

"Like people refusing to wait on the elders in restaurants, refusing to give or sell items to 'em. The town's become a powder keg, and I feel the pressure building."

"You think it might escalate?"

"The elders are having a meeting today. I think they might issue an ultimatum."

"Maybe we should put the reverend under protective custody."

"No." He waved his hand and shook his head. "They wouldn't make a move against him. Not directly. Roman knows it would only make the reverend a martyr. No, what I think's gonna happen is, I think they're going to make the town choose between them and the reverend."

She thought about it. Creel stubbed out his cigarette and sat back in his chair. The room was considerably lighter as the rising sun penetrated the dusty blinds over the front window. It wasn't quite up, but its unobtrusive light had crept in anyway.

"What are you thinking?"

She answered, "We should back him. I never liked the hunt. I never understood the purpose."

Creel said, "You were lucky, in a way. You were spared having to go through that selection process 'cause of your leg."

"Lucky. Yeah." Fern looked down at her hands.

"Ah, I'm sorry, darlin' I don't know what I was thinking. I didn't mean it the way it sounded. I know you've gone through hell with your leg and all that pain."

"No, Sheriff, it's not that. It's... I know there are people in town who purposely hurt their kids to get them out of maybe being picked. They don't admit to it, but it's not like we don't know."

"I never liked it," Creel said. "Sometimes they go too far and the kid loses a limb or ends up in a wheelchair. And all it does is shrink the pool to choose from. Which means someone else's kid gets shortchanged 'cause of it."

His fingers reached for his cigarettes, but then he must have changed his mind because he brushed them to the side.

"When my car slipped off the jack and crushed my leg," Fern said, "at first, I thought maybe my dad had something to do with it. Like maybe he tried to hurt me so I couldn't be picked. Maybe he came into the garage while I was working and he—"

"Made it fall on your leg," he finished for her. "Yeah, I always wondered about that."

She nodded her head and swallowed. "Except he didn't. I was alone in the garage at the time. No matter how much I've tried to imagine it another way, I was by myself. The car slipped off the jack because I was careless. The truth is…" Her eyes were suddenly filled with tears. "The truth is, my dad never cared enough to do something like that."

Creel stood and came around the desk. He put his hand on her shoulder.

"Fern, your father, and pardon me for saying this, is a damn fool. There were plenty of times when I wished you was my daughter. Still do, in fact."

She said, "I wish I was your…"

The tears came. Creel hugged her and stroked her hair. He kissed the top of her head and said, "There now. It's alright."

But it wasn't. He probably thought she was going to say, "I wish I was your daughter." In truth, she had wanted to say, "I wish I was your wife," but she had chickened out.

She did love David. Of that, there was no doubt in her mind. But her unrequited love for Sheriff Creel had never abated. She loved both men. The love for David was one of passion and sex, giddy and exciting like the kind she read about or heard about from couples who were in newly formed relationships. Her love for Creel was safe. Boring perhaps, and impossible, but safe nonetheless.

It was funny. She loved two men. One was perfect for her, except he was twenty years older and would forever see her as a surrogate daughter. The other man was totally wrong for her, but made her feel sexual and alive. He made her feel attractive and desirable, but for some reason, he was slipping away from her. She was sure of it. David would be leaving soon. Leaving Tanneheuk and leaving her.

If she could combine the two men, she would probably still have a man that didn't love her as much as she loved him. It was funny. Damn funny. She laughed as she cried, while Creel stroked her hair and tried his best to comfort her.

\*\*\*

Drake was in his element. He delivered his sermon about false gods and idols, a particularly fitting theme, he thought, and the congregation soaked up every word. He felt it, felt their love come in waves and the way they hung on his words with rapt attention. Drake basked in their love, which was a reflection of God's glory. Life was good.

He had shaved off the goatee. He still had scars on his cheek – three razor-thin lines that had faded, and he hoped would continue to do so, but they appeared to have healed as much as they were going to for the foreseeable future. The scars were so thin, that in certain lighting they were barely visible. Still, they remained, and he saw them every time he shaved or combed his hair. Three thin reminders of his dalliance with the demon.

He no longer used the sound system in the church. He didn't like the faint feedback it emitted. His voice was powerful enough on its own. It boomed out to the back of the church, which was always filled these days. He looked out and saw the men, women, and children of Tanneheuk.

What he didn't see were the faces of the elders. In the past, it was not uncommon for him to spot one or two of them sprinkled throughout the crowd. Why they came, he didn't know. Curiosity, perhaps, or simply to check up on the people they claimed they lived to protect. But now that Drake's sermons had turned anti-elder and anti-pact, and focused on God and the elders' connection to Satan, they had stopped coming. In fact, Drake hadn't seen an elder in town in days.

It gave his voice more power and his words more conviction. He knew he was having an effect. He was God's instrument; God performed His wondrous work through Drake. Through him, God's power and love shone out over the congregation. Hallelujah.

He finished the sermon with his new customary recitation of steadfast mantras:

"Who are we?" he asked the congregation.

"God's children!" they shouted in unison.

They knew their lines perfectly. Drake had them perform the same rote at the end of every sermon. He saw it as positive reinforcement.

"Who are the elders?"

"Servants of the devil!" they answered.

They were fervent, with the glazed look of devout followers. He had won them over so fast and so easily. He had a talent for preaching, but he was humble enough to know a more powerful force was at work. He wondered if this was how the writers of the scripture felt. Had they experienced the same intoxicating power flow through them as they composed their ordained sections of the Bible? Surely they must have, and praise God for choosing him as a vessel to bring salvation to the people of Tanneheuk.

"Brothers and sisters," he said. He stepped down from the raised platform and walked up the left aisle. He looked into their eyes. "Who do we serve?"

"God!"

"Do we serve the elders?"

"No!"

Some were vehement in their response, while others merely shook their heads. Drake walked around the back of the congregation. Most of them strained to follow him with their eyes as he crossed behind them and began to walk up the right aisle. They twisted in their seats to keep sight of him.

"Do we make sacrifices to the elders?" he asked.

"No!"

"So," he softened his voice for effect, "will there be a hunt this year?"

"No!"

They weren't in unison this time. The "no's" came from all over the church because this last part was a new addition. Also, some of the congregation said it more than once. They said it loud, then several more times to themselves. They repeated it as if it was a word that contained power and repetition would increase it.

"No hunt," Drake said.

"No hunt!"

This was his calling, what he was meant for. He no longer suffered from doubt, nor did he question himself.

"No hunt," he said again.

"No hunt!"

"No hunt!" he said louder.

Again and again, they repeated it back and forth to each other, louder each time, until he thought the walls shook from the sheer force of it. He wanted them to shout it loud enough so the elders would hear it up in the woods. Loud enough that Satan would hear it down in Hell.

"You dare?" The voice cut through: loud, sharp, and tinged with madness.

Everyone was silenced, even Drake who was shocked to see Roman in the back of the church. He had appeared suddenly, as if magically transported there, but that wasn't it. Everyone had been too absorbed in their group recitation to notice him enter.

Drake was shocked, too, by Roman's appearance. His shirt was open to the waist and displayed long scabbed-over cuts down his chest and torso. He was covered with dried blood, too much to be his own, Drake thought, although he couldn't be sure. Sheriff Creel had told him the shapeshifters healed incredibly fast.

Roman also had crusted puncture wounds on his face and neck, deep ones, or at least they once were. They were closed now, but from the darkness of the dried blood, Drake guessed the wounds had once been quite serious and had bled for a long time. The wounds looked like they could have been fatal…to a normal person.

This flashed through Drake's mind in the split second after Roman made his presence known. That, and the frightening way Roman appeared – not so much the dirty clothes and dried blood, but the wild-eyed look he had. He appeared to be on the edge of insanity, which made Drake reaffirm his conviction: The shapeshifters were demons.

"You dare," Roman said, "to dictate to us whether there will be a hunt?"

Roman strode up the aisle towards him. Drake saw people in the pews literally cringe at his passage. Despite their bluster and vocal readiness, Drake realized the townspeople were still very much afraid of Roman and his pack.

Roman came close enough that Drake saw the burning embers of rage in his eyes. He experienced a moment of doubt, of fear, but his faith restored his courage. He would not be bullied by Roman. Not in God's house.

"This is my town," Roman hissed. "These people belong to me."

"They belong to God."

"Don't speak to me about your God. I am a god."

Drake said, "You're a demon. You have no power here."

"No? You intend to stop me? You intend to challenge me?" Roman's voice grew from a snarling whisper to the commanding tone of a dictator. "You come to my town and dare to call me and my people demons, and you think we'll slink away? This town has belonged to my people for generation upon generation, and we will gladly destroy it before we are forced to relinquish it to a false prophet."

"Don't threaten me, Roman."

"Threat?" Roman threw his head back and laughed.

There was something disturbing in that, Drake thought. Roman had always presented an image of composure. Now he seemed partially unhinged. He wondered what had changed.

Roman said, "I offer no threats. What I offer is an ultimatum." He turned to the congregation. "There will be a hunt this year, and you will continue to pay respect to my pack."

"Or else?" Drake said behind him.

Roman didn't turn; he kept his eyes locked on the audience. "Or else we will tear this town apart. We will kill all the dissenters and feast on your corpses."

"Don't you come into our church and threaten us!" Drake was fueled by anger and righteousness, and yes, perhaps a little fear. "We will not be ordered about by the likes of you!"

Drake heard the snarl, then Roman was upon him too fast for him to react or attempt to defend himself. With one hand, Roman snatched him by his throat, while his other hand took hold of the hair on the back of Drake's head. Roman pulled him backwards. Drake tried to free himself, but Roman's strength was unearthly. His hands were like steel. Drake struggled to breathe and fought to keep his balance. He was bent back far enough that he looked straight up at the ceiling. He repositioned his legs to brace himself, although if Roman was to suddenly release his grip, Drake would have immediately fallen on his back.

Roman leaned over him until his face was inches away. Drake saw his features ripple like waves across water. Roman's nose and mouth elongated; his teeth lengthened. Drake was looking into the face of a monster. Roman opened his mouth wide and slowly brought it down, intending to bite Drake's face in half.

Roman was suddenly pulled away and Drake found himself on the floor, sucking in deep lungfuls of air. Roman was mobbed by men from the congregation: Roger Sparco, the owner of Tanneheuk's sole service station; Carl Beardsley, a beefy guy who made his living by refurbishing tractors, and his eldest son, Carl, Jr.; Cal Dennison, the owner of his namesake bar, and his son, Lloyd; and at least four others.

They swamped Roman in a tangle of arms and pulled him back. At least a dozen other men were behind them, ready to lend a hand. Despite the manpower, though, they could scarcely keep hold of him. Roman continued to change and the men that held him struggled against his strength and shifting form. Roman's body tore through the shirt and jeans he wore. The transformation caused the men to lose their grips.

Then Roman changed halfway back to the monstrous form of a man with wolf-like features. It was more horrifying, Drake thought, than being completely in his wolf form. That way, at least, one could forget what he really was. But seeing the creature stop in mid-change stripped away all pretenses of nature and normalcy.

Roman's neck, trunk, and legs were still roughly humanoid, albeit with more hair than normal, but his face was completely wolfish and his hands ended in claws that resembled miniature daggers. He slashed at those around him. Drake heard cries of pain and screams of horror from the children. Carl, Jr. fell back and Cal Dennison clutched his jaw with both hands, blood seeping between his fingers.

Drake stood and pushed himself through the circle of people around Roman. The group had stepped back, but they still surrounded the monster. Drake knew he had to do something before anyone else got hurt.

"That's enough!" he shouted.

Roman growled. Up close, the sight of him was more unsettling. *They truly are demons*, Drake thought. Roman moved menacingly towards him, slightly hunched because his spine was midway between human and wolf. Drake knew what Roman's intentions were: He was going to kill Drake because he saw him as the cause of everything that had happened recently. That was okay, because Drake knew Roman was right. He had been the cause, and he would make no apologies for it. He was prepared to die for performing God's work.

A hand holding a gun forced its way through the circle of men and stopped inches from Roman's head.

"The reverend said that's enough," Sheriff Creel said. "Ya best listen to him."

Roman shifted fully to human form. "*Et tu*, Sheriff?" His eyes stayed on Drake. "Really, I would have thought you were too smart to align yourself with this rabble."

"They ain't rabble," Creel said. "They're the majority of this town, which is to say, most people have come to care for the new minister. And I don't think they'd be too pleased if I let ya rip him to pieces."

Roman slowly turned to face Creel. He looked unblinkingly down the barrel of the gun. His clothes, stretched and shredded, hung on him like rags.

"This isn't the majority of the town in here," Roman said. "This is a small group, comparatively."

"Don't matter. Those that come to his services pass the word on to the others, and they're mostly in agreement. The town is behind him on this, and my job is to protect the town's interests."

"No, Sheriff. Your job is to protect the town. You're not doing that by allowing this insurrection."

"Reverend Burroughs didn't start this. The resentment against your people has been building for a while. He just gave voice to it, that's all."

"I could knock that gun from your hand and have my teeth into you before anyone could move."

"Maybe," Sheriff Creel admitted. "But even if ya did, somebody else would pick up the gun and use it on ya. Or they'd attack ya all at once and probably be able to take ya down."

"Maybe."

"Yeah, maybe," Creel conceded. "Either way, I think ya know this ain't the time or place."

"Perhaps, Sheriff," Roman said. "But a reckoning is coming. You never should have sided with him." He motioned with his chin. "Clear a path."

The crowd parted and Roman walked to the back of the church, his steps proud and purposeful. Drake thought of an emperor cast into exile. He shook his head to dispel the image. He mustn't feel admiration for the creature. It was a soulless abomination, forged in the pits of Hell.

When Roman reached the doors, he turned back to them and said, "You have until sundown to pack whatever you want and leave Tanneheuk. Tell your friends and family. I offer the same amnesty to them, as well.

"But if you stay, you must abide by my condition, which is this: The reverend will be the quarry for our hunt. You must deliver him to the designated spot at the end of Lawson Road within an hour of sundown. If not, my people will destroy this town. And believe me, there will be no mercy."

Everyone, Drake and Creel included, stared frozen and open-mouthed at Roman. When he was through the doors and they had swung shut behind him, everyone began speaking at once. Over the din, Drake shouted to Creel: "Can he really do that?"

Creel shrugged. "I guess we're gonna find out."

# Chapter Thirty-Five

Roman had bathed and changed his clothes, and now he stood on the porch of his cabin. All of the cuts and bites had closed and were fast fading. Very slowly, he was beginning to resemble his old, regal self.

Scattered before him in a large semicircle was the entire pack. He had called for them to gather in front of his cabin, and without hesitation, they had complied. Salacia stood in front with her father. She had been strangely distant the past few months, but Roman attributed it to his own distractions with his sister and the minister.

David was there, too. He had shown up earlier, as he had been since their initial meeting, and Roman had invited him to stay and listen to what he had to say. Although David was a human, Roman didn't lump him into the same category as the townspeople. David was a neutral party, and for some odd reason, he kind of liked the smart-mouthed little human. So he thought it best to give David the opportunity to choose a side.

"My people, I have announcements to make. One is that Salacia is to become my mate, and therefore will be your Alpha female."

The news caused little reaction. Many of them had already learned of their relationship and had probably thought it only a matter of time, especially now that Diana was…gone. The expressions on Mars' and Salacia's faces were the ones he found troublesome. He had expected to see happiness, but Mars appeared pensive and Salacia had a smile that did not reach her anxious eyes. He would have to speak to both of them in private later.

"Our mating ceremony will commence another time, however," he said, "for now we must discuss the festering problem in Tanneheuk. My people," he looked out at the faces of his pack – men, women, both young and old, and a scattering of children dispersed among the crowd – "we are an old race. Not as old as the humans, but an old race just the same. We were once more mighty than we are today. We didn't live in secret. We were a proud race that walked freely among the humans. We were worshipped by them, as rightly we should have been.

"Then things changed. The humans, led by scared religious zealots, banded together against us. They hunted us and drove us into hiding. The last time our people could congregate in public was during the 1500s when a hundred and fifty of our pack leaders met in Constantinople to discuss what should be done. The leaders decided a direct war with the humans would drastically thin their numbers, and it was a chance they were not willing to take. Which is a pity. Had they taken that initiative, I believe they would have been successful. Now, five hundred years later, it's much too late. We are neither as strong nor as many. Our leaders decided we should go into seclusion…hiding. And look what has happened.

"Like a flower that is blocked from receiving sunlight, as it withers and fades in the darkness that envelopes it, so too we fade away. Two hundred years ago, half the world knew our kind existed. Now we're relegated to plot devices for bad movies. Our history has been distorted or forgotten, and we are portrayed as special effects monsters." Some of them nodded as he voiced what many of them had thought themselves over the years.

"The town…our town…has allowed an outsider to come in and sway them away from us. This outsider, this interloper, has stirred them up and put thoughts of rebellion into their heads. He has sown dissent among us, as shown by my sister's actions over the past few months. He is the reason she is no longer with us, and he is the reason we are not given proper respect anymore."

Many of them nodded. No one appeared to disagree with what he said, which is what Roman expected.

"Now, due to the machinations of this interloper, the town wishes to dictate to us that there will not be a hunt this year."

There were cries of outrage among the pack followed by

murmurs and grumbling.

"My people," Roman drew their attention back. "We must remove the cause of this dissent. It has already spread its venom and poisoned the minds of many of the townspeople against us. We must cut out the cause, eliminate it, destroy it, before the damage is irreparable."

Most nodded. The ones that didn't watched him fervently, an indication that although they were keeping their thoughts private, Roman's words still struck a chord with them. The only two who remained unreadable to him were Mars and Salacia. He resisted the urge to frown at them.

Roman looked for David, but he was gone. He hadn't seen him leave, but David's absence didn't surprise him. In fact, he had counted on it. He thought David would probably leave town, but before he did, he would most likely tell the sheriff and some of the townspeople about what he witnessed. Roman wanted the sheriff to know he was serious about his ultimatum, and surely David would warn him about what he saw and heard at the elders' settlement.

He wasn't worried that David, or any of the others in town, would call for outside help. The story of a threat from a pack of shapeshifters was too outlandish. Besides, Roman was sure the townspeople would give in. Where else would they go? Their homes were here. They grew up here. Most of them only had enough money to live on. The majority couldn't afford to leave their houses and businesses.

"This is what I told them," Roman said to the pack, "and this is what we shall do. They must give us a hunt tonight, and they must give us the minister as our quarry. They have until an hour past sundown to comply. If not, we will raze the town."

Mars spoke up. "Roman, destroy the town? Isn't that extreme?"

"No. If they do not comply, then they are outright defying me. Defying us. We can't have that. They have the option of leaving before the deadline. If they stay and choose to oppose our will, we must kill them."

To the pack, he said, "Over the years, many of you have expressed dissatisfaction with our status in Tanneheuk. Many of you have told me privately that you wonder why we are not the ones who live in the center of town rather than the fringe. This is our opportunity to change the status quo. If they defy us, we will use it as our opportunity to remake Tanneheuk in line with what we want."

He felt the approval from the pack…most of them, anyway. He knew the idea of reshaping the town would appeal to them. And so he had played that card last.

"Prepare yourselves," he told them. "Go to your homes and rest and make yourselves ready. As dusk approaches, I may call on some of you for special tasks. For tonight, one way or another, we will hunt."

The pack dispersed. They walked to their cabins, many of them engaged in conversations. All except Salacia and Mars, who seemed more troubled by the news than what he would have expected. He would talk to them shortly and ascertain what their concerns were.

An unfamiliar scent alerted him to a visitor. He spotted the girl as she walked up the path to their settlement, unafraid, as if she belonged there. Despite his recent troubles with the humans, Roman was impressed. He stepped off the porch and approached her. Several of the pack members had also caught her scent and/or heard her come up the path. They started towards her with a hint of aggression in their movements. Roman signaled them to stay away.

He met the girl on the path. She gave him an appraising look, then met his eyes without a trace of fear in her own.

She said, "My name is Maryam. I came here to offer you a deal."

"I'm listening," Roman said.

# Chapter Thirty-Six

Jonas had been up most of the night making phone calls, and had spent the better part of the day chain-smoking cigarettes and drinking bottle after bottle of beer, so when David arrived home, he was snoring loudly on the living room couch. David didn't waste time; he packed a suitcase, helped Philo pack his, and then practically dragged him out to the car. He wished he could have gotten Jonas's gun and the cash he had on him, but he didn't want to chance his father waking up. David decided to make do with what he had – the revolver, the gun in the glove compartment, the sawed-off under the front seat, and the bundles of cash in the hidden part of the trunk. Enough to start a new life with, or at least get a head start on one.

Philo whined once they were outside. David was curt with him for two reasons. One, he was afraid Jonas would wake up and catch him in the act of absconding, which would inevitably lead to the mother of all smackdowns on David's slight frame. Two, David saw Fern's Charger parked on the street in front of her house. It gave him a sharp pain in his stomach. He pictured her inside her house, probably in the shower now, getting ready for her afternoon shift at the radio station. He thought of her warm bed and the many mornings they had spent in it together while Fern had whispered sweet words in his ear. Now he was leaving without a word to her.

But hey, those are the breaks. Right? He thought, *I never promised her anything, never made a commitment to her, never led her on. She should have known it was a short-term thing. I mean, look at me and look at her. I'm cute, funny, personable… I can get girls way out of my league, and in fact, have…quite often, too. Now look at her. She's…she's…*

David couldn't bring himself to think negative thoughts about Fern. She was cuter than he had originally thought, especially when she invested time into it, had her hair done and wore something other than her town deputy shirt and blue jeans. She was affectionate, too, and very sweet once you got to know her.

David pushed it out of his head. He couldn't get soft now, not when all hell was about ready to break loose. He had to get out of town, away from the crazy werewolves (shapeshifters, whatever) and away from his homicidal father.

He got into the passenger seat of the Caddy and told Philo to drive. He tried not to look at Fern's car or her house. He tried not to think about her. It was a struggle, but one he ultimately won.

There was a line of cars on the road out of town, like half the town had decided to leave on a vacation at the same time. *More likely*, David thought, *the rats are deserting the sinking ship.* Word must have gotten out about what was coming. Did Roman tell the townspeople? David couldn't remember if Roman had mentioned that during his speech to the pack, but he wouldn't put it past that prick to march into town and issue a threat.

The whole thing surprised David, in a way. He knew Roman was a dictator-type, sure, but he would have pegged him as a levelheaded one. During his speech, David looked at him and thought, *He's become unhinged.*

The cars moved slowly through Main Street. Many of them were packed tight with suitcases. David and Philo made their way through town and out to the outskirts. The procession of cars moved freer and slightly faster. Fulman Bridge would be coming up soon.

Philo said, "I still don't understand. Why are we leaving Dad?"

"I told you already. That's just the way it is."

"But why? He's our dad."

"Yeah, no kidding," David said. "Look, just trust me on this. Dad's…Dad's not one of us anymore. He can't be trusted."

"It's not right. First Amber leaves. Now we're leaving Dad behind."

Philo kept turning his head to look at David and stopped

paying attention to the traffic. The cars in front had braked and Philo didn't see it. David jammed his foot on the brake pedal and mashed it down. The Caddy screeched to a halt inches from the rear bumper of the car in front of them.

"Jesus!" David yelled. "You fuckin' idiot! Will you pay attention to the road? And stop bitchin' about Dad." In a quieter tone: "And Amber."

Philo was silent for a while. They crossed the bridge. David clenched his fists and stared at the floor. He looked at the floor mat, his shoes, his tight fists, knuckles white on his lap. He looked at everything except the rushing blue water that thundered under the bridge.

When they made it to the other side and were on the regular roadway again, David let out a tight breath and relaxed. His fingers flexed and muscles in his shoulders loosened of their own accord. He vowed one day to figure out the cause of his phobia and see if, perhaps through therapy, he could overcome it. For a man who prided himself on his confidence and ability to manipulate people, the fact that he was so unexplainably afraid of crossing a body of water perplexed him. He wondered if his psychotic father had something to do with it. He could picture Jonas tossing his infant son into the water and saying, "Sink or swim, kid. It's a rough world and you gotta learn to swim with the sharks," and thinking it was a form of tough love.

Not that David recalled any such traumatic episode from his childhood. It was certainly possible, though. Anything was possible. His father had murdered Amber. David had never expected the old man to do something like that. Sure, he was a bastard and all. But coldblooded murder?

The rules of the game had changed drastically, and David had not been given fair warning. He didn't like the fact that he couldn't tell what the rules were and what the playing field was like. When your father kills your cousin, and the town you're living in is about to be besieged by werewolves (shapeshifters, whatever), then maybe it was time to run away and get your bearings.

That was what he intended to do. Go somewhere, probably someplace warm with lots of beaches and pristine water where he could watch the girls in their skimpy bikinis parade by, and get his head screwed back on straight.

Philo said, "I still don't understand—"

"Oh, for the love of God, will you stop your bitchin'?"

"But Dad—"

"Forget Dad. Okay? Fuck him. Just drive. Trust me," David said. "I'm doing you a big favor by dragging your sorry ass away from that town and away from our father."

"We shouldn't have left Dad behind. He wouldn't—"

"He wouldn't what?!" David screamed. "He wouldn't leave you?! I got news for you, Philo. He'd do a lot worse than that if he thought it meant saving his own ass!"

"He wouldn't—"

"Pull over!" David had bits of foam at the corners of his mouth he was so frustrated and angry. Why did his idiot half-brother have to make it so difficult?

Philo failed to react fast enough, so David grabbed the steering wheel and jerked it to the side. They skidded onto the side of the road, Philo with both feet on the brake and attempting to keep them from heading into the brush. The people in the car behind them leaned heavily on the horn as they drove by. David flipped them off.

"Look," he said to Philo, "I'm gonna say this one more time. If you don't get it into your pea-brain that what I'm doing here is for the best for both of us, then you're gonna be on your own. Got it?"

Philo refused to answer. He stared straight ahead and stuck his bottom lip out in what David recognized as his usual pouting expression.

"C'mon," David said. "Let's go. We've gotta put some distance between us and the town."

Philo stared out the windshield. David clenched and unclenched his fists. He really didn't have time for this. Why didn't he leave the idiot behind? Why the loyalty? Was he really going to babysit his half-witted half-brother from now until, Jesus, forever?

"We going, or what?"

Nothing. Anger flashed white hot through David. It boiled up inside him, up to the back of his throat and threatened to erupt. As if he had to vomit, except instead of bile, it would be a volley of harsh words and insults.

"Sometime today?" David's voice was stretched taut, but he didn't yell.

"I don't think we should leave Dad behind. He wouldn't—"

"Oh, for Christ's sake! Get out!"

Philo didn't move.

"Get out! Get out of the car!"

"Here? But—"

David opened the glove compartment and pulled out the gun. He stuck it roughly into Philo's fleshy side.

"Get out of the car," he told Philo. "Get out now or I'm gonna shoot your dumb ass and push your body out. I'll leave you lying on the ground like a big stupid piece of road kill."

Philo must have seen the conviction in his eyes. He got out of the car. The driver's side door was nearly clipped by a passing car. David slid over and shut it. He put the car in drive and pushed the button for the window. It slid down with a grinding hum.

"Amber didn't skip out on you," he told Philo. "Dad killed her last night. He bashed her head in with a shovel."

David hit the gas. Dirt and gravel spat out behind the rear tires as the car fought for traction, found it, and shot forward. He caught a glimpse of Philo in the rearview mirror, standing on the side of the road dejectedly as the cloud of dust and dirt slowly covered him.

David merged into traffic and wondered why the hell he had considered taking Philo with him in the first place. Well, fine, now Philo could go back and confront Dad. Good riddance to the both of them. He was better off on his own. Taking Philo with him was the act of a nice guy. David Rafferty knew he was a lot of things, but "nice guy" wasn't one of them.

Slade Grayson

# Chapter Thirty-Seven

He came to slowly, reaching for consciousness from across a great distance. His eyes blinked open and took in his surroundings. He was outside in the woods. It was near sunset with the sun dipping below the horizon and the shadows deepening. His body hurt, as did his head.

Drake opened his mouth to speak. His lips and tongue were dry and it took a moment for him to work up a bit of saliva. His mouth was arid and he had a distinct metallic taste. The side of his tongue was sore. He realized he must have bit it, but he still couldn't remember where he was or what happened.

Somewhere near the edge of the mountain range, that much he could determine. He was on the ground, sitting upright with his back to a tree. Images were slow to come, but they began to flicker in his mind like a television with a faulty power connection. His memory was sluggish and disjointed.

He remembered being in the church and talking to Sheriff Creel. Creel told him half the town had embarked on an exodus. They were afraid – afraid to take sides, and afraid of what would happen if they did. So they packed what they could and headed out of town until…whenever. Until things settled down to a semblance of normality or until the new status quo was firmly established, *i.e.* the shapeshifters left or accepted their lower rung on the social scale. Or, quite possibly, the people didn't expect to return.

That was half the town, give or take. The other half was split, with fifty percent willing to fight the shapeshifters to protect the reverend and their newfound independence, and the other fifty percent staying inside their homes and pretending it was just another day. Stupid, but that was human nature for you. When the going gets tough, there is always a group of people prepared to stick their heads in the sand and pretend that everything is fine.

Drake was pleased, and relieved, he had to admit, that no one suggested giving in to Roman's demands. Either he had truly touched the town with his staunch faith or they were primed for drastic change. He was probably just the catalyst. The town was ready for the fire of change and Drake had been the match that had ignited it. He liked to think that maybe it was a bit of both.

He climbed unsteadily to his feet as the memories slowly revealed themselves. Creel had suggested he leave town, but Drake had steadfastly refused. Creel became angry, even threatened to put him in cuffs and forcibly take him out of Tanneheuk. But Drake remained resolute. He would not bow down to Roman and he would not abandon his congregation. Despite Creel's anger and sharp words, Drake thought he saw a glimmer of approval in his eyes. He had finally earned the sheriff's respect.

They briefly discussed their options. Creel wanted to arm some of the remaining townspeople. Not that he had enough arms to do so, but he had some firearms in the storage room of his office. Also, he could commandeer the rest from the small sporting goods shop in town. It was Fred Hurley's shop and it mainly catered to the fishermen in Tanneheuk, but he had a few shotguns for sale, too. They were old and dust-covered, for who needed a gun in Tanneheuk? There was no crime, and hunting was forbidden. Hurley kept them for aesthetic purposes, but they would certainly come in handy now. Some townspeople had their own personal guns for when they went on vacation. Creel said he would make the rounds and either recruit the owners, or collect their weapons for those who were willing to fight.

Drake had been against it. He wouldn't advocate violence, not even to protect his own life. He talked to Creel about God and scripture and trusting in a higher power for strength, guidance, and protection. Creel didn't believe in his words, but it didn't deter him from his argument. They had to trust in God. Besides, he doubted anything was going to happen anyway. Roman was too levelheaded to carry out his threat. His people, supernatural though they may be, were vastly outnumbered.

When Drake was sure his legs would support him, he walked between a stand of trees and saw a dirt path that led up into the woods. His natural inclination was to proceed down the slope to where he would presumably come to a road. But up the path he saw a vague outline of a building. A house or a cabin, he couldn't be sure. He trudged up the slope, his boots heavy on the path.

Where was he? It was quickly turning dark and he feared he wouldn't be able to find his way if the light left him completely.

So he had a disagreement with Creel, he recalled, then had the urge to urinate. He excused himself, walked to the back and entered his living quarters, peed, flushed, and washed his hands. When he came out of the bathroom, there had been a knock at the back door. Celia?

No, Drake remembered it was Celia's younger sister, Maryam. He had opened the door and she stood there. She looked... surprised? No, that wasn't right. Anxious was a more apt description. There had been something in her hand – like a black box. He opened his mouth to ask her what was wrong, then... What? It was a blur.

Something had struck him. Maryam. She touched the box to him and the world turned upside down. It was a stun gun, he realized. That's what had happened. She used a stun gun on him. More than once, too, because he remembered trying to get up after the first assault. She had used it again and again until he lost consciousness.

Why? Why would she do that to him? And what happened after? Did she drag him to her car and drive him to this remote area to dump him off like refuse? For what purpose?

He came to the building, up the path and around a slight bend. It was a cabin, and there were more beyond that one. Cabins with people, walking to and fro in the midst of chores. He recognized a few and his blood turned to ice. Drake stopped dead in his tracks when the familiar figure sauntered towards him.

"Hello, Reverend," Roman said. "It's almost sundown. You best start running."

Slade Grayson

# Chapter Thirty-Eight

First thing Creel did when he discovered the reverend missing and the back door open, was call Celia. He thought he caught a glimpse of Celia's sister's VW leaving the parking lot. He wondered if Reverend Burroughs had rushed off with the girl because Celia was in trouble. But why leave without saying anything to him? Celia was unable to explain it either, which made Creel concerned. Something was amiss and his gut told him Roman was somehow involved.

Creel got on the phone. He called his oldest friends and the people he thought he could trust the most. He gave them each a brief rundown and told them where he wanted them to go and what to bring. He reminded them about the elders and if they were forced to engage one of them, to aim for the brain or heart. Preferably both.

Creel would go over all of that with his makeshift posse once he met up with them in person. He would remind them that the only sure way to kill a shapeshifter was to stop their heart and/or brain for twelve to fifteen minutes. After that, their natural healing abilities would no longer revive them or heal their damage. They would remain dead. Fire was a sure way, too.

He got in his jeep and sped to the radio station. He spotted Fern's Charger in the parking lot and experienced a momentary flash of warmth around his heart. No other car was there, not the receptionist's nor the other part-time disc jockeys. But Fern could be counted on to report to work. Bless her heart, she would never miss a shift at the station, even in the face of a major catastrophe.

He entered the station. As he suspected, the building was empty except for Fern, who was playing music and fielding phone calls in the control booth. She spotted him outside the glass and waved him in.

"Hey, Sheriff," she said.

"Fern. How ya feelin'?"

"Better. Sorry about…" She shrugged and appeared uncomfortable.

"Never mind that," he said. "Sometimes it's good to talk to someone. A good cry every now and then does wonders, too."

Fern smiled.

"I cry sometimes just to let off a little steam."

Fern giggled. "Oh, go on, Sheriff. You never cry."

"Sure I do. I cry sometimes."

"Like when?"

"Well," he said, "after the missus died."

Her smile faded and he regretted saying it. She had felt better, was laughing and smiling, and he had to ruin it by bringing up a tragic event.

Fern said softly, "I never knew. You seemed to handle it so well."

"Oh," he waved his hand. "I didn't mean to bring that up."

"No, it's okay. I want to know. Why didn't…at the funeral, you seemed so… I mean, I knew you were hurting, but…you hid it so well."

"Ya mean, why didn't I cry?" Creel said, "I'm not the type for public displays. But believe me, I cried plenty in private. Even though she was sick for so long and when she died, it was almost a relief. So I cried for thinking that, and I cried 'cause she was gone and I missed her."

There was a catch in his voice. He fought to regain his normal stoicism. Luckily, it was practiced enough that he could slip easily back into it. But Fern's eyes were wet and she no longer smiled.

"Now, don't get all misty-eyed on me," he told her. "Go back to smilin' and feelin' good. I like ya better that way."

"Okay." She tried to smile, and nearly pulled it off.

"I need ya to do some stuff for me, Fern. Make some announcements to your listeners."

"Sure, Sheriff. Anything you want."

Creel outlined what he wanted her to say and how often she should make the announcements. He thought again about calling the state police as Reverend Burroughs had suggested, but he couldn't bring himself to do it. What would he say? Tell them the werewolf pack that watched over Tanneheuk might have kidnapped the town minister and was preparing to go on a rampage? Probably not a good idea, not one that would be taken seriously, anyway. Besides, Creel saw this as a town matter. He was the law here and he would deal with the town's problems. He and anyone else he could enlist.

When he finished with his instructions to Fern, he had her repeat it back to him. She did, word for word. When she finished, he kissed her on the forehead.

"That's good, darlin'." He turned to leave. "I'll be in touch. Stay safe."

"Sheriff?"

He stopped at the door. "Yeah?"

"I love you."

"I love you, too, darlin'. Now mind what I said and stay safe."

He headed out to meet with the others.

***

The phone rang most of the afternoon. Jonas didn't answer it. It was the old woman's phone and most likely it was one of her friends calling to gossip or blather about nothing. Jonas could have picked up and made up some story, said Mrs. Dallway was out shopping or visiting someone out of town, but why take the chance of getting tripped up in a lie? Bad enough those two ungrateful bastard sons of his skipped out on him.

David was behind it, of course. No way Philo would come up with the idea of ditching his father. Only David would come up with underhanded, lowdown dirty shit like that. Even took the car, the little bastard. When Jonas caught up to him, he planned to wring his scrawny neck.

Jonas spent the afternoon stripping every valuable item he could from Mrs. Dallway's house. He packed it all in her car in the garage, including the jewelry and silverware that Amber had originally planned to steal. He waited for it to be fully dark before he planned to leave. He didn't want to take the unnecessary risk of being spotted driving out of town in the old woman's car. It would be too suspicious, especially in a tightknit community, and Jonas wasn't about to make a rookie mistake. Especially now that he faced multiple life sentences, maybe even the death penalty, although he wasn't sure if Montana had the death penalty. To him, life in prison was a death penalty.

Dusk arrived. Streetlights came on and a few neighbors put on their porch lights. Jonas readied himself.

He would go to California first, put together a crew, and pull off the big con he had planned for the better part of a year. Then, most likely, he would screw his partners out of their shares. There was no loyalty among thieves or con men. After that, he would search for David and Philo. He wouldn't kill David, but would certainly beat him until he wished for death. Probably leave him somewhere destitute and broken. It would serve the little shit right.

He wouldn't hurt Philo; he knew he wasn't to blame. He would grant Philo forgiveness and allow him to come back into the fold, which is what Philo probably wanted. Philo was, Jonas was sure, probably giving David a hard time about leaving him behind. It made Jonas smile…barely.

He took two cans of kerosene and a small can of gasoline that he found in the garage and spread it throughout the house. The kerosene covered much of the downstairs. He spread it liberally on the carpet and drapes, and anything else he thought would burn quickly, including the couch and chairs. Each room received a generous amount. The gasoline went to the second floor, with a trail up the stairs and into the master bedroom where Jonas drenched the bedspread and curtains.

His plan was to light a fire as he left, and by the time he was on his way out of town, the whole house should be one big bonfire. Once the local yokels finished sifting through the ashes, Jonas would be far away. He would switch cars. Probably buy some nondescript heap somewhere. Once he got to California, he would buy a car more suited to his tastes. The idea was, inconspicuous but comfortable.

He heard a sound down in the living room. David and Philo?

Jonas actually had a momentary surge of happiness. He was

glad they had come back for him. Almost immediately his happiness was replaced by a sense of self-loathing because he knew it wasn't them, and he hated himself for wishing that it was.

It was the old woman's son and daughter-in-law. He heard their voices.

The son, Barry, called out in a weaselly voice, "Mom? You here? We've been trying to call you." In a lower tone, Jonas heard him say, "Maybe she's at the neighbors."

He heard Barry's wife say something, but he couldn't make it out. He heard the next part, which was, "I hope that girl isn't here," referring to Amber.

Jonas was well aware of the tension Amber caused. He had seen her walk around in her bikini in front of Barry, who obviously couldn't help but stare at her pale freckled body. Barry's wife was on the plump side and wasn't a very pleasant person. Barry always sounded like he was asking a question in everything he said because he lacked confidence. His wife sounded like she was constantly nagging him. Which she probably was.

Point was, Jonas understood why June didn't like Amber and why she hoped Amber wasn't around. Nobody likes it when their spouse, no matter how wimpy and pasty-faced they may be, looks at a member of the opposite sex.

He decided to put in an appearance. As he came down the stairs, he heard Barry make a comment about the kerosene everywhere. He was going for the phone in the kitchen. Jonas pulled the gun from his waistband and pointed it at him. June gasped and put a hand on her husband's shoulder. Barry saw the gun, too. His mouth made an "o" shape, but no sound came out.

Jonas walked to them and brought the gun to within inches of Barry's jowly face. "I'm only going to say this once, so make sure you listen. There isn't going to be any screaming or calling for help. No running, either, and no talking. Just the two of you doing what I tell you. Got it?"

"Yeah. I—" Barry started to say.

"No," Jonas said firmly. "No, no, no. We're already off to a bad start. I told you, no talking. Got it this time?"

The two of them nodded their heads.

Jonas directed them up the stairs to the bedroom he had, until recently, been occupying. June's legs were trembling, and he had the urge to tell her to relax, to reassure her everything would be okay. He shook his head and wondered what the hell was wrong with him. Why would he lie to them at this point?

Barry and June walked in front of him, the slow zombified shuffle of the condemned. They were both pale, monochrome… every ounce of color had been leached from their skin. Jonas found himself fascinated by it. He observed them impassively as they entered the bedroom. He motioned for them to get on the bed. The smell of gasoline was strong.

They sat on the edge. He motioned for them to lie down. Barry laid stiffly on his back. June laid on her stomach, her head turned to the side so she faced Barry. Interesting, Jonas thought, then considered what to do. Tie them up? What would be the point of that? Lots of work on his part. Plus, he was going to set the house ablaze. Would that be humane? To let them burn to death? No, Jonas knew what he had to do, the humane thing to do.

"Is my mother okay?" Barry asked.

"She's fine."

Jonas yanked the pillow out from under his head, placed it between Barry's face and the barrel of his gun, and pulled the trigger. There was a muffled pop and June whimpered. Jonas quickly shifted it so the pillow was over her head and pulled the trigger again. He did it fast before either of them could cry or scream or beg. He wasn't in the mood for that.

Feathers from the pillow drifted in the air. It made him think of snowflakes, big ones like you see up in the mountains. He tried to think of the last time he went for a walk in the snow. *A long time ago*, he thought.

What the hell had happened? Twenty-three years of living the con artist way and never a moment of violence. Now, four deaths in twenty-four hours. Jonas sat on the floor with his back against the wall, knees drawn up to his chest, and the gun still in his hand, but hanging loose and forgotten. He strained to figure out how it all turned out like this. How it all turned to shit around him.

# Chapter Thirty-Nine

*I'm a bad man*, David told himself. *That's all there is to it. I was born bad, raised bad, and I'll always be bad.* There was no use trying to change now.

He sat at the counter in the rundown diner he and his so-called family had stopped at all those months ago. As the sun sank below the horizon, business, which had been dead when he arrived earlier that afternoon, steadily increased. The waitress, Beth Ann, had been right: After dark was their prime time.

Beth Ann was on duty, along with two other women who appeared to have their best days behind them. The clientele was mostly truckers, either headed for the interstate or headed for Lake Dulcet. There were some teenagers, too, though not from Tanneheuk. David could tell because they weren't maimed, crippled, or shell-shocked looking. Plates of greasy, burnt food passed to and fro, and the truckers devoured it greedily. The teens were more interested in gossiping and sucking back soda than eating.

David sat two stools down from old Clem. He was starting to think the old fossil was surgically attached to his seat. He hadn't even seen the old man get up to piss.

Maybe he was once like David. Maybe he ran out on a girl and stopped at the diner to try and talk himself into the fact that he did the right thing. Much like David, maybe he found he couldn't work up enough lies to tell himself. So he just stayed and stayed. Like David seemed to be doing.

He had come in earlier, sat down, and ordered a grilled cheese and a Diet Dr. Pepper. He told himself he was just stopping for food before moving on, but the soda got him thinking about Fern. Except that wasn't quite true. He had already been thinking about her. He had been thinking about her nonstop since he made the decision to cut and run.

What the hell was wrong with him? Was he really in…?

No, he couldn't bring himself to even *think* that word. He was afraid if he did, it would make it real. He couldn't be in love. Not with her. Maybe a rich supermodel. That he could understand. But Fern? No.

A guy like David would never fall in love with a perpetually stoned, small town, unsophisticated, tomboyish, plain-looking woman. No way. Not even a Plain Jane who lit up every time she saw him. And made sure she got him a soda when she got herself one. And gargled with mouthwash first thing after she smoked a joint because she wanted her breath to be fresh so she could kiss him. And once picked a small flower and gave it to him, and he almost made a snide comment about it, but then saw her face and saw the affection she intended the gesture to convey, so he took the flower and laminated it and put it in his wallet where it still resided, even now, so why the pretense that he didn't care about her?

*I'm a bad man*, he told himself again. *I only look out for myself. I leave pain and misery wherever I go. I care nothing for anyone else. Mothers and fathers warn their daughters about me. Fiona Apple writes songs about guys like me. I'm bad news and trouble rolled into one smooth-talking package.*

He had long since paid the check and it had been a while since one of the waitresses had asked if they could get him something. Now they ignored him while they scurried to serve the truckers.

David looked at his reflection past his empty soda glass, through the pie display case, and in the mirror that lined the wall of the kitchen. *Look at you, you goddamn schmuck.* His fingers went to the necklace around his neck and absently stroked the small silver ankh.

"You should go get her," said a voice that sounded like liquid sandpaper.

"What?" David looked at Clem. "You say something?"

"You should go get her. That girl you been stewin' over."

Clem's face turned to David. He looked much older than David had originally believed. He didn't have wrinkles as much as he had checkered lines crisscrossing his face. Two red-streaked eyes like over-boiled eggs floating in murky water regarded him.

"What the fuck you talking about, old-timer?"

"Kid, you got that look on your face that only comes from worryin' about a woman. You musta left one behind somewhere, and I'm telling you to go get her."

"You think so, huh?"

The old man shrugged and turned back to the coffee cup Beth Ann kept filled.

*Crazy old fucker. What does he know? Older than dirt. Probably hasn't had a woman since Moses smashed the first set of the Ten Commandments. He thinks he's going to give me advice?* David fingered the ankh.

"Ah, hell," he said and got up. He headed for the door, then turned back and snatched the five dollar bill he had left for a tip. Fuck 'em. He'd never eat in this dump again, so who cared if he stiffed them?

He got in the Caddy, started the engine, and roared out of the parking lot, nearly sideswiping a semi that was pulling in. He raced down the road and took the turn for Tanneheuk. The old man, Clem, had said something as David headed out the door. What was it?

It sounded like, "Watch out for the wolves." That couldn't be right, could it? Did the old man know about the shapeshifters? David shook his head. He probably said something else and his imagination twisted the words around.

When he was close enough to pick up the signal, David turned on the radio. It was preset to the Tanneheuk station. Paramore's "Misery Business" was playing. Trees whipped by, faster and faster. David pushed the speed. He knew there wouldn't be cops with radar guns lying in wait. Also, traffic had died out. Anybody who had the idea to leave town had already done so, and everyone else was set for the night. And nobody was heading into town, except him.

He pushed the buttons and the windows slid down. Wind howled through the car. He turned up the volume on the radio. The song ended and Fern came on. She said something about folks staying indoors, keep their doors and windows locked, and to listen to the station for further instructions. David didn't care what she said. He was just happy to hear her voice.

"Hang on, Sugar!" he yelled out the window. "I'm coming for you!"

Then he saw it up ahead – Fulman Bridge. David stood up on the brake pedal. The tires squealed and left a good forty feet of rubber before the car came to a dead stop. The bridge. The goddamn bridge. David wanted to scream in frustration.

***

She was set. She was sure of it. Pretty sure, anyway. As sure as she could be after all her months of preparation. Today had been the most important part: the abduction of Reverend Burroughs, which Roman had sent one of his minions to assist her with. Maryam had used the stun gun, a loan from Roman, which made her wonder why he had such a device and what he could possibly need it for. Whatever, she didn't question it. She simply accepted it and promised to give it back. At some point, anyway.

The man Roman ordered to go with her and help transport Burroughs' unconscious form was a twitchy, brown-haired, scraggly bearded man who didn't speak a word during the entire road trip to the church and back. Maryam wondered if the man could speak. She supposed she would find out once she became a member of the pack.

Maryam was excited, and anxious, and yes, maybe a little scared, too. But that was okay. Maryam wasn't the type to freeze up in the presence of fear. On the contrary, fear sharpened her mind and enhanced her reactions. She became more attuned to her body and environment when she was afraid. Fear worked to her advantage.

She was ready. All week she had collected her urine in the plastic bottles. Then this morning, she poured it over various areas around the hunting ground. She knew the route she would take, so she purposely scattered her scent in opposite directions. Also, Maryam had done so many practice runs over the last six months that the entire area was flush with her scent. The wolves would find it difficult to pinpoint her location. Many of them would be running in circles.

She smiled at the image. They might be angry about how she tricked them, but it wouldn't matter. She would join them, be one of them, and they would have to accept her.

She waited at the end of Lawson Road. No sheriff escort, and it was hours before midnight. This hunt was different than the others, but that was okay. Roman had agreed to it, had agreed to the whole deal as a matter of fact. She offered him what he wanted in exchange for what she wanted. All that was left was the ironing out of details.

Maryam looked at the sun. There was a line of orange and yellow at the horizon. The sun was almost gone. Maryam was supposed to wait until it was completely dark before she began her run. She decided to go anyway. So what if she was a few minutes early on her start time? If she had intended to play fair, well, she probably wouldn't have a chance in hell of winning, would she?

\*\*\*

Not the bridge. He couldn't be stopped by a fucking bridge. This was comical. David stood outside the car and stared at the concrete causeway ahead of him. He heard the roar of the river thundering underneath the bridge. It was like the snore of a slumbering leviathan. He thought of it that way, too, like the water was a giant snakelike beast that couldn't wait to snatch him into its black jaws. The headlights of the Caddy didn't reach it, but he sensed the blackness roiling underneath the bridge. Damn it.

The windows were down and the radio blasted into the night. David waited for something. Inspiration, maybe. Maybe a miracle. Like if he stood there long enough, the bridge would disappear and there would be just a road. He could drive in, snatch Fern, and drive back out again. They could live happily ever after.

Yeah, right.

"Fuck," he said.

It was dark. The sun was completely down. It was now or never. Songs streamed from the radio. Puddle of Mudd went by, as did Scissor Sisters, Gavin DeGraw, and Molly Hatchet. David wasn't sure what Fern's theme was tonight, nor did he much care. All he cared about was how the hell he could get across that bridge.

The song started, familiar in its refrain. It was Elton John's "Saturday Night's Alright (For Fighting)."

"Okay," David said. He paced back and forth alongside the car. "Okay."

He listened to the song. It soaked into his head and filled his mind and body. It energized him.

"Okay. Okay. Okay." He said it each time just a little bit louder than the last, until he was screaming it. "Okay!"

He jumped into the driver's seat, put the car in reverse, and mashed the gas pedal. The car shot backwards. He hit the brakes, yelled, "Okay!" one final time, put it in drive, and floored it. He smacked the volume button until the song was an explosion of sound in the car. David yelled the lyrics along with Elton.

The car shot out onto the bridge. His hands gripped the steering wheel, his knuckles white and his muscles taut. Sweat broke out on his back and the back of his neck.

"Don't give us none of your aggravation!" he yelled. "We've had it with your discipline!"

The end of the bridge was in view. He saw good old terra firma under the concrete pillars now. He relaxed and eased up on the gas.

Suddenly, trees were falling, two of them, one on either side of the road. They were big, massive things with branches as thick as beer kegs. They fell together, synchronized, one toppling to the right and one to the left, and they were going to cross in front of his car. The road would be blocked and David would be stuck on the bridge.

He slammed the pedal to the floor and the engine screamed. *Come on, come on, come on,* he mentally pleaded. For a split second, he thought he might not make it. The trees were nearly on top of him and he thought he and the car would be flattened. *This is how I'm going to die.*

He squeaked through, barely. He made it under the first tree and just missed the trunk of the second. The branches caught the car and made a huge smacking sound on the roof and trunk, like a giant wooden fly swatter attempting to squash a tiny metallic bug. The back window exploded and the back end of the car was driven down. He heard the crunch of the metal when the tree dented the trunk.

*Dad's going to be pissed I fucked up his car*, David thought, and laughed out loud. In the rearview mirror, shadowy figures crawled around the stumps of the fallen trees. Bastards cut the trees down to block the road. He wondered if it was the townspeople or Roman's pack.

His gut told him it was the pack. But were they trying to keep people from getting into town? Or getting out?

# Chapter Forty

He hadn't run since… when? College? He wished he had stayed with it. His lungs burned, his legs ached, and he had the overwhelming inclination to vomit. Unfortunately, he couldn't spare the time to stop and do it. They were coming for him.

Drake's first instinct was to run back down the dirt path, thinking it would lead him to the main road, but Roman said they were coming for him as soon as the sun set. He thought the road might not be a good idea after all. For one, he wasn't sure of the distance back to town. He remembered when Creel had brought him to the elders' settlement. The drive hadn't seemed overly long, but he remembered there wasn't much traffic that passed them. Also, he hadn't paid much attention to the mileage because he spent the time thinking about what he was going to say to Roman.

What was it? Five minutes? Ten? He wasn't sure. He knew, though, that running down a road with a pack of wolves behind him was not the soundest of ideas. It would be too easy to follow him, like an action movie where a man is chased by a speeding car and decides to run down the center of the street. That sort of behavior never made sense to him. So instead of staying out in the open and running in a straight line, he thought the cover of the trees and a zigzag pattern would help him evade his pursuers.

It wouldn't matter, though. They were faster and stronger, and their senses were more attuned. He was sure they could hear the noise as he crashed through the brush, and they could easily follow his scent. Sweat dripped from him and left a trail that any animal could follow. He was sure, too, that Roman had lied. They wouldn't wait for sundown to begin the chase.

Roman had told him to run, that if he stopped or couldn't elude them, that they would kill him. Not just kill him, but tear him to pieces like any other prey.

"Where am I supposed to run to?" he had asked in a voice he fought to keep steady.

His mind raced. Was Roman bluffing? Was this an elaborate ruse to frighten him and possibly convince him to bow down and renounce his position?

Roman answered, "It doesn't matter where you run to, Reverend. We're going to catch you. Doesn't matter if you run back to town or away from it."

"Aren't you supposed to give me a destination? The river?"

"The river isn't far from here," Roman said. "But your run isn't part of the pact. In fact," he shrugged, "there is no pact anymore. You convinced the town to break it."

"It was unholy. Evil. I only told the people to do what was right in the eyes of the Lord."

"I'm glad you feel that way, Reverend. Your faith can carry you through the next hour, maybe more, depending on how fast you run and how determined you are to keep living. But rest assured..." He smiled. "We will catch you."

"Just do it now. Kill me now, Roman. I'm not afraid. If it's God's will, then so be it. Killing me won't change the fact that the town's eyes have been opened to what you really are."

Roman laughed. "What, demons? Is that what you call us? Reverend, you might believe yourself to be a martyr, but all you really are is an agitator. Once you're gone and we've gnawed your bones down to dust, we'll make a new pact with the town. A better pact. One that benefits us the most."

"You won't get away with this."

"Of course we will. Even your God won't stop us." He looked at the strip of red that bordered the horizon and the darkened sky. "It's time for you to go now. Run. Or you can stand there with your moral indignation and your ancient beliefs and allow us to kill you. Which will it be, I wonder?"

He ran. It wasn't that his faith was shaken or his beliefs

shattered. It was that he was born with the innate human desire to survive. He couldn't stand still and allow himself to die a violent death any more that he could have stood calmly and quietly in front of a firing squad.

He removed his clerical collar as he ran and loosened his shirt. The night air was cool with a hint of dampness, but still he sweated from the exertion and the fear. He heard the howl of the pack behind him.

Was Roman leading them? He immediately thought that they sounded too close to have really given him a head start. Maybe they did and he simply couldn't compete with their four-legged forms and heightened senses. His trek took him uphill and down.

At first, he ran without thought, desperate to put distance between himself and the elders. Then he considered strategy. He ran serpentine. He headed away from the town and headed for the direction of where he thought the river ran.

Drake stopped for a moment. It was a mistake; he knew it immediately. His legs shook and he gasped for air. It would be tough getting his body to respond to the command to run again when every fiber of his being wanted to double over and suck in oxygen.

Vague shapes were visible through the thicket of trees. He knew what they were. They were the hunting party, and they loped easily through the darkness in his direction. They would catch up in minutes. He hadn't thrown them off his trail and he hadn't managed to lose them. He ran again and mentally recited a prayer. His faith was unshakeable; he knew whatever happened, it would be God's will. But he still didn't want to die.

His legs and lungs screamed. His heart tried to pound a hole through his ribcage. The most he had ever run in his life was four miles, and that was so long ago... How long could he keep going?

Conceivably, it should be possible to run for hours and hours. People ran marathons. Could he run twenty-six miles? Didn't marathons originate because a messenger in ancient Greece ran twenty-six miles to warn a town of an impending attack? As Drake recalled, the messenger dropped dead as soon as he delivered the message. He wondered how far the messenger would have run with a pack of large wolves chasing him.

Drake wouldn't make twenty-six miles. They were close, and quickly closing the gap. He had minutes left. He topped a ridge and looked down on the river. It rushed by in a fury, black and violent, too wide and too powerful to traverse. He would drown if he tried, but what other choice did he have?

He turned back towards his pursuers. They were mere feet away and in a semi-circle formation that left him no room for escape. A black wolf weaved among them. The other wolves deferentially gave him room to pass. The wolf stood up on its hind legs and simultaneously transformed into human form. Roman shook off the excess fur and smoothed his hair back behind his ears. His smile was one of smugness.

"Congratulations, Reverend. You made it to the river. Generally, that would mean you were safe and had beaten the pack. Of course, the hunt usually starts far from here, which makes it much more difficult for all concerned parties. What we did here didn't follow any of our pre-described rules."

"What was this, then? Just a big game?"

"Maybe some of us simply like to play with our food."

He stepped forward until he was within reaching distance of Drake. His eyes were bottomless. All trace of humanity was wiped away. The veil had dropped and all Drake could see was the savage animal that wore a human suit.

He reacted from survival instinct. He punched Roman, first with his left fist, then with his right. Roman's head rocked back and forth from the blows, but he stood his ground. His head turned back to face Drake, one eyebrow raised.

"Really? This is what you resort to, Reverend?" A line of blood slipped from the corner of Roman's lips. "You made me bite the inside of my mouth."

He wiped it with his middle finger and held it up to study it in the moonlight. He looked from the blood on his finger to Drake, then back again.

Roman grabbed him by his shoulders. His fingernails pierced Drake's shirt. He struggled, but Roman had him pinned in place. Roman's face extended and his teeth elongated. It was the horrific amalgamation of man and wolf that Drake had witnessed in the church. He leaned in to Drake, who squirmed under the grasp, but failed to free himself. Drake saw thick drool tinged with blood on

Roman's teeth and lips. The hideous face came in and chomped down on Drake's collarbone. He leaned his head back to scream at the pain, and at the same time brought his knee up into Roman's groin.

He was suddenly released from Roman's grip. He fell back to the river. Before he dropped from sight, he saw Roman hunched over, still in his half man form.

Drake tumbled down and hit his injured shoulder against an outcropping of rock. This time, he did yell out, but then he was in the river and the current had hold of him. He struggled to stay afloat and keep his head above the water, but he was pulled under.

# Chapter Forty-One

The front door opened and Jonas heard someone enter the house. He clutched his gun and steeled himself. Three murders in and he was prepared to commit more.

What the hell, what did it matter now? The state could only fry you once, right?

He heard a familiar nasally voice call out, "Dad?"

*Philo*. Jonas should have known Philo wouldn't abandon him. He had probably insisted David turn around and come back to get him. He rushed to the stairs to prevent Philo from coming up. He didn't want Philo to see the bodies, see what his father did, what his father was capable of.

"Philo," Jonas said when he got to the top of the stairs. He slowly made his descent and looked for David's traitorous face, but Philo was alone. "Where've you been?"

"I'm sorry, Dad. It was David. He said… I didn't want to, but he said…"

The poor kid was near tears. Jonas tucked the gun in the waistband of his pants behind him, below the small of his back. Philo didn't seem to notice it. Jonas put his hand on his son's shoulder to reassure him. He wasn't to blame, and Jonas wanted him to know it.

"Where's your brother?"

"I don't know," Philo answered dejectedly. "He made me get out of the car and I walked back. Dad, where's Amber?"

"I told you, son. She left us. She left last night. Ran off. Said she had enough of us."

Jonas saw something in Philo's eyes. David had told him.

He said, "David put ideas in your head. But don't believe it, son. I love you and I'd never do anything to hurt you. Understand?"

Philo looked at him with a blank expression. "David said…. that… that you…" His eyes teared up.

"Never mind what he said. He's a liar and a traitor to this family. Amber left. That's all you need to know. Okay?"

A light came on in his son's eyes, a light of acceptance. Jonas saw that Philo had accepted what his father told him. He had to because the alternative – that David had abandoned him and his father had murdered the woman he loved – was too terrible to contemplate. Philo accepted his father's words not because they rang with truthfulness, but because the alternative meant he was alone in the world.

Jonas gave him the keys to Mrs. Dallway's car and told him to take it out of the garage. He wanted to put distance between them and the town, and he wanted to get on David's trail. He had an idea the kid was going to California, then heading down to Mexico. Jonas thought he had a good chance of catching up to him. When he did… He clenched his fists at the thought.

He took a duffel bag of clothes, the hell with the rest of it. He would buy new things later, and whatever Philo needed. Let the rest burn up. He didn't care.

He stood at the front door and smoked a cigarette. Once it neared the end, he would toss the lit butt into the living room and ignite the kerosene. He hoped the house would burn fast, because he wanted the sheriff to be busy for a while. Jonas smiled at the thought. He was sorry he couldn't kill Sheriff Creel before he left town. It would be payback for the hard time he gave Jonas when he arrived in Tanneheuk back in May. Maybe he could stop off at the sheriff's place on the way out of town.

From the front door, while Philo backed out of the garage, down the driveway, and into the street, he saw them: wolves. Big ones. It was a group of nine or ten, and they walked down the center of the street as if it was the most natural thing in the world. Jonas stared and wondered if he was imagining it. Philo pulled alongside the curb and stepped out of the car, and then noticed the wolves, too.

*Shit.* It wasn't a dream.

Jonas pulled out his gun, and just as suddenly, realized he might have made a mistake. All of the wolves stopped and regarded him. Four trotted in his direction, while the rest squared off around the car and Philo.

*This can't be*, Jonas thought. *How do they know? They're just stupid animals, aren't they? How could they know I'm a potential threat?*

Jonas fired two shots at them. He thought one hit its intended target, and although the wolf stumbled and fell, the others kept coming. Even the one that fell wasn't down long. Jonas saw it get to its feet and run at him, a few steps behind the others.

He threw the door shut and heard Philo yell from the street, "Dad!" Before the door was fully closed, he felt the impact from one of the wolves throwing itself at it. He managed to block its entry, but the others barreled into it and he was thrown backward. The cigarette flew from his mouth and hit somewhere on the rug. There was a whoosh of ignition and a fire started in the living room.

Jonas was on his back. Two wolves pounced on him, one black and one brown. He had his arm under the throat of the black one, its gnashing fangs inches from his face. The brown one had its front paws on his shoulder and ribcage, but its attention was on the rapidly expanding fire that raced throughout the room. Jonas still had his gun.

The weight was crushing; both wolves weighed as much as a full grown man. Jonas managed to get the gun underneath the chest of the black one. He pulled the trigger and the wolf suddenly became dead weight. He shoved it to the side and pointed the gun at the brown one. It had turned at the sound of the shot, but it was too late for it to react. Jonas shot it twice in the face.

He was up on his feet and prepared to race out the door, but the other two wolves blocked it. They growled at him. One took a menacing step towards him, but neither would commit to entering the house. Jonas saw that the fire scared them.

The heat in the room became overbearing. The black wolf

wasn't moving. The brown one, however, the one that took two bullets to the face, was struggling to its feet.

*It's not possible*, Jonas thought. *How…?*

The wolf glared at him, one side of its face bloodied, the flesh torn by the two bullet holes. One eye bulged unnaturally over a ripped piece of its fur.

Jonas ran. Not out the front, because the other two still kept their vigil, snarling at him yet unwilling to enter the burning house. He couldn't go out the back either because the fire had already spread throughout the bottom floor and created a wall between them and the back door. Jonas ran up the stairs. The brown wolf gave chase. A line of fire caught the trail of fuel and followed closely behind. Jonas fled down the hallway to the bedroom that held the bodies of Mrs. Dallway's son and daughter-in-law. Jonas leapt on the bed and trampled the corpses underneath. He turned and pointed the gun at his pursuer.

He was still in the process of turning, his legs facing one way and his torso twisted, the gun up and firing, when the wolf slammed into him. They both hit the wall with a crunch that Jonas felt in his bones. Even so, he knew his shots had hit home. Jonas was on the floor in a seated position, his back against the wall and the body of the wolf in his lap. He managed to extricate himself from under it and stood on unsteady legs.

The fire had spread down the hallway and licked at the open doorway. Jonas went to the window. He opened it and punched his fist through the screen. It bent outward and fell to the ground with a clatter.

He heard a snarl. Jonas turned and saw the wolf struggling to get to its feet. *How*? He had shot it multiple times! The damage to the wolf's face looked better. It was healing at an incredible rate. He decided it didn't matter. What mattered was that the house was now engulfed in flames and he had to get out. He put the gun back in his waistband, deciding not to waste any more rounds on the wolf. It wasn't in a position to hurt him at the moment, anyway. It appeared to be having trouble shrugging off the last few shots it took to its body.

Jonas climbed through the window and swung his legs around so he was hanging from the sill. His intention was to hang as far down as possible, then drop softly to the ground. But when he let go, he dropped fast and landed hard on his ankle. It shot a sharp pain up his leg. Jonas let out a groan and collapsed to the ground. The gun had fallen from his pants, too, and through the pain, he pulled himself along the grass in search of it.

Out on the street, Philo was under siege.

He shouted, "Dad!" over and over and swung his large fists at the wolves. He was slashed and bloody, and the group of wolves had grown in number. But Philo refused to quit. Jonas saw a handful of neighborhood residents attempt to help him, one with a shotgun that fired two bursts before three wolves brought him down.

Philo put up a valiant effort, but he was outnumbered. The wolves were too big and too plentiful. They seemed to multiply in numbers, coming from between the houses and up the street unbidden, but somehow knowing they were needed. Residents of the neighboring houses came out to see what was happening or to lend a hand. Some were chased back inside. One person fired a handgun. A woman brandished a kitchen knife. It didn't matter; the wolves were unafraid and they moved in a concerted effort to take down all potential threats.

Philo punched one, then another. One jumped on his back and he flipped it over his shoulder and slammed it down on the car hard enough to dent the trunk. The wolf was momentarily stunned, but it recovered and came back for another attack. Philo fought and fought, but they were too strong, too vicious, too many...

Jonas had his gun. He tried to stand. Pain exploded through him and nearly caused him to black out. He tumbled over and lost hold of the gun again. He retrieved it and stood back up, more cautiously this time. He stood in time to see Philo get ripped to shreds. The wolves swallowed him up in a big pile of claws and teeth, ripping and tearing... Jonas thought he could still hear him shouting, "Dad!"

Jonas pointed his gun, but he knew it was futile. Philo was dead or dying, and shooting at the pack of beasts wouldn't change that. All it would do would be to alert them to his presence. At the moment, they were intent on devouring his son and a few others who had made the mistake of getting involved.

Jonas's survival instincts overrode his paternal ones. He limped into the shadows between the houses and worked on putting distance between him and them.

# Chapter Forty-Two

Fern made the announcements regularly as Sheriff Creel had instructed. She told the townspeople that the elders were to be considered dangerous and potentially lethal, and that they should stay indoors and arm themselves as best they could. Those that possessed firearms were asked to go to Creel's office and wait for him to give them further instruction. Anyone who showed up should consider themselves temporarily deputized. Also, the church was being utilized as a makeshift command and information center, and folks were encouraged to come there for further information.

She hadn't smoked a joint since the start of her shift, and she felt it, too. Her leg ached, more so than usual. Fern loaded the next five songs, then left the control booth. She was alone. The others had either left town or barricaded themselves in their respective residences. Probably the smart thing to do in either case. Smarter than what she was doing, but what else could she do? The radio station was her life, especially now that David…

It didn't matter. She lit a joint and took a slow easy drag. She held it in her lungs and looked at the unlit phones. No calls, which was highly unusual. Where were her fans? Probably gone away, like the others, or cowering in their bedrooms with the doors locked and heavy pieces of furniture piled in front of them.

Fern limped to the door and looked out at the parking lot. The lights mounted on the outside of the building cast it in a large pool of light, with additional support from the streetlights. She cracked the door an inch and exhaled the smoke into the night air.

The air was crisp with a hint of the coming winter. Not quite cold yet, but summer was on the wane. Fern thought by the time she finished and headed home, she might need her jacket.

She smoked her joint and looked down the road towards town. She thought she heard noises in that direction, like yelling and...

Was that *gunfire*? No, it couldn't be. Could it? Fern found it hard to believe it had come to that, but apparently Sheriff Creel's call to arms had been answered.

She heard the rising roar of a car engine pushed to its limits. It sped closer and closer until she saw the headlights, along with hearing the occasional squeal of tires as it fought to navigate the sharp turns of the side streets. Through the warm buzz she experienced from the joint, apprehension began a slow climb up her spine. The car came close enough that she was able to identify it as the Raffertys' Cadillac and her apprehension became something else. Something unfamiliar, like... happiness?

It was David; she knew it. He had come back, or maybe he had never left. Maybe she jumped to conclusions. It didn't matter. It was David, and her heart thumped in her chest.

The Cadillac roared down the street and jumped the curb. It raced across the sidewalk and over the grass divider that separated the parking lot from the street. Tufts of grass shot from behind the rear tires and the frame of the car lurched like a rampaging rhino as it tore across the parking lot curb and dividers. Sparks ignited as the bottom of the car scraped against concrete, and Fern heard a loud thunk and clatter when something fell off, most likely the muffler. The car came to a screeching halt directly in front of her. David popped out of the driver's side with a sawed-off shotgun in his hand.

"Rum Raisin, get your purse and let's get the fuck out of here. There's werewolves all over the place, and they've gone bugfuck crazy."

Fern laughed and ran to him. He had time to put the shotgun down on the hood of the car before Fern threw her arms around him. She leaned down and kissed him more passionately than she had ever kissed a man before. David was surprised, but after a moment, he responded and kissed her back with the same intensity. When she pulled away, her eyes were shiny from the myriad of emotions that swelled within her.

David said, "What was that for? Not that I'm complaining."

"You came back," Fern replied happily

"Of course I came back. Did you think I'd leave without my woman?"

She kissed him again and thought her heart would burst through her chest. She said, "I love you, Peanut Brittle," and meant it. She realized now that she didn't truly love two men. She only loved David. Her feelings for Sheriff Creel were, at best, infatuation borne from a childhood crush. It was a fantasy.

Her love for David, though, that was real. She had been too afraid to admit because she had believed it to be one-sided.

"I love you, too, Chocolate Éclair," David said. "Now let's get the hell out of here. The wolves are attacking people. People are attacking the wolves. All kinds of mass hysteria. There's shooting, and fires, and biting... Oh, and the road out of town's been cut off."

"I'll get my keys," Fern said. "We'll take my car. We'll figure out something."

"Yeah, sure, but let's move before Roman and the rest of his fang gang make their way here."

She moved as quickly as she could with her bad leg. She got her purse and car keys from the central booth, and loaded two more songs to play just for the hell of it. She hated to leave the station with dead air, but her man said they had to leave, so...

*Her man.* She liked the sound of that. When she came back outside, the trunk of the Cadillac was open and David was transporting a bag of what looked like bundles of cash to her Charger. Fern also saw two handguns on top of the money – a shiny revolver and a black semi-automatic.

"What's that?"

"That's our new life," he said, "If we can get away from this nutty town."

He got in the passenger side of the Charger and tossed the bag into the back seat. The shotgun was braced in his lap with the barrel pointed at his open window.

Fern slid in and started the engine. The radio was already switched on and "The Hand That Feeds" by Nine Inch Nails blared through the car speakers. David chuckled.

As she drove out of the parking lot, Fern said, "If you like this song, you'll probably love the next one."

"What's the next one?"

"Werewolves of London."

"Cute," David said.

\*\*\*

They had come close a number of times. Maryam had seen the wolves follow false scents, then become perplexed when the trail took them in a circle or led to a dead-end. She stayed downwind and moved cautiously. Sometimes she stood perfectly still and held her breath, willing herself invisible while the wolves crossed the path in front of her or off to the side. It wasn't just the urine she had spread around that threw them off, but that her scent was everywhere because she had been all over the woods in the last six months.

Maryam had also memorized the landscape to the point that she knew every potential hiding spot. She was able to move from cover to cover until the wolves moved on, at which point she would continue her full out run towards the river. Even with all her preparation and planning, however, there had been several close calls. Luckily, another dirty tactic had come into play: Maryam had spread copious amounts of chili pepper throughout the woods over the last two weeks. Much of it, she was sure, had been dissipated by the elements, but some of it had clung to the area. One of the wolves occasionally came across a patch of it and would succumb to a sneezing attack. The others would carefully skirt the area and continue their hunt, eventually followed by a sniffling, sneezing wolf.

She thought it odd that the number of wolves looking for her seemed so small. She had counted eight, but that couldn't be right. The pack consisted of much more than what she observed on her trail. So where were the rest? She knew Roman was leading a group that planned to hunt Reverend Burroughs, but that should still have left several dozen more wolves.

It was no matter now. She was in the clear. They had moved on to another false trail. Maryam was close to the end, close to her destination. The wolves would try to cheat, she knew, by reaching the river ahead of her and following its course until they could cut her off. Maryam had planned for that contingency.

There was a spot she had visited only twice to keep her scent from saturating the area. It fell between two outcroppings of rock, a small path that led to the river. It was perilously close to the elders' settlement, which was probably why they wouldn't think to look for her there. Most people would try to put as much distance as possible between themselves and the source of their threat. Maryam wasn't most people.

She was close. She heard the rustle of the river, a sound like rain filtered through tree branches. It gurgled and thrummed with movement. She took the narrow path through the rocks.

*It's all over*, she thought. *I won.*

Except the path was blocked by a snarling white wolf. How? How did he know she would come this way? As if he intended to answer her unspoken question, Merc shifted to his human form and stood before her with an evil grin.

Maryam rushed at him. His grin slipped to a look of surprise a moment before her body collided with his. She planned to knee him in the groin, then deliver a crushing blow to the back of his neck with her elbow. But Merc was much too fast. As soon as she moved towards him, he reacted.

He leapt at her and wrapped his arms and legs around her. His weight pulled them down. Maryam twisted to ensure she landed directly on him, hoping her weight would stun him or at least knock the wind out of him. If the fall affected him any, he didn't show it.

"I'll eat you!" he screamed at her. "Eat you! Eat you!" over and over.

He bit her ear and Maryam howled in pain. Warm blood flowed from the wound and coated the side of her neck. She hit at him in a fury and they rolled back and forth until he released her flesh from his mouth. She raked at him with her nails, short though they were, and bit at him as she rained blows on his small frame. Merc was just as savage, if not more so. He didn't punch back; he stuck to biting and clawing, but his nails were much larger and his teeth were sharp and jagged.

They ripped and tore at each other. Maryam was fueled by

adrenaline, frustration, and rage at the fact that she was close, so goddamn close. Through the haze of animal savagery, she heard the river not more than a hundred feet away. She wouldn't be denied this, not by him.

She punched his kidneys. She bit and tore. Her teeth sank into his cheek and her nostrils filled with the sickening stench of his blood and the foulness of his breath. For a split second, their eyes met. There was a flicker behind his eyes and Maryam thought, *God, he's actually enjoying this.* It spurred her to fight more frantically.

With a mighty effort, she lodged one arm against his throat and pushed her upper body away from him. His eyes bulged and his teeth snapped. She knew she couldn't hold him for long. His strength was incredible.

She moved her free hand behind her to the backpack she wore. She still had the stun gun, but she couldn't retrieve it from that angle, so she reached into the space between the backpack and her back where she had the hunting knife stashed in its sheath. She was reluctant to use it, but she refused to lose because of Merc. If the pack killed her because of it – so be it.

Her hand closed over the handle and she yanked it free from its sheath. At that moment, Merc exploded with a burst of strength that knocked her up and off of him. She landed on her back, but managed to keep hold of the knife.

Merc jumped up, pounced, and landed square on the knife that Maryam managed to put between her body and his leaping form. She felt the thunk as it lodged between his ribs. He stood up suddenly and looked with puzzlement at the handle that protruded from his chest.

"Girlie-girl," he said. "Why'd ya do that?" He sank to his knees. His hands came up and feebly worked to wrap themselves around the handle.

"You should've stayed in your wolf body," Maryam said. "You would've had me then. But no stinking human is going to stop me from winning."

She threw herself at him and buried the knife to the hilt. It hit his heart and the light went out of his eyes. He had become a lifeless lump of flesh.

Maryam struggled to her feet. Her hands were soaked with

blood – both his and her own. She gingerly touched her ragged ear and winced at the sharp pain. Her movements were stiff and sore from the many scratches and bites she had received from him.

She staggered to the river and nearly collapsed on the bank. Through her cloudy vision, she saw a group of wolves lope gracefully towards her following the river, as she knew they would. The two wolves in front stopped and transformed. One was a female with short blonde hair. The other was a barrel-chested man with long silver hair. They looked at her with surprise, confusion, and perhaps a little awe.

Maryam looked up at them and laughed.

# Chapter Forty-Three

Creel saw Reverend Burroughs shambling along the side of the road. He almost clipped him with the Jeep, but managed to swerve away in time. Creel braked and swung the Jeep around so the headlights and roof mounted spotlights lit up the reverend's soaked and battered frame.

He stepped out of the Jeep and walked up to Drake. The reverend was dripping wet, his skin a bloodless white and his lips tinged with blue. His shirt was torn and his feet were bare. He stared at Creel with a vacant expression.

"You okay, Reverend?" Creel knew it was a dumb question, and thought for a moment that he wouldn't get an answer.

Drake said in a shaky voice, "Y-yeah. F-fine."

Creel walked him to the Jeep and helped him climb in. He took a fleece-lined denim jacket from behind the seat and placed it on Drake's lap. He thought Drake would put it on, but when he walked around to the Driver's side and got in, Drake still had it on his lap. He stared straight ahead and hadn't seemed to have moved.

He shifted the Jeep into first, turned the heater on high, and aimed the vents at Drake. Eventually, with much prompting, he was able to get the story of what happened, up to the point when Drake went into the river.

"I'm gonna take ya back to the church. We're using it as a command post of sorts. Ya can get cleaned up and provide moral support, but I don't expect ya to do no fighting."

"Command post? What's going on?"

"The town's under siege," Creel answered. "The elders have been attacking anyone they catch on the street or not locked up in their homes. They even cut off the road out of town."

"Why?"

"My guess, they're isolating us. Herdin' everyone together. Roman's... well, my thinking is, he's pulling the leash tight on the town. Figurin' out who he's gonna get rid of."

"He's restructuring," Drake said. "Clean slate."

"That's my guess, too."

A few minutes later, they turned into the church parking lot. The building was lit and the parking lot held an assortment of cars and trucks. One was leaving as they entered. It stopped so its window was lined up with Creel's. It was Carl Beardsley, looking more sober than Creel had seen him in a very long time. Sober and worried.

"Where ya headed, Carl?"

"They took out the phone lines, Sheriff," he said. "So now we're forced to drive around to check on everyone. There's been report of a couple of fires, too."

"Fires? What the hell are they trying to do? Burn the town down?"

"Beats me. Seems that the fire started at Mrs. Dallway's place and it's spread to a couple of other houses. We're not even sure the elders started it, but when the fire crew showed up to put it out, they got attacked."

Creel shook his head. "It's been a pretty dry summer. That fire could get out of hand." He thought for a moment. "Head out and see what's going on. Pass the word around, then come back and report in. Stay in your car as much as possible. Ya got your gun?"

Carl patted the seat next to him. "Right here."

Creel thought he could make out the vague outline of a handgun on Carl's passenger seat. "Just be careful," he told him.

Carl drove on and Creel drove the Jeep to the back of the church. From the corner of his eye, he saw Drake wince when they came to a stop.

"What is it?"

"Just my shoulder. Roman bit me there. Feels like... it's hot. Burning a little."

"He bit you?" Creel felt his stomach clench. He reached across to the glove compartment and took out his flashlight. He switched on the beam and focused it on the shoulder Drake kept rubbing.

His shirt was punctured between his neck and shoulder. Creel ripped the material open and studied Drake's skin.

"Not too bad," Creel said. "The wounds are already closed. Couldn't have been too deep."

"Really? Felt like he bit me to the bone. It burns like…" He shook his head, unable to finish his thought.

"The virus they carry," Creel said, "the virus that makes them what they are. It's in their saliva. It doesn't interact well with us, like an allergen."

"Does it… will it… turn me…?" Drake swallowed hard. "Into one of them?"

"No. It has to be a concentrated does of the virus, like a blood contact. And even then, it kills most people."

Drake shivered, either from being cold and wet or from what Creel said, he couldn't be sure. He studied Drake's face in the reflected glow of the flashlight beam, and thought he saw something there. Worry or concern maybe. Maybe fear.

"Reverend, did Roman's blood get mixed with yours?"

"No."

"Then you should be fine."

Drake nodded and Creel shut off the flashlight. They exited the Jeep and entered Drake's apartment. People were moving back and forth into the church area.

A radio on the kitchen table was set to the local station. Creel heard "Werewolves of London" and chuckled. Good old Fern. That girl was something else.

People came up to the reverend, concerned, as if he had been a missing family member. They inquired how he was. They truly cared about him, Creel realized, which shouldn't have surprised him. After all, they had gone against hundreds of years of tradition based solely on the reverend's directive.

He saw, too, that the people were relieved. They looked to the reverend for guidance, and now that he was here, they naturally flocked to him for direction. Creel should have been insulted, for he had guided the town for many years. He should be the person everyone looked to for leadership. But he didn't feel slighted.

In a way, it was a relief not to have the pressure of being the person who was supposed to have all the answers. He was tired of being the moral rock to which everyone in town went to for strength. Let the young minister assume that role. Creel knew it was ultimately going to end badly, and he didn't feel an ounce of guilt because he hadn't been the cause.

Besides, the reverend truly came alive in his role. Creel saw that he was changed, no longer in the zombie-like state he had originally found him in on the side of the road. Now Drake answered questions and gave words of reassurance. He'd gone from the shivering wreck that had been in Creel's Jeep minutes ago, to a strong and confident leader. Creel hoped it would be enough to carry them through the long night ahead.

***

They entered the settlement in a flank formation with Maryam in front. An outsider would have found it difficult to determine whether she was their prisoner, or if she was the leader of the ragtag band of wolves and humans. Mars and Salacia, still in their human form, marched on either side of her. The rest of the wolves brought up the rear. Maryam appeared to have difficulty in remaining upright. Mars and Salacia helped balance her as she half-marched, half-stumbled ahead. She was injured, and probably weak from blood loss. Still, she kept her head up defiantly.

With a select few of his pack, Roman had waited for the hunters to return. They had driven off gunmen Creel had sent to look for the missing reverend. They had fired on Roman and his followers; one shot had been lethal. One of Roman's trusted lieutenants had taken a shotgun blast to the head that had removed a sizeable chunk of brain matter. The damage was too extensive for the shapeshifter virus to repair. Too much damage to the brain, too much loss of oxygen. The elder had died, and remained dead.

Roman and his followers had killed four of the humans and driven the others off, back to their vehicles and presumably back to their homes. They had their scents, however, and had every intention of following the killers and exacting vengeance. Roman swore to kill them and their families for raising arms against his people. He swore to kill Creel, too. If not for him, Roman believed the townspeople would have stayed in their homes and been as docile as sheep.

Maryam fearlessly walked up to him and said, "I won. Now give me what I want."

Roman couldn't help but grin.

"She killed Mercury," Mars said. "She used a knife."

"Mercury wasn't one of the pack," Roman said. "The rules against using weapons don't apply to him."

"He was the Omega, but he was still one of us."

*What was this?* Mars's eyes challenged him. His Beta had openly questioned his judgment. Roman looked to Salacia, who avoided his gaze.

"She won the hunt. My word on this stands." He fixed Mars with a glare, but the man refused to submit.

Mars said, "I wish to speak with you in private."

Roman considered his response. His first instinct was to lash out, physically if not verbally. If he refused to submit by Roman's sheer force of will, then Roman's inclination was to resort to savagery. But there was Salacia to consider. Despite her emotional distance lately, Roman still cared for her and still intended to make her his mate. He didn't want to cause her pain by physically harming her father.

He motioned to Maryam. "Bring her inside with us."

The four of them entered Roman's cabin. Roman experienced a fleeting pang of longing for Diana. The lack of her presence in their home, even the absence of her scent, caused a stir of remorse down deep inside. He shook it off and mentally chastised himself. How could he feel remorse for killing that whore, that traitor to her people? She had received nothing less than what she deserved, and his only regret was that he had been unable to inflict more pain on Reverend Burroughs before his death. He was sure the reverend drowned in the river, and although that particular form of death was effective, it had been much too good for him. Roman had entertained thoughts of slowly devouring Burroughs piece by tiny piece.

Inside the cabin, Mars and Salacia each picked up a blanket from a folded pile and wrapped it around themselves. It wasn't for modesty, as nudity was the norm in their culture. But the small bite of coolness that permeated the night air held an edge to it. Without their furs, Mars and Salacia felt it. Roman had already taken the opportunity to slip into a flannel shirt and pair of jeans before their arrival.

"Salacia, see to the girl's wounds." Roman sat in the center of the couch and laid his arms on top of the backrest, his fingers pointed straight out from his body, completely comfortable and at ease.

Mars took the chair across from him, the same one Creel always sat in when he visited. Used to visit. Roman would have to choose a new town sheriff once the "purge" was over.

Salacia sat Maryam on the floor, then retrieved a towel and basin of water from the kitchen while Roman observed from the corner of his eye. Salacia dabbed Maryam's cuts with a cloth. The girl winced from time to time, but didn't utter a sound. She stared at Roman, enraptured.

"You have concerns?" he asked Mars.

"Yes, Roman, of course. Don't you think this has gone too far?"

"Too far? It's gone as far as the townspeople have allowed it to. I gave them a choice."

"You told them to go against their religious beliefs."

Roman said, "He was a troublemaker. An instigator. An anarchist posing as a reformer. I could not allow that to continue."

"But you forced the town into a corner," Mars said. "Can't you see that? Now, people are dying. *Our* people are dying."

"Perhaps." Roman nodded thoughtfully. "But perhaps if our ancestors had been willing to sacrifice themselves for a worthy cause such as this—"

"Such as what?"

Roman glared at him. His voice tight, he said, "Such as the principle I've set forth, which is that we should not be the ones who live in the shadows. We should be the ones who are rightfully worshipped and treated with deference."

"We were worshipped, Roman. The townspeople—"

"The townspeople paid us token homage, and that was all. What did they really do? One hunt a year? Allowed us to eat for free if we chose to enter their establishments? Gave us their castoff clothing and furnishings?" He waved his hand in a dismissive gesture. "Scraps is what they gave us. And to think I nearly let myself be convinced by Sheriff Creel to do away with the hunt." He shook his head. "I will never allow a human to dictate anything to me, nor allow them to cajole their wishes through conniving or clever pleading. Never again."

Mars sat back and folded his arms over his thick chest. He looked to Salacia, but her attention was on tending to Maryam.

"You don't agree with my decision," Roman said. "But I still expect your loyalty."

"I am, and always will be, loyal to the pack."

"No. You must be loyal to me."

Mars wouldn't meet his eyes. The wolf inside Roman quickly surged to the surface and nearly effected a transformation. Roman held it down; he placated it with soothing internal words.

Yes, it was an insult that Mars wouldn't submit to his will. However, he was still Salacia's father, and this wasn't the time or place. He promised his animal side that there would be an accounting. Soon.

Roman stood, walked to where Maryam sat, and looked down at her. Salacia had her wounds clean and had draped a blanket over her shoulders. Maryam stared unwaveringly up at Roman.

"Give me what I want," she said.

"To be one of us? I don't have to."

"Yes, you do. I won. I made it to the river."

Roman smirked. "Yes, I know. You upheld your end of the bargain. I didn't mean to imply that I wouldn't uphold my end. What I'm saying is, you're already infected with the virus."

"How?"

"Mercury's blood mixed with yours, is my guess. You cut him or scratched him or stabbed him, and his blood leaked into one of your open wounds." Roman shrugged. "Whatever the case, the virus is in your system now. I can tell." He placed the back of his hand against her forehead. "Warm now, but your fever will increase. You'll begin to feel a lot worse over the next few hours. If you survive, then you'll be like us."

"I'll survive."

"Perhaps."

"I will," she said.

Roman hoped she would survive. He liked her spirit.

# Chapter Forty-Four

"Uh, Spice Cake? Why are we heading towards your house?"

Fern answered, "We have to get Jethro."

*The dog*?

"Listen, that's probably not a good idea." David gripped the shotgun tight in his hands and scanned the abandoned streets. The abnormal quiet exacerbated his anxiety rather than curbed it. "I like Jethro. He's a great dog. But…"

"But what?"

"But they do this shit all the time in horror movies. You know, go back for the family pet and something bad happens. Usually to the guy first, and then the girl."

He thought Fern might have flashed a quick smile at that, which was funny because he hadn't been kidding. It did his heart good, though, to see her smile. She had done that a lot since he showed up at the station to get her. He wanted to see her smile a lot more from here on out – like for years and years. He wanted that very much. Unfortunately, he also knew they were stuck in Tanneheuk.

Fern said, "I want to get Jethro, and my mom, too, although I don't know if she'll go with us."

David caught that she didn't mention her father. No big surprise there. He knew Fern wasn't close to the man, and he certainly wasn't one to lecture on the whole "Honor Thy Father" doctrine.

"How're we going to get out of town? I told you they blocked the road," he said.

"We'll walk across the bridge if we have to."

"Fine by me."

Well, not really. Walking across a bridge wasn't any more of an appetizing idea than driving over one, but since he had already overcome part of his phobia, David figured, what the hell. May as well crash through all of his mental barriers.

When they turned onto Fern's street, David saw the flames. Were they burning the houses?

It turned out to be two houses. Mrs. Dallway's house was one of them. He couldn't be sure where the fire started, but it had spread to the house next to it. Or possibly the fires had been set at both houses, but he didn't think so. Fire was as dangerous to the shapeshifters as it was to the humans. So why would they put themselves at risk? No, it had to be an accident.

Mrs. Dallway's car was parked on the street and several bodies were scattered around it. One of them... the body was torn apart, but the size and approximate shape...

"Philo?"

Fern had slowed down to make the turn into her driveway when David stepped out of the car. He stumbled a bit since the car was still in motion when his feet connected with the asphalt, but he didn't fall. He ran to the body of his brother.

The glow and heat cast by the flames gave him an eerie failing of standing on the outskirts of Hell.

"Why?" he whispered.

Why didn't the big idiot continue walking out of town? Why did he have to come back for their father?

"He wasn't worth it, Philo," he said quietly.

"David!" Fern called to him. She stood next to her car in the driveway.

"Coming."

He ran across the street, surprised to find that his eyes had teared up. *Really? Over Philo? I never would've guessed I gave a damn about him.*

"What is it?" Fern asked. "Are those people your family?"

"My brother. The others I don't recognize."

"Our neighbors, probably. We should get inside."

"Let's get the dog and your mom and get the hell out of here."

He still couldn't believe they stopped for the dog. Fern's

mother he could almost understand. Almost.

All the lights were on inside the house. Fern's mother sat at the dining room table. A full ashtray, plus the lit cigarette in her hand, attested to the fact she had chain-smoked most of the afternoon and evening.

"Mom," Fern said, "we have to go. I'll get Jethro."

"I can't. I can't leave without your father."

"Where is he?"

"He…" Her mother shook her head and took a drag of her cigarette.

"He what, Mom?"

"He went outside to see if… if he could help put out the fire." Tears rolled down her cheeks. "He hasn't come back yet."

She couldn't meet their eyes, keeping them locked on the table in front of her. As if she believed that if she moved her eyes from that single point, her worst fears about her missing husband would be realized.

Fern looked to David, the unspoken question heavy between them. Was her father one of the bodies he had seen out on the street? He shrugged his response. He didn't know, and probably wouldn't say if he did. Admittedly, he was an insensitive bastard, but he wasn't cruel.

"Jethro!" Fern called.

The dog came into the room quicker than David had ever seen him move before. *Like he knows*, David thought. The dog knew there was serious shit happening and he'd shrugged off the older, good-natured pet persona. He was ready to get out of there. David didn't blame him.

"Okay, so we're going?" David asked. "Mrs. Wilde? Maybe we should just get out of here. Okay? We can come back tomorrow after everything's calmed down."

Actually, David had no intention of coming within a hundred miles of this crazy ass town ever again. But there was no point in letting Fern's mom know that. Once he got himself and Fern far away, Mrs. Wilde could do whatever she wanted.

"I can't leave without him," she sobbed.

David resisted the urge to roll his eyes.

"Mom, we have to. Like David said, we can come back."

Mrs. Wilde shook her head and took another drag off her cigarette. Fern looked to David. He shrugged.

"Let me get the dog in the car," he said. "You talk to her. Try to convince her. But be quick."

Fern nodded. David led Jethro out to the Charger. The fires across the street still radiated heat, though he thought the intensity had diminished slightly. Up the street, he heard a scream followed by a succession of gunshots. David shook his head. What the hell was he thinking coming back here? He opened the door and Jethro jumped in.

"Hello, son."

David felt the barrel of a gun pressed to the side of his head, at the same time the shotgun was pulled from his grasp.

"Dad," he said. "How've you been?"

His father came into view from the shadow of the house. His face was damp with sweat and pale from pain. He favored one leg and seemed unable to put his full weight on it.

"You came back," Jonas said. "For what? The girl?"

"Something like that."

"You should've stayed gone. That's the last lesson I'm ever gonna teach you."

"It's a good one, too, Dad."

"Now give me the keys to the car."

David smiled. "Would you believe... I don't have 'em?"

Jonas stared at him hard, his eyes searching. Then he smirked. "I do believe it." He used the gun to motion for David to back away from the Charger. "I don't need keys to start one of these antiques."

In the passenger seat, Jethro growled loudly.

"Get that mutt out of there or I'm gonna shoot his ass out the other side."

David tried to think of a way out of the situation, a way to stop his father from taking the car and, more importantly, the money. But there was nothing he could say or do. He opened his mouth to call the dog.

A large brown wolf leapt onto the roof of the car and shoved its muzzle to within inches of Jonas's face. It opened its mouth to reveal long rows of sharp teeth. A line of drool fell from its bottom lip as it growled. Jonas fired just as the wolf threw itself at him.

Another wolf came out of the shadows. Jonas fired again, but David was already running for the door to the house. Behind him, Jonas yelled out and the two wolves roared as they tore into him.

David tripped and went down hard. He scrambled to get up, to get the revolver out of his waistband. He saw the second wolf— a large red one with white streaks in its fur— advance on him.

*Oh, Jesus*, David thought, *this is going to be bad.*

Jethro attacked it by jumping onto its back and biting into its meaty hide. The red wolf let out a yowl that was equal parts pain and surprise. David aimed the revolver, but couldn't get a clear shot. The red wolf moved too much as it attempted to shake Jethro off. The dog was unable to keep a tight hold, but as soon as his grip was loosened, he immediately dove back in for another attack.

From the doorway behind him came a volley of gunshots. Fern, the armed and trained deputy. *God bless her*, David thought. Two of the shots hit the red wolf dead center. It was alive, still moving, but not very well.

From behind it, the brown wolf came up and chomped down on the back of Jethro's neck. Its massive jaws engulfed the poor dog. David heard the crack of bone and saw Jethro's body go limp. Now the red wolf was getting to its feet. David was up and throwing himself back inside the house. He grabbed Fern around the waist and hauled her in with him. She cried and screamed for her dog.

"I know, I know," he said. "It's too late. Jethro's gone."

He locked the door and half-dragged her back to the dining room.

Fern's mother was on her feet, her face ashen from fear and despair. "What's happening?"

Fern sobbed, "They killed Jethro."

David thought it odd that she cried over the death of a dog, but her missing and presumed dead father had failed to elicit a scintilla of emotion. Then again, he wasn't feeling anything over the brutal death of his own father. *So, there you go.*

The picture window behind the table where Mrs. Wilde stood suddenly exploded. The two wolves crashed through and knocked Mrs. Wilde to the floor. Fern and David both fired their guns. They hit both wolves, but only the brown one appeared to be affected. It collapsed and didn't move. The red wolf clamped its mouth on Mrs. Wilde's arm. She screamed. Fern fired again until her gun was empty. The red wolf stopped moving.

*Christ*, David wondered, *what does it take to stop those things*? It was like you had to keep shooting them and shooting them.

Two more jumped through the smashed window. Mrs. Wilde struggled to free her herself from under the body of the red wolf. Her arm, the one the wolf had bitten, was a mass of shredded tissue. David tossed his gun to Fern, then grabbed a long carving knife and a meat cleaver from a block on the sideboard next to him.

He shouted to Fern, "Help your mom!" and rushed at the two wolves.

He jabbed at one and swung the cleaver in a wide arc at the other. His intent was to keep them at bay until Fern could get her mother to safety. In essence, David had decided he had gone completely insane because he was sacrificing his life for someone else. Go figure.

He jabbed and slashed. The two wolves, both of them brown and not quite as large as the other two, growled and attempted to circle around him. He slashed at the one on his left with the carving knife. He made several cuts on it, which didn't appear to bleed much. David chalked it up to either his inability to make more than a superficial wound, or the creature's enhanced healing ability.

Behind him, Fern had dragged her mom out from under the red wolf. The wolf on David's right feinted a move, but for some reason, call it intuition, David didn't fall for it. The wolf on his left made a jump to get by him. David lunged and struck out with the carving knife. It caught the wolf flush in the stomach, and he let go of the handle as the animal fell to the floor.

Unfortunately, the maneuver left his guard down on the right. The wolf took advantage and snatched David's knee between its vise-like jaws. David cried out, a bit unmanly, he knew, but he couldn't help himself. It felt like an iron bear trap had sprung closed on his leg, such was the explosion of force that he felt.

He fell backward, but was able to keep hold of the cleaver. Somehow, through the thick haze of shock and blinding pain, he managed to draw up a resource of strength, and brought the cleaver down on top of the wolf's skull. It broke through its skull and cleaved its brain; the sound was not unlike a cantaloupe being halved. The wolf was dead.

"David!"

He looked to see if Fern was warning him of impending danger, but her cry was merely one of concern for him, which he thought was quite considerate.

"Okay," he said. "I'm okay." He pried the wolf's jaws from his leg.

Movement on his left drew his attention. The wolf he had stabbed was on its side. It moved its legs in a feeble attempt to either get away or to dislodge the blade, David wasn't sure which. The body rippled and took the shape of a boy in his late teens. His newly formed hands grasped the handle of the knife and withdrew it from its stomach. It was the most horrific sight David had ever seen, and that said a lot in light of recent events.

The boy fixed David with a hate-filled glare. "Bastard," he hissed through a mouthful of blood.

"No, I'm Conan the fuckin' Barbarian," David said, stood and hobbled to where Fern and her mother waited by the side door.

Fern didn't wait for David to say anything. She walked to the boy, who now knelt in an upright position and clutched together the slit in his gut. He growled at Fern, leaking small bubbles of blood at the corners of his lips. He continued to growl even as Fern placed the revolver to his forehead. David saw hatred and rage in the kid's eyes, then a small flash of fear right when Fern pulled the trigger. He fell over, dead.

"Now, please can we go?" David asked.

"I can't," Fern's mother whined.

*Christ*, David thought, *not this again.*

"Let's go," Fern told him.

They left Fern's mother in the carnage of the room, holding her gouged arm. She stared wide-eyed at the floor, lost in another reality. Perhaps it was one where she still baked pies and tended to her surly, ungrateful husband, and not one where bloodthirsty werewolves had destroyed her dining room.

They ran for the car. David stopped long enough to pick up the fallen shotgun next to his dead father. Jonas's face was locked in a clenched teeth expression, one of those World War II battlefield faces. His father had to be the ultimate hardass, all the way to the end. David studied his father's face and decided to keep that as his last image of the man, and not the slashed and bloodied form crumpled between the trashcans of Fern's house.

He got in the car. "You're leaving your mom?"

"She cares more about her husband than she does me. She hesitated and now Jethro is dead. I'm not going to lose you, too, because she doesn't want to believe her husband is dead."

"Well, okay then."

Fern backed out of the driveway. Her eyes faced behind them towards the street so she couldn't see what David saw. And David had trouble believing it himself. It was the red wolf. It burst through the side door of the house and stood in the middle of the driveway like a bull preparing to charge.

"Look at that shit," David said. "What does it take to kill those things?"

"Aim for the head," Fern answered.

The wolf ran at them. David leaned out the passenger window, gritting his teeth at the pain in his leg, and fired the shotgun. The shot missed. The wolf jumped and landed atop the Charger's hood. David fired again. A chunk of the wolf's shoulder exploded in a mass of blood and gore that splattered the air behind it. Still, the wolf didn't go down.

It shifted partially to human, to an even more horrible sight that David thought would drown out the other horrible sights he had witnessed. It was now part red-haired man and part red-furred wolf, and its body was covered in small puckered wounds where they had repeatedly shot it. The wounds were closed; the only evidence of their existence was small red indentations that appeared to be fast fading. Its left arm and shoulder had a huge chunk missing. David could see the exposed muscles working, and although he couldn't be a hundred percent positive, he swore the huge wound was attempting to stitch itself back together.

It used its damaged arm to reach out and grab the shotgun. David yanked on it, but it wouldn't let go. Fern stepped out of the car, took aim, and fired the last two shots into the red monster's head. The first bullet went through its cheek. The second must have been a brain shot because it went limp and slipped off the hood onto the pavement.

Fern sat back in the driver's seat. "I told you, aim for the head."

"Yes, dear."

She turned the wheel, floored it, and asked, "How's your leg?"

"Hurts like hell," he answered. "How's yours?"

"Hurts like hell."

She raced through the streets until she reached Main. Whenever David saw one of them, he fired a shotgun blast in their direction, sometimes more than one. He went through the box of shells, lighting the night up in a series of tiny explosions, then he switched to the handguns. He wasn't sure how many he hit and in reality, figured his odds weren't that good considering his lack of marksmanship. But still, he thought he should try to hurt or kill as many of the four-legged bastards as he could on their way out of town.

Slade Grayson

# Chapter Forty-Five

Drake showered and put on clean clothes. He examined his wounds in the bathroom mirror. He found bruises here and there, but nothing serious. The shoulder injury struck him as odd. There were red marks where Roman's fangs had punctured his flesh, but the wounds were closed, which was strange because Drake had felt the fangs tear through his flesh and connect with bone. But the skin wasn't broken. It wasn't even scabbed over. The flesh was smooth, and when Drake stepped out of the shower and toweled off, the red marks were gone, too.

He could almost believe the bite had never happened, except the area throbbed and burned. Worse, the burning had slowly spread over a larger area and seemed unlikely to abate. Drake wondered what would happen once the burning sensation enveloped him completely.

He already felt feverish. It reminded him of the times after he had spent the night with Diana, which brought on a quick bout of guilt over the fact that not only had he given in to temptation, but that he had been unfaithful to Celia, too. It also brought on unwanted thoughts of infection.

Creel had said there had to be blood to blood contact. So there was the possibility he was infected. Roman had blood in his mouth when he bit him, so conceivably, Drake might die. Creel said that was the likely outcome when a human became infected.

Drake pushed the thoughts away. Whatever happened, he believed it was all part of God's plan, and he refused to believe God would bring him through all this just to smite him when he was so close to delivering the town out from its demonic influence.

He left the bathroom and went to his bedroom. He put on socks and boots and checked to see that his hair was neatly combed and his collar was straight. Drake had wanted to put on jeans and a t-shirt, but decided to wear his minister vestments. The people needed to see him as a figurehead of spiritual strength.

He entered the church area. The church was being not only used as a communication and command center, but also as a sanctuary of sorts. Families were camped out in blankets and sleeping bags on the pews and the floor. It made Drake think of victims of natural disasters, forced to leave their homes and possessions, bundled together in a temporary shelter until things returned to a semblance of normalcy.

Celia was near the front of the building talking to her parents. Off a little ways in a corner, Creel was talking to a small group of armed men. Most he recognized from town or from his congregation. People looked at Drake as he walked through the room. He had spoken to many of them earlier and reassured them. He spoke to some of them again and bolstered their spirits. He talked of God's love and His Divine Plan for all of them. Now that he had cleaned himself and appeared rejuvenated, despite the burning infection in his body and the slight lightheadedness it gave him, the people drew strength and inspiration from him.

Celia made eye contact and walked over to him, followed by her parents. Drake noticed three small children asleep on the pew next to him – two little boys and an older sister on the floor in a sleeping bag. The sister held the hand of one of the boys as they all slept. It was an unguarded moment of tenderness, and Drake didn't wish to disturb it. He moved to an unoccupied space in the back and motioned for Celia and her parents to join him.

Celia's father apologized for his younger daughter's actions. Celia's mother simply cried, too overcome with emotion to say anything let alone apologize. Drake assured both of them that it was all right, that he didn't blame Maryam for what she did.

"It's not truly her fault," he told them. "She's been bewitched by demons who, until recently, were idolized by the townspeople and allowed to roam unchecked throughout God's creation. She can still be saved, and I promise I'll do everything I can to see she is brought back to her family, and to God's grace."

With a shaking hand, Celia's mother reached out and clutched Drake's arm. She was on the verge of collapse and he was her sole support.

Drake took her arms and held her, as if they were afloat in a pool of water and he was her lifesaver. He wanted to instill a feeling of serenity in her. With a warm smile, he stared into her eyes and sent her thoughts of peace and love. When she returned the look and her anxiety had lessened, he turned to her husband and clasped one of his hands between his own two. He held it for a moment and repeated the same look and smile of love and calmness. He took their hands and put them together so husband and wife were now each other's support, as it should be.

Drake took Celia's hand and led her into the back rooms. His kitchen was filled with people topping off their thermoses with coffee and filling the tense night with idle chitchat. It was a tactic to relieve anxiety. Drake understood it. People talked as if it was a friendly gathering at a neighbor's house, and it worked, too, because he could see the tension would lighten briefly.

He led Celia into his study and was surprised to find Reverend MacDonald slumped tiredly behind his desk.

"Who's that?" MacDonald barked.

"Just me, Reverend Burroughs," Drake answered, "and Celia."

"Oh, yeah, well…" MacDonald perked up in the seat. "They won't let me go outside to smoke my cigar. And they won't let me smoke in here. So what the hell am I supposed to do? I need a drink, too."

"I'm sorry, sir. All I have is water. There's coffee in the kitchen though."

MacDonald stood and walked to the doorway with the practiced ease of someone who had made the trip several thousand times before. Since Drake had neither rearranged the furniture, nor changed the décor, MacDonald still knew the layout and was able to navigate it without sight.

On his way out of the room, he said, "I need something stronger than coffee. And don't give me that 'sir' bullshit."

Drake shook his head at the man's curmudgeonly behavior. He closed the door and took Celia into his arms. He kissed her with a wealth of passion that surprised both of them. When he pulled back, she was flushed and slightly out of breath.

"I... Drake..." She shook her head. "What brought that on?"

"I wanted you to know how I feel. And to know that I'm sorry for being distant. We started something, something wonderful, I think, and I allowed myself to... Well, never mind."

"It doesn't matter," she said.

"Yes. It does. I want you to know how I feel about you, that I think you are the best person I know. And that I love you."

She smiled, and they kissed again. And again. When he pulled back this time, Celia glowed with emotion.

"I love you, too," she said. "You know that, don't you? I think I always have."

They kissed again. Drake felt the passion build until they stood on the precipice of something more serious than necking.

"Drake," she said in a breathless voice, "let's.... let's make love."

"Here? Now?"

The idea was ill-timed and completely inappropriate, yet he had to admit he was aroused enough to take her up on it. Part of him, the physical part, wanted to say yes.

Instead, he said, "We can't. I want to." Lord, did he want to. "But we can't."

"Please. We might not be alive tomorrow. Who knows what's going to happen? I want the memory of being with you. I love you. I want to experience the feeling of having you inside me."

She kissed him and his resolve threatened to melt away. He was almost lost, but somehow found the willpower to pull back and hold her at arm's length.

"We can't, Celia. Please believe me when I say that I want to, but it would be better if we waited."

"I love you."

"I love you. And I want to make love to you. With you. But not now. Not this way. We'll survive the night. I promise. There's too many of us. The elders can't possibly win. We'll survive, and then we'll be married. We'll make love as a married couple, the way it should be. The way you deserve."

"Married?" Her face lit up. "You want to marry me?"

He nodded. "As soon as this is all resolved. Okay? We'll get married."

She grabbed his hand and pulled him out of the room, hyper and joyous now. He was caught up in the moment, too, happy at her obvious enjoyment.

*How could I have been blind and foolish before? Anyone in their right mind would fall in love with this woman and want to make her his wife. How could I have been led astray by Diana?*

When they entered the kitchen again, they found MacDonald by the open back door. He blew cigar smoke out into the night air. Sheriff Creel was in the middle of telling everyone that the fire crew had managed to get the house fires under control. For some reason, and no one was sure why, the wolf attacks had stopped. They were able to fight the fires unmolested. Creel said he thought maybe the elders realized that allowing the town to burn might not be in their best interests.

Drake took it as a positive sign, but for different reasons. He figured Roman had likely realized the futility of his actions. The elders couldn't possibly win, so maybe he had called for a strategic retreat.

*We're going to get through this*, he thought. *It's all going to be okay.* The forces of good would triumph over the forces of evil.

Then the power shut off and everything plunged into darkness.

Slade Grayson

# Chapter Forty-Six

There wasn't much of a gap between when the power went out and the wolves attacked. When the blackout hit, Creel immediately thought, *I expected this.* And he had, too.

He figured it was only a matter of time before the elders took out the town's power. Lack of electricity had a tendency to cause irrational fear in folks. It was a genetic throwback, back to when the darkness of night concealed countless hidden terrors.

Creel reacted fast. He gave orders for the men to dig up flashlights and candles. He heard Reverend Burroughs tell someone where they could find a flashlight in one of the kitchen drawers. Reverend MacDonald barked that he knew where there were some candles in one of the closets, and he certainly didn't need any light to move around, so he would get them.

People were accidentally jostling each other as they moved in the dark. He thought it was under control, that the blackout was simply a minor inconvenience. Until all hell broke loose.

Large, heavy shapes burst through the windows, shattering the glass. There were similar crashes in the church section of the building. Something big and black on four legs filled the open back doorway. There were screams throughout the church.

Creel had his gun out. He aimed and fired at the shape. It was a dangerous reaction because a civilian could have moved into the line of fire during the confusion. He calculated that possibility in the split-second before he fired, but decided to chance it anyway.

Maybe his shots hit, maybe they missed, Creel couldn't be sure. It didn't matter. The wolf leapt into the room and the screams intensified. Creel's gun was nearly knocked from his hand in the commotion. People rushed to get through the doorway to the outside.

He heard the sound of people being attacked. There were more gunshots, but not from him. The gunshots lit up the room in quick bursts of lightning.

During the flashes, Creel saw a wolf rip into one of the men while another fired shot after shot into it at point blank range. He tried to focus on it, pinpoint the location so he could add his own gun to the fight, but it was much too quick and too many bodies were rushing out of the room. Creel was pulled along with the crush of people as they forced themselves through the narrow doorway.

Outside, he took stock of the situation. Reverend Burroughs was there with his arm around Celia. His face was set in grim determination, while Celia cried quietly. Other men and women were there, while others ran out of the church and joined them. The problem, as Creel soon discovered, was that they had nowhere to run. They were surrounded by a circle of wolves.

From the front came the rest of the people, men, women, and children, their eyes wide with fear and barely restrained panic. Another line of wolves forced them to the back parking lot where Creel and the others stood like a herd of cattle forced into a pen. Creel cocked his gun and waited.

Not everyone was there. One or two were missing, maybe more. Ones who had put up a fight, probably, like in the kitchen. Reverend MacDonald was one of the missing. Creel shook his head. Attacking innocent civilians was bad enough, but an old blind man?

By snapping their teeth and emitting intermittent snarls and growls, the wolves corralled everyone into one giant circle. The men, and two of the women, still clutched their guns, but no one dared to fire. Creel knew they wouldn't make a move without his say-so. It would be suicide if they did.

"What'll we do, Sheriff?"

The question came from behind him. It was a man's voice, but Creel didn't see who it was.

"Hold tight," he answered. "Let's see what they're up to. If they make a move to attack, open fire. And keep the circle tight.

Men on the outside. Women behind them. Kids in the center."

Positions were shifted as everyone followed his orders. Men with guns took the outside perimeter of the circle and kept aim on the wolves. Even Burroughs, who was weaponless, took the outside line and kept Celia behind him. Creel thought, *He's more of a man than I originally gave him credit for.*

The wolves quit their advancement and stood menacingly in place. Everyone waited. Creel wasn't sure what they waited for, but it was the elders' game and they held all the cards.

The sound of a car engine drew closer and the sweep of headlights rolled over them as it turned into the church parking lot. The wolves didn't turn to investigate, as if they had expected the new arrival.

It was Carl Beardsley's car, but Carl wasn't at the wheel. Roman was driving, Mars was in the passenger seat and two women he guessed were Salacia and Mars's mate, Flora, were in the back. The wolves moved aside so the car could enter the outer ring of the circle.

The car stopped and Roman stepped out. He was bare-chested and barefoot, dressed only in an old pair of jeans, with a smug look on his face that Creel wanted to perforate with a bullet. He willed himself to keep his temper in check.

He wondered what had happened to Carl Beardsley, but figured deep down he probably knew. Creel shook his head.

*I told him not to get out of the car. Why didn't he listen? Maybe it wasn't by choice…?*

"Sheriff," Roman said. "I told you there would be consequences. You should have listened. You chose the wrong side."

Creel kept his gun at his side, pointed at the ground. He was tempted to shoot, but he was unsure of the distance and whether it would hit its target. Once he fired, he knew both sides would instantly attack. The only chance was to take down Roman immediately. It had to be a kill shot. Take out the leader and maybe the rest would falter or run.

"Well," Creel said to Roman, "maybe I did. Maybe I didn't. That remains to be seen. The question is, what are ya planning on doin' now? The numbers between us look pretty even. And we've got guns."

"That you do, Sheriff. That you do. But you know guns aren't a sure thing when you're fighting one of us."

Creel nodded. "We'll get some of ya. That's for certain."

Roman stepped closer. Creel tensed.

*A little more*, he thought. *Just step a little closer.*

Behind Roman, Mars, Salacia, and Flora stepped out of the car. They all wore similar ragged jeans and the women had on ill-fitting t-shirts. Creel saw uncertainty on Mars's face. Flora was a blank, as usual, but Creel knew she would do whatever Mars wanted her to. Salacia was an unknown element. The question was: What was Mars going to do?

"Roman!" Mars yelled.

An expression of surprise crossed Roman's face. He looked over his shoulder at his Beta male.

"Yes?"

Creel heard disapproval in Roman's voice. He didn't like that Mars interrupted his villainous gloating.

"This has gone far enough. I've struggled with this decision, perhaps for too long," Mars said. "Nevertheless, you have to stop this. Leave these people alone."

Roman turned to face Mars fully. Creel considered shooting him in the back of the head. He still wasn't a hundred percent sure of hitting the right spot to put him down for good. With Roman, Creel knew, you only got one chance. Then you died.

Roman pointed an accusatory finger at Mars. "You think I haven't sensed your dissension? I'm disappointed that you would side with this cattle over your own kind."

"No, Roman. I'm not siding with them over my own. I'm siding with them over you."

"Traitor," Roman spat.

"Why? Because I dare to question you? I dare to question the man who killed my leader and best friend?"

Creel brought his arm up and steadied himself. Much as everyone else, Roman was focused on Mars. Creel took careful aim and lined his gun up with the back of Roman's skull. No one paid attention to what he was doing. The focus was on Roman and Mars.

"You don't know what you're talking about," Roman said.

"You killed Jove. You killed your father."

"You don't know what you're talking about," Roman said again, this time through gritted teeth.

Creel held his breath and slowly tightened his finger on the trigger. From the edge of his vision, he saw Salacia take notice of him. As he squeezed the trigger, she yelled, "Roman!"

Roman ducked instinctively, a blur of movement that Creel couldn't compensate for. The bullet continued on its path and caught Mars in the throat. Salacia screamed. Roman whirled and fixed Creel with a fierce look.

"Kill them!" Roman shouted to his followers. Then the bloodbath began.

# Chapter Forty-Seven

Drake had Celia behind him. She stood so close that her breath caressed the back and side of his neck. She was scared, which was understandable because everyone was scared. He had to admit, he was scared, too. Not for himself or of dying, he was scared for the people and especially scared for Celia. If he could just get her safely away… His mind raced as he looked for an escape route.

The attack broke out and he quickly pushed Celia through the crowd to the back door. He tried to pull some of the children along, too. Although a few moved with him along with their mothers, many stayed rooted to their spots, transfixed by the firing guns and the savage wolves attacking the first line of defense. Drake didn't have time to coax them; things were happening fast and he needed to act now.

At the back door, a wolf stood guard. It was the same one that had rushed inside the open doorway and attacked them so as to force them outside. Now it kept them from going back in.

Drake stepped to the front of the small group he was trying to protect. He would sacrifice his own life if it meant getting Celia and the children to safety. He braced himself and hoped he could put up a long enough fight that the others could slip around them.

Reverend MacDonald appeared from out of the gloom behind the wolf. He was bloody and haggard, and although he looked to be in no condition to be of assistance, MacDonald fell on the wolf.

The wolf was taken by surprise, and Drake didn't hesitate to take advantage. He jumped at the animal and shoved his fingers into the wolf's eye sockets. It let out a high-pitched yelp that sounded unnervingly like a human scream.

Drake moved back in time to avoid the reflex snap of the wolf's jaws. It shot past him, stopped, and shifted back to human form. A naked middle-aged woman stood before them and rubbed her eyes.

"That stung!" she yelled.

Celia's father came up on her side and landed a haymaker to her jaw. The power of it surprised Drake. Celia's father was a short, slight fellow, but the force of his punch equaled that of a man twice his size. The woman collapsed in a heap on the ground.

From the doorway, Drake called to them: Celia's parents, the children he had missed, and the other unarmed townspeople. Some of them didn't respond because they were under attack or blocked by wolves. Those that could get by raced to where Drake beckoned to them.

He let them pass into the back room, then turned to observe the fight as it progressed outside. The armed men and women fired round after round into the wolves. Some shots were fatal, as Drake could see several wolf bodies on the ground, but the majority of the shots didn't appear to faze them. They tore into the crowd and rendered destruction through fang and claw. People screamed, and people fell.

Creel fired multiple shots. Either he was a true marksman or perhaps he was lucky, but many of his shots were fatal or caused great wounds in their targets. Creel ejected an empty clip, popped in a full one, and went back to shooting.

Roman and Mars were locked in combat. He thought Roman must have used the fact that Mars was wounded to his advantage and attacked him immediately after he gave the kill order to his followers. Although Mars had size on his side, he appeared to be having trouble holding his own against Roman. They were both in mid-transformation, the horrific half-man, half-beast form that Drake had witnessed Roman use earlier that day in front of the congregation.

Drake saw, too, that Mars's wife or mate had attempted to assist him, but Salacia had intervened. The two of them struggled with each other, then transformed simultaneously to their wolf forms. They were evenly matched, or so it seemed, but Salacia was more ferocious, and Drake knew that she would probably be victorious.

"What should we do, Reverend?"

The question came from somewhere behind him. Drake's head swam; his elevated heart rate acted against him. The excitement of the attack and the fight was causing his cardio-respiratory system to go into overdrive, which meant the infection in his system, the virus, was racing through his bloodstream at an accelerated rate.

"Drake?" Celia's voice.

He wanted to answer, but the world tilted on him. He had to use every ounce of willpower to remain on his feet.

"Burroughs! You need to lead these people!" shouted MacDonald.

Drake turned to them. The room was dark, but he managed to make out several scared faces. The children especially struck a chord within him. He couldn't give up, couldn't let himself fall apart now. He steeled himself and mentally commanded the room to stop spinning.

"Out the front," he told them. "Reverend MacDonald, you lead the way. Everyone hold hands and move as quickly as you can. We'll go out the front while the elders are distracted in the back parking lot."

As he spoke, Drake noted that the gunfire had decreased. The fight was already winding down.

"We have to go. Now!" He used as much force and conviction as his sick body could muster.

He sensed more than saw the people follow his directions. Celia's hands found him in the dark. She touched his face.

"We'll be all right, won't we?" she asked.

"Yes. Just go out the front and we'll find cover out there. Maybe in one of the houses."

She took his hand, but he pulled it away.

"I have to be last. You go ahead."

She hesitated.

"Go. I'll be right behind you."

MacDonald was leading them through the door to the front of the church. Drake pushed Celia along, then made sure everyone else was going. The chain of people eased its way through the doorway.

Drake didn't follow. He wanted to; the voice in his head yelled for him to move. *Go!* it said, but his body rebelled. The world continued to tilt and spin. His thoughts became vague things that floated in the ether.

He took a step, and another. The next step he missed. He put his foot down, heavy, and slipped as if he had stepped off a ledge and there was nothing solid to catch him. Drake fell. His chin banged on the table and his body twisted from the impact so that he landed hard on his side. His mind blinked out.

*** 

It was still dark when he came to. There was a moment when Drake couldn't decide if he was awake or not. But he turned his head and saw the hazy outline of the back door. Beyond it was the slightly brighter shade of the night sky.

He got to his feet and managed to stay upright. Every joint and every muscle in his body ached, and his insides continued to burn with a terrible fever. It felt like the worst case of flu he had ever had, except worse because he knew he was not going to eventually get better. All the bed rest and fluids in the world were not going to help him overcome the virus in his system. He was going to die, plain and simple. Strangely, the thought didn't bother him much.

He was disconnected. The world was an abstract puzzle and he was so far removed from it, the pieces blurred. It was as if he was looking at a piece of 3D artwork and he was unable to focus on one point long enough to cause the picture to spring to life. Or, quite possibly, Drake didn't care what the picture was anymore.

The flashlight was still in the kitchen drawer. No one had time to retrieve it before the wolves attacked. Drake switched it on and surveyed the room. There was a body on the floor – a human. It was familiar to him, but other than the fact that it was a man's body, he couldn't identify it.

He walked to the door that separated his apartment from the church section of the building. Everything was deathly still. He walked through the church.

There were more bodies by the front doors: men, women, and

children. All of them had been savaged mercilessly. The wolves had caught them as they tried to escape through the front of the building. Drake studied them in the glow of the flashlight beam with detachment. He was hollow inside; the fever had consumed his emotions.

He had to step over bodies to move outside. There were more on the pavement. He found Reverend MacDonald's lifeless body right away, and Celia's parents'. He couldn't be sure, but he thought this wasn't everyone. A few had managed to escape.

When he spotted Celia's body, he heard a long sustained moan. He thought it came from her, but when he moved closer, he realized the moan came from within himself.

Her throat had been ripped apart and she had deep gouges that ran vertically down her cheek and jaw. Her eyes stared ahead, devoid of life or any of the sparkle he used to see in them. He crouched down and brushed a lock of her hair back. He thought she was still beautiful, even dead and mangled as she was.

Drake stood and walked back through the church. He wasn't as careful when he stepped over the bodies this time. No one complained when he stepped on them.

He walked back through the church to the back door and out into the parking lot. His motorcycle was still there, still standing next to his road-worn car. He walked to the bike and slung his leg over it, then gave a cursory glance at the bodies scattered on the ground.

There was Creel's body, and a few others he recognized. Mars had obviously lost his battle with Roman. Mars was fully in human form now, a large chunk of his throat gone. Other than that, his naked body appeared undamaged. Next to him was the wolf body of his mate. There were other wolf bodies, but not nearly as many as the human ones.

"Help, please," a woman's voice called to him. "Please help."

Drake saw a naked woman on the ground a few feet from where he was. She was approximately his age, maybe a year or two younger, with short red hair and dark eyes that stared at him.

"Please," she said. "I can't move."

She was on her stomach, her head turned to the side facing his direction. There was a dark red splotch on her back, a little bigger than the size of a bullet hole. Drake stepped off his bike and walked over to her.

She said, "I was shot in the back and now I can't move. The bullet's still in there. It's stuck in my spine."

He knelt down and examined her back. There was dried blood from where the bullet had struck her, but the hole was closed.

"It's healed up," she said, "but the bullet is still in there. If you could... if you could get it out, it'll heal completely and I'll be able to move again."

He looked at her back and touched the area where she had been shot. Without the dried blood and except for a slight redness to the area, he would have been unable to tell where she had been shot. The skin was closed and unmarred.

"Please. Please, I'm afraid. Please help me."

He looked into her dark eyes and saw fear and rising panic.

"Dig the bullet out," she said. "I don't care how you do it or how much it hurts me. It doesn't matter because I'll heal as good as new."

Drake stood and her pleas became more desperate.

"No! Please don't leave me like this! Get the bullet out. I'll... I'll... I'll do anything you want. I'll give you anything. Anything!"

"You'll do anything I want?"

"Yes! Yes, anything!"

"This is what I want you to do for me." Drake pushed her onto her back and placed a boot on her throat. "When you get to Hell, tell the rest of your demon kin that there's more coming." He slowly applied his weight down until he cut off her breathing.

He stared into her eyes the whole time until her skin turned a bluish tint and the life had long left her body. He stood on her throat for a long time, longer than he needed to, but he wanted to ensure she was truly dead. No last minute reprieve or surprise healing from her demon shapeshifter virus.

Drake climbed back on the motorcycle, gunned the engine to life, and rode around the side of the church. He saw the body of another wolf and a small wolf cub trying to nuzzle it back to life. The cub yipped and howled for its dead parent. Drake aimed the bike to take him close to the cub. As he rode past, he stuck his foot out. His steel-toed boot caught it hard in the hindquarters and sent the cub into a huge flip over the body of the dead wolf.

If Drake had felt better, he would have stopped and attempted to kill it. But the fever was taking its toll. His vision blurred and doubled, and it took tremendous concentration for him to keep the motorcycle on the road

On the road out of town, he came to the two fallen trees. He swerved and went off into the grass, and nearly slid the bike sideways. Through a herculean effort, he kept the motorcycle upright and shot through a narrow gap between the fallen trees and the edge of the forest. The rear tire barely kept traction, but he made it and got back up onto the road.

He thought he saw two wolf shapes come at him from out of the darkness, but he kept the bike gunned and sped away. He wasn't sure if the shadowy wolf shapes were real or products of his feverish mind. No matter. He sped down Fulman Bridge and left Hell on Earth behind.

# Chapter Forty-Eight

Fern parked in the middle of the road. The engine ticked as it cooled. The two fallen trees blocked the view of the bridge on the other side, but David knew it was there. Its presence was tangible; it was a monster that lurked beyond the crushed branches and waited with a malevolent patience. David didn't find it nearly as imposing as he once had. The monsters he had seen over the last few hours were far scarier.

Fern smoked a joint. They had their windows up most of the way, except for a small one inch gap at the top. David stuck out his hand in a silent request for a toke.

"Really?"

She was surprised, because he had never asked before.

"Yeah. My leg's killing me."

And it was. Once the adrenaline subsided, his leg had begun to throb. The pain pulsed with his heartbeat and his pants leg was soaked with blood. The material had turned stiff, so whenever he moved his leg, the hardened pant leg worked against him. It made his leg hurt more. Plus, a large section of it stuck to the area of the bite, which sent sharp daggers into it when he moved and the material tore loose.

The marijuana burned his lungs and made him cough. He couldn't remember the last time he had smoked a joint. He handed it back to Fern. She gave him an amused look.

"Okay," he said. "So I'm a lightweight."

She grinned and smoked some more.

David checked the ammo. He had shot almost all of it. The shotgun shells were gone and the bullets for the handguns were nearly depleted. He found one round for the revolver and two for the automatic. Fern gave him a questioning look.

"Three shots left."

"You did a lot of shooting." She said it like she was stating a fact rather than making an accusation.

She couldn't possibly be upset with him for shooting at every wolf they saw (and probably a few things that looked like wolves...maybe even a couple of very large dogs). The point was, Fern was the one who decided to drive up and down the side streets and around every cul-de-sac while David fired out the window at any oversized four-legged creature they happened upon. He had hit quite a few, too, which made him happy. It made him feel like he was doing something, like he was contributing to the war.

Fern wasn't upset that their ammo was almost gone. If anything, she seemed ambivalent. Or maybe resigned was a better term. She was resigned to the fact that that they weren't going to make it anyway, so why not kill as many shapeshifters as possible?

"Think we can get across the bridge?" he asked.

She shrugged and smoked. She didn't appear to be in a hurry to get out of the car.

"What do you want to do?"

"I want... I want to hear you say you love me."

"I love you."

She shook her head. "Say my name when you say it."

"I love you, Fernandiaz."

She sighed and slid back in her seat with a satisfied expression. If David didn't know better, he would have thought she just had an orgasm. He put his hands up, like, *What was that all about?*

"I just wanted to hear it one last time, in that perfect way with my name at the end. That's all I wanted," Fern said. "All I ever wanted."

"You talk like we're going to die."

Fern met his eyes. The dreamlike glaze had faded and was replaced with a look of compassion, love, and a little bit of sorrow.

"We are," she said.

"Oh. Well, okay then."

"We can't drive around the trees. We could go back, but to where? They've got our scent now and wherever we try to hide, they'll track us. And believe me, they will, because we've killed some of them. The rest of the pack will be out for our blood."

"What happened to the idea of walking across the bridge?"

"We could try, but I'm willing to bet there are sentries watching us right now. Roman wouldn't have sent them here to cut down trees, then left the area unguarded. There are probably still a couple of elders watching from the woods."

David looked out his window and stared into the inky blackness of the forest. He didn't see anything that resembled the shape of a man or a wolf, or anything really, other than pitch blackness. But what did he expect to see? Glowing red eyes like something out of a horror flick?

That was not to say that he didn't agree with her. It made perfect sense that Roman would leave a few of them to guard the road. But how many? Two? Four? Eight? David hoped it was two.

"We could sit here," he suggested.

"Not for much longer. If we sit here too long, they'll probably try to come through the windows to get at us."

"We could keep driving around town."

Fern nodded. "I thought about that. Except we're low on gas. Fuck it, let's make a run for it across the bridge."

He checked his window again. "Okay, we get out, make a beeline – whatever the fuck that is – around my side." He pointed to the right edge of the fallen trees. "Get around there, and run like hell across the bridge."

"Can you run?" She pointed to his injured leg.

"Probably not. Can you?"

"Probably better than you. But not very well."

"Then I guess we're all set."

"I guess so."

He handed her the gun with the two remaining rounds, then double-checked the revolver. Still only one bullet.

"Ready?" she asked.

"Not really. You know… I still can't figure out how this all happened. How did my life end up like this?"

"Any regrets?"

"About a million," he said. "But not about you."

She reached across and tenderly stroked his cheek.

"One last kiss?" she asked.

"Until we get to the other side of the bridge."

"Until then."

She leaned in to kiss him. David leaned to meet her halfway. The pain in his leg was searing, a red hot poker that some invisible sadist twisted around in there. He gritted his teeth against it and met her lips.

For the brief moment that they kissed, the pain was forgotten. When they finished and pulled away, however, it came back twice as strong.

*I don't care*, David thought. *It was worth it.*

"Okay," he said. "Let's rock and roll."

They got out and made for the edge of the fallen trees. David hobbled on his damaged leg while Fern limped along on hers. Four-legged shapes burst from the shadows. They came at them from all directions at once. Fern fired twice. David fired once.

\*\*\*

Salacia followed Roman back to the elder settlement. They shifted back to human form and walked the last several hundred feet to Roman's cabin. They reached it just as a light rain began. Her muscles ached, not only from all the miles she had traversed over the last twelve hours, but also from the fight. She was weary all over, especially down deep in her soul.

Picus and Janus came out of the woods opposite them. Their expressions mirrored her own, though she suspected for different reasons. Salacia had overwhelming guilt from siding with Roman over her father, and although she hadn't actually raised her hands against him, his death was as much her fault as it was Roman's. For the rest of her life, she would have her father's death on her conscience. If she hadn't killed Flora, Flora would have aided Mars in fighting Roman. It would have turned the tide. The worst part was, she now questioned whether siding with Roman was the right choice.

Picus and Janus spoke to Roman in hushed tones. She couldn't hear all of it. Picus spoke in Russian and she wasn't fluent in that language. What little she did catch was bad news.

The fight had not gone well for the elders. Despite casualties on both sides, the deaths had been close to three-to-one in favor of the elders. Which was still bad because there were many more humans than elders. Picus estimated that there were only a dozen or so elders left alive, while there were close to a thousand humans.

Apparently, Roman had not counted on the number of firearms available to the townspeople. She saw the surprise on his face when they told him of the newcomer, David Rafferty, who had several guns and had driven around Tanneheuk with the deputy and shot at the elders. Some of his shots had been fatal.

She knew what Roman would think: that he should have killed Creel right away before he had the chance to organize his private militia; that he should have killed Burroughs weeks ago; that he should have killed David Rafferty instead of letting him walk away from the camp earlier that day. She knew Roman would have to come to terms with the fact that he simply wasn't a brilliant tactician and had acted out of anger rather than divine destiny.

"Gather the remains of the pack. Tell them…" Roman looked to the overcast sky that sprinkled water down on them, perhaps seeking answers in the pattern of raindrops. "Tell them we'll regroup up north. It might be better if we split up, no more than two or three of us traveling together. We'll meet up after the first of the year and I'll decide the next phase then."

Salacia saw he struggled with what to tell them. He hadn't counted on not being successful, and now that defeat was obvious, Roman was lost as to his next step.

Picus asked something in Russian. He must have wondered where the pack was supposed to meet because Roman responded, "Janus can tell you. We've always kept a location far away from here as a possible safe haven in case something happened to disrupt our lives here. It's near the Canadian border, far from the humans." He spat the last word as if it disgusted him to have to say "humans."

Picus and Janus nodded and headed back into the woods, shifting into wolf form before the darkness engulfed them. Their departure was as silent as their arrival had been.

Roman stared into the woods, but not at the spot where Picus and Janus had gone. He was lost inside his head. It was the only time Salacia had ever seen an expression of despair and uncertainty on his face.

Gods, how she hated him. She hated herself, too, for believing he was something more than what he was. He wasn't a god among mortals; he was power mad and delusional. He was an emperor who had allowed his empire to crumble due to his own lustful needs.

His face showed the totality of his loss. It was a mask of absolute dejection, until he caught her watching him. Then he replaced the mask with one of confidence.

She wished she could take back her decision to side with him. She wished Roman was dead and her father was alive. She wished it with every fiber of her being.

Salacia would stay with him, of course. What choice did she have? Go off on her own? Try to find another pack? The idea of attempting to blend in with the humans, or worse, searching for another pack of shapeshifters that would accept her, was too frightening to consider. So, too, was the notion of living on her own. Salacia had never been alone her entire life.

No, she was stuck with Roman. Stuck with him and the remnants of their pack. She'd made her decision and now she would suffer the consequences.

She followed him into the cabin. He didn't speak to her; he barely acknowledged her presence. He treated her like she was one of his followers rather than his mate. It made her decision to side with him seem trivial.

Inside, she smelled the human. The cabin reeked of sickness, sweat, and fear. Maryam wasn't where they had left her. The nest of blankets they had put on the floor for her was empty. They followed her scent to the bathroom. Maryam was naked and unconscious on the floor. Roman knelt down and placed his palm on her forehead.

"She's burning up with fever," he said. "We have to get her temperature down before it kills her brain."

"I thought you said she'd survive this."

Roman ignored her. He turned the cold water on in the bathtub, plugged the drain, then picked Maryam up and placed her in the tub. He had his arm behind her shoulders to support her and keep her head from slipping below the waterline. With his free hand, he scooped small handfuls of cold water and bathed her face, head, and neck. It was an act of gentleness that Salacia had not seen from him in months. It reminded her of the man he used to be.

Maryam's eyes fluttered open. She whispered, "How much longer?"

"For what?" Roman asked.

"How much longer until the pain goes away?"

"Not much longer." He continued to bathe her head with the water.

Maryam's eyes fixed on a spot on the far wall. They were glassy and distant.

"I want to be one of you. Am I one of you yet?"

"Yes. You're one of us," he told her. "You're one of us. You're one of us."

He told her over and over, long after the last breath left her body.

*** 

Drake drove through the rain. The coolness of the night air mixed with the cold drizzle should have soothed his feverish state, but he barely felt it. He burned inside. He was drenched on the outside by rain, but sweat also soaked his clothes from the inside out.

He drove until his vision stayed blurred and he nearly lost control of the motorcycle. He turned off at the very next rest stop, which was an outpost of gas stations, restaurants, and several motels. He took the motel that appeared to be the most rundown, and therefore the least likely to ask questions. Drake wanted to find a dry place to lie down, not answer a bunch of questions from a bored night desk clerk about where he was from or why he was driving coatless and helmetless through the rain.

He pulled into the parking lot of a shabby, two-story courtyard motel. He didn't pay attention to the name of the place, but the lit VACANCY sign registered in his ebbing consciousness. He parked the motorcycle and lumbered to the well-lit office that beckoned to him like the sole light in a raging storm. Not that the weather had turned that bad, but Drake's mind had slowly dimmed until his vision held a blurred border around every object and he saw everything as if it was at the end of a very dark tunnel.

He staggered into the office. Behind the front desk, a woman with a long gray ponytail and lots of turquoise jewelry looked up from behind a computer screen. Drake saw her lips move, but he couldn't make out what she said. He realized he couldn't hear anything except his heartbeat, which sounded erratic.

"Room," he said. "Please." He reached into his pocket for his wallet and the world turned upside down.

One minute he was standing in front of the woman, the next he was staring up at the ceiling. He thought it odd and wondered how he had gotten himself into such a strange position, then realized he was flat on his back on the floor.

The woman's face peered down at him. She must have come around from behind the counter. Her lips moved again. He suspected she was asking if he was okay, if he needed help.

Drake wanted to reply that he was all right, really, all he needed was very cold water to drink and a dry place to rest, but his mouth no longer worked. His vision grew worse until he could barely see the woman. She seemed so far away now, that he doubted she would hear him if he could manage to speak anyway. Maybe if he shouted…? But no, he was much too weak to shout. Instead, he decided to close his eyes and allow himself to die.

# January

Slade Grayson

# Chapter Forty-Nine

Daniel Goodis entered the midtown eatery and was struck by the similarity between this visit and his last one the previous Spring. It was the same time of day as the last time he patronized the establishment, and the décor and the look of the customers appeared to not have changed. Even the hostess was the same woman who had been there the previous time. The only difference was that the patrons were dressed in warmer clothing.

Daniel stood for a moment in the foyer. He shook off the bitter cold that had carried in with him from outside and that still clung to him in a frosty aura. He removed his knit hat and gloves and put them in the pocket of his overcoat. He walked to the hostess stand and returned the young woman's smile.

"Hello," he said, "I'm meeting a party here. My name is Daniel Goodis and I'm meeting—"

"Oh, Reverend Goodis?"

"Yes."

"Your party is waiting for you at the bar." She motioned to the left side of the restaurant. "If you'd like a table, I have one open. Or you can be served lunch at the bar."

He smiled again at the hostess and threaded through the restaurant to the bar. The person he had come to meet was a surprise to him. To clarify, he was surprised when the man called.

*Is that…? No, it couldn't be him, could it?*

The man at the end of the bar, several seats away from the other bar patrons, was more broad-shouldered than Daniel remembered. His blond hair was down to his shoulders, longer and thicker than the last time he saw him. When Daniel moved closer, he recognized the man's profile and realized it was indeed the person he had come to meet.

The bartender was a portly older man with hair gelled to his scalp. He was talking to Drake and as Daniel approached, he caught the conversation in progress.

"…kind of hard this early in the day," the bartender was saying. "That's all I was saying, Father."

"Reverend," Drake stressed. "I'm a minister, not a goddamn priest."

"You're allowed to talk like that?" the bartender said with surprise. "I thought the Bible said not to take the Lord's name in vain."

"The Bible says a lot of shit. Now, you going to keep preaching to me? Or you going to get me another whiskey like I asked?"

The bartender picked up a bottle of Jack Daniel's and refilled Drake's glass. Daniel noticed he took it straight, no ice. Drake muttered a "thanks" that sounded more like a growl. The bartender moved down to the other end of the bar and pointedly kept his eyes off his surly customer.

When Daniel approached, Drake turned suddenly, somehow sensing his presence. Drake's upper lip had a curl to it, as if he had stopped himself in mid-snarl. When he saw it was Daniel, his lip relaxed, but Daniel still had the impression Drake's body was coiled and tense.

From what, though? And what had happened to change his friend so?

Besides the piratical hair, Drake's face was covered in blond stubble. Like his shoulders, his chest was broader than Daniel remembered, and he had a tautness about him, like a steel spring cranked down and held in place by the thinnest of levers. Daniel had a sense that his friend was on the verge of leaping from his seat.

The biggest change was his eyes. Drake's eyes, Daniel recalled, had always been warm and filled with compassion. Now they were predatory. Colder. Even when Drake made eye contact with him, and Daniel expected the recognition to cause an expression of warmth at seeing his old friend and mentor, there was little change. Drake's eyes became less narrow, perhaps. That was it.

Daniel took the seat next to him and had the urge to give him a hug in greeting, but he saw no opening for such. In fact, he was too nervous to make the gesture. He was afraid of how this new version of Drake would react to someone suddenly invading his personal space.

"Drake, I was surprised, but also quite happy to hear from you. I've been very worried, as have your parents. They call me on a weekly basis. How have you been? *Where* have you been?"

Drake grunted and turned back to stare at the wall behind the bar. "Fine," he said, and Daniel noticed the deeper timbre of his voice. "Better than fine," he said after a moment. "I'm good. Real good."

Drake still wore his black shirt and clerical collar as if he was still the minister of a church. Daniel noticed, too, that he wore black jeans and motorcycle boots. Slung over the seat opposite him was a black leather trench coat and a black wool scarf with silver threads woven throughout that gave it a hint of a metallic appearance. The whole ensemble was completely unlike the Drake he knew. This Drake looked dangerous.

"I was very happy that you called me," Daniel repeated. "Your parents have been worried about you."

Drake grunted.

"What happened out there?"

Drake took a healthy swallow of whiskey. Without turning his head, he said, "The wrath of God. That's what happened."

"I don't…" Daniel shook his head. "They said on the news that there was a riot of some sort. People were killed. They said many people have packed up and left without a forwarding address, leaving much of their possessions behind, and that Tanneheuk is almost a ghost town."

Drake didn't answer. He was silent and still, until Daniel couldn't wait any longer.

"Please, Drake. Talk to me. Tell me what happened and why you haven't contacted me until now. And why haven't you contacted your parents? They think something terrible happened to you."

"Something terrible? No," he said. "Not terrible." His face

turned to Daniel. "Something miraculous happened to me. I was reborn."

When Drake's eyes were fully on him, Daniel tensed. Sweat formed on the back of his neck and under his arms. His former protégé, the innocent and compassionate yet flawed young man, was gone. The man next to him was something different. It was a savage animal that had taken on the skin of his friend. It certainly wasn't Drake.

The bartender broke the spell. He came over and inquired if Daniel wanted anything. Daniel shook his head and managed a weak smile, grateful for the interruption. Looking into Drake's cold eyes had been hypnotic, but at the same time frightening.

"Did you do what I asked?"

Daniel kept his eyes averted. "I placed a call to Harker Lang's church as you requested. He's not there. They said he travels extensively and they couldn't be sure when he would check in next. It was all very vague and somewhat…strange, I guess."

"Strange, how?"

Daniel shrugged. "I thought it strange that a church would be so unsure as to the whereabouts of one of its ministers. But then again, I didn't know where you were these last few months."

Daniel wouldn't make eye contact again. Now he was the one staring at the back wall. He felt Drake's eyes on him, though, like two laser sights. He sweated more. Slowly, he slipped off his overcoat. He wasn't sure why his movements were so tentative other than the unexplainable feeling that he thought it unwise to make any fast or sudden movements around Drake.

"Doesn't matter," Drake said finally. "I wondered what Lang's connection was to everything that happened. I thought he might be one of them. But I don't think he is. I think he's something else entirely."

"One of what?"

"Maybe he's an agent of the Lord," he said. "Like me."

Daniel glanced at him. "Drake, what… What are you talking about? What happened to you?"

"I told you, Daniel. I was reborn."

He stood, slipped his scarf around his neck, and pulled on the leather trench coat. Daniel noticed there was a motorcycle helmet on the seat that the coat had covered. Drake picked it up along with a pair of leather gloves.

"You're driving a motorcycle? Awfully cold weather for it, isn't it?"

For the first time, Drake smiled. It resembled more of a sneer, with the left corner of his lip rising up. The right corner rose, too, but not quite as high. The expression could have been a smirk, but Daniel didn't think so.

"Cold weather doesn't bother me much," he said.

"And you're driving after you've been drinking?"

"You'd be surprised at how much it takes to get me drunk these days." Drake paused, then: "Thanks for coming, Daniel. I have to go. I have God's work to do."

He moved to leave. Daniel put his hand out to stop him, but stopped short of touching him. Instinct had kicked in and Daniel was glad of it because the sharp look Drake gave him confirmed the notion that it would have been a mistake to grab him.

"Something else you want to ask me?"

"What should I tell your parents? Are you going to call them?"

"You call them," Drake said. "Tell them their son is fine." He leaned down and sniffed the air around Daniel. "You're not a vegetarian anymore. You smell like you've been eating meat."

He walked away, the snap of his boots on the floor echoing unnaturally loud. He walked past a group of businessmen being led to a table by the hostess. One of the businessmen, not watching where he was walking because his eyes were locked on the hostess's legs, collided his shoulder against Drake's. Drake continued walking as if he had brushed past the outstretched leaf of a houseplant or something equally insignificant.

The businessman was knocked hard, as he hadn't seen the collision coming. He reacted like he intended to say something to Drake.

*Please don't,* Daniel mentally pleaded. *Don't say anything to him. Just let him go.*

Either the man picked up on Daniel's silent prayer or, more likely, the sight of Drake's long hair and leather clad frame intimidated him to keep quiet. The man let Drake leave without a word, and when Drake was well out of earshot, only then did he turn to his lunch companions and comment on the incident.

Daniel couldn't hear what the man said, but his impression was that the man attempted to make light of Drake's rudeness. It was evident, too, that the man was relieved he didn't have to confront Drake face-to-face.

*I know how you feel*, Daniel thought. If that was what Drake Burroughs had become, Daniel hoped he never had to see him again.

# Chapter Fifty

Roman caught the scent a half mile from the cabin. It puzzled him because it was familiar, yet he had trouble matching it to his sense memory. When he did recognize it, he smiled.

He followed the scent to tracks in the snow: wolf prints, big ones, the kind made by one of his own. He smiled again.

He followed the tracks to his cabin where they changed to human footprints. There was smoke coming from the stone chimney. His unexpected guest had taken the liberty of building a fire in the cabin's fireplace.

Roman walked up the two wooden steps to the front door. The top step creaked loudly under his moccasin. He wasn't concerned about stealth; his guest expected him.

He entered the cabin and shrugged off the oversized parka he wore over his t-shirt. He let it drop to the wood floor and stepped out of his moccasins. He watched with curiosity as the blond-haired man poked at the fire in the fireplace. His back was to Roman and he appeared not to have taken notice of his entrance, though Roman was sure he had. He was sure the man knew everything Roman was doing.

Roman sat in a rocking chair directly across from him. Even from the back, he noted the physical changes in Reverend Burroughs. He wore a flannel shirt and a pair of jeans, both of which belonged to Roman. His feet were bare. The jeans fit him, though they appeared a little short. The shirt was too tight. Burroughs's upper body was thicker than it used to be. Roman was fascinated.

Drake turned finally and faced him. He sat on the stone ledge of the fireplace. The flames crackled and hissed. He had used the wood stored out back and the water frozen in the wood made sounds as it turned to steam.

"You survived it," Roman said.

"Apparently."

Roman shook his head and smiled. "I would never have guessed. I found you, you know, inside the church, unconscious. I smelled the sickness in you. I thought you were dying. I would never have suspected… I wonder if Diana knew. If that was the reason she was drawn to you. Somehow, she sensed you could survive the changes the virus puts the body through."

Drake said, "She used to scratch me, bite me a little. I would feel feverish afterwards. Perhaps she was testing me to see how my body would react."

"Or perhaps she thought she could help you build up tolerance to it by exposing you to it little by little."

"Well, whatever the case…"

"Yes," Roman said, "whatever the case. Here you are."

"Yes."

They regarded each other for long moments.

"I suppose now we fight," Roman said.

"Yes, but not just yet."

"The wolf is close to the surface in you, I can tell. It's evident by your hair and beard stubble, and the changes in your body."

Drake stared at him without emotion, to the point that Roman wondered if his mind had drifted. He had expected more anger, more passion…

Roman asked, "How does it feel?"

"How does what feel?"

"Oh, come now, Reverend." Roman laughed. "Don't play games with me. This is an amazing opportunity. There's so much we can discuss now. You're still new to this. You must have questions, and I'm sure some interesting observations since you were once so convinced we were demon spawn, or constructs of the Devil, or whatever foolishness you spouted back then." Roman leaned forward. "How does it feel now to know how wrong you were? How does it feel to be one of us?"

"I'm not one of you," Drake said. "This is my punishment. And my gift. Just as God marked Cain for his sin, so He has marked me. But He's also given me this ability to use in His service."

"You…" Roman sat back, disappointed.

He had hoped for something revelatory, a vindication of sorts for their past debates. Even godhood, apparently, was not enough to shake Burroughs's close-minded, antiquated beliefs.

"It's wasted on you," Roman said. "All of this, all of what happened. If you had finally seen the light, then I would have almost thought it was worth it. I see, however, it was all pointless."

"No, I have to disagree."

Roman spread his hands as if to say, *Please explain.*

"For a long time, I wondered about my place in the world," Drake said. "I questioned my calling. I questioned God's plan for me."

Roman sighed loudly. "Really, I—"

"Shut the fuck up!" Drake snapped. "I listened to your petty tyrannical speeches back in Tanneheuk. The least you can do is sit there quietly and listen to what I have to say. Especially after everything you've cost me."

"My apologies, Reverend. Please continue."

Roman wouldn't admit it to himself, but besides the surprise he experienced at Drake's outburst, he also felt a twinge of…apprehension? Yes. Apprehension was a good word. Certainly not anxiety or fear.

"I used to wonder about my place in life and what God wanted of me. Now I know. After I came to terms with what I'd become, I hunted down surviving members of your pack. It was surprisingly easy for me to follow their trails." He shrugged. "Not that there were many left. Still… I saved you for last. I expected to find your whore here as well. I see she left you a few days ago."

It was true. Salacia had left without a word, though Roman couldn't say it had taken him by surprise. She harbored guilt over her decision to side with him over her father. The guilt enveloped her over the months until she became a mere shadow of her former vibrant self. He knew shortly after they left Tanneheuk together that it was not a question of *if* she would leave him, but *when.*

"Doesn't matter," Drake went on. "I had intended to save you for last, but I suppose in the grand scheme of things, it won't matter who I send to Hell first."

"Oh? Is that where I'm going, Reverend?"

"Without question. And then I'll track down your consort and dispatch her as well."

"What makes you think we won't be waiting for you down there?" Roman couldn't help but indulge the man's fantasy.

"If the Lord decides I'm unworthy and I must pay for my sins in Hell, so be it. I'll deal with you and your kind down there just as I have up here. At least now I know my purpose in life, and I'm content with that."

"And what is your purpose?"

Drake said, "God wants me to seek out and kill all the monsters."

"I find," Roman said, "that I've grown tired of this, and tired of you."

"On the count of three?"

"Very well. One."

Drake said, "Two."

"Three," Roman said, and leapt from his chair. He changed in mid-air.

Drake changed, too, much quicker than Roman would have believed possible. While Roman's speed at changing was legendary, Drake's change was nearly instantaneous. Roman was midway through his change when Drake simultaneously transformed and ripped through his borrowed clothes. It was as if...

It was as if the wolf had been there all along, pretending to be human, and when Roman called "three," it shook off the human form of Drake Burroughs to reveal itself.

Roman was impressed in spite of his own pride and the fact that someone had finally beaten him.

Drake crossed the distance between them, fully transformed into the wolf he had always been. His fangs ripped into Roman's half-changed throat.

Roman's last and final thought was, *Too fast. It was too fast. And him...of all people...him...*

# The End

# About the Author

Slade Grayson hates talking about himself in the third person, but that's generally the way these things are done, so...

Slade is a former freelance journalist turned novelist, who occasionally writes book and movie reviews. He hasn't won an award since grade school, but that's okay. He's not in this business to win awards. He wants to make money! Oh, and tell stories, of course.

Slade lives outside Washington, DC and currently has so many books in his TBR pile, he probably won't live long enough to read them all. Unless he wins the lottery and can spend all of his spare time reading. Wouldn't that be nice?

And before you ask: Yes, that really is his name.

Made in the USA
Middletown, DE
22 June 2025

77289736R10239